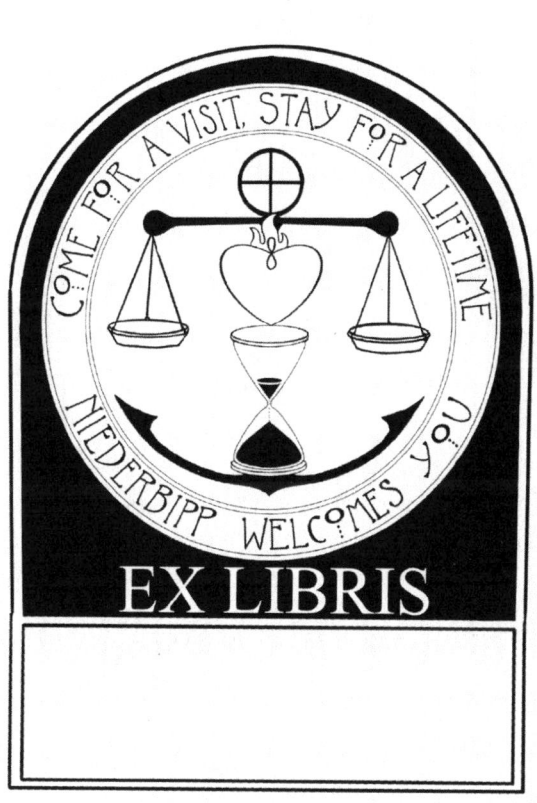

Other books by Ben Behunin

Remembering Isaac
Discovering Isaac
Becoming Isaac
Forget-Me-Notes
Borrowing Fire
Put A Cherry On Top
The Lost Art of Wooing Rabbits and Other Wild Hares
The Disciple of the Wind
How to Seduce a Sasquatch
Authentically Ruby
Splendidly Ruby
Pleasantly Ruby
Persuasively Ruby

Ben's books are available from his website, www.potterboy.com, www.amazon.com and wherever above average books are sold.

GRACEFULLY RUBY

The Legacy of Joy

Book 5 in a series

by Ben Behunin

Gracefully Ruby
The Legacy of Joy

Copyright © 2022 by Benjamin A. Behunin
All rights reserved. Manufactured in the United States of America

The contents of this book
may not be reproduced in any part or by
any means without written consent from the author
or Abendmahl Press except by a reviewer, or lecturer
who may quote passages in a review or lecture.

First printing, November 2022

Published by
Abendmahl Press
1150 East 800 South
Salt Lake City, Utah 84102

ISBN 978-0-9838025-5-6

Designed by Bert Compton and Ben Behunin
Illustrations by Ben Behunin
Layout by Bert Compton
Editing by Sharon Ellsworth-Nielson

Tell all the truth
but tell it slant —
Success in Circuit lies
Too bright for our infirm Delight
The Truth's superb surprise
As Lightning to the Children eased
With explanation kind
The Truth must dazzle gradually
Or every man be blind —

—Emily Dickinson

Table of Contents

Chapter 129 An Uncommon Character 1505
Chapter 130 Matt's Question 1520
Chapter 131 Acceptance 1534
Chapter 132 Cold Showers 1545
Chapter 133 Forbidden Fruit 1559
Chapter 134 Pancakes 1575
Chapter 135 Surprises 1590
Chapter 136 Lemon Drops and Stones 1598
Chapter 137 The Phone Call 1609
Chapter 138 Promises 1616
Chapter 139 Plans 1626
Chapter 140 Permission Granted 1641
Chapter 141 Balances, Deposits, and Bank Accounts 1648
Chapter 142 Cinco 1655
Chapter 143 Perseverance 1663
Chapter 144 Of Motes and Beams 1669
Chapter 145 Emma 1679
Chapter 146 עץ חיים 1695
Chapter 147 Conscientious Partakers 1723
Chapter 148 The Parkins 1737
Chapter 149 The Gazebo 1765
Chapter 150 The Work of Joy 1770
Chapter 151 Of Socks and Green Tomatoes 1785

Chapter 152 17927 1802
Chapter 153 Success in Circuit Lies 1815
Chapter 154 Confessions 1827
Chapter 155 Buttercup 1844
Chapter 156 The Final Frolic 1855
Chapter 157 The Last Sermon 1867
Chapter 158 A Quaker Wedding 1885
Chapter 159 Finale 1890
Afterward 1897
Postlude 1911
About the Author 1920

PRELUDE

I've delayed beginning this book for very selfish reasons—I don't want it to end. That, and I realize how much work this is going to be to wrap things up in a way that will keep both my readers and the campers on Harmony Hill happy.

After four Ruby books already—and three more if you've read the Isaac series—you're probably well invested. You've learned to care about Ruby and Pops. You've alternated between wanting to punch Genevieve in the face and wanting put your arm around her and tell her everything is going to be all right if she would just_____.
(fill in the blank)

Somehow I've heard you talking back to the characters you've both loved and loathed. I've sensed your frustrations and disappointments, and I've noticed how you've recognized a piece of your own heart in this summer's quirky set of campers. I've listened to your predictions, and I've resisted telling more than I know, not wanting to make promises I didn't know if I could keep.

When I packed my bags for my first visit to Harmony Hill, I really had no idea what I was getting myself into. A real writer might have been able to guesstimate the time required, but I'm not a real writer. I'm a potter. I write when I can, in between shows, or whenever the folks from Harmony Hill refuse to leave me alone.

When Ruby and Pops began dropping by the studio, more than a dozen years ago, they had some great stories to tell that made me laugh, made me think, and occasionally made me weep. I was impressed and felt compelled to do what I could to share their stories, but I had a hard time knowing how and where I would fit it all in. I had pots to make and had overextended myself, making promises to many other stories that were begging to be told. They've been patient with me—they've had to be, but they were old when they first showed up, and have only grown older with each subsequent visit.

After several years of small talk and random stories from their time on Harmony Hill, they finally got down to business and told me why they'd made the many journeys to my door. Their motivations, they admitted, were based in love and hope, but they couldn't deny that they were laced with fear—fear that what they had to share might be forgotten and lost if more people did not learn the keys of joy.

Perhaps, like me, you've tried to guess the keys. By now you've learned four of them. This last one was the most difficult for me to learn, but I suppose that shouldn't be a surprise. I've never been a natural at it. Few of us are. And thus, joy—real joy—is rare.

As keepers of the ancient keys, Pops's and Ruby's biggest concern has long been that they would pass on before the keys could be shared with a broader audience than just the twelve campers they bring to the farm each summer. Sure, Niederbipp has many inhabitants who know the keys and live their lives by them. Folks like the Parkins, who run the marriage retreat center out of their home just north of town, are helping to spread the word as well. But they've all agreed that the important work of joy needs a broader platform, one that could reach far more people and help spread the historic truths which the broader world has largely forgotten.

From all my experiences with Pops and Ruby, and the time I've spent on Harmony Hill, I know two things for certain. 1. Joy truly does exist, and 2. Most of us are unwittingly living contrary to the formula that might produce it.

But it doesn't have to be that way. Joy is light. It is hope. It is elevating, ennobling and empowering. And it's available to anyone, male or female, rich or poor, regardless of where you come from or who you voted for. There is, however, a formula, a recipe—one that cannot be ignored and one which all true seekers of joy must embrace.

These keys may be new for you. They may be difficult to live at first. But I invite you to set your prejudices and preconceived notions aside and embrace them. Ultimately, you have very little to lose, but the greatest joys in the universe to gain.

Let me know how it goes.

Thank you for being patient with me as I've learned the art of writing. I hope you've enjoyed this journey so far. I've enjoyed traveling with you, running ahead a mile or so each night when we pull into camp, and returning with stories of the vistas up ahead.

Though this will be the last of Ruby's stories, there are many more characters who've been knocking on my door, begging me to share theirs. I'm not making any promises, but know they will come when the time is right and the circumstances provide. Until then, I hope you'll enjoy this last tale from Harmony Hill.

It may be some time before I get back to Niederbipp, but the Niederbippians have carved out an indelible place in my heart. I hope they have in yours as well. They are each as real to me as you are, and I'm grateful to have been able to introduce them to you. Now that you know each other, I hope you'll have occasion to hang out together more regularly. They remind me a lot of you, and I knew you'd find many things in common.

Friends, cheers to the journey, and Viva Niederbipp!
Ben Behunin

December 2022

CHAPTER 129

An Uncommon Character

God is not looking for extraordinary characters as His instruments, but He is looking for humble instruments through whom He can be honored throughout the ages
—Albert Benjamin Simpson—

Genevieve couldn't help but smile as she and Matt walked across the stony riverbank, hand in hand. She couldn't help but smile as he helped her up the steep stairs cut into the earthen bank. Nor could she help but smile as they walked along the path, still holding hands, all the way back to where the path crossed in front of the Engelhart Ebenezer and ended at the highway.

But before they reached the blacktop of the highway, the joyful sounds of children's voices alerted them to the fact that they were no longer alone. Matt squeezed Genevieve's hand softly before letting it go just as two children broke through the tall grasses and willows that obscured the perpendicular path. Two adults followed close behind them, looking winded as they jogged to keep up.

"Oh, hello there," Genevieve said, recognizing the woman with the bright, red-rimmed glasses and the middle-aged man who followed close behind.

"Oh, hey," the man replied. "I hope our kids didn't run you over."

"No, but it looks like they're ready for an adventure," Matt responded, turning to see the young boy attempting to scale the rocky face of the Ebenezer while his sister playfully spanked his bottom.

"Mom said you're not allowed to climb that," the little girl insisted. But the little boy wasn't listening, quickly climbing above the reach of his younger tormenter.

"Mom said, P.J.!"

"It looks like you've been blessed with two strong personalities," Matt said, taking a step closer to the kids. "If I remember right, your daughter's name is Hazel, right?"

The man turned and smiled. "I'm sorry, have we met? You guys look familiar, but I can't place you."

"No, I don't think we've ever officially met, but you've probably seen us at church, and I helped you guys a few weeks ago at the farm stand," Matt replied. "My grandmother's name was Hazel, and I remember thinking when your wife gave her sermon a while back that it's cool that some of the old names are being used again."

The man peeled the young boy off the monument and set him down on the ground. "I'm Paul Meier," he responded, turning to take Matt's hand.

"Matt Owens. And this is Genevieve Patterson. We've bumped into your wife a couple of times in town, but it's nice to finally meet you."

"Yes, it's nice to see you again," Susan responded. "I expected to hear from you after seeing you at the grocery store. You're the writer, aren't you?" she asked, turning to Genevieve.

"Yeah, that's right. I'm sorry. We've been busy on the farm and I haven't had a chance to get away, but I'd still really love to chat. Maybe a Sunday afternoon sometime?"

Susan chuckled as she turned to see that P.J. was taking advantage of his parent's diversion to scale a different face of the Ebenezer. "If you don't mind being distracted by constant interruptions, colorful shenanigans, and capricious capers, Sunday afternoons are usually a great time to chat," she said with another chuckle as she walked to the monument and peeled her son off the perch he had found four feet off the ground, returning him to terra firma. "As you can tell, we have two very busy children."

"That's the way they should be," Matt said, tousling the young boy's hair.

The boy looked up at him and smiled before stomping his small foot down on Matt's shoe.

"That's not nice, P.J.!" Hazel protested.

"Mind your own beeswax," P.J. responded before running off to chase a butterfly.

"I'm sorry about that," Paul replied. "P.J. obviously has some energy to burn."

Matt laughed. "Not a problem. Your kids look like a lot of fun."

"Fun and exhausting," Paul replied. "There are plenty of arguments for having your kids early, and I'm a living witness that all of them are true. On days like today, when we'd rather be napping than galivanting off to throw rocks in the river, we have to remind ourselves that we're lucky to have them. But most days are more fun than a barrel of monkeys around here. They do a great job keeping us young while simultaneously reminding us how old we are."

Susan stepped closer to her husband, wrapping her arm around his waist as he rested his arm on her shoulder. "They make me crazy every single day, and yet I can't imagine my life without them."

"I'm impressed that you're still finding a way to be productive," Genevieve said without thinking. "Sorry, that sounded...bad. But didn't you also just publish a new book?"

Susan nodded. "Almost. *Zen In The Art Of Wrestling with Angels and Demons* will be released in three weeks."

"Congratulations, that's quite an accomplishment, especially considering your *extracurricular activities*," Genevieve said, nodding toward the children. "I've always wanted to write a book."

"Oh, in which genre do you normally write?"

Genevieve quickly glanced at Matt before responding. "I work for a woman's magazine, and until recently wrote mostly about international fashion and trends."

"That sounds exciting. But not anymore?" Susan asked.

Genevieve shook her head. "I...I still work for the magazine...but my assignment is changing. I...I guess I still don't know exactly what it will be, but I think it will be more...substantive."

"That sounds exciting as well," Susan responded, letting go of Paul as he and Matt rushed to help P.J. untangle his T-shirt from the low branch of a scrubby shrub he'd been attempting to climb.

"I think it could be," Genevieve continued. "I'm still working on wrapping my head around it, but, as it turns out, it requires some pretty big changes, including relocating here."

"To Niederbipp?" she asked, looking quite surprised.

"Yes, and more specifically to Harmony Hill."

Susan nodded thoughtfully, looking at Genevieve carefully. "That can mean only one thing."

"What's that?"

"That you've been asked to become the next matchmaker of Niederbipp."

Genevieve couldn't hide her surprise. "What do you know?"

Susan chuckled. "It's no secret that Ruby's getting older. There's an incredible story there, as I'm sure you know. I tried chasing it myself a couple of times, but she always said she was waiting for the right time. I think what she really meant was that she was waiting for the right person. And it sounds like that person is you."

Genevieve smiled weakly. "I'm sorry. The last thing I would want is for you to feel like I'm encroaching on your turf."

"No. Not at all," Susan responded. "I couldn't possibly do it the justice it deserves. I wondered what medium her story would be told through, and I have to admit I never considered it being told through a woman's magazine. I would imagine they'd probably have to dedicate the better part of a year's worth of content to her story."

Genevieve nodded, feeling overwhelmed with her assignment once again. "It's supposed to start with a ten-thousand-word photo essay and go from there."

"Wow, that's amazing! How are you feeling about it?"

She shook her head. "It depends on the moment, but generally overwhelmed. She has such a legacy, you know. And then there are the keys of joy, and the history of the farm, and the rest of the town, and their life's work, and Pops, and…"

"Yeah, I can see how you would feel overwhelmed. And you're going to ultimately take her place on top of that?"

Genevieve grimaced. "It's taken me a couple of months to think about, but I…I've just decided accept Ruby's offer."

"You mean like…today?"

Genevieve nodded sheepishly.

"That's exciting news! And Matt…is he planning on being…?"

Genevieve turned to look at the others, noticing how Matt had knelt on the ground next to P.J., who was standing tall with his mouth wide open while the boy's father and sister looked on.

"What are they doing now?" Susan asked.

"I'm not sure, but Matt's a dentist. He's planning on taking over for Dr. Cummings at the end of the summer."

"Well, that's great news! Don't get me wrong, you'd have trouble finding a nicer dentist than Dr. Cummings, but his hands aren't very steady anymore, and I'm not sure if his mind is either. Paul and I were just talking the other day—when P.J. showed us his first loose tooth—that we're going to have to find a new dentist. That would be great to have a younger dentist in town, so we don't have to drive all the way to Warren. But wait...if you're taking over the farm...and Matt's taking over the dental office...? Is there someone else?"

Genevieve blushed.

"Sorry, that's none of my *beeswax*, is it?"

"It seems like everybody shares a whole lot of beeswax around here. This is all new, and we've obviously got a lot of things to figure out."

"So, are you saying Matt is your?...do you plan to?...Sorry to be nosey."

Genevieve smiled, watching Matt as he pointed to each of P.J.'s teeth and helped Hazel keep her numbers straight as they counted them together.

"He's a man of uncommon character, isn't he?"

"You know him?"

She shook her head. "Not much more than I get to know most of you campers. I've been watching Ruby's summer recruits from a distance for more than thirty years as they've come and gone, but I'm sure I've probably paid more attention in the years since moving back. You see a lot of personalities and characters in that amount of time, and, if you're at all observant, you see a lot of change and progress over the course of a summer. Of course, our observations are limited, based mostly on what we see at church, and the farm stand, and your irregular comings and goings in town."

"And what have you seen?"

Susan thought for a moment. "If I had to boil it down to one word, I think I'd call it hope."

"Hope? You mean like in the keys of joy?"

"Yes. I don't think I understood what hope really is until I came here. The hope around here is a full, rich, all-inclusive hope—almost like a light that penetrates all things with encouragement and fortitude."

Genevieve nodded thoughtfully.

"It's inspiring to watch what I'd generally consider *boys stuck in men's bodies*—how they somehow grow up and mature over the course of the summer, most of them waking up to the fact that there's a whole lot more to life than living for the weekend. And then to see women, dusting off their eyes and recognizing their innate physical and spiritual strengths that they'd never known before…It's really quite remarkable… the magic that happens up there on Harmony Hill."

Genevieve considered the changes that had taken place in her own life over the past three months, the appreciation she'd gained for her personal strengths and the awareness of her many weaknesses which she'd never previously considered.

"Yeah, it's inspiring to watch beautiful changes as confidence grows," Susan continued. "I know the recruits that come here each summer are usually looking for something more, something better than the mediocrity and indifference that popular culture is serving up hot in cities across the world. Y'all are a different sort, arriving ready to work on yourselves, to face your challenges and demons, to become better humans. Watching that evolution gives me hope that character and integrity are not dead, and that my children *will* have strong peers and mindful, whole-hearted people with whom they can pursue their own joy."

She stopped speaking for a moment and turned and pointed to the Ebenezer. "You probably already know that this town—the people who came here and built this place—they understood things that most people have forgotten—if they ever knew them at all. Reverence for God and creation. Living and loving with compassion and charity. Learning how to take control of your life and your appetites through self-discipline. Developing patience for yourself and others…"

She shook her head, turning back to Genevieve. "If you think about it, these are the answers to all the world's troubles. Paul and I have yet to come up with even one challenge to marriage, family, or life in general that couldn't be made better if not completely avoided if more people would embrace the keys of joy. It's a beautiful thing to watch evolution in motion every summer as new campers arrive in Niederbipp, then leave five months later with a richer appreciation for the purposes of life and a determination to set a new course toward a life filled with meaning, whole-hearted ambition, and joy."

Genevieve nodded solemnly, recognizing how the course of her own life had taken just such a turn over the last three months. She turned and smiled at Susan. "It took me a minute to fully appreciate it, but I know now that this is where I'm supposed to be."

Susan returned the smile. "Then welcome. This town could use another writer. I'm glad you're here."

They turned to see that P.J. was now counting his sister's teeth as she stood before him, her mouth agape.

Susan nodded toward the men and her children. "A friend once told me that deciding who I married would be the most important decision of my life. I had no idea how right he was. I'm so grateful that my heart and head were in a place where I could make that decision with clarity and understanding, and that we've been able to build our life together on the foundation of joy."

"That's what this town is all about, isn't it?" Genevieve responded. "Joy!"

"Yes, but it's curious that only those who are ready for joy see it for what it truly is, especially in the beginning. To those who aren't ready, Niederbipp is just another backwater town at the crossroads to nowhere."

"I'll admit that may have crossed my mind in the beginning."

"What changed?"

Genevieve thought for a moment. "Maybe everything. The first couple of weeks lasted an eternity, and now…now I can't imagine having to leave at the end of the summer."

"I've recognized that for those who open their heart to the possibilities of joy, the humble yet resolute voices of generations of

Niederbippians rise up from the ground beneath our feet and sing out across time and space, joining with unseen choirs of angels in affirming joy's most ennobling truths."

Genevieve nodded slowly. "And you…do you consider yourself a Niederbippian, or an angel?"

Susan looked at Genevieve with a warm smile. "When it comes right down to it, the song is the same, either way."

"Joy?" she asked after a moment's thought.

"Yes, joy, but also grace and hope."

"And your new book, *Zen In the Art of Wrestling With Angels and Demons*…can I assume part of it is your story about finding your way to hope and joy?"

Susan nodded. "The best stories we can write are the ones we know the best."

Genevieve took a deep breath and exhaled slowly. "There's a lot I still don't know about all of this."

"Of course, there is. But remember you're only a few months into a formula that was designed to be fully understood over the course of a lifetime."

"Doesn't that ever feel overwhelming and discouraging?"

"Sure, especially in impatient moments when we want to see the whole picture. But you have to remember that when you sign on to live according to the keys of joy, you're never doing it alone."

Genevieve thought for a moment, then nodded. "I assume you're speaking about God?"

"Yes. Except the Lord build the house…"

Susan's words surprised Genevieve, but without missing a beat she completed the proverb. "…they labor in vain that build it. That's the first lesson of the farm."

"Yes, but that's also the first lesson for everyone who chooses to walk the path of joy. Paul and I learned that from Ruby and Pops ourselves shortly after we got married and began our own foray into more deeply understanding the joys which we, until then, had only flirted with."

Genevieve nodded slowly. "Is that what you would call moving them from your head to your heart?"

"Exactly. But like you, and everyone else who has ever pursued the path of joy, we've only built what we have by adding one brick at a time."

"I'd say you guys have created something beautiful together."

"Thank you, but this *house* we're working on together is far from finished."

"Really?" Genevieve looked quite surprised.

Susan nodded. "We've come a long way, and we're grateful every day for the understanding we've gained over these past several years. But God is still working with us, teaching us, helping us to see that He has much bigger hopes and plans than we have for ourselves. We catch glimpses of His grand design from time to time, but most days we are each placing one brick or one stone upon another, patiently persevering as the three of us build this thing together."

Genevieve nodded thoughtfully, looking a little discouraged. "So, does it ever get beyond being work?"

"I don't know. I'm not sure it's supposed to." Susan mused.

"No?"

"Look at Ruby and Pops. Look at Hildegard. They're the oldest people I know and they don't seem to be doing much coasting."

"No, I guess you're right."

"Yeah, they're still building, aren't they? They're still laying bricks, and planting trees, and even worrying about the small stuff like cleaning windows and sweeping the front porch. As far as I can tell from watching them, all of those things are part of moving things from your head to your heart."

Genevieve shook her head but smiled. "I really had no idea what I was signing up for when I came here three months ago."

"I don't know if anyone ever does. But if you knew then what you know now, would you still have come?"

Genevieve thought for a moment, but her answer was clear. "Yes. I didn't know…and I guess I still don't know a lot, but yes, it feels right…it feels good. I have this undeniable feeling that this is what I'm supposed to be doing…what I was made to do."

Susan smiled again. "Then I'd say you've discovered the power of moving what matters most from your head into your heart. That's where all good things happen."

Genevieve nodded slowly, thoughtfully. "What does that mean to you?"

"How long have you got?"

"How long do you need?"

"I'm still figuring it out myself. I know how it feels more than I have words to describe it. As one who spent most of her life in academia where empirical evidence and tangible proof defines all acceptable truth, I've had to learn a new way of processing and understanding truths that can neither be weighed or measured by any scientific method."

"You're talking about spiritual truths—about the keys of joy?"

Susan nodded. "The scientific method works great for most things in our physical world, but it quickly falls short when it comes to discerning things of a spiritual context. You can't physically weigh the value of a charitable act for example. You can't chart the innumerable changes that come into one's life when they begin to experience the world through the lens of reverence. Hope, so far as I can see, quickly becomes a natural byproduct of even just attempting to live life at the intersection of charity and reverence. But you start poking around, start taking a closer look at how the keys interact with each other, how they build on each other and support each other, and pretty soon you see that the keys—if one will embrace them—have the ability to change even good lives into something better and richer. And there's really no end to the possibilities that living a life of joy can provide."

"I'm beginning to see that. But if it's so good, why don't more people know about it? I never would have imagined that really any of the keys might have the power to produce anything like what I've seen and experienced here."

Susan nodded. "I remember wondering the same thing when we first began opening our hearts to the deeper understanding of joy that the keys offer."

"And what have you come up with?"

"Well, the keys are relatively simple, aren't they? And they cost nothing other than the setting aside of a little pride and embracing a conscious change of pace and mindset. What corporation would ever be tempted into marketing such an enterprise when there's no status, no wealth, no honors or glory to be gained? In a world that's defined by all of those things, where pride and greed and financial status have become the driving force of most individuals, the keys quickly become a trifling amusement or dusty relics of a forgotten past which are easily blown aside by the roaring winds of narcissism.

"Knowledge may be power, but as long as that knowledge remains undigested or unassimilated, its power is limited in its ability to truly nourish and improve one's life. My father could recall libraries full of *knowledge,* yet he was either unable or unwilling to recognize the simple yet elegant truths of the keys of joy. He must have walked along this path thousands of times in the years he lived here, yet to my knowledge he never took the time to sit on one of Isaac's benches and allow the truths that surrounded him to percolate into his heart."

"That sounds familiar. I'd guess we probably all do that to some degree, right?"

Susan nodded. "It's sad, but true, and I suppose there are as many reasons and roadblocks as there are people who cling to them. But until we choose to overcome those reasons and roadblocks, until our sincere craving for truth and joy overpowers our hesitation or indifference, we are doomed to languish, separated from all that can be by our holding too tightly onto what is comfortable."

"So, basically…fear?"

Susan chuckled. "You almost sound like you've read my book."

"Maybe it's just that I've been wrestling with my own angels and demons."

Susan smiled and nodded. "Just as any sincere seeker must."

Genevieve turned back to the men and the children who had turned their attention to stacking small stones along the edge of the path. She watched silently for a moment, observing the playful, energetic children and their patient, older companions who sincerely seemed to be enjoying a chance to play.

"There's something you're not asking," Susan said, waiting for Genevieve to turn and look at her. "It feels like there was a deeper reason you wanted to talk to me."

Genevieve nodded, turning again to the men and the children. "I wondered when I heard your sermon, and every time I've seen you since, if you'd do it all again—if you'd leave your presumably comfortable job with its salary, and perks, and independence, and throw it all…or…I mean, set it all aside to move here and have a family instead?"

Susan remained silent for a moment, watching her children interacting with their father and Matt. "Let me ask you this," she said. "Knowing the little that you know about me, what would you guess would be my answer to your question?"

Genevieve smiled as Hazel stood from her pile of rocks, threw her hands up in the air and joyfully proclaimed, "Daddy, I got one in a row!"

She turned again to Susan. "I'm pretty sure I never would have said this before coming here this summer, but I think you made the right choice—the best choice!"

"Thank you. I have colleagues who told me I was insane to leave my tenured position, a respectable income, and the gravitas and respect I'd accumulated over my nearly two decades of teaching. But knowing what I know now, my biggest regret is that I didn't do it sooner. Becoming a mother was a colossal change of pace, and there are still plenty of challenging moments, questions and concerns. But I love this," she said, motioning to her family. "I love my life. I love my husband and my children. And I love this chance to explore so many aspects of this beautiful, joyful world I never could have known had I stayed in my comfortable position and not taken the chance to move my hopes and dreams from my head to my heart. That's really the only place dreams can take flight—that the full extent of the magic can be realized."

Hazel stood and excitedly ran to her mother, grabbing her hand and pulling her toward the others. "Look, Mommy," she said, pointing to the small stack of rocks on the ground. "I got three this time!"

Genevieve followed close behind, catching Matt's eye as she drew close. He smiled warmly at her, and in that moment there was a flash of magic that passed between them, an undeniable understanding and connection that made it difficult for either of them to look away. But Hazel had other plans, and she was not about to let something as ethereal as that momentary connection interfere with her agenda.

"Mr. Matt, you're coming to the river with us, right?" she asked for the third time, tapping him on the shoulder where he knelt on the ground near the rocks they'd been stacking.

"Huh?" he responded, finally breaking his gaze and turning to the girl.

"Are you coming with us to the river? I'm learning to skip rocks. It's fun. You should come. My dad can teach you."

Matt smiled at her, placing his hand on top of her head. "I would love to do that, but I already promised Genevieve I would go with her."

The little girl looked very disappointed.

"But can we come with you another time?" Matt continued.

"Tomorrow?"

"Uh, tomorrow might be tough. Genevieve and I have to work on the farm and sometimes we don't know how long that will take. But we could maybe come by in the afternoon if we get our work done early."

The girl's face brightened quickly. "Mommy, he's going to play with me tomorrow!" she reported loudly as if her mother had missed the entire interaction.

"That sounds fun," Susan replied.

"Yep, and did you know he knows the Tooth Fairy? And he helped me count P.J.'s teeth."

"He sounds like a good guy," Susan acknowledged.

"Yep, he pretty much is. Can he come to my birthday party?"

"Uh, sure Honey, but that's not until next spring. Why don't we just plan one day at a time?"

"He can come to my birthday, too, Mom," P.J. announced.

"Well, it sounds like we have the next ten months all planned out," Susan replied, turning to Genevieve. "It seems," she whispered to Genevieve under her breath, "that even my kids can appreciate his uncommon character."

Matt stood, patting each of the kids' heads before dusting off his knees. "I'll do my best to see you two tomorrow." He shook Paul's hand before approaching the women. "You've got a couple of great kids."

"Thank you. We like them," Susan said. "Thanks for taking the time to play. I understand you may be taking over for Dr. Cummings to be the next dentist in town."

Matt glanced at Genevieve quickly before turning back to Susan. "I thought I would be, until recently. I…we…we have a lot of questions to answer over the next couple of months."

"Then I'll try to mind my own business and let you guys figure things out. It sounds like there's a bright future for both of you."

"I hope so," Matt said, smiling at Genevieve.

"There will always be questions," Susan said, smiling at both of them as they turned to her, "but living according to the keys of joy will help you remember that all good, sincere, honest questions have answers that are waiting patiently to be discovered. And in quiet moments, when the clarity is rich and pure, you will know—if you care to see it—that there's a blueprint for your life that's bigger and better than you ever could have dreamed."

CHAPTER 130

Matt's Question

All my discoveries have been made in answer to prayer.
—Isaac Newton—

Matt and Genevieve watched until the small family had disappeared into the willows that grew along the trail before they turned away and continued their quest. They hurried through the town's quiet streets, hoping they might find Ruby and Pops among Jake and Amy's Sourdough Sunday gathering. And though the crowd included many of the campers and a few dozen other visitors, Pops and Ruby were not among them.

Learning from Crystal that their elderly hosts had headed back to the farm after church, they quickly greeted Jake and Amy, thanking Amy for her sermon. Then snagging a couple slices of bread, they made a quick escape from the courtyard.

While they biked back to the farm, Genevieve shared with Matt the things she'd learned from Susan, and Matt shared with Genevieve the things he'd learned from Paul and the kids. They briefly discussed the idea of raising kids according to the keys of joy until the reality of having children began to feel overwhelming. As they dismounted their bikes and began pushing them up the steepest part of Harmony Hill, the conversation ceased. Of course, part of that was due to them both being out of breath, but there was another part that felt strangely awkward for both of them. What had felt comfortable and right on the banks of the river just an hour earlier was now less than comfortable. In addition, the reality of what they were about to commit to had also begun to weigh heavily on their minds and hearts. The descent down the farm's rutted drive was made without any conversation at all, and by the time they'd parked their bikes in the shed, the silence had grown deafening.

Matt reached for Genevieve's hand, and they stood shoulder to shoulder at the bottom of the front step, looking up at the big house and the porch where they'd spent most of their evenings over the last three months.

"Are we really doing this?" Matt asked.

Genevieve smiled weakly. "Are you already having second thoughts?"

"I'm having a hard time knowing exactly what I'm feeling, to be honest. Part of me is excited, and another part of me is completely scared of the commitment."

She turned and looked up at the house, considering the extent of the commitment they were about to make. "Are you talking about the farm, or marriage?"

Matt turned and looked at her, his eyes filled with uncertainty. "I feel like I've got some catching up to do."

"Huh?"

"I think you're at least one step ahead of me. You've got your answer about how you're going to be spending the next fifty years of your life. Me...I'm still trying to figure out how to work that idea out of my head and into my heart."

Genevieve nodded after a moment, turning to look up at the house. "That's fair. Do you need some time?"

"I'm not sure what I need. I've just been thinking about how I've made a lot of decisions over the last twenty years—many of them relatively big decisions. I came here because I wanted to get married and move on with my life, and now that it's a real possibility...I guess I'm just reeling from all that's changed over the course of a couple of hours. I mean...shoot, this feels like the biggest decision of my life—actually the *two* biggest decisions, neither of which existed this morning when I got out of bed. It's kind of a big deal, isn't it?"

Genevieve laughed. Turning her back to the house, she stood in front of Matt and looked up into his eyes. "You do recognize that you don't have to do any of this alone, right?"

Her words brought a sudden halt to Matt's internal struggle. He knew she was right. Saying yes to any of this meant he was no longer flying solo. There would be far more to consider than he'd ever known before, but there would also be more to share, more to talk about, more than just his own thoughts to regard and consider. The idea of having someone to help him make choices and decisions felt both exciting and clunky, liberating and heavy. Why had he never considered this? He looked deeply into her eyes, surprised to recognize the connection he found there. But it was more than just a connection to her. There was some totally foreign yet strangely familiar sense of calm, an unmistakable reassurance that made it difficult for him to look away. He took a deep breath and let it out slowly, calmly, the spent air drawing out a lifetime of fear and hesitation.

Raising his hands to her shoulders, he gently pulled her closer. She responded in kind, wrapping her arms around his chest until they could feel each other's hearts beating.

"This is crazy, right?" he said, holding her even tighter.

"Probably, but which part of crazy are you talking about?"

"Committing to spend the rest of our lives doing something we knew nothing about just three months ago?"

"Maybe, but do you think it's much different than any other couple who's ever committed to run this farm? I can't imagine it was much different for Pops and Ruby, and it seems like they've done okay, right?"

"Okay, but they have all the answers. They know what to do when the chickens stop laying or the milking machine stops working. They know how to trim the fruit trees and plant the garden and stop the campers from killing each other."

Genevieve laughed, pulling her head back from his shoulder so she could look into his eyes again. "I'm pretty sure they didn't know how to do any of that before they came here, either."

"Okay, but I'm sure they knew more than us. Look at us! A dentist and a writer! What could we possibly teach anyone about making a good marriage?"

"Well, we could start by having the kind of marriage that would inspire campers to hope and believe they could create a good marriage of their own."

"Do you really think we have what it takes to inspire anyone?"

"Probably not on our own, but look what Ruby and Pops have created together. From everything we've learned, they came here very different than they are today."

He nodded, looking thoughtful. "And you really want to get tangled up with an old guy like me?"

Genevieve rolled her eyes. "How old do you feel?"

"What does that matter?"

"It's an important question. How old do you feel?"

"Most days I feel like I'm about twenty-five. Why?"

"I've always had a hard time considering myself older than twenty-four, so really, what's the difference? Sure, you've had a few more years to read and travel and learn than I have, but that feels like more of an asset than a liability. I've already told you that our age difference really doesn't matter to me."

"It might not now, but what about in forty years when I'm eighty-three and you're not even seventy?"

"Then you'll have to work a little harder to keep up."

Matt laughed. "I already do."

She rolled her eyes. "You really are a terrible salesman!"

"I just don't want you to feel stuck with an old man who's slowing you down."

"Are you sure that's all it is?"

He looked at her for a moment before letting out a long breath. "I've never had much confidence, and I definitely never would have thought that someone as put-together and beautiful as you would be interested in a dud like me. I'm just afraid that you're going to wake up and realize I'm a loser and that you could've done a lot better."

Genevieve shook her head before burying her face in his shoulder, holding him tight. She didn't let go for what felt like at least a full minute. "I can't imagine ever feeling this close to anyone else," she finally said. "I'll admit that the love I feel for you has grown slowly, but I really can't imagine what this summer would have been like without you here to help me open my eyes and heart to so many things I've been missing."

She lifted her head and studied his face. "I know it's only been three months since you pulled me out of the mud, but the patience and kindness you've shown me…the beautiful moments we've shared together…the way you always know what I need to hear even when I hate to hear it…I love you, Matt. You could turn around and walk away and never speak to me again and I'm sure I'd have to spend the rest of my life searching for the love and kindness you've given me because now that I know it, I know I could never be truly happy without it."

Matt smiled, shaking his head as he looked up at the big house, then back at Genevieve. "I love you, too."

"That's almost enough for me," she said, moving her arms from around his ribs to over his neck, pulling his face down till their noses touched. She kissed him softly. The kiss was short, but it was enough for them both to know that the spark of physical attraction they felt for each other was sufficient for love to continue to grow between them without worrying about potential incompatibility issues down the road.

Matt licked his lips and smiled. "Don't get me wrong…that was really nice, but I don't think we can be doing this. Not yet. We can't make this weird for everyone else and risk messing up the magic with the other campers."

She laughed. "Hey, I never signed a contract."

"But I did."

"Relax, I know. I just needed to check to make sure it wasn't…you know…weird."

"Was it?" he asked, looking almost fearful of her answer.

She shook her head, smiling broadly.

The sound of the screen door closing behind them caused them both to jump and they turned quickly to see Pops and Ruby walking across the porch, hand in hand.

"Well, what are you kids up to?" Pops asked.

"Uh, we…uh…we were hoping to chat…with both of you," Matt replied.

Ruby smiled. "About this," she said, pointing to their still-entangled arms, "or something more pressing?"

Matt and Genevieve looked at each other, trying not to smile before turning back to Ruby.

"Both," they said in unison.

"I see. Well, Pops and I were just heading down to visit the Ebenezer behind the milking barn. Would you like to join us?"

Genevieve turned to Matt.

"Um, sure, but I need a couple of minutes to myself. Can I meet the three of you down there?" Matt asked.

Ruby glanced at Pops before nodding. "If we don't see you in half an hour, we'll send ol' Rex to find you."

Matt smiled weakly, untangling his arms from Genevieve's. "I'll meet you there. I just have to catch up with Genevieve." He turned and left in a quick jog, hurrying past both bunkhouses and disappearing into the woods.

"It's a beautiful day for love to grow," Ruby said when Matt could no longer be seen.

Genevieve turned to find her elderly hosts smiling at her. "Yes, it is. I hope you don't mind, but I kissed him."

Ruby laughed. "Well, it's about time."

"Excuse me?"

"You heard me. I've been wondering what you were waiting for."

"But I…I thought that was forbidden."

"Well, for those who've signed contracts, it is. But for you…let's just say it's strongly encouraged that you not tell any of the other campers about it. And, I might add, that I'd suggest you not do it again until October. Matt signed the contract, and he'll be held accountable for his actions, both those today and those in the future."

"What are you going to do to him?"

Pops laughed. "It will all depend on what you kids have to talk to us about. If it's what we hope, I'd say ten lashings with a wet noodle ought to suffice."

"And if it's not?"

"Then we'll have to think up something dreadful." He smiled and winked at Genevieve. "I promised Mom a stroll after our power nap. Would you like to join us now or wait for your Mr. Darcy?"

Genevieve smiled brightly. "I think I better join you. I'd hate to miss him."

"We wouldn't want you to miss him either, Dear. Come, let me take your arm. I'm feeling tired today," said Ruby.

"Would you like to just stay here on the porch?"

"No. The porch is my favorite room in the house, but it's not much of a place for privacy. You never know who'll be joining us, especially on a Sunday afternoon as glorious as this one. Come. It sounds like we have some things to discuss." Ruby held out her hand and Genevieve was quick to move her elbow within range for the matriarch of the farm to take it. Together they descended the stone steps and walked the well-worn path in the shadows cast by the ancient cottonwoods. The talk was pleasant and easy and the walk was slow as Ruby set the pace.

Genevieve wondered to herself how she'd been so blind as to miss most of Ruby's gradual physical decline. Her presence and wit were as strong as ever, but her speed and strength had certainly changed in the three short months since Ruby and Pops had whisked her out of the restaurant and driven her up Harmony Hill, sandwiched between them in the front of the pickup as if they were expecting an escape attempt. But this had also been the woman who'd taken her turn at the milking machines and on Bessie's saddle on the nights they made ice cream. She was nearly always in the kitchen before the campers arrived in the morning for KP duty, and to Genevieve's knowledge, she had yet to take even a few hours off, even though it had been nearly three months since her cancer diagnosis.

As they made their way slowly but steadily down the path, Matt continued to jog toward his destination: the old bench that overlooked the orchard. Genevieve had shared with him the things she'd learned about Thomas coming there to work on his sermons and other important questions. And Matt remembered Pops telling all the campers that it was there that he'd gone to pray for direction and inspiration about marrying Ruby and taking over the farm. The fact that Genevieve had her answer to both her marriage question and how she would be spending the next fifty years left Matt feeling hopeful.

Very unlike the girl he'd met just three months ago, Genevieve now wanted to be married. And what was even more thrilling was that she wanted to be married to him. Matt was not opposed to it. He'd learned to love her as he'd worked with her and they'd spent time talking during their free time. She had become only more beautiful to him with each passing day. And though he knew she was way out of his league, she had somehow, mystically, learned to love him, in spite of his best efforts to talk her out of it. But was that enough?

Matt had been inspired several times by conversations at the dinner table and other things that Ruby and Pops had shared with the group about the added strength that can come to a marriage when you know that heaven is behind you. Coming from a broken home, the only child of ill-matched parents, it had been impossible not to be affected in negative ways by their divorce and messy custody issues. And though it had been two-and-a-half decades since he'd left home and struck out on his own, the memories and baggage of his parents' failed marriage had always followed him on a short tether.

But somehow the tether had been cut this summer, and the unwanted baggage had been largely left on the road at the top of the drive. In the void, hope had flourished like a seed finally finding a fertile oasis after blowing across a barren desert for decades. Sprouting slowly at first, beginning when he heard of the farm from his co-worker, it had grown significantly with the arrival of his acceptance letter, a merciful boon to his impoverished self-confidence. But with it had also come a growing sense of anxiety and fear that he'd already wasted his best years and would be found too old or too odd for anyone to love.

Most of those anxieties were quickly put to rest upon arriving at the farm and realizing that though he was older, he wasn't much different than any of his comrades. They all had their strengths, but also their weaknesses. And somehow they'd all quickly come to the conclusion that their only real contenders or rivals were themselves. According to Pops and Ruby, they'd reached this place of wisdom far earlier than most years' campers, allowing each of them to focus their attention and efforts on working on themselves rather than wasting any precious time or energy focusing only on the weaknesses of others.

So far, it had been three great months full of growth and enlightenment. Thanks to Genevieve, Matt had been able to discover strengths he'd never recognized before. But she'd given him much more than that. Her early acceptance of him as a friend, an ally, and a confidant had filled a void he hadn't even recognized. That friendship had grown to warmth as they'd spent time together, working their way toward a better understanding of the keys of joy. Through it all, she had not only accepted him and befriended him, she had also loved him, quirks and all.

He loved her for that. But he also loved her for who she was. He'd watched her transformation from a prickly prima donna, full of piss and vinegar, into something far more approachable, even lovable. Somehow he'd been able to not only see through but *cut* through her more sassy and cantankerous fits and starts to find a soft and easier part that very few had ever been allowed to see. He knew the sass she was capable of transmitting, but it had been some time since he'd felt like he needed to watch his back or felt compelled to do what he could to smooth over her ruffled ego. Like the wild pony on the neighboring farm that she'd been visiting since shortly after her arrival, Genevieve had somehow been transformed from a petulant, unapproachable wild creature into an amenable and thoughtful woman with incomparable promise.

Arriving at the bench, Matt looked over the orchard, most of its trees still heavily laden with fruits of all kinds. He sat down, resting his back against the embedded ceramic tile. "Be still, and know that I am God," he repeated several times softly as he listened to the heartbeat pulsing in his ears slowly decrease.

Prayer was not entirely new for him. There'd been many short periods over his lifetime when prayer had played a role. He remembered several times from his youth, when his father was largely absent, that he'd sought God in prayer. Help had often come. But once the trouble had passed, his desire to pray had often gone with it. He'd learned meditation and mindfulness from local spiritual leaders in some of his travels. These less structured spiritual practices had been his closest thing to prayer in the recent years prior to coming to the farm. Pops and Ruby had created a safe space for prayer of all kinds, first by example, and later by invitation as soon as the campers felt comfortable enough to share. There had never been any pressure to participate, but there had been daily invitations to be both voice and ear.

Matt had learned to appreciate these moments of prayer and the chance it gave him to slow down, to focus, and to hear the reverent tones of communion with someone or something in a space both near and far away. Listening to his fellow campers learn to pray and watching them grow had softened his own heart. There were still hundreds of questions. He was quite certain there always would be. But he'd learned there were also answers. Through the foundation they'd been taught of reverence, hope, and charity, he'd also learned that there were answers to be had, answers to be shared, answers to offer direction, guidance and ultimately liberty and joy.

The recently common talk of marriage being life's most important decision had somehow imbued prayer with an even greater gravitas. Seeing the difference it had made for Genevieve just an hour earlier had left Matt with his own yearning to know. Somehow he knew that an answer now, in either direction, could influence all future decisions. But an answer, he knew, could also form a breakwater to challenges that arose in the future. He knew he needed help. And he knew that need would only grow increasingly larger if he chose to move forward with the course of action he and Genevieve had discussed.

As he sat listening to his heart and his head playing tug-o-war, Matt felt a calming surge of humility wash over him. He was facing what he knew were the biggest changes of his life, changes that would bring about untold sorrows and challenges, but also the potential of unprecedented joys. He needed to know. He needed answers.

He closed his eyes, hoping to focus. But in the sudden darkness he found light as he spoke the words of his heart. Following the pattern Pops and Ruby had demonstrated from the beginning, Matt began with gratitude. This quickly opened his mind and heart to a flood of people and experiences that had brought him to this point. He was here, sitting on this bench, asking these questions because of a million choices that had been made by himself and countless others. He opened his heart to all of those choices, the good and the bad, but especially those which had opened his heart to the possibility of finding joy.

Though his eyes remained closed, the light that filled his heart and mind continued to grow as his words asked the question. He'd committed to spend this summer on the farm because he wanted to be married. And now with the possibility of obtaining his desire standing right in front of him, was it right? Was Genevieve right for him?

He took a deep breath and listened, blocking out the soft purr of insects and birdsong. He repeated his question, rephrasing it this time as though he'd already made the decision to be her husband and only needed a thumbs up from the universe to move forward. With this there came an even greater light to his heart and mind, causing his heart to swell with a previously unknown quality of joy that caused his whole body to smile. The joy he felt in that moment was well beyond anything he'd known before and exponentially bigger than anything his mind could manufacture on its own. It was lush and full and seemed to nourish and fill him with both excitement and a unique sense of peace. He knew! He knew what he needed to know! He could marry Genevieve with confidence in knowing that, despite the many questions which remained, the heavens and the universe would help him.

But there remained another critical question: the farm. He'd come here to become a husband, not a farmer. This had never been part of his agenda. And though he'd grown to love the farm and the community that surrounded it, this would require additional changes—infinitely bigger changes—abiding, indelible, lifelong changes. Was he ready for that? Was he ready to give up his work and travels as a dentist; work that for twenty years had provided him with purpose, meaning and identity? It had been the source of great satisfaction as he'd helped people around the world be able to do such basic things as eating and smiling. Dr. Cummings had generously offered him his practice and a place to live and work for as long as he wanted. Could he just walk away from such a generous gift and exchange it for something that would require far more work, provide far less pay, and remove all future possibility of vacations, four-day work weeks, and travel?

Matt took another deep breath, weighing his options. He knew that Genevieve was ready to commit herself to the work of being the next matchmaker of Harmony Hill, if she hadn't already offered that commitment to Ruby and Pops. She was also ready to commit herself to being his wife. For a moment his mind was flooded with a deluge of unanswered questions about the potential of parenting young children while running a matchmaking farm, the loss of freedoms to travel at will, and the loss of all real income. Was this not simply too much to ask?

He was growing flustered when an image moved into his mind, bringing with it a sudden sense of calm and light. It was the balance scale that had been presented to them just two evenings earlier when they'd learned the fourth key of joy: self-discipline. This image and remembrance brought with it a quick end to the deluge of questions, allowing some semblance of peace to return. As he asked himself why these scales should appear to him now, his mind's eye was drawn to the Latin phrase inscribed at the bottom of the brass stand, TRADE NON QUOD VIS MAXIME QUOD VIS NUNC.

He paused, going back in his memory to Friday evening. What was it that Ruby had given as the translation? As the memory came, Matt took another deep breath, allowing the answer to permeate his lungs and fill his body with peace. "Trade not what you desire most for what you desire now," he whispered, repeating it several times, the light in his mind and heart growing brighter with each repetition.

What did he want most? He wanted marriage. He wanted to be a father. He wanted to help people. He wanted to make a difference in the world. Sure, he could do all of those things as a dentist, but at that moment he recognized that his vision had been limited to what he already knew. As Genevieve's husband and partner on the farm, the lives of twelve fortunate individuals could be changed for the better every summer. Those twelve individuals could go on to create marriages and families that could influence the lives of countless others. But with Genevieve's platform as a writer, the rare truths and the keys of joy they'd learned here could be shared with many more—infinitely more!

Matt's eyes filled with tears as he imagined the hope and goodness that might flood the world from the small trickle that could flow down Harmony Hill and out into a world that was starved of both hope and goodness. This vision was so filled with light and possibility that Matt felt his whole soul vibrating with the intensity of it. It wasn't the clarity he'd hoped for. It was vastly better! His recent dreams of becoming the dentist of Niederbipp evaporated in the bright glow of the higher light, taking with it every hesitation and unanswered question. He knew what he needed to do. He knew!

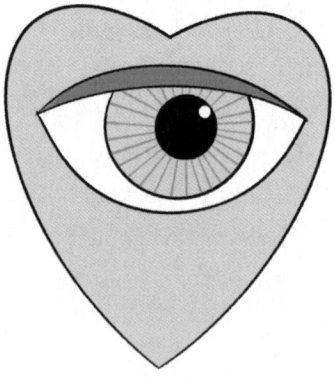

CHAPTER 131

Acceptance

The test of every religious, political, or educational system is the man that it forms.
—Henri Frederic Amiel—

Matt nearly floated back through the woods and across the path that led to the milk barn. He found Ruby and Genevieve sitting on the shadowed bench, quietly watching Pops as he wrestled with two low stones that were refusing to come into balance.

Genevieve looked up at Matt, her eyes filled with questions.

He smiled broadly and winked at her before moving in to help Pops who'd been startled by Matt's approach and had upset all but the two lowest stones. Pops, his forehead covered with beads of perspiration from the August sun, was quick to let Matt take over, taking a seat next to Ruby on the bench.

After adding a couple more of the largest stones, finding both his balance and his voice, Matt turned to face the spectators.

"Ruby, Pops, Genevieve and I have something important to talk to you about."

"That's what Genevieve told us," Ruby replied.

"You've already told them?" Matt asked, looking surprised.

"No. I wanted to wait for you," Genevieve said. She stood and walked next to Matt, sliding under his arm and wrapping her left arm around his waist. She looked up at him and smiled a smile that chased away all fears. He beamed, surprised that he still had tears left to roll down his cheeks. She brushed them away before squeezing him tight and turning back to face the watchful matriarch and her adoring husband who'd rested his arm on her shoulder, both of them waiting patiently for whatever was to come.

Genevieve turned and smiled again at Matt who nodded, encouraging her.

She cleared her throat, trying to swallow the joyful emotions that swirled all about her.

"Ruby, Pops, I…we…if the offer is still on the table, Matt and I would like to accept it."

They watched as Pops and Ruby turned to each other, wrapped their arms around each other, and wept openly. Their response was so emotional that Matt and Genevieve couldn't help but respond. They rushed toward them, sitting down on either side of them, embracing them as they embraced each other.

"This is the best news we've had since…ever!" Ruby managed; her voice still drenched with emotion. "What? How? I…we…we need to know."

Matt and Genevieve both laughed, their own emotions making it difficult to do much more.

After a moment, Matt stood, walking quickly to the assemblage of round log stools that stood ten feet away, rolling one at a time into the shadow of the scrubby tree that sheltered the bench, standing them up within inches from the older couple's knees. He took Genevieve's hand, helping her to her feet before they both turned and sat down to face their benevolent hosts.

"When did you make this decision?" Ruby managed.

Genevieve glanced at Matt before speaking. "We've been talking about it since you first offered it to me, but I only made the decision this morning, after church."

Ruby turned to Pops. "I told you not to give up hope."

"You know I'm no good at patience," Pops responded.

"Yep, I do. But, boy, you kids had us worried. With only two months left, we're quickly running out of runway. I didn't think I'd be so worried about it. I'd resigned myself to just letting it go, to trusting it would all work out the way it should, but I've lost a lot of sleep over the last ten weeks."

"I'm really sorry about that," Genevieve responded, resting her hand on Ruby's knee.

Ruby placed her own wrinkled, farm-worn hand on top of Genevieve's, squeezing it softly before reaching for Matt's hand, placing it on top of Genevieve's. "I've had good feelings about you two from the very beginning."

"You weren't ever concerned about our age difference?" Matt asked.

Ruby smiled, shaking her head. "What's fourteen years in the realms of eternity? I'm a little more than eight years older than Pops, and it's never given us anything to sneeze at."

"On the contrary," Pops said, leaning forward. "Being married to a woman of maturity has had plenty of advantages over the years. I, frankly, think it's silly for two adults to care much about age. If there's magic between two single folks of any age, they ought to keep their hearts and minds open to the possibilities of love to grow into something beautiful."

Matt turned to Genevieve and nodded. "I think we've discovered that."

"I hope you have. You'd be blind if you hadn't," Ruby responded.

"You saw it?" Genevieve asked, looking surprised.

"From that very first Sunday when Matt fished you out of the mud, and again the next Sunday when he fished you out of the river and brought you back to the farm."

"You saw all of that?" she asked, sincerely surprised.

"I wouldn't be much of a matchmaker if I hadn't."

"But…where…how?" asked Genevieve.

"I was picking berries on the other side of the pond when you allowed your emotions and frustrations to land you in the mud bog. As for your rescue from the river, in all honesty, I wasn't there, but a friend of mine watched most of it and shared with me her observations."

"Hildegard?" Matt asked.

"Do you know any other nosey German woman who could pass so flawlessly as a harmless old lady?" she asked with a wink.

Genevieve smiled, shaking her head. "Do you think she'll provide the same intelligence service for me once I become the matchmaker of Harmony Hill?"

Ruby laughed. "Whether you like it or not. She helped Millie Smurthwaite long before I arrived, and I'm certain it's safe to assume she'll be interested in helping you for as long as she can. And when she's gone, there will be others."

"Who?"

"Well, there's Thomas, and Gloria and Joseph, and Bev, and Sam the baker, and Kai and Molly, and the mayor, and Jake and Amy, and the Parkins."

"And don't forget Susan and Paul," Pops added.

"They're all your spies?" Genevieve asked bemusedly.

"Oh, heaven's no. But we're on the same team. We're Candle Lighters, you know? Protopians. Sincere people who are proactively working to help build a better world, community, families and individuals."

Matt smiled, shaking his head. "And these Candle Lighters...they are your eyes and ears in town?"

"You didn't think we could possibly do this all by ourselves, did you?" Ruby asked. "No, it quite literally takes a village."

"So, that day Thomas spent the day fishing with Spencer...did you set that up?" Genevieve asked.

"No. I don't set any of it up. Pops and I learned our first summer on the farm that God puts people in our paths who can help us open our eyes and hearts so that we can feel and experience the magic taking place all around us. I came to believe many years ago that there are people, perhaps angels in disguise, whose main purpose is to keep us from falling asleep at the wheel and missing out on the most important things in life."

"But how do they know what to say?" Genevieve asked. "It seems like every time I turn around, Hildegard was there to tap me on the shoulder or gently beat me over the head with something I needed to hear."

"Yes, she's particularly practiced. Since she retired from teaching, more than thirty years ago, she's taken it upon herself to make her time count for something positive. Having lost her husband in the war after less than a year of marriage, she decided early that she'd spend her life looking for ways to love and serve in hopes of helping others avoid the sorrow and loneliness she's had to endure."

"But other Candle Lighters and Protopians...they seem very different from Hildegard," Matt suggested. "What about Kai and Molly, and Jake and Amy, Susan and Paul. They're all married and young."

"Is that a problem?" Pops asked.

"Well, no, I guess I was just looking for a pattern...for similarities."

"Then you'll have to look a little deeper than their outward appearances or their marital status. You'll have to look in their hearts," Pops suggested.

"Yes, and if you do, you'll quickly recognize that their hearts always lead them to actions of love and kindness," Ruby added. "They make time to stop and chat with a stranger, or comfort a child, or do their best to lift and encourage wherever they can."

"You've basically described everyone we've met in Niederbipp," Matt suggested as Genevieve nodded.

"Yes, it's contagious, isn't it?" Ruby asked. "There's something that happens within the human heart when one's eyes witness compassion and charity in action. There are few things as contagious as unselfish expressions of love. If you're surrounded by enough of it, it changes everything—everything! Even the most hardened, calloused, cranky individuals can only be surrounded by it for so long before they begin to soften, before they begin to exhale goodness of their own."

"Like James and Spencer?" Genevieve suggested.

"Yes, like James and Spencer...and like yourself," Ruby replied.

Genevieve nodded, wiping a tear from her eye. "I got everything wrong about this place, didn't I?" she finally managed.

"Many do. From the outside, looking at us through the lens of pop culture, we are little more than hicks and tumbleweeds on the outskirts of nowhere; oddities and simpletons in a world infatuated with the endless waves of soulless fads and disposable values."

Genevieve shook her head. "I'm sorry. I didn't know how wrong I was."

Ruby leaned forward, resting her hand on Genevieve's knee until she looked into her eyes. "We all are lost until we learn there's a better way. We all are ensnared until we learn the truths of liberty. We are only human until we discover the portion of ourselves that is made of the same immortal stuff of the gods. If we learn the truth, the truth will set us free—free to pursue liberty and the eternal path of joy."

Genevieve smiled, though tears rolled freely down her cheeks. She shook her head as she took Ruby's hands in hers. "I don't know if I could ever have it in me to share with others the wisdom you've shared with us."

Ruby shook her head, offering a gentle smile. "Don't you see? You already do! You must remember, as De Saint Exupery said, 'It is only with the heart that one can see rightly; what is essential is invisible to the eye.' Wisdom begets wisdom. Light is attracted to light. Truth will always find those who seek it honestly if they do so with real intent and use it to improve the world around them. If we have any real magic or wisdom at all, it has come into our hearts and minds to remind us who we are and where we came from."

Genevieve and Matt both nodded slowly.

"And the benches…" Matt said, pointing to the tile embedded in the wooden plank behind their elderly companions, "…the benches… the tiles…they're the portals to that place we came from, aren't they?"

Pops and Ruby smiled at each other before nodding and smiling at Genevieve and Matt. "Only those who've followed the instructions and put in the time with sincerity and honest desire can know that truth," Pops responded.

"There's nothing particularly magic about the benches here on the farm and those scattered across Niederbipp," Ruby added, "other than the fact that they were built by humble hands out of a righteous desire for others to develop a yearning to know who they truly are: sons and daughters of the Creator and Author of all true joys."

Matt nodded. "We both know that you speak the truth. We've both experienced a connection to another world…to a different, brighter truth."

"And you must never forget it," Ruby replied. "The world will try to rob that from you, filling your heads with doubts if you're not careful. I…we…we encourage you to record the truths you've received deep in your hearts where they can never grow cold, and no fear or doubt can break through and rob you of that most precious of all gems."

"And you mustn't ever forget that truth requires the light of day and regular nourishment if it's to grow and retain its power of goodness," Pops added.

"You mean like having conversations like this one?" Matt asked.

"Yes. Spiritual conversations, prayer, gathering with others to worship, making the time to be still, turning your truths into charitable service, exercising hope, reverence and self-discipline, patiently and thoughtfully working together with others to heal broken hearts and scatter sunshine.... These will all encourage truth to grow and increase in brightness."

Genevieve shook her head. "Those are all the things that most people are cutting out of their lives. It's no wonder so many people are feeling hopeless."

"Truth will never cease to exist when popular culture cuts it from the cool list. It continues to burn bright, even in dark places, offering hope to all those who sincerely and earnestly seek it," Pops added.

"So why don't more people seek it?" Genevieve asked.

"Moral agency is a gift given to all mankind. There are those who accept it from their youth and never lose it. But most of us only come to know the sweetness of the truth after sampling the bitterness of all that is not truth."

"It feels like a very unproductive, or at least, inefficient way of learning," suggested Matt.

"Yes, but most of us refuse to learn any other way," Ruby answered.

"Maybe your articles could help people skip the potholes and landmines," Matt offered, turning to Genevieve.

"I was just thinking the same thing. But will people listen?"

"You don't think they will?" asked Matt.

Genevieve looked pensive. "I don't know. It feels like most people just want to be entertained. They don't want to work on themselves. Sometimes they don't even want to think. They just want to unplug from reality and be rocked to sleep with a happy lullaby."

"I'm afraid you're right," Ruby acknowledged.

"Really? Then what good can we do?" Matt asked.

"I don't have the answers that will work for the two of you. You'll have to find them yourselves. But you know where to go for answers. You've got a whole town full of Protopians who'll be anxious to help. And I believe that those who are sincere will continue to line up for a chance to spend the summer here on the farm, excited for the opportunities of finding hope and joy."

Ruby leaned forward again, laying a hand on each of their knees. "Answers will come as you seek them. You'll make your share of mistakes, but if you learn to work together and counsel with heaven every step of the way, you'll find the light and the hope to guide your feet. You've got truth on your side. You have the keys of joy. You have the blessings of heaven. And with that you have everything you need to succeed."

Matt and Genevieve smiled, feeling both excited and overwhelmed.

"Where do we go from here?" Matt asked.

"And how do we tell the rest of the campers?" asked Genevieve.

Ruby turned to Pops. "I'm not sure, are you?"

Pops shook his head. "We've talked a little bit about this since we offered you the position, Genevieve. Mom is…slowing down. We've done our best to hide most of that from you, but the sad reality is that she…she can't keep up the pace she's been trotting. As for me, after Mom passes, I've made arrangements with Thomas to take his second bedroom in the little house next to the chapel. I'll be available to help you anytime you need it for as long as I am still capable of lending a hand. But this will be your farm."

"We couldn't possibly chase you off like that," Matt responded. "This is your home."

Pops lifted his hands to stop the protest. "It's all part of a plan set in motion several generations ago. When the matchmaker is gone, the husband is allowed to visit and assist, but he no longer has stewardship and must not get in the way of the new matchmaker and her husband."

"I don't understand! We need you here to help us!" Genevieve responded, emotion hanging from her words.

Pops shook his head. "In the next few months, I'll share with you all that I know. You've already learned most of it, but there are still a few nuances about the house and the animals that I'll need to teach you. And like I said, I won't be far away if you get yourself into a bind. My only hope is that when my time is up, you'll bury me next to Mom in the orchard."

Genevieve looked distraught. "It all feels so…calloused…insensitive…compassionless."

"Please, don't feel that way," Ruby replied. "We signed up for this fifty-seven years ago. We knew what we were getting ourselves into. We will stay in the big house until my time is up. There are three bedrooms upstairs and two baths. Once you're married you're welcome to choose whichever room you wish. We'll help you get a hang of things and teach you how to run the farm when there's just two of you to do it through the winter. I…I don't expect to be around till next spring, but if I am, I'll help you sort through the applications and make sure you're ready for next year's campers."

Matt shook his head, turning to Genevieve. "This just got real!"

She nodded, too full of emotion to speak.

"I guess we didn't consider the details that this decision would bring about," Matt replied.

Pops smiled. "Neither had we when we took this on. In many ways it's a lot like marriage; you never really know what you're agreeing to when you say, 'I do.' You can't fully appreciate what 'in sickness and health' really means until you've lived through one cancer scare and are facing the realities of the second. You just have to enjoy the good times and work your way through the hard times, holding tight to the love and hope you share. And when your clock runs out of minutes, you have to do your best to gracefully make way for the next stewards who'll hopefully value your efforts enough to sort through your junk drawers, hold onto the most important elements, and let the rest go to make room for the stuff they'll add along their way."

Matt and Genevieve each wiped away tears with their free hands, their other hands holding tight to each other.

"You'll have to give me a couple of days to decide what we'll do with the rest of the summer while the campers are here," Ruby added. "I'd hate to take you out of the rotations; you've both been so helpful in sharing your light with the others. But assuming you'll be getting married when the summer ends, it might be best to allow you to move through the rotations together for the next two months."

Matt looked at Genevieve. "We're happy to do what you think is best, but it would be nice to at least have some regular time together in the afternoons, if that's not too much trouble."

Genevieve nodded. "I guess we have a wedding to plan, too. And parents and friends to notify."

Matt laughed. "This was definitely not in my wheelhouse when I woke up this morning. I still can't believe we're actually doing this!"

"I'm not sure I can either," Ruby admitted. "We've prayed for at least twelve years that we'd be able to pass this farm on to another couple who'd love it as much as we have. It feels like we've been holding our breaths as we've been watching the end of the runway coming at us faster and faster. I have to admit I feel a mighty burden lifted off my chest."

Pops nodded. "I need you kids to know we appreciate you, but I don't want either of you to have any illusions that this won't be the toughest thing you've ever done, especially the first few years. You'll have to learn to communicate and forgive each other quickly."

"But it will be the thrill of a lifetime," Ruby added. "You'll have more fun than you ever thought was possible, and make friendships that'll keep you going from season to season for the rest of your lives and beyond."

CHAPTER 132

Cold Showers

Good character is not formed in a week or a month. It is created little by little, day by day. Protracted and patient effort is needed to develop good character.
—Heraclitus—

The compromise they'd made of keeping Matt and Genevieve in the regular chore rotations while giving them time to spend together in the afternoons immediately proved to be less than either ideal or practical. On Monday afternoon, after the chores had been completed, the two of them tried to slip away to the bench overlooking the orchard when Greg and Susan invited them to play croquet on the front lawn with the rest of the campers. And though the croquet was fun and filled with engaging conversation about self-discipline as it relates to sex, drugs and rock and roll, it was not at all effective for planning a wedding or talking about the logistics of marriage and the responsibilities they would soon assume.

Tuesday wasn't any better. Though the regular chores were finished shortly after lunch, Pops invited all the men to the tack barn to help polish and wax the nearly endless supply of leather tack for the horses. Meanwhile, Ruby took advantage of what she called 'an uncommon energy surge,' to teach the women the basics of knitting.

And though Matt appreciated the tutorial Pops offered the men on the proper ways of rigging up a draft horse with the tack they'd just cleaned and polished, and Genevieve appreciated the camaraderie of the women and the little she was able to learn from Ruby about knitting, progress on their own agenda was once again postponed.

On Wednesday night, after the campers had all headed for the showers in their respective bunk houses, Matt and Genevieve stole away for a moment, escaping under the moonlit sky to the bench by the Ebenezer behind the milk barn. Knowing their absence would not go unnoticed for long, and not wanting to cause any suspicion or inadvertently start any rumors, they kept their rendezvous short. It was really only long enough to check in with each other and see how the other was feeling about their joint decisions and the growing list of ramifications. And though the list was overwhelming and the questions mind-boggling, they both were grateful they were doing it together. As they sat close to each other on the bench, looking up into the night sky, they were both flooded with a calm and peaceful sense that everything would be all right, that somehow everything would work out.

The feeling returned Thursday morning when they were surprised to discover that it was their turn to work the farm stand together. They both had difficulties hiding their excitement as they helped the others gather produce, eggs, cream and cheese to the pickup truck. They smiled at each other as they pushed their bikes all the way up the rutted drive. They smiled to themselves as they coasted all the way down Harmony Hill. And their smiles remained while Pops helped them unload the truck, which was somehow mercifully accomplished in record time.

"Mom asked me to remind you kids to have fun, but not too much fun, if you know what I mean," Pops said through the open passenger window.

They laughed as they wrapped their arms around each other.

"If you don't mind, I think we'll just try to sell out early and spend some time in town," Matt suggested.

"I don't mind at all," Pops said. "Should we hold dinner for you?" he asked with a wink.

Genevieve looked at Matt and shook her head before turning back to Pops. "If we're not home by midnight, it'll be safe to assume we've eloped to Tionesta, and we'll drop by after the honeymoon to check in on you."

Pops laughed. "If you run into any trouble or plan to be delayed, send word with Thomas. He'll be comin' up for dinner this evening."

"Thank you," Matt said.

Pops nodded. He turned and looked out at the highway, his hand on the shifter. He took a deep breath and turned back, emotion already in his eyes. "I want you kids to know how grateful I am for what you're doing…for what you've agreed to do. It would've killed us both to let the farm go. I've slept better over the last three nights than I have in months, knowing that everything is going to work out." He smiled, wiping a tear from his cheek. "We have a lot of hope and trust in both of you. Thank you."

"Thank you for trusting us," Matt said.

"Yeah, and thanks for seeing more potential in us than we see in ourselves," Genevieve added.

"I love you both," Pops said with a nod. "I love you both."

"We love you, too, Pops," Genevieve replied.

"Well, you better get busy so you can enjoy some time together in town."

They waved as he left in a cloud of dust, but watched as the old pickup truck swung onto Harmony Hill Road and disappeared into the curves.

Without wasting a moment, Genevieve wrapped her arms around Matt again. "I can't believe we have a whole day together," she said, leaning her head into his shoulder.

"What if we get sick of each other?" Matt joked.

"Pfff. I don't think that's possible."

"I don't know. We've never had the chance to get sick of each other. We're entering unmapped territory. I don't remember the last time I spent the whole day with a beautiful woman." He laughed. "Come to think of it, I don't remember the last time I spent the day with a woman at all. I might be totally boring. And I already know I'm going to have to practice a lot of self-discipline not to kiss you."

"Then I guess I'll just have to kiss you."

"Uh, that's a problem."

"Why?"

"Hello! The contract! James and Crystal have had to play it cool. They'd be ticked if they found out we'd been snogging while they're not even allowed to hold hands."

Genevieve looked at him and shook her head before she began to laugh. "What the hell have we gotten ourselves into? We have almost two more months of this! Two more freakin' months before I can kiss your face!"

Matt laughed.

"What are we going to do?"

"I don't know. I've already volunteered to take that last shower for the past few weeks."

"*The last shower?*" she asked, looking confused.

Matt couldn't help but laugh at the look on her face. "The last shower's always ice cold. It...it tends to cool off feelings that have no outlet."

"Oh, right. Does it wor... Wait a minute..." she said, screwing up her face. "You've been taking cold showers *for weeks?*" She laughed out loud. "*Weeks?*"

"Well, obviously it's not cold enough, either that or I'm building up immunity to it like Wim Hof."

"Who?"

"Yeah, you know, Wim Hof, the guy who meditates on icebergs for hours, wearing nothing but a Speedo. He's a YouTube phenomenon."

The look on Genevieve's face suggested she was somewhere in between amused and confused.

"Why would anyone meditate on an iceberg in a Speedo?"

"It's...I don't know...good for self-discipline, I guess. There's a book about him in the library. Spencer's been reading it. Maybe you could have it when he's done."

"Thanks, I'll keep that in mind," she said, just as the first car of the day pulled onto the gravel shoulder, stopping at the stand. An older couple got out and purchased twenty dollars' worth of assorted produce and a dozen eggs, leaving a five dollar tip and asking Matt and Genevieve to give their best to Pops and Ruby from Howard and Betty.

As the car pulled away another one pulled up, giving Genevieve only a quick moment to say what was on her mind. "You've been taking cold showers *for weeks?*"

The look on Matt's face got both of them laughing and they greeted the new customers with wide smiles. These, too, purchased a decent amount of produce, making quick work of the rest of the bushel of tomatoes, six large onions, and a whole cheese wheel. Matt helped them to the car and found Genevieve laughing when he returned.

"*Weeks*?" She stopped her teasing only long enough to laugh some more. "*Weeks*?!"

"Yeah, that was obviously a mistake to open my big fat mouth and admit that. Thanks for the warning. I'll be sure to hide my vulnerable bits a little more carefully next time."

She didn't have time to respond as the next customers arrived. They were carrying off a basket of green apples when two more cars drifted off the highway from opposite directions. It stayed busy like this for the next forty minutes, quickly clearing off the counters and significantly diminishing the backstock. They filled the counters again, Genevieve continuing to laugh every time she caught his eye, while Matt did his best to ignore her.

Just before noon, the sounds of children's voices drew their attention to the far side of the highway. They watched as Susan, holding onto her kids' hands, stood at the white painted line, waiting for safe passage. She didn't have to wait long, but Genevieve and Matt watched and listened as she explained to her kids the important rules for crossing the highway.

"Hello, P.J. and Hazel," Matt said as soon as their feet hit the gravel on the farm stand's side of the pavement.

"Hello, Mr. Tooth Fairy!" P.J. shouted back, laughing as though it was the funniest thing he'd heard in weeks.

Matt and Genevieve laughed good-naturedly. "How'd we get so lucky to get a visit from you guys today?"

"Well, we came because P.J. has some business to take care of," Susan replied.

"Is that right?" Genevieve asked, looking down at the boy who was suddenly quiet. "I think we still have some cookies around here. Are you looking for some of those?"

The boy didn't respond verbally, turning suddenly very shy. He moved behind his mother's legs, hiding his eyes.

Genevieve searched Susan's face, wondering if she'd said something wrong.

"P.J.," Susan spoke softly, kneeling beside him. "Remember, this is why we're here. I need you to use your big boy words and tell Matt and Genevieve what you did."

P.J. bit his lip, his eyes quickly filling up with tears.

"Go ahead," his mother encouraged. "Like we practiced."

The young boy, obviously filled with anguish, stood still as tears began to roll down his cheeks and dampen the neckline of his striped T-shirt.

Matt, recognizing the boy's discomfort, approached him slowly, sitting down cross-legged on the ground in front of him so their eyes were at the same level. P.J. stood frozen with fear and shame. Matt reached for the boy's arm, rubbing it gently until P.J. looked into Matt's compassion-filled face. "How can we help you, P.J.?"

"I stole a cookie yesterday, and I'm very, very sorry!" He was weeping before the last words escaped his small lips. But he stood tall, obviously coached by his mother, awaiting his punishment.

"Ruby makes mighty tasty cookies, doesn't she?" Matt asked.

The boy looked up, watching Matt carefully. He nodded. "I didn't like the raisins, but it was mostly good."

"Yeah," Matt said, biting his lip and trying not to smile. "I'm not a big raisin fan either."

The boy smiled as his mother, sister and Genevieve looked on silently.

"It doesn't feel good to steal, does it?" Matt asked gently.

P.J. shook his head, looking down at his shoes.

"Yeah. But it's brave of you to come back and make it right. It takes a real big boy to do something like that."

"My mom said that I need to do some work for you or something, and that I need to give you this." He plunged his hand into his pocket and pulled it out, turning it over, his palm open to reveal a crumpled dollar bill.

Matt accepted it, unwrapping the moist bundle to find three quarters and dime. "This is a lot of money. Did you earn it yourself?"

The boy nodded. "Sometimes I pull weeds for my neighbors, Mr. and Mrs. Lemon Drop."

"Is that right?" Matt asked, working hard to keep a straight face. "Are they nice people?"

The boy nodded.

"And do they have a house made of lemon drops?"

"Pfff. No, but that would be cool if they did. They knew me before I was even born, at least that's what they tell me sometimes. And they give me lemon drops most Sundays at church. They're really nice."

"Boy, I'd say! Maybe you could introduce me sometime?"

"You like lemon drops, too?"

"Who doesn't?"

"Yeah, I know, right?"

Susan cleared her throat, and P.J. looked up at her. A wordless communication passed quickly between them.

"So, what do I have to do for you?" P.J. asked.

"I think what he's trying to ask is what work he can do to make this right?" Susan explained.

Matt glanced quickly at Genevieve who had no answers. He turned back to P.J. "Did you say you know how to pull weeds?"

P.J. nodded.

"Well, I just noticed this morning that we have some weeds behind the farm stand. Would you like to help me pull those?"

P.J. turned his head, looking at the back side of the farm stand.

"Maybe you could offer to sweep as well," Susan suggested.

"Yeah, I'm kinda good at sweeping, but not as good as Mom."

"Well, you're in luck," Matt said with a big smile. "We've got all sorts of sweeping practice around here. But if you pull weeds and sweep, I'm gonna have to insist that you don't go home until you've tried out our swing."

"You have a swing?" P.J. asked, his face lighting up with pure excitement.

"Pretty much the best swing on this side of the Allegheny. Maybe

Miss Tooth Fairy here could show you and Hazel the swing while I help your mother."

Genevieve looked uncertain but was quick to oblige the two excited children who followed her without needing any further information.

"Thank you for this," Susan said as Matt dusted off his backside. "I swear, to our knowledge, this is the first time he's ever stolen anything. We've purchased cookies as rewards for good behavior before, but we definitely didn't buy a cookie yesterday. He might have gotten away with it if it weren't for the raisins I found this morning under his pillow."

"Well, he obviously needs to learn to cover his tracks better," Matt said with a broad grin as he turned to look at Genevieve lifting Hazel onto the swing next to her brother.

"How did you learn how to work with kids like that?" Susan asked.

Matt shrugged. "I try to remember that it wasn't too long ago that I was a kid myself. That, and I'm a dentist."

"Yeah, but kids don't usually like dentists."

"That's just because they don't know dentists are just kids in big bodies. I had a good teacher, the first dentist I ever worked for. He was great with kids. Had a few of his own grandkids, too. I never met a kid who didn't come out of his office with a smile on his face. They could have had ten cavities filled and four teeth pulled and they'd still come out of there like they'd been to Disneyland…or at least the Disneyland parking lot."

Susan laughed. "What was the first thing you ever stole?"

"Me? A pack of gum. Banana flavored as I recall. I don't think they even make it anymore. Stuffed it in my pocket when my mom wasn't looking at the checkout stand at Kmart."

"How old were you?"

"Not much younger than P.J.. Probably five."

"And your mother…what did she do?"

"About what you did. Marched me back to the store and had me tell the manager what I'd done. Probably the most traumatic experience of my life to that point. I handed him the money I'd taken from my piggy bank and cried my eyes out."

"Did he make you sweep?"

Matt laughed. "No, he talked my mother out of it as I recall. How about you?"

"Cherry lip gloss, from the grocery store. I was five. It somehow found its way into my pocket when my mother wasn't watching. She found me basically eating it in the closet an hour after we got home. It was smeared all over my face."

"And the manager made you sweep?"

"Yeah. Scared me straight. I was grateful for it. I still am."

Matt nodded. "Self-discipline," he said, wiggling his ring finger. "It's a big one, isn't it?"

"It's actually pretty scary how big it is. As they say, it's what separates the boys from the men. You're fortunate you had a good mother."

"Yeah, and so is P.J.. Is it as tough as it looks?" Matt asked.

"Parenting?"

Matt nodded.

"Mmmm, it depends on the day. It's a beautiful thing finding someone who you love enough to want to complicate your life by creating a family and raising kids together. It's been a big adjustment for both Paul and me. Maybe ask me again in ten years when the kids are teens."

"I will, and I'll be sure to ask for any advice you're willing to share."

"So you're planning on sticking around then?"

Matt nodded, his gaze drifting to Genevieve and the kids at the swing.

"As a dentist or a gentleman farmer?"

He looked surprised. "Genevieve must have mentioned it the other day, huh?"

Susan shrugged. "It's a small town."

"Yeah, well, Genevieve accepted Ruby's offer on Sunday, right after we saw you guys."

"That's great! I assume you also have a wedding to plan?"

"Among at least a million other things."

"Then I won't keep you. I also came to pick up a couple tomatoes for some sandwiches and a dozen eggs if you've got them," she said, looking over her shoulder at the nearly empty counter. "Am I too late?"

"You are if you were looking for Romas and Beefsteaks, but we still have some gorgeous Amish Brandywines."

"The yellow ones?"

"Yeah."

"I'll take four."

He bagged up the tomatoes and the eggs and made change while Susan watched Genevieve playing with her children.

"Would you like us to bring them home?" Matt asked.

"Excuse me?" Susan responded, obviously distracted.

"With any luck we'll be sold out within an hour. I know you barely know us, but we were planning on heading to town when we were done here. We'd be happy to drop the kids off on our way."

"Are you serious?"

"I…only if you're comfortable with that."

"After watching you interact with P.J., yeah, I'm comfortable with that. But you want them both? That's a lot to handle."

"I'd guess that P.J. would be more comfortable if Hazel stuck around, too. It'd be good practice for both of us. But I don't want to be pushy."

"Okay, but only if you promise me to make sure P.J. works off his debt to society."

"It's a deal," Matt said, extending his hand for a fist bump.

Susan walked to the swing where the kids were all smiles in the hands of Genevieve, who looked surprised to be having such a good time herself. She explained quickly to her children that Mr. Matt and Miss Genevieve would be bringing them home as soon as P.J. finished up his work.

Genevieve, upon hearing the plans, turned to Matt for confirmation that what she was hearing was correct.

He winked and nodded before turning back to the farm stand to help a customer. Susan waved and mouthed the words, 'thank you,' before crossing the highway and walking back along the parallel dirt path.

In between customers, Matt helped P.J. uproot the weeds behind the stand. And by the time the floor was swept to the best of a six-year-old's ability, the produce had been reduced to two lonely tomatoes and a bell pepper.

The timing was good for Genevieve, too, since her back was sore after nearly an hour of pushing Hazel on the swing, who was still squealing like it was the grandest adventure of her life. The kids were thrilled to help Matt and Genevieve lock up the farm stand and embark on the next adventure.

With the farm stand secured, they carefully crossed the highway, Matt and Genevieve guiding their bikes with one hand while holding onto the hand of a child with the other, doing their best to mirror the safety approach they'd watched Susan use an hour earlier. With no cars in sight, the stress was low. But reaching the other side and seeing the narrowness of the path was not comforting to Genevieve, who was at quite a loss as to how she could manage both a bike and a young child.

Quickly recognizing her discomfort, Matt came up with a creative solution: the kids would stand on the pedal opposite the road with one hand on the seat and the other on the handlebar while Matt and Genevieve pushed and steadied the bike. The kids, for their part, thought this was the second greatest joyride of the day, second only to the 'best swing this side of the Allegheny,' a phrase both children repeated at least a dozen times before they reached the turnoff to their drive, just fifty yards beyond the turnoff to the Englehart Ebenezer.

At first glance, the overgrown, bush-lined drive felt a little haunted. But with the Meier name on the mailbox and the kids insisting they were in the right place, they proceeded down the winding gravel drive. After thirty feet, the bushes gave way to a large, lush lawn, shaded here and there by giant, old-growth trees.

Susan waved from a chair near the house, setting down a book and coming out to meet them. The kids jumped off the bikes and swarmed her, both of them talking at once about the swing, and the weeds, and playing shop with Mr. and Miss Tooth Fairy.

"Can we go there again tomorrow?" P.J. begged, having long forgotten the reason they'd gone back again today.

"I don't know if Mr. Matt and Miss Genevieve will be there again tomorrow," Susan replied.

"Nope, unfortunately we'll be working other chores tomorrow," Matt replied.

"Well, then maybe you can come to my house and play. You know where we live now. You can come anytime you want, except for when I'm in school. That's supposed to start again soon, but maybe if you came to play, I wouldn't have to go on those days." P.J. pushed.

Matt looked at Genevieve and smiled. "I think we'd like that."

"Actually, I was hoping you both might join us for dinner on a Sunday sometime. I know you're both busy during the week, and rotating through partners, but Paul and I would like to get to know you both better, if you think you could get away for an evening."

Genevieve looked up at Matt and nodded. "I'd really like that. It's been fun being with your kids. I have to admit, as an only child, and having never taken a babysitting job, kids have always scared the heck out of me. I know we only had them for an hour or so, but they really are fun little people."

"And after the rest of the campers go home in October, and we get married, we'd love to have you guys up to the farm." Matt laughed, turning to Genevieve. "Did I really just say that...*after we get married, you can come visit our farm*?"

Genevieve laughed as well. "That does sound really strange, doesn't it?"

Susan smiled. "It sounds like you two have a lot of things to work through. If you find yourself feeling bored or in need of a little entertainment, you're always welcome to borrow my kids or drop by to play. They seem to have an endless supply of shenanigans and energy."

"Thanks," Matt said, nodding to Susan and smiling at Genevieve.

"No, please, I feel indebted to you," Susan replied. "I was nervous bringing P.J. back to the farm stand today, knowing I needed to move quickly while it was all fresh. I wasn't at all sure how things would go, knowing you all rotate chores every day, but I...I really couldn't have asked for a better experience for him. Your response and your understanding were exactly what I was praying for all morning." She turned to look at her kids who'd busied themselves gathering dandelions, lining them up around the edge of a picnic table that stood nearby.

"It really does take a village to raise these little monsters and help them transform into decent humans. I'm grateful they'll have both of you as part of their village. And I hope that when you two have kids, that Paul and I can return the favor."

Matt smiled, reaching for Genevieve's hand.

"We'd be honored," Genevieve replied.

Susan smiled. "I'm sorry to take up any of your precious alone time, but again, thank you for what you did today. I'm grateful, sincerely. Thank you."

CHAPTER 133

Forbidden Fruit

Love is no assignment for cowards.
—Ovid—

They said their goodbyes, the kids running alongside them as Matt and Genevieve pushed their bikes back up the drive to the highway. With smiles and waves, they pushed off, pedaling north a hundred yards or so before they remembered they had no plans or destination in mind.

"Do you even know where we are?" Matt asked, pulling over to the shoulder and looking around.

"Uh, the fairgrounds have to be right around here somewhere, right?"

"Oh yeah," Matt said, turning to look. "And where are we going?"

"Well, it's past time for lunch. Where are you taking me for our picnic?"

Matt smiled. "Sorry. I forgot. Do you prefer finding a place in town, or by the river?"

"How about town?" she said after thinking it over for a moment.

"Lead on," Matt said, motioning for her to pull ahead.

She turned them back around to the shortcut she'd discovered into town on one of their jaunts to visit Ned and Nora. The narrow road led through some of the old town's more residential streets, over cobblestone roads that looked like they could have been laid at the same time as the old-world architecture they butted up against. Hand-carved stone lintels with chisel marks still vividly present hung above every door and window, contrasting with the textures and colors of the multi-hued plaster and stucco. Window boxes and flowerpots showcased bright geraniums, lavender and herbs.

Where the space permitted, they rode side by side, winding their way through the charming back streets, unconcerned with deadlines or external commitments.

"Can we do this again tomorrow?" Matt asked when they stopped and dismounted, realizing they'd driven down a lane with no outlet.

"I'd like that," Genevieve admitted. "But how?"

"We could elope to Tionesta."

She laughed. "You've obviously never tried biking there? It's no picnic. Do you have any other ideas?"

Matt thought for a moment. "None that don't include shirking all or our responsibilities and commitments and just running off together."

She laughed as she turned her bike around and kicked off, leaving him behind. "Sounds like you might be in need of one of those cold showers," she taunted over her shoulder.

He quickly caught up. Unable to think of anything charming to say, he simply smiled and shook his head. "This isn't going to be an easy couple of months, is it?"

Genevieve smiled. "No, but that's probably a good thing, right?"

"How so?"

"I'd much rather be wanting to kiss your face off than to be wondering how I might possibly muster any feelings of attraction toward you."

Matt laughed out loud. "Kiss my face off...? So, if I'm hearing you correctly..." He paused, stopped pedaling, and coasted as he grabbed hold of the back of her saddle, waiting for their bikes to come to a stop so he could stand next to her. "If I hear what you're saying," he repeated, "you think we're going to be okay?"

Genevieve laughed, grabbed his shirt with both hands, and laid a big kiss on his face that couldn't possibly leave him with any doubt.

"Whoa!" he said, catching his breath. He laughed when his eyes finally focused on her smiling face. "I'm pretty sure we're going to be okay..."

"Yeah, that's a relief. We've become such good friends that I was worried that kissing you would be like kissing my brother."

"I didn't think you had a brother."

"I don't," she responded, swatting his chest. "But you know what I mean, right? I figured we'd be all right after that peck on Sunday, but, yeah, this confirms that we're going to be just fine."

Matt nodded, looking thoughtful. "So, now that we know we're okay, how do we keep it from being weird for the next two months?"

She shook her head after thinking for a moment. "Do you think it would have been better not to know until the end of the summer?"

"No," Matt responded immediately. "It just gives me one more thing to look forward to. But you do know that we do have nearly two months, right?"

"Fifty-five days."

"What?"

"I figured it out last night. *Fifty-five days*. It's still a long time, but I've been thinking it'll probably give us a chance to exercise some self-discipline."

Matt nodded.

"If we're going to spend the next fifty years teaching it, I guess we probably ought to know something about it, right?"

Matt nodded again. "So where do we go from here?"

Genevieve turned and looked up the road for a moment before turning back to Matt. "Considering the contract you signed—and I agreed to comply with, albeit somewhat more loosely–and considering the fact that it would make things really awkward if our fellow campers caught us making out, the only sensible answer is…"

He took a deep breath and exhaled loudly. "Cold showers and playing it cool," he responded, finishing her sentence.

"Right," she said, nodding as she extended her hand.

Matt looked at her hand for a moment before extending his own hand and shaking it. "Self-discipline," he muttered.

Genevieve squeezed his hand until he looked right into her eyes. "Self-discipline," she responded, smiling broadly. "I don't know if we could legitimately spend the next five decades talking the talk if we can't walk the walk ourselves."

"You're right," Matt conceded. "You're right. I've been waiting my whole life to find the right girl and get married…what's fifty-five more days?"

"Well, I don't mean to be critical, but it's actually only fifty-five days if we get married on that last day. We've been so consumed with the idea of taking over the farm that we haven't officially set a date, have we?"

"You're right," Matt replied. "When do you want to get married?"

Genevieve looked thoughtful. "How's your tomorrow looking?"

"That would be my first pick, too. But wouldn't it be best to let our parents know? And then we need to arrange for the wedding itself, and plan a honeymoon, and get you a dress, and I probably ought to find a suit, and are we having any kind of a party afterward?"

"Yeah, eloping is actually sounding better and better."

"Really?"

"I used to dream about a big, fancy wedding, but it all sounds so... superfluous now. What if we just got married at the church here in town...a small wedding...on the last day of the summer so the rest of the campers could be here and not have to make special arrangements. Our parents could book a room at one of the local bed-n-breakfasts and we could spend a week in Niagara Falls or on Prince Edward Island. We could just make it...simple."

"Are you serious?" Matt asked, looking surprised.

"Why not?"

"It's just that I expected you to want to make a big deal out of it. You know, something for the magazine. I've been preparing myself for something far more extravagant than anything you just outlined."

"Is that what you want?"

Matt shook his head. "No, but I was ready to support you in whatever *you* want. I only plan to marry you once. I don't want you to have any regrets."

She leaned forward and wrapped her arms around his neck, resting her chin on his shoulder as they awkwardly balanced their bikes against their legs. "I'm not that girl anymore," she said softly. "If I'm choosing to live a simple life in the future, I might as well start now."

"You're sure? I've got some money saved. We can do what you want."

"Yeah, I'm sure."

"What will your parents say?"

"I don't know," Genevieve said, letting go of Matt and stepping back to look at him. "Does it really matter what they'll say or even what they'll think?"

"I guess not. But isn't it better to keep the peace than to start out our marriage with them feeling like we don't care what they think?"

Genevieve shook her head. "I've always felt that too many weddings are little more than a chance to show off status and wealth. Will it hurt my father's feelings that his only daughter won't be having her wedding party at the country club where he can show off to all of his friends?

Probably. And my mom will probably be bent that she can't invite all of her society friends to join her in the party. I spent the first eighteen years of my life trying to fit in with that crowd. I did a pretty good job pretending that's what I wanted, becoming the snob I was expected to be. I don't mean to sound ungrateful, but that upbringing—the wealth and connections it afforded me…it wasn't much more than a whole lot of posturing and pageantry. It took coming here…getting stung by a thousand wasps and head-butted by a sheep for me to recognize there's more to life than all of that.

"The entire world thinks they're chasing the authentic and sincere, but not many ever recognize they'll never find it until they open their hearts and souls to the foundational elements we've been learning this summer. I can't know what I know now and go back to that world and pretend I don't know better. I've been to weddings that cost more than all the inhabitants of Niederbipp combined make in months. I don't mean to judge anyone, but where's the charity in that? Where's the reverence? Those people—the people I came from—I can't think of anyone I knew from that set who understood the place of gratitude or hope, and certainly not self-discipline. I don't miss any of that."

Matt nodded thoughtfully. "Okay, but how can you ever hope for your parents to understand you and the life you've chosen for yourself if you turn your back on them? How do you hope to reach people with your writing if you condemn the very readers you're hoping to help recognize that there's more to understanding life than they've ever known before?"

Genevieve let out a long breath. She shook her head before turning back to Matt with a smile. "Whose side are you on?"

"I hope I'm on the same side as that little voice in your heart."

She smiled and hugged him again. "You're right," she whispered. "Dang you!"

He laughed. "I think you're probably hangry. I know a spot where we can eat. Then we can talk more about this."

"Lead on," she said, letting him go.

They wandered through the backstreets, pushing their bikes and enjoying the beauty of the town and the bright summer day. Leaning their bikes against the fountain basin, they sat down on the stone bench and ate their lunches. As they chatted and reasoned together, the path forward became clear to both of them. They could not deny the reality of their varied upbringing or their parents' stations or status. But they knew they also had to be true to themselves and the new truths they'd adopted since coming to the farm. There could be moderation. They could come to the center. They could invite their families to be a part of their simplified union without casting judgment, being difficult, or inviting unnecessary drama. By the time their bellies were full, they both felt like they were back on track, even though the details had yet to be ironed out.

The shop windows just up from Robintino's restaurant displayed a dress on one side of the door and a suit on the other. They both had noticed it without mentioning it, and so Genevieve gave no resistance when Matt took her hand and walked with her across the cobblestones to have a closer look.

"This must be Lin's shop," Matt said as he peered through the windows to the bolts of fabrics and the cutting tables.

"Who?"

"Lin. You know, the sassy Asian lady from Sourdough Sunday."

Genevieve looked blank.

"Come on. Really? She didn't ask you why you were still single?"

She shook her head. "Did she ask you?"

"No, not exactly…she pretty much *told* me I was still single because I'm a dentist, and no one likes their dentist."

"Well, she's not wrong," Genevieve said, looking through the windows to see if she could spot anyone inside. "I think you might be right."

"Thanks a lot!"

Genevieve laughed. "No, I mean about Lin. Is that her?" She pointed to the back corner of the store where a dark-haired woman sat at a sewing machine.

"May I help you?" a man asked from behind, causing them both to jump.

They turned to see a man wearing a blue smock shirt with a measuring tape around his neck, his gray goatee and hair suggesting he was somewhere in his mid-sixties.

"Uh, maybe," Matt stammered. "We…we're getting married."

"Congratulations," said the man. "When's the big day?"

Matt turned to Genevieve quickly before answering the man. "The first week of October."

The man smiled. "That's coming right up. And should I assume, since you're standing at my door, that you may be in need of appropriate apparel?"

"Yes," Genevieve answered. "Do you make wedding dresses?"

"I don't, but my wife does. I handle mostly suits and men's clothing. I'm Albert Schreyer. Would you like to come in?"

"Sure," Genevieve replied.

Albert reached between them and pulled the worn, brass handle, holding the door open for them to enter. The movement of the door jostled the silver bell that was attached to the upper corner, causing a crisp chime to emanate from it as they walked through the doorway. The woman at the sewing machine rose from her seat and moved quickly to the front counter.

"We have a couple of kids who are getting married," Albert said.

"That's good news," replied the woman.

"This is my wife, Lin," Albert said. "She's a first-class seamstress and tailor and has taught me nearly everything I know. How can we be of service?"

"Oh, I know you," Lin said, smiling at Matt. "You're the dentist who was looking for a wife at Jake and Amy's Sourdough Sunday."

"Yes, it's nice to see you again."

"And it looks like you've been successful and probably won't be interested in dating our daughter, Alice, anymore."

"Uh…no, I suppose that would be a bad idea at this point," Matt said awkwardly.

"It's just as well. She said she wasn't interested in dating a dentist anyway, so it's good you found someone who would."

"I'm Genevieve," she said, extending her hand to the petite woman behind the counter.

"Yes, you're a better match anyway. Closer to his age. Alice, she's too young to marry a man with gray whiskers."

Matt subconsciously rubbed the stubble on his chin.

"Yes, she's only twenty-nine. Better that you marry someone closer to your age," Lin said, nodding to Matt. "You look like you're thirty-three, thirty-five?" Lin said, moving the object of her frankness to Genevieve.

Genevieve forced a smile. "Actually, I'm also twenty-nine, at least for another couple of weeks."

"Ho!" Lin responded, looking only slightly embarrassed. "It must be the yoga. Alice teaches yoga. It keeps her looking young. Maybe you should try?"

"Thank you, I'll keep that in mind," Genevieve responded, trying not to be offended.

"But no yoga talk today. You're getting married!" she said with a big smile that filled her whole face. "How wonderful." She looked at Matt again. "But you…you're camping this summer at Ruby's farm?"

"We both are," Genevieve replied.

Lin turned to the calendar on the wall. "It's only August. Summer doesn't end on the farm till October. You're making plans early!"

"Yes, we wanted to make sure we weren't scrambling at the last minute," Matt replied.

"This is good for an old man like you. Yes, very good idea." She smiled again.

"Please," Albert said, motioning for them to step to the far side of the front counter where a narrow opening allowed them to pass into the workspace. "My wife always gets excited about weddings," he said as he followed them. "And will you be needing a suit then?"

"Uh, yeah, I suppose I would. I don't remember the last time I wore a suit."

"Black or navy?" Albert asked.

"Excuse me?"

"The color? Do you have a preference?"

"Uh, do you have a suggestion?"

"How about gray?" Genevieve replied.

"Gray? Really?" Matt responded.

"Why not? Black's too formal for a Niederbipp wedding, and navy's not much better."

"You'll be married in town then?" Albert asked, moving toward the bolts of gray fabric lined up on the shelves against the wall.

"Yes, that's the current plan," Matt replied after glancing at Genevieve.

"And October…that will be getting a little cooler, though you'll likely be sweating no matter the outside temperature," Albert said with a wink as he pulled three different bolts from the lineup. He laid these on the counter and invited Matt and Genevieve to take a look.

"They're all wool?" Genevieve asked as she fingered the cloth.

"Yes."

"Is that a good thing?" Matt asked.

Genevieve nodded, looking up from the fabric. "It's durable and depending on the weight and weave it's usually breathable, and it wears a lot better than synthetics."

"You know your fabrics," Albert responded, looking surprised. "What line of work are you in?"

"Oh, uh, I'm a writer, but I've always been interested in fashion," she replied, keeping it brief and unassuming. "What do you think about this one?" she asked, turning to Matt.

Matt stepped forward, running his hand over the gray fabric.

"Herringbone. Classic. Timeless. Definitely formal enough for a wedding in Niederbipp, but universal enough to also wear to business events or parties. Not a bad choice," Albert offered. "Do you know your size?"

"Uh…large, sometimes extra-large."

Albert smiled. "I'll take that as a no." He reached for his measuring tape and the notepad on the table. "You look to me like a 43-long, but I've been wrong before."

"But he rarely admits it," Lin added under her breath. "And what about you?" she asked, turning to Genevieve. "A wedding in Niederbipp, huh? Church or outdoors?"

Genevieve looked to Matt for an answer.

"Church," they both said in unison.

"Classic or modern?"

"Uh, I'm not really sure. I don't know if I've thought that much about it."

"Really? A woman of your age who knows at least something about fashion and she's never thought that much about the dress she'd wear on her wedding day?" Lin said incredulously.

Genevieve looked surprised again by the woman's bluntness. "Well, maybe I do have a few ideas, though they've definitely changed a lot over the last few months."

"Let me guess," Lin said with a knowing smile. "You came here wanting a dress that would make you look somewhere between a princess and the Queen of Sheba, and now you'd be happy with a flour sack with a couple of holes cut in it and a sash of raw wool around your waist."

"Well, I don't know if I'd go that far," Genevieve admitted, "but yes, my ideas have been simplified. How did you know?"

Lin tapped the end of her nose. "We've been making clothes in this town for more than forty years. And in those years we've made at least four dozen dresses for Ruby's campers who are anxious to get married at the end of the summer. We've seen the pattern. I don't know if you can spend much time in Niederbipp without it simplifying your tastes and desires. We still make some fancy dresses, but usually only for tourists who are passing through and want to get the kind of dress none of their girlfriends will have. Nope, Ruby's girls, if they don't arrive simple, somehow become more simple by the end of the summer. They become more interested in the sanctity and commitment of marriage than they are about the afterparty or how they'll look for their pictures."

Genevieve nodded slowly. "What is it, do you think, that happens to us?"

Lin pursed her lips, looking at her husband who was still working on Matt's measurements. "Don't get me wrong, but many Western women grow up believing they are princesses. Our daughter thought the same thing, against our will. But she, like many American girls, spent too much time worrying about her outside parts and not enough about her inside—about her heart and the parts that matter most. She married, but it didn't last. Now she's starting to learn the things you kids learn on the farm. But it's hard when you do things out of order."

"Out of order?"

Lin nodded. "When you act first and think later, when you listen to your head but forget to listen to your heart—it makes things messy, you know?"

Genevieve nodded.

"She's a beautiful woman, and she has a charming prince of a son, Freddy. But she's alone. She thinks she was too young," Lin said with a shrug. "Maybe."

"You don't agree?" asked Genevieve

"If you know what's important, and you know how to listen to your heart, you can be young and have it work out just fine. But if your heart is set on things that really don't matter, and you don't want to listen to anyone who says, 'slow down and open your eyes,' you might miss warning signs that the universe wants to show you. If that's where you are it might not be the right time for a big commitment like marriage. It's maybe okay to think shallow about a date to the prom, and maybe we're just old fashioned, but marriage is supposed to last forever."

"Love is blind," Genevieve mused.

Lin shook her head. "Stupid love is blind. Good love is neither blind nor selfish. Good love focuses on what's real, on the voices only the heart can know are true. We tried to tell her what we saw in Jason, but it's hard to help a heart that doesn't have room for truth."

Genevieve nodded slowly. "I'm sorry."

"So are we. You'll learn this too, someday, but your children make choices that don't include you. That's okay. We all must find our own path. We all have choices, but not all of us have wisdom. And wisdom comes only to those who want wisdom—who believe there *is* wisdom. It only comes to those who decide wisdom is more important than what they want this minute."

"Oh, she's coming around, Honey," Albert replied, looking over his shoulder.

"Yes, yes," Lin said, shaking her head. "I know. We're all somewhere in the long process of coming around. Patience is never easy for me, but it's made harder when you watch sadness that could've been avoided."

"But the keys of joy," Genevieve responded, "she knows them, doesn't she?"

Lin shrugged. "Somewhere, somehow, we hope she still does. You'll see. You kids have learned them because you wanted to learn them. That's the only way they have any power to bring light and happiness. You have to want to know them. You have to want to live them. Until then they are only nice ideas."

Matt caught Genevieve's eye and a unique sense of understanding passed silently between them as Albert continued to take measurements, making notes on a scratchpad.

"What kind of dress did your daughter have?" Genevieve asked.

Lin glanced at her husband. "You've heard, of course, of a strapless gown?"

"Sure."

"Well, hers was more of a gown-less strap."

Genevieve couldn't help but smile as she envisioned it. "You made it?"

Lin shook her head. "I offered, of course, but she knew I wouldn't approve of what she wanted. She had one made in Pittsburgh. Itty bitty little thing. Couldn't have used more than three quarters of a yard on the whole dress."

"I've made neckties that use more fabric," Albert added without even looking up. "Like Lin suggested, you don't get to choose much once your children reach adulthood. We tried to teach all of our children the power one wields when they honor their own bodies with modesty and reverence. But those plain words are easy to forget when the trends of the world are going in a very different direction."

"Was the ceremony here in town?" Matt asked.

"No, it was at a sports bar down in Pittsburgh. Jason's best friend got ordained on the internet and turned the whole thing into a stand-up routine," Albert responded. "Seven months later, Freddy was born, and a year after that, Jason ran off with a girl from his co-ed softball team, and the rest is pretty much an ugly cliche."

"Wow!" Genevieve responded.

"That turned into quite a downer for a beautiful couple like yourselves, preparing to make the most exciting decision of your life," Albert said, reaching his arms around Matt's waist with the tape. "It's hard not to be jaded when you're still spinning in the aftermath of a child's divorce."

"How long has it been?" Matt asked.

"Almost three years," Lin said. "Jason's turned out to be mostly a deadbeat. He's at least a year behind on child support and really only takes Freddy when he's trying to impress the next in his long list of *girlfriends*."

"Do you see much of your daughter and Freddy?" Genevieve asked.

"It depends on how much help she needs. She drops Freddy off from time to time for the weekend, but otherwise we don't see much of them," Albert reported.

"Alice teaches yoga at three different studios to make ends meet," Lin added. "We've offered to let her move home to help her get her feet on the ground, but not many folks even know what yoga is around here, and since she moved to the big city, she says Niederbipp is far too sleepy."

Matt and Genevieve glanced at each other again, making it silently clear they had a lot to talk about.

"Did you have a fabric in mind for your dress?" Lin asked.

"I'd probably say satin, but I'd be open to any recommendations."

"How about denim?" Matt suggested flippantly, his arms lifted out to his sides as Albert measured his chest.

"For a wedding dress?" Genevieve asked, looking amused.

"Mmmmaybe not," Matt responded. "Pretty much all I've ever seen you in are your farm duds. It's just hard to imagine you wearing anything else."

"Yes, but weddings are special. White satin, good. Denim, not good," Lin suggested as she pulled three different shades of white satin from the shelves, laying them on the table.

Genevieve ran her fingers over the three choices. "I think I like this one best," she said, looking up from the bolt of soft, French vanilla satin.

Matt nodded, looking a bit uncomfortable as Albert measured his inseam.

"And what for the style?" Lin asked.

"I feel like I've been inspired to go with something classic. How about an A-Line, tea length, and probably a squared neck with half-sleeves."

Lin looked surprised. "Wow, sounds like you know exactly what you want."

"I think I'm getting there," Genevieve said, winking at Matt when he turned to her.

Lin moved Genevieve onto the short, carpeted platform before taking her measurements and drawing a quick sketch of the dress she'd described. Meanwhile Matt and Albert had settled on a three-piece suit with flat-fronted pants, hemmed without a cuff.

"We have time to get this right," Albert said, "But I'll need you to drop in to finalize the length in a week or two."

"Sure," Matt said, looking across the room at Genevieve. "I can't believe this is really happening."

Genevieve smiled. "It feels like a dream, doesn't it?"

Matt nodded.

"Would you like to make a deposit?" Albert asked, bringing them both back to earth.

"Uh, sure," Matt said, reaching for the wallet in his back pocket. As he pulled the card from the leather billfold, he realized it had been more than three months since he'd charged anything, and the first time he'd ever put money down for wedding apparel. He would realize later that he didn't ask for the amount. He didn't need to. He didn't care. He was getting married! He was getting married to Genevieve Patterson in just fifty-five days!

ONE THIRTY FOUR

CHAPTER 134

Pancakes

It is by teaching that we teach ourselves, by relating that we observe, by affirming that we examine, by showing that we look, by writing that we think, by pumping that we draw water into the well.
—Henri Frederic Amiel—

"What do you want to do now?" Genevieve asked as the tailor's shop door closed behind them.

Matt smiled, the reality of what they'd just done hitting him like an electric charge. "We're getting married!" he said, wrapping his right arm around her back.

She looked up into his eyes and smiled. "Yeah, this just got real, didn't it?"

Matt nodded as he took a deep breath, staring at her.

"What?" she asked, when she noticed she was caught in his gaze.

"You're beautiful," he replied.

Her smile broadened as she reached for his face, laying her hand on his stubbly jaw.

"Genevieve?" The voice came from across the street and they turned quickly to see Amy's smiling face. Genevieve dropped her hand, trying to wipe away the look of surprise as Amy waddled across the cobblestones.

"Congratulations!" she said, beaming. "I hear you two are going to be sticking around indefinitely."

Genevieve turned to Matt, an unmistakable look of surprise on her face. "Who told you?" she asked, turning back to Amy.

Amy laughed. "You guys still have no idea how small this town is! We were beginning to feel a little bad that we didn't hear it from you two sooner."

"We're just coming to terms with it ourselves," Matt admitted. "And you should probably know that the other campers don't know yet."

"Oh, really? But Ruby and Pops?

"Yes, of course," Genevieve replied. "We're just figuring out how this is all going to work, and we're trying to not make it weird for the rest of the campers. We still have fifty-five days before the summer's over."

"But who's counting?" Amy replied with a broad smile. "Jake and I are happy for both of you. In fact, we'd like to have you to dinner sometime if you think you can fit it in."

"Uh, yeah, that would be nice," Genevieve replied. "When?"

Amy laughed, patting her belly. "How about tonight?"

"Really?"

"Sure. Why not? I feel like we're in a strange limbo right now, not sure when the baby's coming and not making any plans beyond a few hours. But if it works for you, we'd love to have you."

"That's really nice," Matt said. "Are you sure we wouldn't be putting you out?"

"Not at all. It's nothing fancy. I had a craving for Jake's sourdough pancakes and his famous buttermilk syrup. He's just unloading the kiln so he sent me to the market to pick up some sugar."

"Well, what can we bring?" Matt asked.

Amy thought for a moment. "I can't really think of anything that goes better with pancakes than more pancakes. Just come."

"We'd love that," Genevieve said after glancing at Matt.

"Do you think Jake could use some help at the studio?" Matt asked.

Amy laughed. "Probably! I was just trying to help him unload the kiln, but I turned around and knocked over a stack of mugs with my belly. I'm just so spatially challenged right now. I'm basically a bulldozer everywhere I go."

"Well, let me help him; that is, if you girls can handle the shopping and the sugar schlepping," Matt suggested.

"I was born to schlepp sugar," Genevieve responded, flexing her arm to prove it.

Matt jogged up the cobbled side street to the pottery, grateful to have one more legitimate reason to extend their excursion.

"I'll be right with you," Jake said from somewhere in the back of the studio when Matt entered the showroom. It was the first time he'd seen the pottery from this vantage point and his eyes roamed wildly, taking in the variety of colors, textures and shapes, as well as the rich aroma of earth and the hint of turpentine. He had nearly passed the front counter when he noticed the now familiar design of the five keys of joy etched into a natural-colored tile, embedded into the wooden front of the counter. A basket filled with small, similarly colored tiles sat atop the counter, and Matt smiled to himself as he read the words embossed on one of them, *Be still and know that I am God.*

"I understand you could use some help," Matt said as he stepped over the threshold that separated the showroom from the studio.

Jake looked over the top of the kiln door, a look of surprise on his face. "Oh, hello, Matt. What's going on?"

"Genevieve and I just got invited to pancake dinner, and I figured I better get up here and see how I could earn our keep."

"That's nice of you," Jake replied, reaching for a second pair of leather gloves.

Matt stepped forward to receive them, accidentally kicking a piece of pottery across the floor. "Oops, maybe I'm not the right guy to be doing this," he said, watching the piece disappear under a table.

"That was already broken. I'll be happy when Amy gets her balance back. I can't imagine how difficult it would be to carry a thirty-pound bowling ball attached to my belly."

"Yeah, she just mentioned she ruined some mugs."

"Mugs this week, bowls last week," Jake smiled good-naturedly. "It will all be worth it someday soon."

"Are you feeling ready to become a father?"

Jake nodded, handing Matt a still-warm pitcher from the bowels of the kiln. "We've been waiting a long time for this. After eight years of marriage and three miscarriages, it's hard to believe this is really happening! Dude, I'm going to be a father sometime in the next week or so. It just feels so…surreal."

"I can only imagine," Matt admitted, accepting two more pitchers from Jake and setting them on the table behind him. "Have you settled on a name?"

Jake nodded. "Isaac."

"Isaac…isn't that…the name of the potter who worked here before you?"

"Yeah. We never knew him, but he's the reason I came here, and one of the reasons I stayed. It's hard to explain, but even though he'd passed on before I got here, he's been more of a father figure to me than any other man in my life."

"That's a lot to say," Matt responded, accepting a stack of cereal bowls from Jake's hands.

Jake nodded. "My father left when I was still just a toddler and the only memories I have of him are traumatic."

"I have difficult memories and a complicated relationship with my dad, too."

"Hmm. Families can be messy, can't they?"

"Pretty much. Is your father still alive?"

"No. We didn't find out until just before we got married, but we found him on a Google search. He'd been killed in an accident several years earlier. If my mom had known, she never told me before she passed away herself."

"Wow! I'm sorry," Matt replied.

"Thanks, it's…it's okay. I really don't think about it that often, but getting ready to become a father…I guess it's probably unavoidable to think about where we came from…and where we're headed."

"That's a lot to think about. I've probably been sorting through similar thoughts as I've been thinking about marriage and the mistakes my parents made."

"Those are probably good things to consider, but don't forget to focus on the right things."

"What do you mean?"

"I may be speaking out of turn, but you guys are equipped with tools that your parents probably never had."

Matt nodded thoughtfully. "You're talking about the keys of joy?"

"Yes."

"Yeah, no," Matt said with a chuckle. "My parents definitely didn't have any of those tools."

"Not a lot of people do. I don't know if marriage is ever easy for anyone, but without a foundation to unite marriage partners…it's gotta be really hard, right?"

"Yeah, that's the way it seems. But you and Amy, you've known them since the beginning of your marriage, right?"

"More or less. The foundation was there, and we knew the basics. But I'm sure our understanding of the keys grew exponentially in the first few months of our marriage, and much more in these last eight years."

"And I can only assume they've made your marriage stronger."

"Without a doubt. We each came to our marriage with our shares of both hopes and fears. Amy's parents are still married, but they've spent most of their marriage without much unity. It's really only been the last few years that their marriage has been what I'd consider functional and fulfilling for either of them."

"What changed for them?"

"Have you heard of the Parkin House?"

"Uh, Parkins…yeah, those are the folks on the north end of town who run marriage retreats, right?"

"Exactly. Amy's folks spent a week there shortly before we got married and they've been working their way through the keys ever since. Amy and I feel fortunate to have learned them early on, before we had the chance to build walls between us. It's tough teaching old dogs new tricks when they've spent most of their married lives being selfish and going in different directions. Amy and I noticed early on that there was a big difference between most of the marriages we'd observed over our first twenty-two years and the marriages we found here in Niederbipp."

"Yeah, I've noticed the difference as well."

Jake nodded. "We knew right away there was something different about the people here—these Candle Lighters and Protopians. I don't know if Amy and I ever would've had a volatile relationship—it's just not in our nature. But we've learned a lot about mutual respect and love, and the importance of each of the keys by watching the people here. You can't be around them without wanting to be better, without wanting to improve."

"I know what you mean," Matt said, taking a big bowl from Jake and moving it to the front counter where there was more space. "Are you glad you stayed?" he asked when he returned for more.

"In Niederbipp?"

Matt nodded.

"I can't think of a day that's gone by over the last eight years that I wasn't grateful that Amy and I both stayed. As you know, it's a small town with lots of quirks and very little privacy, but we can't imagine a better place to live, or a better place to raise our kids."

Matt found a place for another stack of cereal bowls, returning for more.

"If the little birds around here are to be trusted, it sounds like we're going to be neighbors," Jake suggested with a warm smile as he handed off two vases.

"Word travels fast."

"Oh, you have no idea!"

"I assume Hildegard told you."

Jake nodded. "Among others. You and Genevieve have become the topic of quite a lot of chatter around here."

"Seriously?"

"In a town as small as ours, you can't expect there to be many secrets."

"What else do you know?"

Jake smiled. "The latest is that you two were recently seen entering the tailor shop about an hour ago."

"What?" Matt asked with a laugh.

"Yeah, it takes some getting used to, but it grows on you. You'll for sure have more privacy than most of us, living up on Harmony Hill. But people are watching. They pay attention to who's coming and going, and maybe even what you're eating for dinner."

"Does that ever bother you?"

"It did in the beginning, but it quickly changed when we realized it was just their way of caring about us. Tomorrow there will be at least a couple of folks who'll drop by to ask about your visit this afternoon."

"What will you tell them?"

"What would you like me to tell them?"

"Uh, would it be best to tell them the truth or would it be better to make up a fun story about…I don't know…starting a side business doing cremations in your kiln?"

Jake laughed. "People are generally used to the truth around here. Your story might throw them off your scent for a minute or two, but I can almost guarantee you'd either have people signing up for your cremation services, or you'd quickly be dealing with the funeral home who'd be upset by the competition, or maybe both."

"Then let's just stick with the pancake dinner," Matt replied, taking another set of warm vases from Jake.

"I have a question for you," Jake said, when Matt had turned back.

"Sure, what's up?"

"I'm wondering what happened to Genevieve."

"What do you mean?"

"I've heard Genevieve Patterson stories since before we got married, and just between you and me, none of them were very nice. I met her the day before the rest of you campers arrived, and I have to say I never would have believed that she was capable of either warmth, kindness or decency."

Matt smiled and nodded. "I caught glimpses of that myself, early on."

"So, I know we don't know each other very well yet, but I've been jonesing to ask you for weeks, *what happened*? How did you learn to love such a porcupine and help her become…something different?"

Matt shrugged. "Maybe she never was a true porcupine."

"I don't know." Jake chuckled. "She was pretty awful the night I met her; obliviously self-centered, obnoxiously entitled and painfully rude. And then…fast forward a couple of months…somehow…she wasn't any of those things, and she was instead almost…gentle, thoughtful, and pleasant. What happened?"

Matt looked thoughtful for a moment. "Maybe she remembered who she really was."

Jake stayed silent for a moment, considering Matt's suggestion. "Do you think it's just a matter of remembering?"

"I don't know," Matt replied, obviously pensive. "What if we're all a bit crunchy on the edges, and we just need to be warmed up a bit? You know, given a new environment and a chance to slow down and really consider who we are and what we want? What if everyone, around the world, had a chance to regularly sit down on one of those benches scattered across town and take an honest inventory of their life and their relationships? What if everyone could experience the power of real reverence...of all the keys of joy? I don't know if this town fully appreciates the power for good that the keys can have if people will put them to work. I've seen it work in Genevieve's life, but I've *experienced* it working in my own."

Jake nodded slowly. "I have, too. Amy and I both have."

"I don't know if you can spend much time here without experiencing a desire to be something more...something better."

Jake smirked. "Talk about poetic justice!" He shook his head but smiled. "You probably know by now that Genevieve came here to destroy Ruby, but she ended up becoming her."

"Yeah," Matt replied, nodding. "The truth can ultimately set you free, right? Even if at first it only makes you mad. I suppose we all have to find that place where the truth has a chance to work its way into our hearts—where its potential can be appreciated."

"You're right," Jake admitted. "You're right. The details were different, but I also found the truth I didn't even know I was looking for."

Matt looked thoughtful for a moment. "This is a really cool town, Jake. I can't even imagine having discussions like this anywhere else in the world with friends I hardly know."

"I remember thinking the same thing when I first got here."

"Have you been able to figure out what it is?"

"I think so. Communication is always different when people share a foundation that includes any one of the keys of joy and a desire to learn and understand each other. In that environment, you can set aside your differences and make genuine and personal connections without fear or insecurity."

"Huh. I think you're right. That's the way it's been on the farm. The discussions and the connections got a lot more personal real soon after we learned the first key."

"But you guys each came with another similarity that allowed you to move in the right direction for the keys to be shared."

Matt thought about that for a minute. "Are you talking about hope?"

Jake smiled, turning to close the door of the now-empty kiln. "Hope brought you here, didn't it?"

Matt nodded.

"That's what brought me here, too. And Amy. And probably most of the people who ever come here. Something changes in your heart and head when you move forward with optimism and hope. It's like you open your whole soul to possibility. Maybe it's only in circumstances like that where your heart can really be open to truth."

Matt nodded as he digested the truths Jake shared. "It's the same with all truth, isn't it?"

"I think so. Without hope, without a sincere desire for growth and understanding, I don't know how much progress a person can honestly make. You have to want it. And there has to be real intent to do something meaningful with any truth that comes along."

Matt nodded again. "Otherwise, you're only wasting everyone's time, aren't you?"

"But most of all, your own. Too many people are afraid of the very first step...of suspending their fears long enough for the light of hope to move them forward."

"Wow, you might have just described my first forty-two-and-a-half years!"

"Maybe, but I don't know if that matters as much as your *next* forty-two-and-a-half years, using what you know now to move forward rather than stagnating or allowing fear to eat up any more of your precious time."

Matt took a deep, unconscious breath and exhaled slowly as he stared off through the back window.

The bells on the front door jangled, causing them both to turn.

Genevieve followed Amy through the doorway, carrying a grocery sack, laughing with each other like old friends.

"Are you boys done yet?" Genevieve asked when they reached the front counter.

"With the kiln, yes. But we haven't filled the shelves yet," Jake responded.

"Why don't Genevieve and I do that and you guys can get dinner going?" Amy replied.

"Uh, only if you promise not to break any more of my pots," Jake replied.

Amy patted her belly softly. "I blame the boy. I'll make Genevieve carry the big stuff."

"Yeah, sure," Genevieve responded. "I've always liked playing 'Shop'," she said, turning around to look at the showroom, noticing the spaces that needed to be filled as well as Amy's paintings lining the top of the walls around the circumference of the showroom. She paused, stepping closer to a still-life painting of a pair of old, rubber boots leaning against a large, colorful flowerpot filled with geraniums. "This looks familiar," Genevieve said, taking an even closer look. "I think I saw this porch earlier today as we were coming into town."

Amy smiled. "I painted that one about a month ago, on site. It's just down the street, Gerda Blumfeld's place."

Matt came to the showroom to take a closer look. "I remember that, too," he said as he looked up at the painting. "That's got to be one of Jake's planters," he said, pointing to a much smaller but similarly glazed planter in the window display.

Jake put his arm around Amy as he nodded. "That was one of the first pots I made after coming here. It's a little wonky on one side, but fortunately Amy captured the good side."

"I always do," she responded, kissing him on the cheek.

"These are all really beautiful," Genevieve said, moving her attention to the next painting of a couple of sheep in a pasture. "There's something familiar about the way you paint…I just can't…Wait a minute. I know where I've seen your style before. I think my boss has your paintings all over the office."

"Really? Who's your boss?" Amy asked.

"Julia Galiveto."

Amy smiled broadly. "She's been buying my work for the past eight years."

"No way!"

"Way! She's one of my best customers. We've probably sold Lawrence and her close to thirty paintings."

Genevieve started to laugh. "What? How?"

"Yeah, they drop in at least a couple of times a year, usually in the spring and then again for the fall colors," Amy reported.

Genevieve turned and looked at the painting again. "I should have known. Your paintings are also hanging in that restaurant down the street, aren't they? I knew they looked familiar that very first night."

"Yeah, Robintino's. David and Nancy Garber, the people who own Robintino's, introduced us to the Galivetos."

"David and Nancy *Garber*?!"

"You know them?" Amy asked.

"Good looking couple, mid-sixties, the husband is a silver fox and his wife's at least as good looking and always classy?"

"Hey, I think I met them at your first Sourdough Sunday of the year," Matt suggested.

"Yes, and yes!" Jake said. "Great couple. Amy and I have often said we hope to be as classy as they are when we're their age." He turned to Amy. "We've got a long way to go."

"A *long* way!" Amy confirmed.

"Oh my gosh!" Genevieve replied, her hand on her forehead. "This is all starting to make sense."

"What is?"

"David and Nancy, they were recently made members of the board of my magazine! I met them at a party just a few weeks before I came here." Genevieve shook her head, smiling. "Julia's probably been lining this up for months, if not years."

The others looked at her blankly.

Genevieve laughed. "I thought I was coming here for a quick weekend interview, but instead I find out I'm a small cog in a machine that's been moving forward for who knows how long. Who knew that so many roads could intersect in a town as small as Niederbipp?"

"We run into stories like this all the time," Jake mused.

Amy nodded. "You'd be surprised how many people have spent time here, either at the Parkin's marriage retreat or the Swarovski's farm, or just passing through for a weekend getaway. People come from all over the country, and even around the world."

Genevieve nodded slowly. "I know I underestimated this place in the beginning, but it just seems like there's way more to it than I ever could've guessed."

"Yeah, we've been here for eight years and we're still learning about connections. The Garbers, for example, were one of the first couples that came to the Parkins for marital counseling."

"I can't imagine *them* ever needing *marital counseling*," Matt responded. "They seem like they have an ideal marriage, like they have it all together…"

"It surprised us as well," Amy admitted, "But then we were also surprised to learn that the Parkins were inches away from a divorce when they bought the deserted mansion."

"*And now they lead marriage retreats?*" Matt asked, dubiously.

"Yeah, Tom and Emma have a really incredible story," Jake responded. "We got to know them just before we got married when they commissioned Amy to do a large painting for their newly renovated dining hall."

"It's still the biggest painting I've ever done," Amy added.

"What did they choose as a subject?" Genevieve asked, looking up at the variety of landscape and still-life paintings hanging on the showroom walls.

"That was kind of a funny thing. They commissioned me to do a painting of a pile of rocks."

"You mean like an Ebenezer?" Matt asked.

"No, not exactly. There were a few of the rocks that were stacked on top of each other and five or six others that were scattered in the foreground."

"That seems like a strange subject for a dining hall. Did they ever tell you why they wanted rocks?" Genevieve asked.

"Yes. As I'm sure you've already learned, a lot of things are very symbolic around here. The rocks represented…"

"Actually," Jake said, interrupting his wife, "I don't know if we could do justice to the meaning to either the rocks or the painting."

Amy nodded. "Are you thinking they should talk to Tom and Emma?"

"Yeah, it seems like it would mean a lot more, right? Plus, it would give them the opportunity to get to know each other. Matt and Genevieve's syllabus is basically the same as the Parkins, right?"

Amy nodded. "And you guys would really love the Parkins. They have all sorts of great insights about marriage and life in general."

"And they're amazing cooks. If I were you, I'd find a way to invite yourselves to dinner," Jake added.

Matt laughed. "The good people of Niederbipp are going to start thinking we're a bunch of mooches. Paul and Susan just invited us to dinner, too."

"Lucky you!" Amy replied. "We love those guys, and Paul and Susan are also amazing cooks."

"Does everyone know how to cook around here?" Genevieve asked.

Amy laughed. "I wondered the same thing when I moved here. My aunt is an excellent cook as well. I guess when there aren't a lot of restaurant options, you either learn to cook, or you starve. Jake and I have learned to love cooking together. I assume you guys have, too, this summer?"

Genevieve nodded. "That's been one of the biggest surprises of my life. It's way more fun than I ever could have guessed."

"You didn't cook much before you came here?" Jake asked.

Genevieve shook her head. "The extent of my cooking was avocado toast or warming up a meal from Trader Joe's. It's a shock to go from that, to cooking for fourteen, three meals in a row."

"But it's been really good, right?" Matt asked. "I enjoyed cooking before, but it's different cooking for so many, and trying to be creative."

"Yeah, and then we try to tempt you with pancakes!" Jake laughed.

"Are you kidding?" Matt replied. "Pancakes are basically the food of the gods."

"Or at least the food of guys who have limited cooking skills, but know how to make their pregnant wives happy," Jake replied.

"Speaking of which, I'm getting hungry," Amy said. "Jake, why don't you and Matt go up and get started? I'll have Genevieve help me put the pots away and we'll join you."

Matt and Jake didn't argue with the ladies. They took the grocery sack up the back stairs and started dinner.

CHAPTER 135

Surprises

Infancy is the perpetual Messiah, which comes into the arms of fallen men, and pleads with them to return to paradise.
—Ralph Waldo Emerson—

After setting aside the fresh pots that had been previously commissioned by customers, Amy and Genevieve moved on to the showroom, finding places and filling in holes on the shelves and in the display window. Recognizing Amy's physical limitations, Genevieve was quick to jump in and help, fitting the pots into both the upper and the lower shelves where both stretching and balance were required.

A few tourists wandered in while they worked, and Genevieve watched as Amy greeted them with warmth and kindness. She also watched how these strangers responded. It was different than most retail interactions she'd experienced in large cities around the world. It was far more personal, even intimate. In this relatively small space filled with items and artwork that had been created by human hands, Genevieve noticed there was a genuine connection formed between the artist and the customer. As she handled the pottery, she felt it too. It was something far different than picking up a random item in a department store display. It was almost as if there were some bit of life that had somehow been magically transferred from Jake's fingers into the clay. But she noticed it was in the paintings, too. The pots had all found places before Amy had finished with the last couple who'd selected a colorful serving bowl and four unique mugs.

Not wanting to interrupt or get in the way, Genevieve walked to the far end of the showroom to take a closer look at Amy's paintings. It had been more than two months since they'd taken the wagon and horses down to the Stoltzfuss farm for the barn raising, but Genevieve recognized it right away. The depiction of the tall, white, clapboard building towering over the line of buggies and the farmhouse brought back warm memories of that day. She moved on to the next painting, a bench looking out on the stony riverbank, dwarfed by the river and the hillside beyond, big, billowy clouds sailing across the sky. It felt like the painting almost invited her in to take a seat and enjoy a moment of tranquility.

As she moved on to the next painting, she listened as Amy told the customers about her husband. She'd heard the customers admiring his pottery, but she watched their interest pique as Amy briefly talked about his humble beginnings and the last eight years since their marriage—two artists living a dream they'd made tangible. They paid with a credit card, but before they left, the middle-aged woman took a bill from her wallet and slid it across the counter. "It's been a few decades since we were expecting our first child," she said, "but we know that diapers and formula have only gotten more expensive. Please accept this as an investment in the next generation of potters and painters."

Amy thanked them graciously and walked them to the door, waving through the window as they wandered back the way they came. "I'm starving! The boys should've been done by now." She descended the steps and locked the front door. She had just turned and put her foot on the first step to climb back up when a sudden look of concern flashed across her face followed immediately by the sound of water hitting the floor.

"Oh no!" Amy said, looking up, fear in her eyes.

"What happened? Did you pee yourself?"

She bit down, clenching her jaw. "My water just broke!"

"That's…bad, right?" Genevieve responded, feeling a pang of panic rush through her.

"Not bad, but very inconvenient. Dang it. I had my heart set on pancakes tonight." She laughed. "I guess you better go tell Jake. I'm sorry, but I think this puts an end to our dinner party."

"Oh my gosh! You're having a baby *now*?" Genevieve asked, her voice rising with alarm.

"Hopefully not right now, but soon. I've been having small contractions on and off since Monday, but…oooof…." She reached for Genevieve's hand, gripping hard as a contraction swept over her, causing her to sway. "I better sit down."

Genevieve helped her come down slowly, kneeling next to her as she waited till the death grip on her hand and forearm slackened. "I'll go get Jake," she said, scrambling to her feet. She ran through the back door and up the stairs, bursting into the kitchen with the news, frightening both the men who were just adding the last of the pancakes to the tall stack.

"She's having the baby now!" she managed.

Jake's face immediately went pale. "Where?"

"In the pottery, by the front door. Her water just broke."

Jake's face flashed a look of panic and excitement as he tore down the stairs, two at a time, Matt and Genevieve following close behind.

"Amy, are you okay?" Jake yelled from the doorway.

"Yeah, this is a mess. They're coming fast, Jake."

"Where's your car?" Matt asked.

Jake turned; his face unreadable. "We ordered it a month ago and it's still not here," he said over his shoulder as they all rushed toward Amy.

"But the hospital, it's close, right?" Matt replied. "Just up by the bus station?"

"Yes," Jake replied, kneeling down on the floor next to his bride. He took her hand, wet from the amniotic fluid, and looked into her face, finding obvious signs of distress. "We gotta get you outta here, Babe. Can you walk at all?"

She squeezed his hand just as another contraction hit. "I don't think so."

Matt looked around, seeing what they had to work with, but the only obvious answer was a chair. He picked it up and brought it to them, setting it down on the floor just behind Jake. "If she can sit on the chair, I think the three of us can carry her up the hill. It's gotta be better than the scooter, right?"

"We gotta go now," Amy replied, struggling to get to her feet as Jake and Matt helped her, her skirt soaked by the fluid.

"What do you want me to do?" Genevieve asked.

"Help us get her out of here," Matt replied.

They sat her down in the chair, then with adrenaline making them stronger than normal, they lifted Amy three feet off the ground and maneuvered her past the potter's wheel, the kiln, and the glaze tables, and out the back door into the early evening light of the courtyard.

"This is the fastest way," Jake said, nodding his head to the side. They raced through the courtyard and onto Hinterstrasse, a back road that ran parallel to Niederbipp's main drag and was free of foot traffic.

Amy held onto the men's necks for stabilization, but when the next contraction hit, her fingertips left deep impressions in their skin. "Stop," Amy said, sounding frantic. Jake and Matt looked at each other before slowing their pace and setting her down.

"Molly," she said, looking at Jake. "We have to tell Molly. She wants to be there."

"Babe, I don't…" Jake began, but quickly stopped when Amy's face made it clear that this was non-negotiable.

"Molly, that's Kai's wife, right? From the market?" Genevieve asked, out of breath from keeping up with the long-legged men.

Amy nodded.

"If you guys have got this, I'll go tell her."

"Are you sure? We can call from the hospital." Jake suggested.

"No, I got this," Genevieve responded confidently. "She needs to be there." She turned and left, leaving the men to carry Amy alone.

"We should have thought of this chair thing last time," Jake said as they hefted his wife again.

"Last time?" Matt asked.

"Eight years ago, Kai and I carried Molly to the hospital when her water broke and the contractions started coming fast."

Amy tried to laugh through her pain. "I ran to the hospital to tell them you were coming. I can't believe this is happening to me, too." Her eyes closed and her jaw clenched as another contraction began, squelching her ability to speak. As Jake watched her, his pace slowed, throwing off the synchronicity of their steps and causing the chair to wobble.

Matt slowed as well, hoping to regain the rhythm they'd had in the beginning when they'd been propelled by their adrenaline. But with Jake focusing on the contortions on his wife's face, Matt knew he would have to concentrate on matching Jake's distracted and irregular gait over the uneven cobblestones. This was made significantly easier as the road leveled off and they entered the church courtyard. But the next contraction was met with a painful groan as Amy did her best to breathe through it.

"I'm gonna be too late for an epidural," she lamented as they carried her though the shadows of the trees to the pedestrian passageway on the far end of the courtyard.

"You kids look like you're in distress," Thomas said, looking up from the side of his home where he was pushing his bicycle through the ankle-deep grass and dandelions.

"Amy's having the baby!" Jake yelled over his shoulder.

"Well, why didn't you say so? How can I help?" He shouted back, quickly jogging alongside them after ditching his bike in the grass.

"You can run ahead and tell the hospital we're coming," Matt suggested.

"Got it!" Thomas responded, heading off through the passageway ahead of them in a quick jog.

They'd just made in through the passageway themselves when Amy cried out again. "This baby's coming now!" she yelped, looking distressed. "Hurry. Oh God, please hurry!"

"Just another hundred yards, Babe," Jake replied.

Matt looked up to see a man and a woman in scrubs coming out of the hospital with a wheeled gurney, racing toward them, Thomas following close behind. For the men, the relief was real, both of them feeling spent from their physical exertions and the stress associated with their sprint. But while their work was done, Amy's was still on-going. The transition from chair to gurney was quick and fluid, leaving Matt and Thomas standing still as Jake disappeared with his wife and the emergency staff.

"Well, that was exciting," Thomas said, clapping Matt on the back. "Good work!"

"Uh, thanks. Did that really just happen?" Matt asked, looking confused.

"I'm pretty sure it did." Thomas thumped the backrest of the chair with his hand. "You just happened to be at the right place at the right time, huh?"

"I guess so. Jake and I were making pancakes, and the next thing I know..."

Thomas laughed. "Life happens fast."

"Did we miss the debut?" Molly asked from behind, causing them to turn as she and Genevieve rushed toward them, looking quite out of breath.

"I don't think so, but you better hurry!" Matt replied.

Molly rushed on, leaving the panting Genevieve next to Matt.

"I was just on my way up to the farm for dinner," Thomas said. "Would you kids like to join me?"

"You're not sticking around to find out how things go?" Matt asked.

Thomas shook his head. "Don't get me wrong, I've been looking forward to this day for a long time, but I'm about as helpful in this situation as a fork in a sugar bowl. I'll swing by in a few hours to offer my congratulations, but for now I'm gonna go get my bike and make my way up to the farm for some fried chicken and cornbread. Should I tell them you'll be late?"

Matt turned to Genevieve, trying to read the expression on her face as she still struggled to catch her breath from her sprint. "I think we'd better take this chair back to the studio and make sure everything's closed up."

"And there's a bit of a mess to clean up in the showroom," Genevieve added with a grimace.

"Then I'll let Pops and Ruby know you're holding down the fort."

"Thank you. Please tell them we'll plan on being home before dark."

Thomas nodded, smiling dumbly at both of them. "I understand congratulations are in order for the two of you as well."

Matt laughed. "We're still not used to the travel speed of news around here."

"Everyone loves sharing good news. Congratulations to both of you. You have a grand adventure ahead of you. And I'd like to volunteer my services wherever you can use me."

"Thank you," Matt said, extending his hand to Thomas. "We've got a lot of things to figure out, and it's nice to know there are sincere folks around like yourself who are willing to help."

"Maybe we could talk to you sometime about the wedding ceremony itself?" Genevieve asked.

Thomas bowed. "At your service, whenever you're ready. I...I've had the great pleasure and honor of being involved with Ruby's recruits throughout most of the last thirty-something summers. Please don't hesitate to ask whenever you feel my support or input could be helpful. If you don't already know, the people of Niederbipp are all happy to help you wherever we can."

Genevieve put her left arm around Matt's waist, nodding to Thomas. "Thank you for your friendship and support. It's comforting to know there are people like you in this community. I know I can speak for both of us in saying we'd love you to be a part of our future and everything we do on the farm."

"Absolutely," Matt said, nodding his agreement.

"With pleasure." Thomas bowed again. "Now, if you'll excuse me, I hate to be late for dinner."

CHAPTER 136

Lemon Drops and Stones

We have to be continually reminded of what we believe. No belief will automatically remain alive in the mind. It must be fed.
—C.S. Lewis—

It seemed a crying shame to let a whole plate of still-warm pancakes go uneaten, and it only made sense to eat the pancakes before they cleaned up the mess in the studio. Though both Matt and Genevieve felt weak after their adrenaline crash and their physical exertions, neither of them were entirely comfortable making themselves at home in Jake and Amy's apartment. Instead, they each pulled a few pancakes onto one of the mismatched stoneware plates stacked on the corner of the table, doused them with buttermilk syrup, and decided to enjoy their meal seated on the front step, looking out onto the courtyard.

"This syrup's even better than Ruby's," Genevieve managed, mumbling through a mouthful of pancakes.

Matt nodded; his own mouth full. "It's supposed to be an ancestral recipe or something. Jake said Kai calls it *Shazzam*, and he's been bugging him for years to figure out a way to package it so they can sell it at the market."

"Sounds like a brilliant idea," she responded, taking another bite.

While they ate, they talked about the profound changes this child would undoubtedly bring to Jake and Amy's marriage. In addition to the change of daily pace, they recognized there would likely be a change in family income as either Jake's or Amy's time would soon be divided, shearing off many collective hours to care for their son. There would be new costs—diapers, formula, and clothing that would rapidly become obsolete as he grew. Then there were doctor visits, and, as Matt remembered, the purchase of a new automobile. In addition, there would be a lack of sleep for one or both of them as they handled late night feedings and other obligatory fussiness.

As they washed the dishes and cleaned up the kitchen, they discussed the realities of their decisions to marry, run the farm, entertain twelve campers each summer *and* start a family. It would be far more difficult than simply showing up at the beginning of the summer, ready for whatever it took to find a spouse. This was a whole different game. And though that game was still exciting and full of the promise of happiness and satisfaction, it wasn't without its concerns, challenges, and complications. It would require hard work, sacrifice, good communication, the ability to quickly forgive each other, and undoubtedly hundreds if not thousands of skills and attributes they weren't yet aware of.

Cleaning up the mess in the showroom took a little longer than they anticipated after they realized that cleaning just one area of the pottery's floor made the rest of it look terrible. While Matt mopped the entire floor of the showroom and the studio, Genevieve made herself useful by dusting the pottery on the shelves. She nearly dropped a large vase when she was startled by Hildegard, her nose pressed against the front window. The old woman smiled and waved before teetering over the cobblestones and disappearing from view.

When they were satisfied with what they could reasonably clean without knowing what they were doing in this unfamiliar space, they turned out the lights and locked the door. They climbed the stairs to do the same with the apartment. They wondered what to do with the now cold, leftover pancakes when an idea came to Matt. He handed Genevieve a small glass jar he found in the drying rack on the side of the sink and asked her to fill it with syrup while he wrapped the plate of pancakes in aluminum foil. They closed the door behind them and retraced their steps to the hospital where they were ushered into a small family waiting room.

A group of nine happy Niederbippians were gathered in a far corner, crowded around Molly who was happily reporting on the speedy, successful delivery of baby Isaac, all eight pounds, fourteen ounces and twenty-three inches of him. The faces of all present were filled with joy. Genevieve and Matt were both feeling a little bit like interlopers when Molly looked up to see them. She quickly invited them to join in the exuberance and explained to the others that it was Matt who'd helped carry Amy to the hospital with Jake, while Genevieve had run all the way to the market, then up the backstairs to their apartment when Kai had been busy with a customer. Molly explained that her father happened to be visiting at the time, allowing her to make the quick change of plans and be there, along with Gloria and Jake, when Isaac had taken his first breath and wailed his first cry.

Molly spoke with such animation and emotion that it was impossible not to recognize how deeply she'd been touched by the experience of witnessing the profound miracle of birth. Even Genevieve was surprised by her own emotions as Molly related how happy Jake and Amy were after so many difficult years of dashed hopes and disappointments. But tonight there was only rejoicing among this happy group of revelers.

A nurse approached the group and a hush fell over them.

"Uh, hi! Amy and Jake would like to invite all of you to come to their room together for a few minutes rather than sending you in one at a time. That is, if you'd like to meet the newest Kimball."

The small gathering of friends unanimously affirmed their desire to do just that.

"Baby Isaac is sleeping, and Amy, of course, is quite tired, so I'll invite you to keep your voices down and your visit short. Please follow me."

Matt and Genevieve joined the small procession, falling in at the end. They quietly wove their way through the hallway, up a flight of stairs to the second floor, and down another hallway to the last room on the right.

Jake, standing at the side of the bed, looked up as the quiet crowd peered in. Gloria, who stood on the opposite side of the bed, smiled brightly, but her eyes were red and puffy. In the middle of the bed, the red-headed Amy reclined, looking somehow regal despite her hospital gown, a tiny, swaddled bundle resting on her chest. The room was bathed in golden twilight, the sun just slightly above the horizon now, sending its beams through the blinds, filling the room with a warm, magical glow. And with that light and warmth came an indelible sense of awe and reverence as they collectively peered in at the bundle of new life.

"Please, come in," Jake spoke softly, motioning for the gathering to join them in the small space. They moved slowly, reverently, each of them touched by the unseen yet undeniable sense of peace and tranquility. They leaned in, but kept their distance, none of them wanting to obstruct the view of another.

Amy, looking tired but strong, gently moved the small bundle so they could see the child's face. His hair, dark and full, spilled out of the top of the blanket, and his pink skin and tiny nose, illuminated by the evening light, almost appeared to glow with an ethereal translucence.

Genevieve watched out of the corner of her eye as Matt wiped a tear from his eyes.

It somehow felt as if the entire world had frozen in time as the small gathering looked on at this Madonna and her child. Few words were spoken, and those that were came only in reverent whispers.

The visit couldn't have been long, a minute—maybe two. But that time was so rich with meaning and significance that its short duration seemed entirely meaningless. Standing at the back of the party, Matt and Genevieve were the last of the small company to leave the room after laying their silver-wrapped offerings of pancakes and syrup on the hospital table at the foot of Amy's bed. Recognizing the simple yet thoughtful gifts laid before them, Amy and Jake whispered words of gratitude as Matt and Genevieve left, following closely behind the others.

"It just occurred to me who you two are," said the tall, gentle looking man as Matt and Genevieve walked out of the hospital, hand in hand. "I've seen you at church. You kids are some of Ruby's recruits, aren't you?"

"Yes," Matt replied. "You looked familiar too. I'm Matt, and this is Genevieve."

The man smiled and nodded. "I'm Joseph. My better half was the second most beautiful woman in that room up there tonight."

"The florist?" Matt said with a nod. "Was it…Gloria?"

"Yes, that's right." He looked at them with a kind yet scrutinizing eye. "I…I think I may have heard something about you two."

Genevieve laughed softly. "Is that right?"

"Yes. Our shop's just up the street from the tailor's, and, well, I understand some congratulations are in order."

"Thank you," Genevieve replied, looking deeper into the man's blue-gray eyes.

"Could it be that you're also the couple who's been chosen to be the next matchmakers of Harmony Hill?"

She looked at Matt. "This is spreading much faster than I ever could have guessed."

"So, it's true then?" Molly responded, stepping away from the other huddle, her own ears tickling for information.

Again, Genevieve turned to Matt.

"Uh, we, uh…yes, both are true," Matt replied. "Though I will say that, to our knowledge, none of the other campers are aware of any of this."

"Then they'll be the last to know," Molly laughed. "As you're quickly learning, there aren't a whole lot of secrets around here. All the windows have eyes, and many of the walls as well."

"Doesn't that ever make you crazy?" Genevieve asked, laughing, but feeling a little uncertain of the voyeuristic habits of Niederbipp's citizens.

Molly offered a gentle and disarming smile. "A few years ago I heard of a woman who was robbed and raped on the streets of Manhattan in the middle of the day as hundreds if not thousands of people walked by, turning a blind eye to her plight as she cried out for help. If that story is on one extreme of the spectrum, our town may be on the other. We're only nosey because we care."

"That's right," Joseph replied. "Millie Banks must have seen you and Jake carrying Amy up here because she called us just as we were closing up shop for the day to let Gloria know that the baby was coming."

"She got there less than two minutes after I did," Molly responded.

"And I'm glad she did! She's been looking forward to this day ever since Jake and Amy asked us to be their children's godparents, and that was at least five years ago," Joseph reported.

Molly nodded. "I learned about one of Amy's miscarriages just by reading Gloria's sad eyes when she dropped by the market. She'd only known for a few minutes herself." Molly patted her chest and blinked her eyes, trying to control her emotions. "We just sat there in the produce section and cried some ugly tears for a few minutes."

"If you can't cry with your grocer or ask your local florist to be your child's godmother, you're probably not in Niederbipp," Joseph added. "Our intentions are good, and our hearts are pure, but it takes some getting used to. You'll soon discover how wonderful it is to have neighbors who care enough to want to know everything about you."

Molly nodded. "But if I were you, I think I'd probably let the other campers know what's going on before they hear about it on the streets."

"That could be awkward," Matt admitted, turning to Genevieve.

"Oh, you have no idea," Joseph continued. "A few years back, one of your male predecessors rode his bike up to Castleton's Fine Jewelry, a shop about eight miles north of here. He planned to propose to one of your female predecessors before the end of the summer, but he never got the chance."

"Why? What happened?" asked Genevieve.

"Oh, it's basically the classic tale of another suitor hearing of the gossip at the Niederbipp Cut-n-Shave. The second fellow rode back to the farm as fast as he could, found the young woman both men had been secretly hoping to make their wife, and proposed to her on the spot. She said yes, and the other guy was stuck with a ring."

"That's brutal," Matt suggested.

"Well, that wasn't the first time, and I'm sure it won't be the last. As they say, 'All is fair in love and war.' As the story goes, the fellow with the ring ended up marrying another girl from that summer's group and they've all remained friends. Ruby claims it was a better match for all of them anyway. But the point is that word travels far faster around here than anybody expects."

"It's a good thing there's no phone service on the farm or the rest of the campers would for sure know already," Molly added. "If I were you, I'd hightail it back to the farm before it's too late."

"I would, too," a female voice spoke from behind them.

They all turned to the older woman with silvery red hair, standing next to a tall, bespectacled man with a bald head.

"I'll admit that if there was a phone at the farm I would've called up there myself just to verify the rumors," the woman continued, stepping forward. "I've got some phone calls to make, including to Amy's parents. But I'd like to shake your hands and offer you a congratulatory gift. I'm

Cindy and this is my husband, George. We had a visit this afternoon from our neighbors, P.J. and Hazel, who seemed to be quite enamored with the two of you." She opened her small handbag and withdrew a couple of small somethings, handing one to Matt and another to Genevieve.

The evening light was faint, but Matt could tell from the weight and texture that it was a stone.

"What's this?" Matt asked.

"Well, around here, that's what we call a rock!" Cindy exclaimed as the other Niederbippians snickered.

"And a nice one too!" George said, looking at the rock in Matt's open palm, his whole face drawn up in a smile as if he were the first to catch the punchline of a very unique joke. He reached into his own pocket and withdrew a small tin. He flipped it open to reveal a dozen lemon drops, offering one to Matt and Genevieve before passing the tin to the others who'd huddled up around them.

"Thank you," Genevieve said, unsure of how she was supposed to respond to these two odd gifts.

"I guess it would be safe to assume your alter egos are Mr. and Mrs. Lemondrop?" Matt suggested, connecting the dots a little faster than Genevieve.

"Well, yes, some of the kids around here call us the *Lemondrops* or the *Rockmongers* and occasionally the *Silly Old Coots Who Live Down by the River*, but most folks just know us as the McLaughlins," George responded.

"We've been friends with Jake and Amy since the day before they were married," Cindy added. "We bought my dad's place—the house I grew up in—a year later when he passed away. We just live on the other side of the brambles from the Meiers Family."

"That must be a lot of fun," Matt suggested.

The older couple smiled and nodded. "They certainly keep us young."

"And the rocks?" Matt asked, holding up the gift he'd been given.

"Yes," Cindy said with a smile. "In his later years, my father was a collector of all things beautiful including, but not limited to, rocks, bottle caps, buttons, acorns and who knows what else. He left the house full of pickle jars overflowing with his treasures and we've spent the last seven years sharing them with others, just as he did. We figure that if we live to be a hundred and forty, we might be able to distribute all of them."

"Sounds like an amusing tradition," Matt suggested. "Maybe we could help you by passing them out at the farm stand."

"Yeah, we tried that a few years back," George replied. "We dropped off a jar of rocks to a couple of your predecessors, but they didn't seem to catch the vision and insisted we take them with us the next time we dropped by."

"Some people just don't get it. No matter how hard you try to help them understand, for some people they'll never see them as anything more than rocks, or bottle caps, or buttons." Cindy reported.

"How would you prefer us to see them?" Genevieve asked.

"As treasures and tokens of friendship. That's what Daddy always had in mind."

"And the lemon drops?" Matt asked.

George laughed. "That's my personal version of a token of friendship. Cindy handles the rocks and other treasures, I follow close behind handing out candy so people don't think we're crazy, though it's been fun keeping people guessing."

"I'll be the first to admit it's kind of a peculiar way to meet people," said Cindy. "But people rarely forget you, and you get a lot of bewildered looks from the tourists when you place a pebble or a rusty bottle cap in their palms and offer them a smile. It may sound like a strange way to spend your golden years, but we never could've imagined how much fun it would be before we tried it."

Genevieve laughed out loud. "I think I'm gonna like it here."

"Me, too," Matt replied.

"There's not a kid in this town who doesn't have a jar or two of his own filled with Bob Allen's treasures," Joseph added.

"I know my kids do," Molly admitted, "along with several pickle jars filled with their own treasures. I'll confess there are times when their collections get a little annoying, but I'm always reminded of your father, Cindy, and the many *treasures* that he shared with me over my first twenty-five years."

"Do you still have your collection?" asked Joseph.

"Some of them, but Kai and I have also been known to pass them along by slipping them into the bags of unsuspecting shoppers at the market." She laughed. "I hope they get as big a kick out of them as we do sharing them."

"I think that maybe that's what treasures are really all about," Cindy said. "Dad's dementia certainly affected his idiosyncrasies, but his childlike desire to share what he had became contagious. When we bought his home and decided to keep up his tradition of making gifts of his treasures, we often found that we returned home with more than we took with us when we left."

"How does that work?" Genevieve asked.

"A rock is just a rock until it becomes a treasure," Cindy replied. "The joy a treasure can produce is limited if it's kept in a jar. By sharing it with others, not only do you pass it on for someone else to enjoy, but you share with them a small piece of yourself, and the joy is multiplied."

"Is it the same with all treasures?" Matt asked thoughtfully.

"We're still working our way through that," George admitted, "but we have yet to discover any treasure whose joy is not multiplied when we've shared it with others."

"Most people don't learn that until it's too late," Cindy added. "My father was a successful developer, businessman and politician. He accumulated great wealth in his early years, but he lost track of his greatest treasures in the process."

"His family?" Matt asked.

Cindy nodded.

"We all played second fiddle to the treasures he valued more than us. It wasn't until many years later, after Mom died, that he began to reevaluate his life and discover the misplaced value he'd given to his professional pursuits, finally recognizing that most of it really didn't matter. But by then, much of it was too late. He did the best he could to make amends for the years of distraction and neglect that took him away from us. I think we all eventually were able to forgive him in our own ways, but that did little to change the fact that he wasn't there when we'd needed him most."

"Wow," Matt uttered involuntarily as he looked down at the stone in his hand.

Cindy nodded. "What the Good Book says about one's heart being close to his treasure is unquestionably true. We must choose our treasure wisely, and thoughtfully evaluate where our heart is. Too many treasures become idols and false gods, demanding devotions while stealing away the hearts and the simple joys from those with whom they become entangled."

Genevieve nodded thoughtfully. "Thanks for the warning," she said, nodding to the pretty stone she'd been given.

"If you kids find yourself in the neighborhood, please stop by for a visit," Cindy responded.

"Yes, we'd love to share more treasures with you, and talk to you about the possibility of you helping us share them with your customers," George added.

"I think we'd like that," Matt replied after a nod from Genevieve.

"We better get out of here so we can let everyone know about Baby Isaac before somebody beats us to it," Cindy said, closing her purse and swinging it over her shoulder.

"I think we better be going as well," Matt replied, tapping Genevieve on the arm.

"Yeah, but…do you remember where our bikes are?" Genevieve asked.

"I think you left them next to the fountain this afternoon," spoke an elderly woman from behind them, her words mumbled by the lemon drop in her mouth.

They thanked her and the others before turning to jog back to the fountain.

CHAPTER 137

The Phone Call

Love that leads life upward is the noblest and the best.
—Henry Van Dyke—

Their ascent up Harmony Hill was quicker than they'd ever ridden before, leaving them both winded and panting long before they reached the summit. Night had fallen and fireflies danced in the air all around them as they discussed how they would tell the other campers. Before they reached the turnoff to the drive, the phone at the top of Harmony Hill began ringing within its booth.

"Who do you think's calling?" Matt asked.

"Probably your mom," Genevieve suggested, laughing as she did.

"Then I better get it," he said, leaning his bike on its kickstand before opening the phone booth's door.

"You're going to answer it?"

"Sure, why not?"

"What if it *is* your mom?"

"I hope it is. It will save me the trouble of calling her with our good news."

"And what if it's my parents?"

"Then *you* can tell them the good news." He picked up the phone. "Hello, this is the phone booth on Harmony Hill. How may I direct your call?"

There was a brief pause before a woman's voice was heard. "Uh, yes, oh…Hello, I…I was hoping to reach Genevieve Patterson."

"Well, you're in luck. She happens to be right here." He handed the receiver to Genevieve, who took it, squeezing through the doorway to stand closer to the phone. Matt leaned in so he could hear.

"This is Genevieve Patterson."

"Genevieve, thank God! This is Julia. I've been trying to reach you all week. The satellite phone you took with you has gone dark. Is everything okay?"

"Yes, everything's fine. It's better than fine, actually. Julia, I don't know how much you know, but I'm getting married!"

"What!?! To whom?"

Genevieve turned and looked at Matt, his nose touching hers for just a moment in the tight quarters. "His name is Matt Owens."

Julie took a deep breath on the other side of the line and exhaled slowly. "This is probably going to sound like a lame question, but do you love him? Is he good to you?"

"Yes, of course. Why do you ask?"

Julia took another deep breath. "I…I'm relieved. I heard from Hildegard on Sunday that you were planning on taking over the farm.

I've been worried all week that you were planning on doing it alone. I've been beside myself, wondering what kind of mess I got you into. And then when I couldn't get a hold of Ruby or Pops, and no one was answering this phone…I told myself if I didn't have an answer by tonight, I was planning on driving down to find out for myself what's going on. Are you sure you're okay?"

"Honestly, I've never been better," Genevieve said, reaching her free hand around to tap Matt's cheek.

"And you're sure this is really what you want?"

Matt wrapped his arms around her middle and squeezed her softly.

"Yes, I'm sure. I'll admit that I wondered what the heck you were thinking when you sent me here, but honestly, this is the best assignment you've ever given me. It's changed…everything. I honestly can't imagine ever leaving for more than quick trips into town."

"And your writing…how's the assignment coming?"

"I was afraid you might ask. I…I've got nothing."

"Nothing? Genevieve…it's been over *three* months."

"I've been a little busy. It's been nearly impossible to find a free minute to sneak away and write anything, what with chores and porch games, and trying to embed myself in all of this and make it look like I'm legitimately invested, and then falling in love and making plans to take over the farm. You remember how it is, don't you? There's not much left at the end of the day."

Julia exhaled again loudly. "You're right. And now with wedding planning and all the extras I'm sure Ruby and Pops are trying to download before…I'm sorry to ask for more, but I really need something. I've pushed this back a month already. My editors are freaking out that we've seen nothing from you."

"Julia, I think I know what you want me to say, but I'm not willing to drop all of this and change the dynamics for all the campers so I can meet my deadlines. I'm sorry. Too much is riding on this for everyone else. I think this has the potential of being everything you want it to be, and more, but it can't be rushed. I can't set all this aside to make a deadline. I'm not willing to sacrifice the hopes of eleven other campers, plus the investment of Ruby's and Pops's time and efforts so readers have something to read. That's not fair to anyone."

Julia laughed. "Are you sure I'm speaking to Genevieve Patterson?"

"Yes, why?"

"Because the woman I sent to Niederbipp three months ago wouldn't have allowed hell or high water to stand between her and her story."

"Well, I'm sorry to disappoint you," Genevieve said, the first hints of emotion hanging on her words.

Julia chuckled. "Actually, you've been anything but a disappointment."

"What?"

"Genevieve, you've been *anything* but a disappointment. I couldn't be more proud of you. From everything I've heard from Ruby and Hildegard, you've endured tremendous hardship and heartache and have worked your way through it better than I ever could have hoped. I knew this would be tough, but I also knew it would change you in powerful ways, if you'd let it."

"It has," Genevieve admitted. "I won't deny that I felt totally betrayed in the beginning, but…thank you."

"*Thank you*?"

"Yeah, I didn't know I needed this, and now that I've experienced Niederbipp, I can't imagine not being a part of what's going on here."

"I remember feeling much the same way at the end of my summer there. As I told you in my letter, I felt incredibly fortunate that Pops and Ruby allowed me to stay on through the winter while I worked on my dissertation."

"Yes."

"And I suppose a big part of me is profoundly jealous of the position they've offered you. I want you to know that you've always had my full confidence."

"But…?"

"No buts. If the timing doesn't work out for you, we'll just have to work around your schedule. I'd much rather start this new direction out right—with your very best work—rather than rush it and offer our readers something less than the full transformational magic Niederbipp has to offer."

"So, what does this mean for my deadline?"

There was a long silence on the other end as the soft sound of papers being shuffled came through the receiver. "I don't know. If we had your article by, say…mid-November, we could rush it through and run it in the January issue. Could that be feasible?"

"Ten-thousand words…," Genevieve whispered as she thought aloud. "I'll…do my best."

"I think she meant to say, *we'll* do our best," Matt added.

"Who's that?"

"That's Matt, my…fiancé."

"Matt, are you still listening?" Julia asked.

"Yes, I'm here."

"I just want to make sure you know that you are one lucky son-of-a-gun."

"Yes, yes, thank you, I'm quite aware of that."

"I'm not sure what I'm going to do without her here in New York, but knowing she'll still be a big part of this vision makes it a little easier to swallow. I look forward to meeting you, Matt. I assume you must have some farm experience?"

"Uh, yes ma'am, exactly three months and five days of experience. I'm actually a dentist."

"Oh, God help us all!"

Matt and Genevieve laughed out loud.

"I couldn't agree more. That's what we're both praying for," Matt replied.

"And the other campers…do they know yet what your plans are?"

"Uh, no, we were just on our way home to tell everyone when we stopped to answer the phone," Genevieve responded.

"Good. Word tends to travel faster than you might think."

"Yes, we're learning more about that all the time," Matt concurred.

"Speaking of 'word traveling fast', you probably haven't heard yet that Amy just gave birth to a healthy baby boy this evening," Genevieve offered.

Julia gasped. "You've seen the baby…he's okay?"

"Yes, Amy and Isaac are both looking good."

"Oh, wow! And they named him Isaac?"

"Yeah."

"What a beautiful name. I can't wait to meet him."

"Will you be coming soon?" asked Genevieve.

"Well, I don't mean to be presumptuous, but if we'd be welcomed, we'd like to come out for your wedding."

"Of course, you'd be welcomed. We haven't set the date yet, but we're thinking about October 8th. That's the last day of our summer obligations and we'd like to enjoy the wedding with the rest of the campers."

"I'm penciling you in now. I know you two have just made it official, but have you thought about whose gown you might be wearing? I hate to be crass, but it would be good advertising for the magazine."

"Actually, I was just fit for my gown this afternoon, and Matt for his suit."

"Mmm. By Lin and Albert, I assume?"

"You know them?"

"Yes, and you couldn't have picked a better shop for a wedding in Niederbipp. Oh, Genevieve, it will be perfect! Will you let the magazine photographers do your wedding?"

"Only if they can do it without making a scene. We'd really like to keep it simple. You know Niederbipp."

"Fair enough. I'll make sure that's clear with whomever we send. What about bridal shots? I'm thinking *American Gothic* meets *Hollywood*."

"Uhh, I think we'd feel more comfortable with far less Hollywood and more American Gothic?"

Julia laughed. "Am I still speaking to Genevieve Patterson?'"

"Yes, but the new and improved, more humble version, who hasn't had either a manicure or pedicure in more than three months, and has no plans to get one anytime soon."

"Got it. I expected this assignment to change you, but I never imagined it would turn you into a granola."

Genevieve laughed. "Do I need to remind you that we do the laundry around here by bicycle power, and I haven't used a blow dryer even once in three months?"

Julia took a deep breath. "Are you ready for a commitment of this magnitude?"

Genevieve turned and looked at Matt, his face illuminated by nothing more than starlight. She smiled at him and reached for his hand, squeezing it firmly. "Yes," she said softly. "I'm sure."

CHAPTER 138

Promises

Truth is ever to be found in the simplicity, and not in the multiplicity and confusion of things.
—Isaac Newton—

From the top of Harmony Hill, the carnival lights, strung across the front porch, made the big house look like center stage in a large, outdoor amphitheater, complete with fireflies blinking like flashbulbs from paparazzi cameras. With their bikes between them, Matt and Genevieve looked down on the happy gathering of their fellow campers and their benevolent hosts, knowing tonight would likely be their last chance to share their news with the rest of the campers before they'd hear it all from the Niederbipp rumor mill.

Matt took a deep breath, whistling softly as he exhaled. "Are you ready for this?"

"I thought I was just a minute ago, but the reality of it…this is kind of a big deal, you know?"

"Are you getting cold feet already?"

"No, it's not that. I've never felt better about anything in my life, but this is…really big. Do you realize we could be spending the next forty to fifty years down there, raising kids and even grandkids in that house?!"

"Are you okay with that?"

"I have to be, right? It's just a little bit hard to think of the next fifty years when I'm not even thirty yet."

Matt watched her, the reflections of the porch lights sparkling in her eyes. "You do remember that you're not doing this alone, right? We get to do this together."

"Thanks for the reminder," she said, turning to him. "I've been flying solo for so long…it's gonna take some adjustments to remember I've got a wingman. I really can't imagine doing this with anyone else, Matt. I love you."

He smiled, leaning awkwardly across both bikes to wrap his arm around her. "I love you, too, Genevieve. I know this is going to be a lot of work, but I want you to know that I'm committed to also making it fun and joyful."

"Promise?" she asked, pulling back from the embrace so she could look into his starlit face.

"I promise," he replied confidently. "That's what this is all about, right? That's what's kept Ruby and Pops here all these years. That's why we're here now."

She nodded slowly. "You're talking about joy?"

He nodded, turning to look down on the farm. "Imagine how this world would be if everyone had a chance to experience what we've experienced this summer—the joy that this place oozes all over everyone who comes here with a sincere heart. I really can't believe I get to spend the rest of my life doing this, and I can't imagine a better partner to share it with."

Genevieve nodded, smiling warmly. "Thank you."

"You still seem nervous?"

"Yeah, maybe I am."

"What's bugging you?"

"I guess I'm still worried how this announcement we're about to make might change the dynamics for all of us over the next fifty-five days. I can't imagine James and Crystal being very excited for us after they've been forced to wait to pursue an exclusive relationship."

"The same rules apply to us, right? We're not asking for any special treatment, other than to have a little time to figure out our wedding."

"Yeah, but don't you think they'll cause a fuss about us moving forward with all of this before the summer's over?"

"I guess we'll have to wait and see, but I don't think we should worry about them."

"No?"

He shook his head. "James and Crystal have to figure out their own stuff. We can't be walking on eggshells for the next two months. We've got stuff to do, and things to learn, and a really small window of opportunity to fit it all in. Besides, I'm sure there are far more of the campers who'll be excited for us, especially when they know that we have Pops and Ruby's endorsement. And it seems like we already have most of the town behind us."

"All of that helps, but…"

"But?"

"I guess I'm just realizing that I'm most grateful for the answers we both got that *this* is what we're supposed to be doing."

"Amen," Matt said with a laugh. "That's the biggest reason to move forward, right?"

She nodded. "So, we know we're supposed to do this, and we know we have the support of Pops and Ruby, and, like you said, most of the town. So, why am I stalling?"

"Is it because you're worried about *us*?"

"No, not at all," she responded quickly. "You and I—us—we're honestly the least of my worries."

"That's comforting. Is it the responsibility of everything?"

She paused for a moment. "It's…*so much* to take on."

"Yeah," he replied, pausing for a moment before he continued. "Remember that day when we learned about the yoke that hangs over the dining table?"

"I think so. What about it?"

"Do you remember what Pops and Ruby said about the yoke being a symbol of a happy marriage?"

"Hmmm. What do you remember?"

"Well, if I understood what they were suggesting…if we do this marriage right, we never have to do it alone. If we do it right, we've got each other to help pull the load. And if I understood the symbolism correctly, what's even better is that if we do this right, we've got the blessings of heaven behind us."

"Okay, but how do we make sure we're doing it right?"

Matt reached for her wrist, gently unfolding her hand so her palm faced up. "I think the answer's right here. He touched her thumb, skipped her index finger, and softly tapped the tips of each of her other fingers as he named the keys of joy. "Reverence, hope, self-discipline, and charity."

"We're still missing one," she said, wiggling her index finger.

"Yes, but we know four of them, and we also know that if we're working on those, we're already working on the last one, too."

She nodded, pausing thoughtfully. "Are they enough?"

"The keys of joy?"

"Yeah, do you really think they're enough to keep us going for the rest of our lives?"

The question caused Matt to pause and think for a moment. "It seems to be enough for Pops and Ruby, right? And Hildegard, and most of the people we've met in town. It's for sure more wisdom and understanding than most marriages have, right? Isn't that why your boss is anxious to share it with your readers?"

"Okay, but just knowing what the keys are…it's not enough. Think about that crazy lady at the library…she's for sure got to know all about the keys, but that's obviously not kept her from being a monster."

"Imagine what she'd be like if she didn't know them at all," Matt responded jovially.

Genevieve laughed. "Okay, but you know what I mean, right? We're learning how they work because we've got each other to help work our way through them. We're surrounded by all of this, plus we get to watch the people of Niederbipp show us what it all looks like in real life. My readers aren't going to have any of that. I can tell them the keys, but how will they see how they work?"

"Are you doubting your skills as a storyteller?"

"I guess I am. How do you find words for all of this wonder? I can write about shoes and handbags and the latest fashion trends, but this… this is entirely different."

"Hmmm. What do you have so far?"

"Nothing…other than some jumbled thoughts and a few random ideas."

"Well, you have been a little busy."

"Yeah, but that doesn't change the fact that I have a deadline and I still don't know what I'm doing."

"But you've watched the magic happening all around you. You've seen each of us transformed by the keys. You've experienced it yourself."

"Sure, but…what I've watched…what I've seen…so much of it is… almost sacred and deeply personal. How do I share any of that without betraying trust and friendship? How do I tell Greg's story about going to that awful bench by the pigs because he didn't believe he was worthy of anything better? How do I write about Holly's hopes and dreams without making her sound two-dimensional and naive? How can I write about

Spencer's change from a chauvinist pig to a decent gentleman and make it at all believable? It's just so much."

"I'm sorry, but that kind of sounds like fear talking."

"It is. This story's way too big for me."

"If you were to take it all at once, yeah, it would be."

"What do you mean?"

"Genevieve, we've learned these things one day at a time over the last three-plus months, beginning with the basics. You'd overwhelm anyone if you gave it to them all at once. Pace yourself. Start small."

"But I've got ten thousand words! There's nothing small about that."

"Okay, so, what if it all started the same way Pops and Ruby began introducing the keys to us? You could lay a foundation with reverence and build from there."

"I don't hate the idea, but it's just that it's so different from anything I've ever written before. Matt, I've spent the last seven years writing about hand-made Italian shoes and handbags and the latest designs of push-up bras. There's a vast chasm between that and reverence."

"Sure, but you've spent the last three months learning things that very few people know about—things that bring people happiness. Imagine how different it's going to be for readers when they open their January issue and see pages and pages of beautiful photographs accompanied by equally beautiful words about a quaint farm at the top of Harmony Hill. The photographs of this place alone would inspire awe and reverence. You just have to follow them up with words that are equally inspiring."

"Oh, is that all?" she asked with a laugh.

"I don't doubt that it won't be easy, but think about it. From what I understand about this assignment, this is the first in a long string of articles. You don't have to tell the whole story right now. You just have to tell enough to get people thinking and asking questions. You want them to come back, month after month, anxious to connect with truth and wisdom that leaves them thinking about what's important and how they can better connect to that little voice in their heart."

"I think you may be giving my readers too much credit."

"And maybe you're not giving them enough. In the end, we're all looking for connection, Genevieve. We all want to discover who we are, find our person, and live happy—even joyful lives. We all want to feel like we're a part of something meaningful, that we're making a difference in a world that might somehow be better because we left our mark on it."

"And you think I can somehow inspire that?"

"If you can't, who will?"

"Matt, I'm a twenty-nine-year-old fashion writer."

"Who's just endured the biggest, world-altering experience of her lifetime, has unparalleled promise and talent, and has a platform to share it with the world that no one else has ever had," Matt added.

"Pfff, I'm just not confident that I'm cut out for this. How can I possibly do it all?"

"I never said you could."

"But I thought you…"

"Genevieve," he said, cutting her off as he took her hand firmly in his. "It's not your job to solve the world's problems. No one's asking you to do that."

She stood silent for several seconds. "So, what do you see as my job with all of this?"

"To tell stories that inspire people to ask questions."

Genevieve looked unconvinced. "I don't know how that will be helpful to most of my readers."

"Maybe it won't be for those who are just looking for the latest handbags or push-up bras—whatever those are. And maybe some people will just read your articles and it will make them feel good—give them a little hope in knowing that a place like Niederbipp exists in a world that's falling apart. But for those who are ready—who are curious and hungry, your articles will inspire questions that will cause your readers to look deeper, and think differently, and open their heads and hearts to the possibility of life having a larger purpose and meaning."

"And you really think I can do all of those things with my writing?"

"No. I *know* you can."

"Matt, you've never seen my writing."

"That's not true."

"What?"

He laughed. "Ruby's not as innocent as she looks."

"What does that mean?"

"She handed me a file on Monday morning filled with every article you've written in the last seven years."

"What? Why? *How?*"

"She told me your boss sent it to her last winter."

"Julia!?" she whispered, stifling a laugh. "Why'd Ruby give it to you?"

"Because she knows you're lacking the confidence you need to be able to do what you've been asked to do."

"She told you that."

"Yes."

"And what were you supposed to do with it?"

"Acquaint myself with your talent so I could offer my support."

"Seriously?"

"Genevieve, you're a brilliant writer. I've been meaning to tell you that all week, but I didn't know how to bring it up until now."

"You really think so?"

"Absolutely. You're creative, and thoughtful, and your ability to express yourself is truly inspiring, even when you're writing about handbags or eyeliner. I have to admit I cried when I read your article about those Greek grandmothers who hand-knit all those stockings to pay for the roof repair on their village church."

Genevieve smiled. "Those women were remarkable, and because of that article, they have more orders for stockings than they'll be able to make in their lifetimes."

"See? You have the gift of influence and persuasion. Did they ever get their roof?"

"Yeah, and a whole lot sooner than they ever thought was possible.

Their ancestors had worshiped in that church for twelve generations. They took a lot of pride in knowing the church would be around for many more generations because of their efforts."

"I don't think you realize this, Genevieve, but you're a Protopian."

"No...I...that's nice of you to say, but it was just one article."

"Okay, but you saw the power that one article had to change the world, at least for those ladies and their village. You know the power of the pen. The question is how you're going to use it. You can use it to promote fancy shoes and lipstick, or you can use it to invite people to ask important questions."

"Why does this keep coming back to questions?"

"Because all wisdom has an honest question at its roots."

"You think so?"

"Yes. Think about it. That yoke was hanging above the dining table, right in front of our eyes for weeks before we started asking the questions that could provide the answers behind the symbolism. I have no doubt that this farm has dozens of things that we won't understand until we're ready to ask and learn. That's what the farm is all about, right? Helping people come to a place where they're hungry enough to ask the hard questions and then do the work to fully appreciate and understand the answers that come. Isn't that what the keys of joy are all about?"

She nodded slowly. "You know, you're going to be a great matchmaker's assistant."

Matt laughed. "Is that what I am then?"

"Did you have something else in mind?"

"I'm not sure, but I think of Pops as much more of a companion than an assistant."

"I think I'd prefer that too, actually. An assistant doesn't ride shotgun in the yoke, does he?"

He shook his head. "If we're really gonna do this, Genevieve, we've both got to be all in; working together, calling the shots together, making the decisions together that matter the most. You'll have responsibilities that only you can do. And I'm sure there'll be some that only I can do.

And there'll be a lot in the middle that won't be mine, or yours, but ours. I've learned that from watching Pops and Ruby."

"Yeah, they do it all together, don't they?"

"I don't know how else you can do much of anything around here. Everything's been built for two."

"Do you think that would ever get old?"

"I don't know. Maybe it's better that way—it keeps you close, keeps you talking to each other, keeps the dust and the cobwebs from building up between you. As far as I could see, my parents never had anything like this to keep them close or remind them why they needed each other. I'd much rather have something comparable to the unity that Pops and Ruby share."

"I'd like that, too. How do we get there?"

"I don't know for sure, but it seems like an important part of it is setting aside the bad examples in our lives and focusing our attention and efforts instead on creating a union that invites God's blessings."

Genevieve nodded slowly. "That's the answer, isn't it?"

"It feels like it."

"Please promise me you'll never let me forget that answer."

"If you'll do the same for me."

"Okay, then let's make this our first promise: that we'll unify our efforts to create a union that invites all of God's blessings."

"I'm a hundred percent in," Matt said, extending his hand to Genevieve.

She took his hand firmly. "I'll match your hundred percent with a hundred percent of my own."

Matt let go of her hand and pulled her close for another hug. He laughed. "Well, now that that's settled, let's go invite the rest of the campers to our wedding."

CHAPTER 139

Plans

In marriage do thou be wise: prefer the person before money, virtue before beauty, the mind before the body; then thou hast a wife, a friend, a companion, a second self.
—William Penn—

"Who goes there?" Pops hollered out to Genevieve and Matt as Rex's barks and howls alerted the company of the intruders. "It's just us," Genevieve replied. "We come bearing good news.

Amy Kimball has given birth to a healthy baby boy, and all is well in Niederbipp!"

"What joy!" Ruby responded, clapping her hands. "They were going to name him Isaac, I believe?"

"That's right," Genevieve confirmed.

"Praise be to God," Thomas said, crossing his chest. "This has been a long time coming."

"What have you guys been doing all day?" Crystal asked, looking suspicious of the latecomers.

Matt glanced at Genevieve and smiled. "It's been a busy day, actually, thanks for asking. We worked the farm stand until we sold out, enjoyed a playdate with P.J. and Hazel Meier, had a picnic at the fountain in town, and then hung out with Jake and Amy until her water broke, at which time Jake and I carried her to the hospital where she had her baby while Genevieve and I cleaned up the mess in the pottery shop. Then we went back to the hospital, met the newest Niederbippian, and rode home. How about you guys?"

"Uh, I think you're forgetting something, Matt," Genevieve replied.

"What was that?"

"That you and I went to the tailor's shop after lunch to get fitted for a new suit and a gown for our wedding."

"*What?* Are you serious?" asked Holly, getting to her feet.

"Yes," Genevieve confirmed as the rest of the campers sprung from their seats and rushed down the stairs to the lawn where the betrothed couple stood next to their bikes, everyone speaking at once amidst the flurry of excitement.

"Silence!" Ruby shouted from the top of the stairs after thirty seconds of chaos. "Silence!" she repeated.

They all turned to look at her.

She smiled broadly, motioning them to return to their seats. "Why don't you kids come back up here and we can learn about this news in a dignified manner that won't startle the animals and leave Thomas thinking we're nothing but a bunch of uncivilized miscreants?"

Thomas looked up from the center of the mob, smiling. "There's a time for civility, but there's also a time to rejoice!"

The campers hooted in response but soon heeded Ruby's call, slowly moving back to the porch, pulling Matt and Genevieve with them

"When did this happen?" Holly asked as soon as Matt and Genevieve had sat down on the wicker loveseat, the rest of the porch's furniture having been pulled into a tight circle facing them.

Genevieve took Matt's hand and smiled at Holly before looking into each of their faces. "It probably would make the most sense to answer that question after a brief announcement from Pops and Ruby."

All eyes turned to their elderly hosts sitting on another wicker loveseat directly opposite Matt and Genevieve.

Ruby smiled, laying her hand on Pops's knee and turning her bright but tired eyes to meet his. They looked at each other for a long moment as the campers and Thomas looked on with rapt anticipation.

She turned and took a moment to look into each of their faces before speaking. "As you know, Pops and I came here as campers just like all of you, fifty-seven summers ago. At the end of that summer, after having decided to marry, we accepted the invitation Millie Smurthwaite extended to me to become the next matchmaker of Niederbipp. Never, in my wildest dreams, did I ever think I'd be spending the next fifty-six summers helping kids, just like yourselves, prepare themselves to make the most important decision of their lives. But here we are. For these past fifty-six summers, our energy and our abilities have been stretched, sometimes beyond their breaking point, as we've learned to love you kids. We've laughed away at least a million hours and cried at least a hundred million tears as we've worked alongside you and learned and shared the keys of joy with hundreds of wonderful young people.

"In the off-seasons, we've recharged our batteries, learned from our mistakes and failures, and worked on each other and ourselves to be brighter, stronger and more prepared for the next summer. Despite our advanced years, I know Pops and I will both agree that this summer has been the most rewarding summer we've spent on Harmony Hill.

We'd love to stick around and discover what next summer brings, but I'm afraid that's not in the cards for either of us. As I'm sure you've all observed, my body is slowing down. And even though my spirit remains vibrant and my mind is relatively clear, my cancer is advancing and I can see the end of the runway quickly approaching."

"But you went to the doctor last week," Ephraim protested. "Isn't there anything they can do?"

Ruby smiled warmly but shook her head. "I've already cheated death at least a few times, and I've outlived nearly all of my peers. For the past fifty-seven years I've been promising Pops that I'd pull my side of the yoke with all my might for as long as I'm able, but despite our best efforts to remain strong, and the ongoing help of the Almighty, the burdens of life have worn me down."

"What can we do to help you more?" Holly asked, her face filled with concern.

Ruby smiled but shook her head. "This is all part of the plan. Humans were never intended to live forever, at least not in our mortal state. We all have to eventually move along to make room for the rising generations. Our bodies are needed to fertilize the fruit trees from which your children and your children's children will pluck their fruit."

"But that fruit...what will happen to the farm?" Sonja asked. "Will this even be here for us to send our children to when they need help finding their joy?"

The old woman nodded slightly. "We don't know who'll be here by then, but we hope your children and even your children's children will have a chance to apply to spend a summer on Harmony Hill."

"But how? No offense, Pops, but we all know you can't do this without Ruby," Josh responded.

"No offense taken. You're quite right," Pops said, catching his breath as he tried to maintain his composure. "There are many things I'll be able to do on my own while I wait to lie down in the orchard next to Mom, but running a matchmaking farm is not one of those. We knew this day would eventually come, as it has for each of the matchmakers who've preceded us. And so, after years of talk and pondering and prayer, we will be passing the torch at the end of the summer and stepping aside so the farm can continue."

"Does this have anything to do with Matt and Genevieve getting married?" James asked as all eyes turned to them.

Matt smiled at Genevieve, encouraging her to answer.

She took a deep breath and looked at each of them as she exhaled. "It's been difficult to keep quiet about this, but more than two months ago, I was surprised when Ruby and Pops invited me to consider becoming the next matchmaker of Niederbipp," Genevieve confessed.

"Two months ago?" Crystal asked. "And you're just telling us about it now?"

"Yeah, well, it nearly killed me to keep it from you, but I had to figure this one out on my own. I'll admit I was—and remain—completely shocked, deeply humbled, and feeling utterly unprepared for this job. So…I told them I was sorry, but I couldn't accept it."

"Wait, what?" Crystal protested. "You're kidding me, right? You lead up with all of this and then drop that on us!?! You're sick!"

Many of the others agreed.

"But then I started thinking," Genevieve continued, undaunted. "I'm a writer, not a farmer, a city girl, who until three months ago spent way too much time and money worrying about my nails and keeping my monthly hair appointment. Every single thing changed for me this summer. I involuntarily traded in my spin classes for a bicycle that actually goes somewhere. I traded a nine-to-five in a city with endless possibilities for the twenty-four/seven aroma of the farm. I exchanged my platinum-class international travel for a ten-mile radius on a bike that's got to be older than I am. I swapped my high-end, fashionable clothes for second, if not third-hand farm duds, and my Christian Louboutin stilettos for manure-encrusted muckers. I hated it. I hated this farm. I hated this whole god-forsaken county." She laughed. "I'm sorry. I know I've already apologized to most of you for being such a prickly prima donna in those first few weeks, but I just need to repeat my sincere apologies for making life tougher for all of you."

She took a deep breath. "While I've got your attention, I suppose it's time for me to tell you all the truth." She glanced quickly at Ruby who gave her the slightest of nods. "I didn't come here for the same reasons you did. I had no intention of getting married. I had no grandiose hopes of finding my prince and living happily ever after."

"Then why did you come?" Susan asked, looking confused.

"I came here on assignment from my magazine."

"Really? A five-month assignment?" Josh asked dubiously, as many of the others muttered in agreement.

"Five months…yeah…nope, that definitely wasn't the plan, at least not as far as I was aware. I came here for what I believed was a two-day interview—three, tops. I was going to be in and out of here and make it back to New York in time for my flight to the Brussels Fashion Show."

"So…that's why you didn't have all of the stuff you were supposed to bring and you were totally clueless in the beginning?" Crystal asked.

Genevieve nodded. "The girl who was supposed to be here—the girl who's place I took—apparently she dropped out at the last minute, and I…" She stopped to laugh, shaking her head. "…and I took her place, pretending I was called up off the waitlist at the last minute."

"So…has all of this just been a big act for you?" Josh asked, looking hurt.

"No," Genevieve responded firmly. "I had to stretch the truth in the beginning to make up for my lack of preparedness and my ignorance. You all had months to prepare for this. I had a few hours. In fact, it felt like I was being kidnapped the night I met Pops and Ruby at a restaurant down in Niederbipp—the night before you all arrived. Instead of having a civilized interview, I was brought up here, shown my bunk, and told to be ready to meet the rest of my campmates in the morning."

"You didn't even try to run away?" Susan asked.

"Oh, no, I did, remember?" Genevieve said with a laugh. "I made it halfway to Tionesta before the wasps and the river brought me back."

The campers looked at each other and smiled, realizing she couldn't have faked that one if she'd spent an entire summer planning it.

"You need to understand that my job—the job I've loved for the last seven years—was riding on this assignment."

"What's your story supposed to be about anyway?" Rachael asked.

Genevieve acknowledged the question but took a moment to answer. "I thought my story was about exposing a fraud."

"Who?" Holly asked.

Genevieve pursed her lips, looking embarrassed. "Ruby."

"But…surely you know she's not a fraud!?!" Spencer responded.

"Yes, of course, I know that now. It's been a few months, but you remember my attitude in the beginning, right? I was awful and cynical and …"

"And scary," Spencer responded as if he weren't even thinking.

Many of the others laughed.

Genevieve nodded good-naturedly. "I'll take that. Heaven knows I deserve it."

"What happened?" Susan asked. "You're not at all the same person you were when you arrived."

"Thank you. Are any of us the same as we were when we arrived?" she asked after a thoughtful moment. She watched their faces as they chewed on her question.

"But you really *were* awful," James said, breaking the pause in the conversation.

She nodded. "I've thought a lot about this, and I've spent a lot of time working my way through it with Matt and Ruby and Pops." She turned to Spencer. "You said I was scary."

"That's in the past," he said, holding up his hands and looking somewhat contrite.

"It's okay, you were right. You nailed it."

"But you're not anymore," Spencer responded assuredly.

"Thank you. I'll take that as a compliment. This has been the craziest summer of my life. Between the bees, and Carlos the sheep, and learning how to use that doggone washing machine…I think…I feel like I've been through a meat tenderizer and come out on the other side a different kind of person."

She looked thoughtful for a moment. "Spencer, I think I may have been scary because I was scared…scared of losing myself and my mind. I was scared of change and truth and…and joy."

"Why were you afraid of joy?" Holly asked.

"Because it was completely foreign to me. I knew nothing of reverence or true charity and next to nothing about hope or self-discipline." She nodded at Thomas. "It had been years since I'd spent any time in church, and even then, it was mostly about showing off my new Easter dress. I remember thinking my life was so big, so full of adventure and travel and all the pride that goes with the lifestyle I'd grown up in and worked so hard to maintain. But to answer your question, Holly, I was afraid of being vulnerable, afraid of being real, afraid of showing my true feelings out of fear of being seen as emotional, or broken, or weak."

"You almost sound like James," Crystal suggested.

"I was. We both were awful. It took seeing part of myself in him to recognize that I didn't want any of that.'

James nodded, understanding slowly penetrating his thick skull.

"Look, we all came here with cracks, flaws, and chips on our shoulders. But to varying degrees, all of you arrived here three months ago with a desire to change your future. I was here for a different reason, or so I thought. My desire for change came later than yours. I had a lot of catching up to do. You'd been working on yourselves, in some cases, for years," she said, nodding to Greg. "You'd been working through your lists of weaknesses and working to make yourselves better and stronger people. You were ready for the keys when they began to be revealed to you because you'd already discovered you needed them."

Many of the campers nodded.

"I didn't come here for any of this, and there were a couple of weeks there in the beginning when I wondered how I could possibly endure the torture of this farm for five excruciating months." She shook her head, trying to stop her emotions from overpowering her desire to control them. "If you would've told me then that there would come a time that I would never want to leave, I certainly would have told you where to go. But the truth is, I can't imagine this farm and this community not being a part of my life forever. I've accepted Ruby's offer to become the next matchmaker of Niederbipp, and I know I'm going to need all your help over the next fifty-five days to get ready for the challenges ahead."

Spencer shook his head and laughed as they all turned to him. "You don't need our help. You were born for this, Genevieve. Remember that day down at the farm stand…how you ripped me up one side and down the other, telling me I needed to man up and be a decent human?"

"I'm sorry, that was…harsh."

"Yes, but it was true. And nobody else could have told me that and gotten away with it. You had the guts to help me see that I was blinded by my own pride and ego. That I'd been…as Thomas taught me that day… fishing with artificial lures, but had nothing real or any true substance to offer anybody. I've got a long way to go, but it was your conversation that opened me to the hope of joy…that got me to the place where I wanted to believe there was something more to life than the next one-night stand. Thank you, Genevieve. You may just be a writer, now, but you've had my vote to do this for months."

"Mine, too," Greg responded. "I told Ruby at least a month ago that she ought to consider you."

"Why would you do that?" Genevieve asked.

"Because you saw me…" He shook his head as tears filled his eyes. "You were the first woman, besides my mother, to ever recognize my many weaknesses and still find some hopeful bit of humanity that was worth saving. The talks I've had with you have changed my life. They've made me want to believe I'm worth something more…that I can do better and be better and leave my past in the past and have a happy future."

Holly, sitting next to Greg, wrapped her arms around him and held him for a moment before turning back to Genevieve. "Greg and I both spent time talking to Ruby about you," she admitted, wiping a tear from her eye. "You've kind of been the big sister I never had, giving me advice, being patient with my curiosity and probably endless questions, helping me see possibilities I never could've imagined. I love you for that. You're going to be a great matchmaker."

"Oh, man, you guys, stop! This is starting to sound like a funeral," Genevieve protested. "We have fifty-five more days until the summer's over. We've got loads of chores and a whole orchard that's still full of fruit, and bushels of tomatoes that need to be bottled, and Matt and I have at least a million things we need to learn before October 8th."

"What's October 8th?" Susan asked.

"It's the day we've decided to get married, and you're all invited," Matt replied. "We wanted you all to be there without having to make a special trip to come back. If Genevieve and I are really going to do this, we can't be gone from the farm for longer than a few days. We'll try to leave for a quick honeymoon and be back the next week."

"Uh, is that date set in stone?" James asked.

Matt looked at Genevieve. "I don't think so. You guys are really the first to know. Why do you ask?"

"Would you consider moving your wedding up a week?"

"Before the end of the summer? What for?" Matt asked.

"Well, Crystal and I…" he stopped and turned to look at her. "We were hoping all of you would come to our wedding before we all part ways, and we were also thinking it would be nice to get hitched on October 8th."

"Wait, what?!? Are you guys engaged?" Spencer asked, looking confused.

"Not officially, but we've been talking about it for weeks," Crystal admitted. "I know it's a shocker considering how we treated each other in the beginning, but…"

"Actually, no…I think we've all kind of been wondering what's taken you so long to make this announcement," Rachael responded.

Everyone nodded, including Ruby and Pops.

"Seriously?" James replied, looking completely shocked.

"You'd be stupid not to marry Crystal," Spencer suggested, turning to James. "She's the only girl in the world who'd ever put up with you."

"That might be true," Crystal admitted, snuggling into James's shoulder as the other campers laughed.

"That's actually not a bad idea," Ruby suggested.

"Which part?" asked James.

"That we send Genevieve and Matt off on their honeymoon while the rest of you are here to help us finish out the season. We've never done anything like this before, but it seems like it would be a good exception to make considering this may be the last vacation they get for a long, long time."

The reality of what Matt and Genevieve were committing to struck each of them with soberness.

"You'd each have to shoulder a little more work while they're gone," Ruby continued, "but it would be nice for them to return to a farm that's ready for them to take over rather than to return to just the two of us old fuddy-duddies with at least one foot in the grave."

Matt and Genevieve looked at each other, each of them wondering how to respond to this offer.

"If we were to be gone five or six days on a honeymoon," Matt responded, looking like he was doing some figuring in his head, "And we needed to back in time for James's and Crystal's wedding, that would mean…getting married no later than October 1st or 2nd," Matt replied, turning to Genevieve. "Could that work for us? Could that work for all of us?" he asked, turning to search each of their faces.

"I don't know if I've ever been consulted about the timing of anyone else's wedding, but I don't hate it," Josh admitted. "It makes sense to me, and I don't think any of us would mind picking up a few extra chores if it means this farm will continue on with you guys as its stewards. I know I can speak for all of us in saying we could have seen this coming, and it feels right."

"Here, here!" cried Ephraim. "I think most of us have been watching you two since you were stung by all those wasps, wondering how long it would take for you both to recognize that you're kind of perfect for each other, despite your differences."

Holly nodded. "We couldn't be happier for you both, and James and Crystal, too."

"What do these announcements mean for the chore rotations?" Sonja asked.

"It means they just became complicated," Greg offered.

Ruby raised her hand after some murmuring from the campers, silencing them.

"There are few things that are democratic on the farm, and we've never considered love interests to be enough of a reason to alter the time-proven chore rotations that have kept this farm thriving for generations."

"But..." James began.

"That being said," Ruby continued, cutting him off, "I wonder if, in these two cases, it might not be better to keep those couples who are already engaged working together rather than splitting them up every day."

"Woohoo!" James responded.

"Not so fast," Ruby replied. "I said there are few things that are democratic on the farm, but this will need to be one of them. There are twelve campers in this company, each of whom have strong opinions, plus one former priest, and two old but wise keepers of the farm who've collected a cumulative total of nearly a hundred and fifteen years of experience on this farm. Each of us should have a say, don't you think, James?"

"Oh, uh, sure," he replied, looking suddenly worried.

"And why does Thomas get a vote?" Crystal asked.

"As a tiebreaker, if one's needed," offered Ruby. "That, and the fact that he'll be around much longer than Pops or me, and may serve as a witness to the decision we're about to make, which may or may not affect the farm for years to come."

"Are you worried about this decision?" Sonja asked.

"I have to be at least concerned about it. It's a decision that will affect each one of you, potentially for years into the future. You each have learned from the chores, which you'll continue to do no matter our decision here tonight. But you've also been learning from each other, how to navigate moods and personality differences. Most of the big lessons have already been learned by now, but with fifty-five days remaining, there are still potentially loads of meaningful lessons to learn."

"But it would also give each of them lots of opportunity to plan their weddings and prepare for their future," Rachael replied.

"Undoubtedly, you're right," Pops agreed, "but it would also potentially detract from the unity and cohesiveness of the whole. You kids learned the value of unity far earlier than most, and we've been impressed by the friendships and connections you've forged with each other. We'd hate to see that negatively affected by four of you being suddenly emotionally unavailable to the others. This is one reason why we have a no-kissing-or-romantic-entanglements rule each summer. We can't afford to have things fall apart at any time, but especially not at harvest time when we need all hands-on deck."

"So, just to be clear, we're voting whether or not we allow James & Crystal, and Matt & Genevieve to be full-time chore partners?" Holly asked.

"That's right," Ruby replied.

"Is there a possibility of a third choice?" asked Josh.

"What did you have in mind?"

"Kind of a hybrid, I guess. That we keep the rotations as they have been, but we allow the sweethearts to spend more exclusive time together in the afternoons and evenings. That way, we're all interacting with each other every week and keeping the good vibes flowing between all of us, but we're also giving the lovebirds time to get their ducks in a row."

"I think I like that," Susan replied. "It feels more inclusive and unified. That, and I'd hate to see this all turned upside down by running into James and Crystal snogging in the laundry shack or find Matt and Genevieve getting frisky in the kitchen."

"I'm glad you brought that up," Ruby said. "Even if we were to vote to allow the lovebirds to be full-time work partners, they would still be held to the same standards each of you would be as it relates to any expressions of sexual interest."

"What?!?" James howled. "But we're getting married in less than two months!"

"Yes, congratulations. You may hold Crystal's hand. And Matt, you may hold Genevieve's."

"But how are we supposed to prepare for marriage if we can't make sure we're at least compatible kissing partners?" Crystal protested.

Pop smiled. "I believe it was Einstein who said, 'Imagination is more important than knowledge. Knowledge is limited. Imagination is powerfully sexy.'"

All of the campers, except for James and Crystal, laughed out loud.

"Listen, we try to run a tight, virtuous ship around here." Pops responded. "We're well aware of the fact that it's probably not what any of you are used to, but then nothing here in Niederbipp resembles much of anything you left behind. Your summer here on the farm included a rare chance to reset all of your thoughts, patterns and plans. You've begun to learn the value of self-discipline, but for most of you, you've really only just begun. We are fully aware of the fact that you are sexual beings, that you have desires, passions and needs. Some of you, I have no doubt, consider yourselves rather expert in the craft of seduction. Others are likely less confident. Either way, self-discipline has the ability to elevate you to maestro status in the nearly lost arts of virtue and honor."

"Yeah, and we certainly didn't bring you this far to watch you nosedive into your past indiscretions or wallow unwittingly in habits and behaviors that can't elevate you to something better," Ruby added. "Engaged to be married or not, let me just remind you all that you agreed to keep your hands, lips and every other body part to yourself while in this county, or until you get married."

"This is crazy!" James protested.

"No," Ruby replied with a wink. "This is joy."

"Are you saying I can't have joy if I kiss my fiancée?"

"Of course not. But I am saying that joy will be awfully hard to catch and hold onto if you don't learn to develop the virtues associated with self-discipline," Ruby reacted.

"Then I think we may be ready to vote," Genevieve replied.

"Good," Pops responded. "We have three options on the table tonight. Each of you may vote only once. Those in favor of option one, leaving the rotation arrangements as status quo, raise your hand."

Ephraim alone raised his hand.

"All those in favor of keeping Matt & Genevieve, and James & Crystal together as working teams, but rotate through the chores with the rest of the alternating teams, raise your hand."

James, Crystal and Sonja raised their hands.

"And all those who wish to support Josh's hybrid model, of continued rotations for both partners and chores, while allowing the virtuous lovebirds to make their wedding plans in the afternoons, raise your hands."

The remaining eleven hands were quickly raised, signifying the obvious landslide.

CHAPTER 140

Permission Granted

True humility is intelligent self-respect which keeps us from thinking too highly or too meanly of ourselves. It makes us mindful of the nobility God meant us to have. Yet it makes us modest by reminding us how far we have fallen short of what we can be.
—Ralph Washington Sockman—

While James and Crystal pouted, the rest of the campers, along with Thomas, Ruby and Pops, openly expressed their joy and relief that the farm would continue on, and that Matt and Genevieve would be guiding the annual summer recruits through the keys of joy for the foreseeable future. After another twenty minutes of congratulatory expressions, Thomas excused himself, citing his early morning shift at the bakery and his need for his beauty rest as his argument to make his way home.

The campers, recognizing the lateness of the hour and their own obligations in the morning, yet still wanting to be together, said goodnight to Pops and Ruby and escorted Thomas and his bicycle up the rutted drive to the phone booth. Huddled together, they watched as his bike light descended into the darkness before turning their eyes to the canopy of stars that filled the night sky from horizon to horizon. They stood quietly in awe for some time, listening to the crickets' rhythmic serenade.

"It's hard to believe we only have fifty-five more nights of this," Ephraim said, his voice piercing the silence as his words pierced their hearts.

"I was just thinking how I wish we could somehow make time stand still," Sonja replied.

"I've wished that many times myself," Susan admitted. "This has been such an incredible summer. I wish we could repeat it every year."

"Why can't we?" Josh asked.

"You mean besides the obvious answers that we have jobs and real responsibilities to get back to, and marriage and commitment that's going to change all of this for each of us?" asked Ephraim.

"Okay, there's that," Josh responded with a laugh. "We all know we could never recreate this and have it be exactly the same, but I've been keeping a list of the things I can repeat."

"What's on your list so far?" asked Rachael.

"Oh, lots of things. Porch games. Star walks. Giving away my TV and spending more time with the people I love or want to get to know better. I used to spend way too much time watching mind-numbing TV shows and playing video games online with people I've never met and probably never will. It just feels like such an empty life after getting to know all of you this summer. I've generally been stingy with compliments and emotional expressions that make me vulnerable, but I need you all to know that I love you and I'm grateful for this time we've shared here."

"I love you, too," Susan replied, putting her arm across his shoulder as a chorus of love and affirmations echoed among all the campers. They moved in closer with a group hug.

"I'm so grateful this won't be the farm's last summer," Greg said. "I'm grateful more weirdos like us will get to come here and learn the things we've learned."

"I've been thinking about that," James admitted.

"Which part?" asked Crystal.

"Maybe we're not such weirdos after all."

"You don't think?" asked Sonja.

"I mean, yeah, we've all got our quirks," James continued, "but doesn't everybody? Aren't we all at least a little bit odd in one way or another? But look what's happened to us as we've either overlooked those quirks or learned to appreciate them. I don't know if I've ever felt closer to any other eleven friends…even friends I've known for years. What's happened here this summer has left me continually realizing how much I've missed, wrapped up in my own little, insignificant bundle."

"*Insignificant bundle*? Are you feeling okay?" Spencer asked.

"No, I'm feeling much better than okay. I'm feeling incredible."

"Even though you have to keep working with each of us rather than just Crystal?" asked Susan.

"You all know I love Crystal, and I'd be thrilled to spend the next fifty-five days working with her, but I also see the wisdom in this."

"I guess," Crystal replied, sounding perturbed, yet resigned. "If we're not allowed to even kiss each other anyway, it's just as well. I was thinking this'll give us a chance to work on our self-discipline while helping us remember that we're part of a bigger group who are all working toward worthy goals."

"And besides, we both missed interacting with the rest of you when

Crystal and I got grounded together during those first few weeks," James admitted. "As much as I pushed back against all of you and was undoubtedly a jerk, you've all helped me recognize that there's so much more to life than I knew before. If it's true that joy requires you to think about someone other than yourself, I think I've pretty much been missing out on joy my whole life."

"That's a bold statement," Spencer admitted, "but I think I know what you mean. I thought I knew what joy was, but this summer's taught me that I've been fishing for joy in all the wrong ponds. My job, my past experiences with women, my ambitions, even the way I used to think…none of that included even one element of the joy we've learned here. None of it was real. I've spent most of my first twenty-eight years foolishly believing the next party, the next promotion, or the next girlfriend was going to make me happy. But it was all a lie. It was all a bottomless pit, a monster that could never be satisfied, no matter the time or treasure I spent to feed it."

Genevieve snickered. "And then we all woke up and realized we've missed the whole point of life."

All of the campers moaned affirmatively.

"So, how do we help other people know there's a better way?" Rachael asked.

"I think we take what we've learned into our marriages and teach these things to our children and anyone who'll listen," Holly answered.

"Okay, yeah, that's great, but the world is big, and we are few," Greg replied.

"I think Ruby's been working on this answer for many years," Matt suggested.

"How?"

"She's been preparing for someone like Genevieve who has a platform and can help spread the word through her writing."

"That's a brilliant idea," Crystal admitted.

"You really think so?" asked Genevieve.

"If not you, who could do it?" Holly asked.

"I don't know, guys. I just feel…overwhelmed by all of it. How do I tell this story about finding joy without making it personal?"

"You can't. That's the point," Spencer responded. "Isn't that what we've all learned over the last few months—isn't that what we've just said tonight? We're here at this point, basking in the light of joy and connection because we've allowed ourselves to make this experience personal, and real, and vulnerable."

"Okay, sure, but Spencer… and no offense…how can I share what's happened to you without making you sound like the self-centered jerk you once were?"

"You can't. I was a self-centered jerk. You can't honestly tell my journey to joy without including where I started."

"But that would mean betraying your trust."

"If it means helping someone avoid the waste of time and energy and dealing with the consequences of choosing all that is *not* joy, it would be well worth the bruise to my ego."

"Are you giving me permission to tell your story?" Genevieve asked, sounding surprised.

"I'm already naked. What have I got to hide?"

"Seriously?" she asked.

"Yeah. Everybody loves a happy ending, right? That's where I'm headed, but it's a much different trajectory than I ever imagined before I came here." He looked up into the stars above them. "I'm light-years ahead of where I was just three months ago. I think we all are."

"Yeah, none of us is the center of the universe anymore, are we?" James asked.

"No, but we still have the ability to shine and offer our humble light to those around us," Holly added. "I think that's why we're here…what each of us is supposed to do with the knowledge and joy our time here has given us."

"You can have my story too, if you think it can help," Susan offered.

"Mine, too," said Holly. "I want others to know there's hope."

The rest of the campers were quick to add their endorsements as well.

"I'll be kind to your stories," Genevieve promised, feeling overwhelmed by the trust they just gave her.

"Kindness is always good, but not at the price of truth," James replied. "Kindness may make the journey sweeter, but it's only the truth that can set us free."

"Then I'll share both," Genevieve responded. "I'll always do my best to share both."

"Maybe that's what one of the definitions of joy is—honest truth coated with sincere kindness and shared in an effort to improve and inspire the world to be a better place." Rachael added.

"I like that," Susan admitted.

"So do I," said Sonja. "It feels like what we've been experiencing here."

"But we still don't know the fifth key," Josh reminded them. "What if it has nothing to do with kindness at all?"

"You don't really think that's possible, do you?" asked Holly.

"I don't know. Probably not, but considering how each one of them has been more difficult than the one before it, I'm not expecting a cakewalk," Josh admitted.

"Do any of you have any ideas of what it could be?" asked Greg.

"Rachael and I think it's mercy," Sonja suggested.

"I like it, but isn't mercy part of both reverence and charity?" Matt responded.

Many of the campers nodded.

"I've been secretly hoping it's chocolate," Crystal added, getting everyone laughing.

"But Ruby said if we were working on the first three, we would be simultaneously working on the last two," Spencer reminded them, "and, so far at least, there hasn't been much chocolate."

"Touché," Crystal replied.

"What about moderation?" asked Greg.

"I've wondered the same thing," admitted Spencer, "But isn't moderation part of self-discipline?"

"And probably reverence, hope and charity, too," Susan added.

"When do you think Pops and Ruby will tell us?" Josh asked.

"Maybe they're waiting for us to gain a better understanding of self-discipline before we'll be ready for it," Ephraim replied. "And maybe a better understanding of some of the other keys as well."

"Then let's get on with it," James suggested. "We only have fifty-five days left, and you all know by now how impatient I am. Let's just put our heads together and figure out how all of this works together."

"I'm in," Josh said, seconding the motion.

All the others agreed. As they walked back to their bunk houses, they each recognized that the already healthy sense of unity they'd learned to appreciate had somehow grown once again, stitching them even closer together as they collectively journeyed toward joy.

CHAPTER 141

Balances, Deposits, and Bank Accounts

Isn't it strange how princes and kings
And clowns that caper in sawdust rings,
And common folk like you and me,
Are all builders of destiny.
To each is given a book of rules,
A block of stone, and a bag of tools,
And left to fashion ere time has flown,
A stumbling block or a stepping stone.
—Robert Lee Sharpe—

Over the course of the next two weeks, the campers soberly watched as Ruby's stamina decreased precipitously. She chose to focus her attention and energy on the kitchen duties, determined to share her very best recipes and experience with the campers before she was no longer able to endure long hours on her feet. With each passing day, she began delegating more and more assignments while offering instructions from her perch on a tall stool Pops had brought down from upstairs. After a week, what began with a need for random, short breaks to sit on the porch or in the library turned into a daily need for an afternoon nap. Her afternoon knitting habits also changed as she began spending more time looking through scrapbooks and sharing with anyone who was interested the stories attached to fifty-six years' worth of campers. And though many other things began to change as she focused her limited energy on the things that mattered most, the one thing she refused to alter were the evening porch gatherings. These remained sacrosanct for Ruby, and therefore for each of the campers, even though it quickly became uncommon for her not to fall asleep before the games and discussions were over.

To the delight of all the campers, these continued to be both lively and informative. Though the group spoke from time to time about their need to learn the fifth key, the discussions around the fourth key—self-discipline—were so rich and meaningful that no one seemed to mind the delayed reveal of the final key.

As they shared and expanded their understanding from night to night, each of the campers took their turns acknowledging their personal difficulties associated with this most challenging key. Though their obstacles to self-discipline were personal and unique for each of them, there were many overlaps. The majority of several evenings were spent fleshing out what self-discipline actually meant and all that it entailed. In the beginning, the discussion focused on what they considered obvious failures of self-discipline. These included things like laziness, pride, apathy and obesity. They went on to identify additional failures of self-discipline that were often easier to hide including addictions, fear, self-loathing and shame.

After listening over the course of several nights as the campers identified the many things that self-discipline was not, Pops and Ruby suggested that they might come to a much better, holistic comprehension of this important key if they would spend more time focusing on what self-discipline *was* and what it required. As their discussion continued and progressed, night after night, they peeled back the many layers of this particularly complex onion, learning from each other and from Pops and Ruby, who often acted as referees when the discussions became loud or heated.

One night, still early on when the discussion was yet finding its footings, Ruby threw the campers another bone of understanding, suggesting that one would have difficulty developing a comprehensive appreciation of self-discipline without at least a cursory understanding of the principle of moderation and the perils that often result from ignoring it. As a result of bringing moderation into the equation, the discussion became significantly more productive. Instead of pointing out the flaws and failures of others, she invited them to look inward and ask themselves where they crossed the line between moderation and into the borders of excess, and even extremism.

"Anything, even that which is good, when taken to an extreme," Pops had told them, "can quite quickly become a vice."

When challenged on this point by James, Pops went on to suggest that even the air we breathe, when more is taken than needed, can quickly lead to hyperventilation. Too much of something as normally harmless as water could cause hyperhydration, a type of poisoning that could kill just as readily as many other poisons.

James ultimately conceded when many of the campers spoke of either their own tendencies, or those of their parents, to overwork themselves, ignoring the body and mind's warning signs while losing touch with those they loved the most and were working to support.

Rachael, having grown up with an overbearing mother who'd

counted her caloric intake from the time she'd been a chubby twelve-year-old, was quite insightful in helping the others gain both understanding and sensitivity about this very delicate topic. Getting out of the toxic environment her mother had created had been an important step, but Rachael had been deeply scarred emotionally. She admitted that when she learned that self-discipline was the fourth key, the news nearly sent her over the edge, but that after a few weeks of difficult processing and conversation, she was seeing the wisdom in it. She also admitted that Ruby's hint about the power of moderation had been helpful, giving her a chance to examine how her mental and physical health had been blessed in the exercise of moderation since coming to the farm.

Ruby explained that many campers came to the same conclusion every year, finding a balance of work, play, nutrition and mental health that they'd never known before. Part of that, she admitted, was the fresh air and the physical work, but she'd watched a curious thing happen every year. Most campers, she explained, when confronted with fresh bread every day, and nearly as much of every other delectable as they could manage, quickly put on at least a few pounds. But when they came to the realization that the bread would be there tomorrow and there'd be enough to go around, they subconsciously began cutting back, finding a natural moderation that still made allowances for things like evening ice cream, cookies and other sweets.

"The greatest and most dangerous imbalances that exist in the world come from taking more than you need and giving back less than you are capable of giving," Ruby had told them one evening. She promised that if they'd take a sincere look at their lives, trim away the excesses everywhere they found them, and commit themselves to give back at least their fair share, they would never stray far from either balance or happiness, and their efforts would bless the world. That same evening, she warned that none of them were strong enough to find either balance or happiness if they carried in their hearts even an ounce of greed, apathy, laziness, anger, jealousy or pride.

To support her position, Ruby cited several of history's most notable moral failures and meteoric disasters who'd fallen prey to their greed, pride, or anger. She suggested each of them could avoid both big and small pitfalls by studying both the lives of those they respected and those they didn't, and then by discerning the truths that led to either their successes or their failures. This practice, she reminded them, would not be very helpful if their hearts were focused more on judgment and criticism than on learning applicable lessons or discerning truths that would allow them to avoid their own failures.

It went on like this night after night, each of them bringing new ideas to the gatherings as they'd had a chance to think from day to day and share their thoughts with each other in smaller groups as they worked side by side. Sometime toward the end of the second week, Pops made a suggestion that got them all thinking. It was a simple idea, but one that offered real-life applications they all could understand. He suggested they look at each aspect of self-discipline as a bank account. If they made regular deposits, there would be money to draw from when it was needed. But if the deposits had been skimpy to non-existent, and the draws large, they could quickly become overdrawn and even bankrupt themselves, leaving only misery and upset.

Looking at self-discipline in this way, the group quickly found applications to diet, exercise, marital harmony, faith, education, dating, friendship, and of course, finances. The bank account model, in fact, proved so universally applicable that the campers had a hard time coming up with any aspect of self-discipline where the model could not easily be employed. One could very quickly draw down his health and nutrition balance, for example, by eating only fast food and ice cream and spending too much time on the couch. But balance could be restored by making regular deposits of whole grains, vegetables, and exercise.

The campers quickly discovered that the bank account model also worked for communication. If one heard nothing but negativity from one's partner, the bank account would quickly be emptied. But by sharing complimentary words of love and support, the account could build up resilience against the time when tough discussions needed to be had or communication failures took place.

Using the bank account model, Matt and Genevieve led a discussion the next evening about faith and spirituality. If the faith account was regularly fed with acts of faith, prayer, service, charity, and reverence, it could withstand the doubts and fears that challenged it. But if doubts and fears came knocking on the door of an account that was already empty, or worse, in the red, it would be difficult for an individual to not feel spiritually destitute or overdrawn.

This spawned a rather long and thoughtful discussion among all the campers about faith and the spiritual things they'd each learned during their time on the farm, their different experiences with prayer and the thinking benches, as well as their attendance at church services in Niederbipp. Formal spiritual services had been something only a few of them had regularly participated in prior to coming to the farm. But they each expressed pleasant surprise at the peace they'd felt and the answers they'd discovered in their own quiet moments when they'd sought inspiration through meditation, pondering, church worship, or journaling.

Without being pushy or preachy, both Matt and Genevieve encouraged the other campers to make their bench time as productive as possible by approaching it with hope and the expectation that answers would come.

Pops and Ruby concurred, adding that for best results, humility, sincerity and honest intentions were critical elements to revelation.

Because of a late summer rainstorm and the fatigue of the campers, two days passed before the next porch gathering. This one was different, more subdued, and thoughtful than the others had been. At first Genevieve wondered if it was because the others had recognized Ruby's declining energy, but the discussion went in a much different direction as Ephraim spoke of his initial reluctance to spend much time at the benches because of the divisive role religion had played in his family of origin. But something had happened over the last two days as he'd approached the benches with a different, more thoughtful and humble spirit. He had trouble describing his experience, working through emotions he'd rarely allowed himself to express or even feel. But what he'd come away with was light—light and a connection with something bigger, calmer, and more interested in him than he'd ever considered possible before.

Holly surprised everyone when she asked Ephraim to close his eyes. Then, reaching around him from behind, she embraced him with the lightest of physical connection. "Did it feel anything like that?" she asked softly. His response left them all touched as he simply wept. As they had many times before in particularly emotional or touching moments, the campers gathered to embrace Ephraim, mingling their tears with each other's, but pulling away with smiles and unconscious laughter that was healing and nourishing for everyone present.

"If this is what it's like to make a deposit in a spiritual bank account, I feel like a millionaire tonight," Ephraim managed, inviting tears from each of them.

Light and connection. It became a common theme to every gathering thereafter. The laughter and horseplay of their early gatherings gave way to deep, thoughtful conversation. No questions were avoided, and all opinions were respectfully considered as they came together to make deposits into both their individual and shared accounts. They were no longer weirdos and oddballs, but geschwister—family. In their sharing of honest feelings and vulnerabilities, they'd created a loving web of beautiful and meaningful connections.

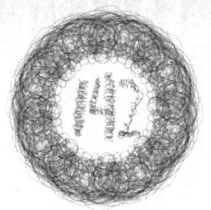

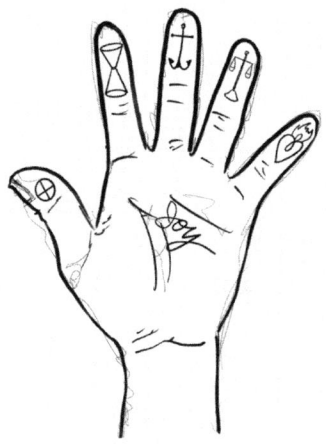

CHAPTER 142

Cinco

...let us fling aside every encumbrance and the sin that so readily entangles our feet. And let us run with patient endurance the race that lies before us.
—Paul, Hebrews 12:1 WNT—

After three weeks of nearly nightly discussions surrounding self-discipline and a variety of balances, deposits and bank accounts, Ruby asked if she might lead the discussion for the evening. While the campers prepared the makings of ice cream, loading them into

Bessie's drum, Ruby sent Greg to the music room to retrieve the game box from the high shelf. With the anticipation of selecting a game, the campers settled in, watching quietly as Ruby unpacked the box, laying the items out on the wicker coffee table at the center of their gathering.

Each of them had handled this box several times over the course of the summer. They'd each pulled items from it to use as props or details required for the games they'd played. As Ruby pulled each of these items from the box now, fun memories were silently triggered by each of them. The magical glow cast by the overhead carnival lights illuminated each object as she organized them atop the wicker coffee table.

Looking quite like the contents of a museum's specimen drawer, there were at least three old shoelaces, five mismatched dice, a small box of matches, three balls of yarn in various sizes and colors, an old hammer with busted claws, the enameled lid of a teapot, seven polished stones, an assortment of acorns, a few sun-bleached chicken bones, several safety pins, a red and white fishing bobber, an antique, hand-crank egg beater, a tarnished silver spoon, a magnifying glass, a bundled extension cord, a pair of lens-less glasses attached to a rubber nose and mustache, a yellow kazoo, several empty spice cans, and a handful of colorful buttons. She drew one last item from the box, setting it in her lap before moving the box, leaving a rectangular-shaped void in the middle of the table surrounded by its neatly displayed contents. Then, with cupped, tremoring hands, she moved the final item from her lap to the center of the table, standing it upright.

All eyes fell on the small, brass hourglass. It had been used to mark the time for many of their games and had been touched by each of them as they'd turned it over to reset the countdown in between contests and contestants. But looking at it now, reflecting the lights strung above it and surrounded by the contents of the game box, it was clear to all of them that this was something more significant than any of them had anticipated.

Matt leaned forward, moving his glasses from atop his head to his nose, looking closely at the top of the hourglass. He shook his head and smiled before sitting back.

"Hey, it's one of those joy clusters," Rachael said, leaning forward to point to the now familiar symbols engraved into the brass.

"Yes, it is," Ruby said, with a gentle smile.

"What is it doing on the hourglass?" Crystal asked.

"We thought you'd never ask," Pops responded, chuckling.

Holly leaned forward to take a closer look and the rest of the campers followed, their heads forming a circle as they leaned over it. "Has that mark really been there the whole time?" Holly asked.

"It's actually been there for longer than we've been on the farm," Pops replied. "As far as we know, it could be as old as the farm itself, maybe even older."

"How'd we miss it?" Greg asked, running the tip of his index finger over the engraved surface.

"Because we weren't looking for it," James replied. "Just like all of the other joy clusters scattered around the farm."

"But I think there's something more to this one," Genevieve replied, leaning forward until her chest met her knees and she could see the profile of the glass within the brass framework.

"What do you mean?" asked Holly, mimicking Genevieve's posture until she saw it, too. "Are you suggesting that X at the bottom of the anchor actually symbolizes the hourglass itself?"

"My gut says it does," Genevieve replied, pointing to the mark.

Again, all heads circled the top of the hourglass, focused on the section of the cluster Genevieve was pointing to.

"Is this really the last key?" Susan asked, turning her head to Ruby.

The others turned in unison, awaiting Ruby's response.

She smiled, her eyes twinkling as she nodded.

"It's about time!" James replied.

Ruby turned to Pops and they both laughed. "You couldn't be more right, James," Ruby replied.

He looked confused. "What do you mean?"

"The fifth key," Ruby responded, looking into each of their expectant faces. "It's all about time—and timing."

"Oh, please don't tell me the fifth key of joy *is patience*," Crystal said, sounding suddenly ill.

Ruby laughed. "I remember feeling the same way when the fifth key was revealed to us, towards the end of our first summer on the farm."

"I was afraid it might be something like this," Ephraim admitted. "But I guess it could be worse, right? I mean, heck, it could be celibacy!" he added, causing them all to laugh out loud.

"Ughh," Spencer moaned, throwing himself back in his seat, looking like he'd been punched in the gut.

The campers all returned to their seats, looking pained and disappointed.

"Couldn't at least one of the keys be easy?" Sonja asked.

Ruby raised her hands to calm the united and growing chorus of moans and whines. She smiled and shook her head as the campers ceased their protests. "If any of the keys were easy, joy would be far more commonplace," she spoke, matter-of-factly.

"Is there a problem with commonplace?" James challenged.

"No, not necessarily. But that which is common rarely calls for respect. It generally requires little to obtain it and is often cast aside as being inconsequential or even worthless. Those attributes could never describe joy."

"I, too, remember being disappointed when I learned this final key," Pops admitted. "Patience rarely comes naturally to anyone, and I'd struggled with it my entire life, always wanting things to work faster and run smoother. I've had to remind myself every day that patience with myself, with Mom, with the animals, and with every camper who's come and gone from this farm over the past fifty-seven years is essential and necessary to finding joy."

"He's come a long way," Ruby said, patting Pops's arm. "We both have. I was at least as impatient as Pops when I first arrived here. And I can't think of more than a handful of campers over the years for whom this key hasn't been difficult."

"I guess I don't understand why patience isn't part of self-discipline?" Matt admitted. "Why does it have to be its own key?"

Many of the campers nodded.

"That question gets asked every year," Ruby replied. "It's actually a really good question and one I struggled with myself for several years. I can't say I know for sure what the earliest founders of this farm and the town of Niederbipp had in mind when they decided that patience was one-fifth of joy, but I have had a few insights over the years that have proven helpful."

The campers watched her, waiting expectantly.

"I want you to close your eyes for a moment and keep them closed until I invite you to open them again." She waited until all their eyes were closed. Then she waited another thirty seconds, allowing the silence of the night to soothe their frustrations and anxieties. "Now," she spoke softly. "Now!" she repeated a little louder.

"Our world—your world—the world you will all soon return to is all about *now*. It's rushed, demanding, intolerant, and full of anxiety and deadlines." Before continuing, she watched silently as many heads bobbed. "You were born into that world, likely coming later than your mothers would have liked. Over the course of your first five years, on a daily basis, you were rushed out of bed, rushed to the breakfast table, rushed to various activities, then rushed back to bed. When school started, your teachers rushed you through your coloring projects, rushed you to learn your numbers and your multiplication chart. You were rushed at lunch, and rushed at recess, and rushed to cram your head full of facts and figures before rushing home to do homework. You were rushed to get a job. Rushed to get your driver's license, rushed to apply for college and get on with your life which, until you came to the farm, was just an endless cycle of rushing here and rushing there, rushing to meet deadlines and expectations by your bosses and others who wanted it now! Now! Now!"

She paused for effect, allowing her words to sink deep into their ears and hearts. She and Pops watched as many of their heads bobbed again, others shook, and some wore expressions of dread and disgust.

"There are some things you and I cannot change," she pressed on. "In order to thrive, each of us has to eat, and sleep, and use the toilet. Most of us must earn our bread and work to pay for the roof over our heads. The majority of us in the first world get to choose how we'll pay our way through life, at least to some extent. But the rush required by *now*, and the impatience we knew from early childhood gets carried with us into adulthood. It affects every choice we make from how we choose to spend our lunch hour, to how we treat our neighbors, to how we take time to feed and groom and care for ourselves.

"It's true that what we demand from our *nows* largely influences our tomorrows, but most of us lose some of the best moments of our lives by rushing from now, to now, to now, seldom taking the time to even notice the flowers, let alone taking the opportunity to enjoy them. We miss the geese crisscrossing the sky. We miss the stars. We miss time with our children and our lovers, too stressed to slow down, too anxious to allow ourselves time to feel, too over-programmed to recognize that life is passing us by and we're missing it all…we're missing the simple, magical, unrepeatable joys."

Again, Ruby allowed the silence to envelope them, saying nothing, allowing the soft, rhythmic ballad of the crickets to wake them in their own time to their own awareness. One by one, they opened their eyes. When she saw that each of them was awake and alert, she leaned forward and picked up the hourglass. She sat back in her seat, lifted the glass at arms-length to the bare lightbulb above her. Then turning it over so the sand within began to fall, she handed the hourglass to Greg.

Greg looked at her, uncertain what to do, so he simply did the same as Ruby had done, holding the glass to the light, watching the grains of sand slide effortlessly through the glass's tiny orifice. He passed it on to Holly who did the same, the hourglass slowly making its way around the circle. Only once was the hourglass turned over in an attempt to make time run backward. But James, quickly recognizing the futility of his efforts, passed the hourglass on to Crystal. The sand ran out before the glass had made it all the way around the circle, providing each of the campers three minutes of cricket song, three minutes of stillness that allowed them to experience the sound of their own heartbeats, three minutes to awaken each of them to a new awareness.

When it was handed back to her, Ruby placed the hourglass back in the center of the table and turned it over again. No one wanted to speak, each of them mesmerized by the falling sand. After another minute had passed, Holly spontaneously reached for Greg's hand with her left hand, and Ephraim's hand with her right. It was a small gesture of friendship and connection, and it didn't stop, quickly spreading in both directions until the circle was closed. Together, without any words being spoken, they watched until the last grains of sand had fallen through the top half of the glass.

"Can we do this again tomorrow?" Greg asked, causing them all to smile.

"I hope you will," Ruby replied. "In fact, I hope you'll do something quite like this every day for the rest of your lives."

"I, for one, am feeling far less impatient than I was just ten minutes ago," Ephraim said, inviting the laughter of all of the campers, as well as the resumption of dialogue.

The exercise had changed the tone from one of whining and discontent to one of honest inquiry and sincere desire to learn how something that came naturally to no one was an essential ingredient in the acquisition and accumulation of joy.

Very quickly a common theme arose as they each shared personal experiences of how patience, or rather their lack thereof, had led to regrets, anxieties, bad habits, and damaged relationships. While they were mentally wrestling through these challenges of their former lives, it was Holly who recalled an earlier conversation when they'd collectively and rather impatiently bemoaned the fact that they only knew three of the five keys. She reminded them once again of Ruby's response: that if they were honestly and sincerely seeking to understand the first three keys, they were already working on the last two.

This shared memory opened each of their eyes and hearts, as they recognized how their growing understanding of reverence, hope and charity, along with their newly acquired understanding of self-discipline, had indeed already influenced their patience towards each other and the challenges they faced. Now, finally, with all the keys identified, they could focus their efforts on understanding each one of them, as well as recognizing how they each overlapped and intersected. And even though some of the keys were less appealing, or at least less nimbly acquirable than others, they now at least knew the attributes, habits and character they needed to develop in their progress toward joy.

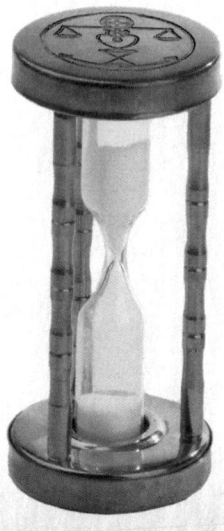

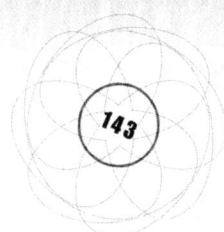

CHAPTER 143

Perseverance

True godliness does not turn men out of this world, but enables them to live better in it, and excites their endeavors to mend it.
—William Penn—

As had been arranged three weeks earlier when both Matt & Genevieve and James & Crystal announced their plans to marry, both couples had been allowed to spend time together in the afternoons when their chores had been completed. This allowed for each of them to make plans for their upcoming weddings, contact family and friends, and spend time together dreaming of their futures.

A few days after the fifth key had been revealed, Crystal and James, fearing they may already be too late, rode their bikes into town on a Monday afternoon to order their wedding clothes. Unlike Geneveive, Crystal didn't know exactly what she wanted in terms of design and fabric and struggled for nearly two hours with the many choices and options before finally settling on an empire-waisted dress with cap sleeves, a lace-enhanced bodice, and twenty-one pearl buttons up the back.

James chose a tuxedo-style suit coat with tails that fell below the backs of his knees, blue and black pinstripe trousers, and a purple taffeta vest. They returned to the farm late that afternoon looking both physically and emotionally drained; an already difficult discussion concerning who would handle which of the expenses had turned heated and boiled over. The temperature between them remained unstable until Wednesday when Ruby walked them both to the pond and invited them to have a seat in the old wooden rowboat. They reluctantly complied with her invitation and had no sooner sat down when Ruby unhitched the boat from the dock and firmly set them adrift with a strong push from a long stick, telling them not to come back until they'd learned the importance of working together and the beauty of companionable communication.

The boat drifted rather quickly to the center of the pond, where its occupants, like miffed children, retreated as far away from each other as they could, each claiming exclusive rights to the space on opposite ends of the boat. Over the next few hours, James and Crystal independently attempted to coax the boat to shore, but to no avail. The obvious lack of oars or paddles inspired them to resort to using their hands, which quickly proved awkward and highly ineffective. But despite their inefficiency, they continued making plenty of noise and churning up a lot of water as they grunted and cursed and mocked each other's feeble attempts. Still, their efforts brought them no closer to the shore and accomplished nothing more than to aimlessly turn their wooden craft in circles. After watching and listening to the foolishness from a distance, the rest of the campers lost interest, turning their attention instead to more productive activities.

It was shortly after dinner that evening before James and Crystal finally wandered back past the big house, soaking wet and sunburned from their long exposure to the afternoon sun. But to everyone's surprise, they seemed happy, even chummy.

Pops called them to the porch where the family had gathered and asked them to share what had happened to turn their obnoxious behavior into something obviously far more friendly. The campers watched and listened as the waterlogged couple explained how, after hours of turning in circles, James had thrown himself into the pond to get away, forgetting in the heat of the moment that he was not a very confident swimmer. Crystal had tried to help bring him back into the boat, but she had lost her grip on his slippery, wet hand. Flying backwards, she went sailing into the pond on the opposite side of the boat.

All the campers laughed with them as they described bobbing in the cool of the water, fully clothed and feeling stupid, both of them clinging onto to opposite sides of the rowboat. After exhausting their upper-body strength trying to hoist themselves back into the boat, they eventually found themselves together at the stern where they discovered the name of the watercraft, hand-painted across the back in bold lettering: S.S. Perseverance.

While the campers laughed at the irony, Ephraim suggested the boat may have been misnamed, pointing out that S.S. stood for Steam Ship and was not actually applicable for a human powered rowboat.

Pops explained that in this case, it was in fact very applicable as the boat had been used many times over the last fifty-seven years to allow couples to blow off steam and come to their senses.

And so it had been for Crystal and James, who explained that the discovery of the boat's name, while treading water behind it, had given them each a chance to take an honest look at themselves. Somehow, in that humble and desperate setting, they'd been able to find the good sense to laugh at their foolish pride and stubbornness which had led them, once again, to lose control. The silliness of the situation also provided each of them a smack of sobering truth that if they did not take this opportunity for a hard reset, they would likely carry their undesirable attitudes and shortcomings with them into their marriage. They shared with the rest of the campers how they had committed to each other, in that soggy state, that they'd never again allow their differences of opinion, passions, or experience to stand in the way of kindness, love and respect.

After that, through no small effort of working together, they'd finally been able to swim the old rowboat back to the dock and the shallow water where they could help each other get out of the mess they'd gotten themselves into.

Ruby and Pops shared that night with all of the campers how, when both partners in a marriage are committed to living according to the keys of joy, harmony between two very different people can both grow and be maintained. But they also warned that whenever any of the keys are neglected by an individual or within a marriage, the harmonious flow of joy will inevitably be restricted.

Painting a picture that they all could understand, Ruby compared living according to the keys of joy to a river that is allowed to flow freely, nourishing and giving life to all that are near it. But, she warned, like a dam is to a river, the progression of all things joyful will be slowed, if not all together stopped, if any of the five keys or conditions of joy are neglected. The constant exercise and regular fine-tuning of reverence, patience, hope, self-discipline, and charity, she and Pops explained, allows the flow of joy to continue uninterrupted and unobstructed.

The next afternoon, James and Crystal made another trip to the tailor shop, this time to simplify their earlier decisions. The lace and pearl buttons were scratched from the order, along with James's entire outfit. Instead, he settled on a classic and simple blue and white seersucker, which Albert warned was traditionally not worn after Labor Day, but he seemed happy to still have an order. While in town, they learned of Castleton's, a small, locally owned jewelry shop, eight miles north

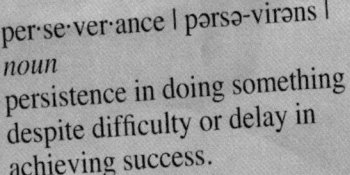

per·se·ver·ance | pərsə-virəns |
noun
persistence in doing something despite difficulty or delay in achieving success.

of town. With money back on James's credit card, and both of them feeling a desire to continue to keep things simple, they rode the distance to find a ring.

They returned to the farm much happier than they'd been the day before, Crystal wearing a thin, simple gold band on her ring finger, and a slightly wider gold band in a box for James for their wedding day.

When asked about their ring choices that night at dinner, they explained they were the results of a conscious and mutual decision they'd made to keep joy flowing by exercising self-discipline and entering their marriage without debt. All the campers cheered when they learned the simple message they'd engraved on the inside of each band: SS Perseverance, to serve as a reminder of the things they'd learned the evening before.

The porch discussion that evening continued on the themes introduced by James and Crystal and their experience gained in the pursuit of simplicity. As they listened to the conversation turn toward the merits of moderation, Pops shared with them a quote from Benjamin Franklin: "It is the eye of other people that ruin us. If I were blind, I would want neither fine clothes, fine houses or fine furniture."

Each of them had stories to share of friends and associates who'd entered marriages with unrealistic expectations of grandeur and ease, only to discover it was more work than they'd expected. Expensive rings, lavish weddings and exotic honeymoons had also added to the marital adjustments, creating divisions and stress when the party was over and credit card bills came due. So much of this, they collectively decided, could be avoided through the simplification of wants and the humble application of both modesty and moderation.

They recognized that these truths were easy to accept in a place where second-hand clothes were the norm and homemade bread nourished both their bodies and souls every day. But with just one month left before they returned to their homes and lives, they all felt some sense of anxiety associated with falling back into old habits and uninspired patterns that had already cost them years' worth of anxiety, distress and difficulties. Though the openness of the discussions they had over the next two nights helped each of the campers verbalize their desires to live simpler, more moderate lives, the Sunday sermon at church solidified their resolve.

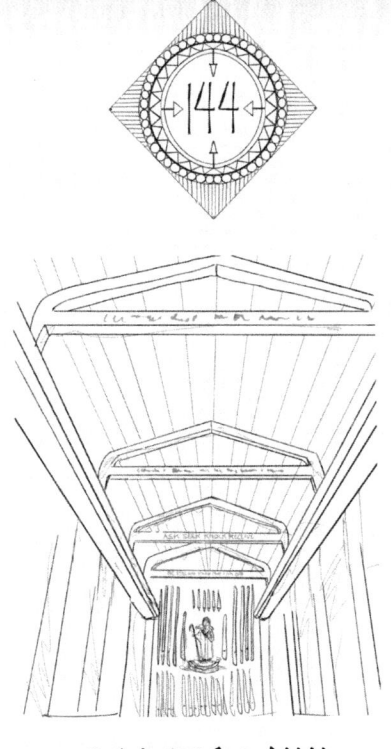

CHAPTER 144

Of Motes and Beams

You can find God if you will only seek—
by obeying divine laws, by loving people,
by relinquishing self-will, attachments,
negative thoughts and feelings.
And when you find God it will be in stillness.
You will find God within.

—Peace Pilgrim—

Unlike many other Sundays, with everyone running late or just barely on time, Matt and Genevieve led out early, inviting anyone who was interested to join them. They hoped that the empty chapel would allow them the time and space to examine the subtle messages painted on the overhead beams. Ephraim, Holly and Greg accompanied this early expedition, happy to be out in the sunshine on a glorious morning that brought with it the first hints of autumn.

The chapel was nearly empty when they arrived, forty minutes before the services were to begin. Only Thomas was there, turning to greet them from the front of the chapel where he was arranging the moveable numbers for the morning's hymns on the hymn board.

"What a nice surprise," he said, jumping down from the stool he'd been standing on, quickly checking his wristwatch. "Is my watch slow or are you kids early?"

"We're early, but deliberately," Matt said. "We came to learn more about the messages on the overhead beams."

"Then you came to the right place," he said, smiling as he pointed to the ceiling. "There aren't many people who even notice the writing on the wall anymore, and even fewer who arrive early to examine them more closely. How can I help?"

"Well, so far, we only know the saying on that beam at the front, but there are four other beams," Genevieve pointed out.

"Indeed, there are, and if you haven't noticed, there are messages painted on both their fronts and their backsides."

Greg looked up, turning around to better examine the nearly inconspicuous shiny white characters on the matte white beam.

"What does it say?" Holly asked.

"I can't tell. It's hard to read." He moved sideways, sliding between the pews until he could make out the word, the individual letters reflecting the light of the sun as it shined in through the tall windows. "I don't think the word is written in English."

"No, it's probably German," Matt said, opening his journal and uncapping his pen. "Can you spell it out for us?"

"Uh, sure...N...A with the two little dots on top...C...H...ST...EN...L...IEB...E."

"What does that mean?" asked Ephraim.

Matt turned over several pages in his journal before looking up. "'Nächstenliebe'...according to the dictionary in the library, that's the German word for charity."

"Seriously?" asked Holly.

"Sounds like you've been doing your homework," Thomas responded.

"I...we have," Matt replied, winking at Genevieve. "The Ebenezer behind the cowshed...each of those rocks has German words carved into them, and we figured it'd be worth working our way through them."

"There's another there," Ephraim said, pointing to the second beam from the back.

"What does that one say?" asked Genevieve.

"It says...oooh, this one must be German, also. It's ...SE...L...BST...DIS...ZP...LIN," he read slowly as he walked down the row between two pews.

Matt smiled as he looked up from his journal. "That one's a little easier. It's almost the same in English."

Holly looked over his shoulder. "Self-discipline?"

"That's right. Is this beginning to sound familiar?" Thomas asked.

"They're the keys of joy?" Ephraim asked, looking surprised.

Thomas nodded. "You're welcome to check if you doubt me, but you'll find *Hoffnung* written on the forward face of the center beam, *Geduld* on the next, and *Ehrfurcht* on the front beam."

Genevieve, Holly and Greg moved forward different distances into the church, their eyes turned heavenward to examine the beams.

"I've got 'Hoffnung'," Genevieve exclaimed.

"This one says 'Geduld'," confirmed Greg.

"Yep, this one says 'Ehrfurcht'," Holly responded, leaning against the rich, wooden frame of the pipe organ to be able to decipher the writing.

"Has that really been here the whole time?" Ephraim asked.

Thomas smiled. "To my knowledge, it's been there since the scaffolding was taken down when the building was built more than three hundred years ago."

"But in that book you wrote…you were still looking for the keys of joy…?" Genevieve replied.

"Yes, I was. It wasn't until several years after my book was published that I discovered I'd been walking and singing and worshiping right under the answers I'd been looking for. They were there the whole time, waiting to be discovered."

"But Hildegard…Pops and Ruby…the old timers…they must have known them the whole time. Why didn't you ask them?"

Thomas smiled. "I did."

"They didn't tell you?" Matt asked, looking surprised.

"I…I wasn't asking the right questions, nor did I have the right heart."

"What does that mean?" asked Genevieve.

"I think I told you once before that I was interested in knowing them for the purpose of selling them."

"Selling them?" asked Holly.

"So to speak. I recognize it was silly, looking at it now, but at the time I thought I might make some money being a tour guide around here…take people on the *Keys of Joy Tour*. I planned to write a book about it and get rich selling the secrets that make this town different. I'm ashamed to admit that now, but at the time I still hadn't learned that life was something more than just being about me. I was neither humble nor sincere in my desires to know the truth. You don't get very far on the path of truth if greed and wealth are your primary motives."

"So, what changed for you?" Matt asked.

"The same thing that's changed for each of you," Thomas responded. "After some humbling and developing a sincere desire to know and understand what I was missing, answers came, as they always do to those who search for them with a sincere heart and a genuine desire to improve one's life. The writing, as they say, was always on the wall, but

I wasn't ready to see it. I expected something grandiose...something big and bold and exciting. When you're looking for grandiose, it's really easy to miss the simple truths that are right in front of your nose. You tend to stumble right over those beautifully subtle truths when you're used to seeking and collecting things that sparkle. It took me nearly half my life to recognize that God rarely works that way. His truths, carried on the whispers of angels, have to find you in quiet moments. And when they do, they reach out and touch you softly in personal ways you may never be able to adequately describe. But they can fill your entire soul with energy as if every one of your trillions of cells has been softly stroked by fire."

Matt looked up at the beams and shook his head. "And to think it was here the whole time!"

Thomas nodded and turned to look up. "It always is."

"What is?" asked Ephraim.

"The truth of God's love. It's never far from any of His creations. You just have to be willing to wipe away the dust of your everyday cares so you can see the love that's all around you."

"Be still and know that I am God," Genevieve said softly, pointing to the words written on the foremost beam, subtly reflecting the light all around them.

"Exactly," Thomas responded. "Until you purposefully, intentionally, and wholeheartedly have a desire to know, and see, and feel God's love, you probably won't be ready to recognize you've been surrounded by it all along." Thomas turned to the foremost beam and took a deep breath, letting it out in the silence of the quiet chapel, its echo moving through the space between them like a gentle whisper.

"There's more written on this beam, too," Holly said when the whisper had faded away.

Thomas smiled and nodded.

She moved gracefully through the empty rows to where she could read it all. "ASK, SEEK, KNOCK, REPEAT."

"Yes, you're beginning to see," Thomas said with a warm smile.

"This one says… 'I AM…THE RESURRECTION…AND…THE LIFE,'" Ephraim read as he moved between the pews. "I assume that's a scripture."

Thomas nodded. "That's a beautiful passage in the eleventh chapter of John. You might look it up to understand the sources from which the founders of this town drew their greatest hope."

"I can see this one, too," Greg said from several rows back. "It says, 'Let us run…with patience…the race that is…set before us.'"

"Mmmm. One of my personal favorites. Hebrews 12, verse 1," Thomas offered.

"What's the last one?" Matt asked, looking up from his journal to Genevieve who was sitting on the last pew, looking up with wonder in her eyes. "It says, 'Love thy neighbor as thyself.'"

"Yes," Thomas replied. "You'll notice that each of the scriptures ties in nicely with the corresponding key on the other side of the beam."

Matt looked down at his journal, drawing lines between the keys and the scriptural verses.

"I have a question," Matt said, looking up again. "If these are so important, why are some written in German and others in English?"

"I wondered the same thing when I first discovered them," Thomas replied.

"What have you come up with?" asked Ephraim.

"What makes the most sense to me is that they promote questions and reverence and wonder."

Matt nodded, looking back to his journal.

"The stones that make up that Ebenezer on the farm," Thomas continued, "were just a pile of rocks until you noticed they had words—messages—meaning hidden just beyond what could easily be seen. Those messages created questions, and all sincere questions lead to the honest search for answers."

"And the answers are all around us, just waiting for us to open the door with a question, aren't they?" Matt asked thoughtfully.

"I believe they are, Matt. But until one sincerely wants to know and is willing to put in the work the answer may require of him, the truth will always remain hidden from his eyes. Many of us are afraid of answers that require work, or change, or discomfort. Until we're ready to hearken, to heed, and to move forward with reverence and humility, any answer will be wasted on us. Until then, our desires for truth amount to little more than immature flirtations, incapable of producing much more than momentary and fruitless infatuations."

"Whoa!" Greg responded, sitting down on the bench, like his mind had just been blown.

"Yeah," Ephraim seconded.

Holly nodded, looking up at the beams. "But each of these are antidotes to stagnation, aren't they?"

Thomas nodded. "They're antidotes to stagnation, and indifference, and pride, and fear, and uncertainty, and apathy, and indecision, and every other human weakness that we choose instead of doing the work that will enable us to progress toward our potential and our destiny. Every one of these sayings is an invitation to not only do something more, but to do something different—something that's uncomfortable or contrary to the self-centered patterns and habits we generally follow."

"I still can't get over the fact that all of this has been here the whole summer," Greg said, shaking his head.

"Yes," Thomas said, leaning forward and pointing to Greg's chest with his finger. "But the answers you've been seeking were in *there* long before you came here." He stood up straight and looked into each of their faces. "The apostle John spoke of the light that is given to all mankind at the time of their birth. I'm a firm believer in that light. I've recognized the beauty and wonder of it growing warmer and brighter with each step we take to understanding our true natures as the sons and daughters of God."

"You almost make it sound like a spiritual homing device," Ephraim suggested.

"I was just thinking it sounds like the hot and cold game," Holly added.

"Yes, I think those are both apt comparisons, and I'm sure there are many others."

"And the benches...the ones around town and those on the farm—they're all connected, right? They all share the purpose of all of this, don't they?" Genevieve asked.

"Absolutely! There are many places around here, as well as around the world, that vibrate with an energy that promotes honest questions."

"Like this church?" Greg said, looking up.

"Yes, and every church and synagogue and temple that have been built out of a hunger and a desire to somehow connect heaven and earth. Some people are born with reverence already in their hearts and their spiritual lamps burning bright. But for the rest of us, we discover our lamps only when we find ourselves in some degree of darkness and recognize the strings of grace and mercy connecting us to eternity."

"Yeah...that's the way it was for me," Greg admitted. "My mother tried to teach me as a child all the things I've learned here this summer, but it wasn't until I hit rock bottom that I could finally sense that there was something more to life than chasing my appetites and impulses."

Thomas nodded. "Reverence often begins at a place of deep humility."

"Why do you think that is?" Genevieve asked, remembering her attempted trip to Tionesta.

"Because we're often too busy or distracted until then," Thomas replied, nodding to an elderly couple who quietly wandered into the chapel and shuffled into a pew several rows ahead. "Until we discover a need to connect with heaven, many of us don't. In the same way that we have to be hungry before food appeals to us, most of us must find ourselves in darkness before we can appreciate the value of light—both the light within and the greater light without."

"But the light...it's always there, isn't it?" Matt asked, pointing to the overhead beams.

Thomas nodded. "I think so. If it's not right before you, one need only to look around or sit and be still and wait for it to reveal itself. Jesus said, 'I stand at the door and knock. If anyone hears My voice and opens the door, I will come in to him and dine with him, and he with me'."[1]

Greg nodded. "I missed a lifetime's worth of knocks."

Thomas smiled. "If God is anything, he is patient. We each find our own pace. There's no shame in that. Life is all about learning and progressing."

"But there's so much time...I missed it all."

"No, there's no sense in thinking that way. Sure, days have passed that might have been spent in the light, but what matters most are the days ahead and what you choose to do with the light you have today. If you humbly choose to pursue light, applying the keys of joy with every step, you'll discover the truth of the proverb: 'But the path of the righteous is like the light of dawn, which shines brighter and brighter until full day.'[2] You kids have discovered truths here today that many people never encounter. Some who discover what you've seen make no note of them or choose to forget them. But for those who are ready, who are hungry for truth and light, these keys open portals into grand and glorious worlds filled with unlimited possibilities and eternal potential."

"Why don't more people know about this?" Greg asked thoughtfully.

"Because our world is noisy, and busy, and we're easily distracted by the color, and shimmer, and excitement of other things."

"But all of that's hardly comparable to what we've experienced this summer," Holly argued.

"Yes, I agree. But for most of the world, until they're ready to see it, the keys of joy, along with most virtues, have little value to people whose hearts are set on riches, who thrive on sensationalism, or who are apathetic to things of a spiritual nature."

The campers turned to watch as several other congregants walked down the aisles to find their seats.

"This may need to continue on another day," Thomas said as he nodded his greeting to a middle-aged couple. "You'll stay for services today, I hope."

"Yes, we were planning on it," Ephraim responded.

"Good. Our sermon today will be given by Emma Parkin. You'll enjoy her. She's got quite a story."

"That's the same Parkins who run the marriage retreat?" Matt asked.

"That's the one. She and her husband Tom have been great additions to our community. I have no doubt she'll leave you all inspired."

Notes
1. Revelation 3:20
2. Proverbs 4:18

CHAPTER 145

Emma

A very little key will open a very heavy door.
—Charles Dickens—

With the congregation now filing in quickly, Matt, Genevieve, Holly, Greg and Ephraim moved closer to the front, settling in on the second row behind a well-dressed couple who looked like they were in their early seventies. Matt, sitting in the middle between Genevieve and Greg, opened his journal to the notes he'd just taken. The German words, written quickly in a blocky hand, were tied with pen lines to the sayings they'd discovered. The five campers leaned in, whispering quietly as they spoke of the things they'd learned from Thomas that morning.

The chapel was filled to capacity when they looked up again, with many faces in the congregation they'd never seen before. The organ prelude filled the hall with melodic energy, providing a stark contrast to the quiet that came as Joseph, the town florist, walked to the lectern to share a simple yet beautiful invocation. At the utterance of "Amen," the campers on the second row glanced sideways at each other with shared looks of respect, having felt the undeniable yet unexplainable sense that more than just mortals had heard his words. They followed Joseph with their eyes as he returned to his seat, sitting down next to his wife.

"Are you thinking what I'm thinking?" Genevieve whispered in Matt's ear.

"That we need to pay them a visit?"

She nodded as Thomas returned to the lectern to introduce the speaker.

"Good morning, friends," Thomas said with a broad smile. "I recognize there are many visitors with us today and we want to welcome you to Niederbipp. Labor Day Weekend often draws some of our biggest crowds of the year, but I think this one may set a new record. Of course, part of that may be due to the fact that Emma Parkin is speaking to us today. Knowing the Parkins are generally welcoming guests to their marriage retreats forty-something Sundays each year, we do our best to schedule them to speak whenever they have a free Sunday and haven't run off to visit their family. Most of you probably know the Parkins, but for those who don't, Emma and Tom became Niederbippians nearly thirty years ago, when they purchased the dilapidated, and some might say, *haunted*, Whitmore Manor. They've spent much of these last three decades renovating their home and turning it into the gem it is today. Tom and Emma will be married fifty years tomorrow and are the parents of three boys, all married and living from coast to coast. But their greatest joys are their seven grandchildren, who are all here this weekend to help their grandparents celebrate their golden anniversary. Without further ado, Emma Parkin."

Thomas motioned to the older couple on the front row, sitting just in front of the campers. The woman stood, walking confidently to the lectern as Thomas, without any other option in the crowded chapel, took Emma's seat next to her husband.

The woman stood silently at the lectern for a moment, taking in the faces of the congregation, smiling and nodding at many of them, waving to a few others. "As Thomas mentioned, it's been nearly thirty years since we discovered Niederbipp. Many of you have come here quite intentionally for one reason or another. Our reason for coming was quite different. We were lost, in many more ways than one. After twenty-four years of marriage, having recently sent our last son to college, Tom and I were at a crossroads—a rather ugly crossroads, I might add. Even though we were both successful family therapists, we'd somehow grown apart, allowing dust bunnies and tumble weeds to fill the space between us until they'd piled up high, becoming a thick and prickly wall. If anyone would have told us we'd make it through that time, and that the next twenty-six years would be the most rewarding and exhilarating years of our lives, we would certainly have wondered what delusions they were suffering from. We were lost before we even left home that day, twenty-six years ago, and we became even more lost, recognizing with each mile we drove that we were nowhere we wanted to be.

"And then…Niederbipp." She smiled, opening her arms as if she were embracing the whole congregation. Many responded with chuckles as if they recognized this unusual punchline.

"I wish we could all take more moments for reflection in our lives instead of waiting for big days to recognize how far we've come. Fifty years is a milestone in nearly any contest, but fifty years of marriage… fifty years of marriage between two broken souls…you have to think we were either too dumb to fail, too stubborn to give up, or that God and His angels had better things for us to do. In our case, Tom and I have made it this far only through the merits and mercy of all three scenarios.

"It's often said that it takes a village to raise a child. And though that's true, the broader world often forgets that it takes a village to do a lot of things. Niederbipp, on the other hand, never forgot that. Our marriage is what it is today because a handful of people stuck their noses into our business when we needed them the most. Ruby and Lorenzo, Hildegard, Joseph and Gloria, Isaac Bingham, and many others who I hope are smiling down on us from heaven. They not only helped us see where our choices were leading us—it surely wasn't difficult to recognize our many weaknesses and failures—but they knew somehow that we were capable of change and progress, and that the strength and experience we were gaining here could help others.

"Many of you know our story. Some of you have lived through it. Others have worked by our sides as we've labored for the last twenty-six years to strengthen and remodel marriages—including our own. You've been there to both laugh and cry with us, to lift us and love us, to encourage and cheer us, to comfort and direct us. There are millions of towns across the world where marriages are failing for lack of hope and direction. But you've helped us put Niederbipp on the map as a place where marriages and families can thrive and bask in the light of hope and joy and in the grace and mercy of God.

"Many of you have recently been out to our home to watch and even participate in the slow work of helping us build what's been dubbed as *The Joy Pavilion*. This was something we'd considered building for years, wanting to create a space where music and dancing could be enjoyed for at least eight months a year, but also provide covered space for creating art, and yoga, and gatherings of all kinds for our weekly guests. As with most things on the ranch, we also wanted to create a space that was filled with meaning while offering a place of reflection and thought.

"Not having the money for an architect, Tom and I drew up our own plans over the course of at least two decades, incorporating symbols for the things we've learned from you and the keys of joy which have entirely changed the way we think and live and love.

"Over the two-and-a-half decades that we've lived here, we've discovered that each of these keys have become pillars of strength and possibility, not only for us, but for the hundreds of couples that come through the ranch each year. In a world where virtues are quickly being replaced by vice and indifference, we wanted to create a space where goodness and time-honored, noble principles formed the structure and provided the integrity of the space they created.

"In addition to the keys of joy, we drew our inspiration from the Old and New Testaments. We searched the Bible for inspiration, combing through verse after verse in an effort to understand the mind and heart of God, his will for each of us, and his patterns and revelations to those who seek him. We studied virtues and connected the dots, recognizing that the keys of joy incorporate all virtues in beautiful and inclusive ways that have left us inspired and uplifted and striving to be our best selves.

"This week, with the help of our children and grandchildren, we finished the last details of *The Joy Pavilion*. We'd like to invite you all to join us this afternoon, if you're up for it, in dedicating it to the author and finisher of the keys of joy and all virtues in general. We've been envisioning this gathering for three years, ever since we first attended one of Jake and Amy Kimball's Sourdough Sunday events. It caused us to recognize that we hadn't fully included all the elements of joy we would like to. We'd always planned for a large wood burning stove to be at the center of the pavilion, to offer both stability and warmth in the spring and fall when the temperatures are still cool. But we realized after that first Sourdough Sunday that a bread oven needed to share the central smokestack with the stove. I will add that our preliminary trials have proven that it also works well for wood-fired pizza. Jake and Amy have been out twice in the last month with their new baby, Isaac, to help us learn the nuances of baking bread in a primitive oven, and I think we've finally discovered the sweet spot of temperature and timing. Which brings me, rather circuitously, to the topic of the thoughts I'd like to share with you today."

Many of the congregants laughed as Emma opened the portfolio she'd carried with her to the pulpit.

"You can learn a lot about temperature and timing over the course of fifty years of marriage. I say *can* because it is certainly not guaranteed that you'll ever learn it, and many couples don't, at least until they come to learn the secrets and value of patience. But patience is tough for most of us. Few of us look forward to the time we have to wait before we can get a driver's license, or fall in love with our person, or buy our first home. No, most of us want all of it now, the minute we think of it, and we certainly don't want to have to wait around for graduation, or till we can scrimp together a down payment, or for our ship to finally come in, and for all the stars in the universe to align in such a way that we can move forward with life without delay. But life doesn't work that way, at least not for most of us. Our dreams of grandeur rarely include the details of the thousands of hours of work and toil required to get there.

"When we first began dreaming about turning our home and ranch into a marriage retreat, we were told that we really ought to spend some time talking to Ruby and Lorenzo Swarovski and learn more about the farm at the top of Harmony Hill. We decided to do just that one autumn Sunday on our way back to Pittsburgh. This was back when we were commuting here on the weekends. We'd just finished a long weekend of working on our house. As I recall, we were dirty and tired and probably short-tempered after recognizing we'd been spending all of our free time and extra funds on a money pit that was returning only marginal bits of happiness.

"We'd met Ruby and Pops at church some weeks before, and we'd heard of Harmony Hill, but we'd never been there and we really weren't prepared for what lay ahead for us and our 1982 Chevy Citation. What we thought would be a quick visit changed abruptly when Tom made the mistake of turning onto their farm's rutted drive. After only a few feet, we heard the bottom of our car rubbing on the higher ground between the ruts. Tom tried turning the wheel to steer us to higher ground when we heard a pop, and the front tire immediately lost its air, slamming us back into the rut. Without the air in the tire, we were hopelessly high-centered, incapable of moving either forward or backward. What made matters worse was that the loss of air in the tire lowered the car into the rut so deeply that when we tried to open the doors, they immediately hit dirt on either side, making them completely non-functional and trapping us inside the car."

Many in the congregation laughed while several of the campers nodded their heads, finding this picture easy to imagine after their own experiences with the rutted drive.

"With nightfall coming on, on a Sunday evening when we knew every towing service would be either closed or wanting to charge double, we surrendered to the same sense of the universe guiding us as we had when we bought our home. We rolled down our windows and climbed out of our car and walked down the drive to the Swarovski's home where we were welcomed like family. They agreed that there was no sense in even attempting to do anything until the morning. But treating us with the kindness and generosity of old friends, they offered us lodging, warm showers, and leftover roast beef and potatoes from their dinner that evening. When we were showered and fed, Ruby and Pops invited us to join them in their library where we learned about the multi-generational history of the farm and the thousands of successful families that had been rooted and nourished by the five keys of joy.

"As I recall, we visited late into the evening, talking together about the keys and the foundation they laid for happy marriages and happy lives. As the Swarovskis spoke, Tom and I felt the truth of the keys speaking to something deep within us, resonating profoundly with the truths we'd gained over our careers as therapists. The things we learned that night were not entirely new to either of us, but in that setting in which they were shared, and having been recently tenderized by a series of humbling circumstances, the keys were a revelation to each of us.

"After Lorenzo and Ruby went to bed, Tom and I stayed up most of the night, designing the format of our marriage retreats. We were so excited, sleep felt like a burden. And though it eventually overtook us, we rose with the rooster's alarm, and carried on talking. While Lorenzo and Tom hitched up the draft horses to pull our car out of the rut, I spent the early hours of the new day picking Ruby's brain and extracting gold nuggets of wisdom from her heart as we made breakfast. Tom did the same as he helped Lorenzo with the farm chores and while taking the tire into town to be repaired. And by the time we were back on the road late that afternoon, we had all the motivation we needed to get our retreat open and operating as quickly as we could.

"I mentioned that learning the keys was a revelation, but actually *living* the keys changed everything. That twenty-four hours we spent on the Swarovski's farm became the catalyst for all sorts of changes in our life and our marriage. Neither Tom nor I had grown up with any religion to speak of, and we began to recognize how our lack of reverence for anything spiritual had limited our understanding of a deeper meaning of both life itself and the relationships that have the greatest potential to bring us joy. For the first time in our marriage, we began to pray together. It was awkward at first, but we followed the simple pattern we'd learned from the Swarovskis, praying from our hearts, expressing gratitude, and asking for help with the challenges we were facing. Something amazing happened over the course of the next few months. We both began to feel a real connection to a God we'd always believed in but had never before considered might be interested in us. And if he was interested in us, a middle-aged couple trying to figure out our purpose and direction, surely he'd be interested in everyone else.

"We began looking at people differently, trying to treat others with the same kind of kindness and charity each of you extended to us every weekend we were here. Our kids began asking what was going on; why we weren't arguing anymore, and why we were treating each other with unusual portions of patience and love. When our clients independently began commenting that we seemed happier and more sympathetic to their challenges, they often wanted to know what was going on in our personal lives. And though it was never our practice to share much of anything personal, their questions often led to beautiful conversations.

"As Tom and I shared with each other what was going on in our separate practices, we recognized the power the keys of joy had to change hearts and minds that had been unable to make much progress using the techniques and practices we'd each learned in graduate school. While those things focused on the things of the head and occasionally the heart, they often neglected the spiritual needs for connection and nurturing. Our conversations around these recognitions only made room for more reverence, humility, charity, and patience for each other, which in turn improved our work with our clients.

"When our clients began sharing what they were learning from us with their families and friends, an interesting phenomenon began taking place. Clients who'd been meeting with us, sometimes for years, began opening their hearts and attitudes to things they'd never considered before. Instead of looking for answers in medication or expensive long-term therapies, they began looking inward, discovering root causes of their anguish, and working their way toward brighter futures by allowing themselves to make sincere and honest inquiries into their past, to learn from them, and to move forward with a new and improved brightness of hope. In some cases, clients who'd been meeting with us every week for many years began skipping appointments, then skipping months, then letting us know they'd figured things out and didn't need us anymore. For a minute, we worried if we were working ourselves out of our jobs by providing our clients with exercises and patterns of truth that brought about real, long-term change. But word began to spread that we had answers that worked, and soon we were both busier than we wanted to be.

"When Tom's office lease was coming to an end and my secretary informed me that she would not be coming back to work after her maternity leave, we decided to take two weeks off and kick our remodel into high gear. Three weeks later, we began welcoming folks to our very first marriage retreats. Looking back, I still can't believe we did it. With only four partially finished rooms and half a kitchen, our early clients worked alongside us as we put the south wing of the house back together, a century after it was destroyed by its previous owners. It's hard to believe, but it took more than eighteen years to bring the house back to its original glory. Today, we have the space to welcome twelve couples each week to learn the invaluable lessons we've learned over these last fifty years, the best of which have come from our interactions with all of you.

"Tom and I have become convinced over the years that there are great things to learn every day—lessons about life and love and the secrets of joy that God and his universe are anxious for us to learn. After living our first twenty-four years of marriage in the fog of spiritual apathy and indifference, we woke up to what has become for us the undeniable truth that God loves us and wants us to be happy. Not only happy, but he wants us to find joy. And though happiness may be acquired fairly easily, joy has a definite recipe. It has required ingredients that generally don't grow spontaneously on any tree or bubble up from untapped springs. The keys of joy have taught us that joy is within anyone's reach, but it does require effort, and humility, and sincerity, and intentionality. It requires looking outside of the small confines of our own heads and recognizing the beauty that comes from doing what we can to lift and love and lighten the burdens of others. It requires us to stop thinking small or shortsightedly and look to the future while focusing our efforts on the present. It requires letting go of disappointments, forgiving others and ourselves, and making each day better than the one before it.

"Each week as we teach these principles to couples of all ages who've been living their lives without some of the key ingredients of joy, we watch as lights turn on in hearts and heads when they recognize they've been impossibly trying to make joy with little more than the ingredients needed to make mudpies. Many have described this awakening as the biggest breakthrough they've ever experienced. Others call it a shot in the arm of pure enlightenment. However you choose to define it, this recognition has the power to change everything, to lift us to a higher plane of consciousness and to set us on a course bound for excellence, transcendence and self-mastery. And with that comes the realization of a much greater light being available to each one of us, if we'll only open the door and invite it in.

"Many of you know the story of the first owners of our home, James and Josephine Whitmore, but for those of you who don't, please let me share. James was a lumber baron, making much of his fortune before he was even thirty. To show off his success, he purchased forty acres of land just across the highway from the old Rutherford bridge and constructed a large mansion in the finest fashions of the era. He employed at least a dozen talented craftsmen to bring his vision to fruition: a stately home built largely of native river stone. At age thirty-one, he met and married Josephine, a spirited young woman of twenty-two, and the couple moved into what became known as the Whitmore Manor, living in the north wing while construction continued on the south wing.

"Four children joined the family over the next six years. With Mr. Whitmore often away on business, I imagine Josephine and the children spent their days enjoying the natural wonders all around them. But one night the peace and serenity of their surroundings came to an abrupt and definite end. That night, James arrived home earlier than planned from business in Pittsburgh. He was drunk and enraged and surprised his wife by pulling her from her bed and brutally rebuking her in front of her children and housemaids over some youthful indiscretions from her past. Apparently, James had learned of these indiscretions from a former classmate of Mrs. Whitmore, whom he'd met at a social club in the city. With sorrow and humility, she admitted the transgressions she'd long forsaken, but to no avail. Infuriated even more by her regretful admissions, he banished her to the south wing of the house, launching a civil war between them. Over the next several years, the war raged on, fought quite literally with the sticks and stones that held the house together until both the family and their home were destroyed.

"We learned of this sad story the weekend we purchased the remnants of their home. Of course, by then, more than a hundred years later, there was little left beyond a few strong walls, the remnants of a turret, and a decrepit stairway that led to the open air of the ruined second floor.

Nature had nearly completely reclaimed her, with a small forest of trees growing up through what was left of the rotted floorboards.

"Looking back now, we often wonder what could have possessed us to believe it had any hope at all. But that house, this community, the last few decades…they've all taught us an awful lot about life, its purposes, and the joy that can only come from enduring difficulties and rebuilding when things are broken.

"As I look out at all of you today, at our children and grandchildren, I feel like I'm catching a glimpse of the richness of eternity and the joys that can await each of us there. It's shocking to me to recognize that Tom and I could have missed out on all of this had we chosen to walk away rather than to sort through the rubble of our marriage and rebuild instead. None of us have to look very far to see the carnage that comes from not forgiving and avoiding working through the tough issues. Too often, in our efforts to dodge contention and heartache, we give up the fight, often plunging us into even deeper heartache.

"At this milestone of fifty years of marriage, Tom and I will both quickly admit that marriage has been the most challenging experience of our lives, but from this challenge have come the greatest joys we've ever known. It feels like that's the way life is—that we usually can't appreciate the value of the sweet without first experiencing that which is bitter. I've often wished this were not so, but that doesn't seem to be the way of either heaven or nature.

"The Greek writer, Aeschylus, once wrote, 'He who learns must suffer. And even in our sleep, pain that cannot forget falls drop by drop upon the heart, and in our own despair, against our will, comes wisdom to us by the awful grace of God.' In short, we suffer our way to wisdom. We see it every week: the wounds and hurt of those good men and women who come to us for help, believing, despite their pain, that there are answers to be had and battles worth fighting, and deeply seated hopes that love can prevail. My dear friends, let me confirm and testify that love can prevail! Tom and I have seen an endless supply of challenges in the couples we've served over the past forty-seven years of practice, and hundreds more of our own. There are surely reasons for divorce, but since learning the keys of joy, and teaching them to our clients, we've become convinced that there are very few problems that can't be avoided or overcome by the humble acquisition and practice of reverence, patience, hope, self-discipline, and charity. Few, if any of these, are found commonly or naturally in anyone. But as Paul shared in his first epistle to the Corinthians, "… the natural man receiveth not the things of the Spirit of God: for they are foolishness unto him: neither can he know them, because they are spiritually discerned.'[1]

"A client, from some years back, pointed out that in her Aramaic translation of the Bible, the reference to the *natural man* was actually translated to '*selfish man*.' I've thought about this at least a thousand times since then. We each have great possibilities for good, but each of us are at least as capable of great selfishness. The keys of joy have many opposites, but it's hard to think of any vice that would be more universally contrary to the keys of joy than is selfishness. As marriage therapists, we have come to recognize over our combined ninety-two years of experience that selfishness is at the root of all marital strife. For years we counseled couples about the need for good communication, financial integrity, and affectionate intimacy, without recognizing that selfishness can quickly steamroll decades worth of work, love and devotion, not to mention the trouble selfishness brings to the character of spirituality.

"As we've taught the keys of joy over these last two-and-a-half decades, we've watched every week as lights have turned on inside heads and hearts that have grown dark and disillusioned by the tarnish of disappointment and compounding acts of selfishness. There are few things as rewarding as watching hope and love return and begin to flow again between partners when the dams of selfishness have been removed and the stale, brackish backwater is allowed to drain. Without the boulders of selfishness to hedge up the way, even a basic understanding of the keys of joy invites hope and infinite potential to begin to flow again.

"As I mentioned earlier, Tom and I both come from a non-religious upbringing. We both grew up with the notion of a higher power being out there, somewhere, but the thought of that power being at all interested in our lives was completely foreign to either of us. Despite our lack of religiosity, there were always questions. These came and went throughout our lives as we raised our sons and looked for the meaning and purpose in life. A god without 'body, parts or passions', as the Council of Nicaea defined God, felt empty and indifferent, incapable of either love or concern. It wasn't until we found Niederbipp—or Niederbipp found us—that we discovered our missing piece.

"The first Sunday we attended church here, we listened to an elderly man share his convictions of the love of God. I remember well the quote he shared from St. Francis, 'You have made us for yourself, O Lord, and our hearts are restless until they rest in you.' That quote triggered in both Tom and me a renewal of a spiritual longing and a recognition that we were adrift and spiritually restless. We admitted to each other on our way home that afternoon that we were hungry for a community of faith—not just a calm, safe harbor where we could take shelter from the storms, but a regatta of excitement and possibility where we could raise our sails and enjoy the excitement of learning and stretching our sea legs through adventure on the open water.

"As John Augustus Shedd once said, 'A ship in harbor is safe, but that is not what ships are built for.'

"Tom and I have found both our harbor and our regatta in you. Our retreats, as many of you know, generally run from Saturday to Saturday, forty-five to forty-eight weeks a year. This makes it impossible for us to join with you every Sunday, but our hearts are never far from you. It brings us great satisfaction each Sunday to share with a smaller gathering, just a mile to the north, the simple truths perpetuated by the founders of this town. And it brings us great peace in knowing your door is always open to us, to gather here with you and enjoy the fruits of God's love and spirit as we check in with each other. God is indeed great, and we take seriously the charge we've been given by all of you and by the eternal author and finisher of the keys himself.

"In closing, I'd like to share a beautiful piece of wisdom that came to us through the hands of Ruby and Lorenzo Swarovski at the end of our first fortunate visit to their farm on Harmony Hill. It was given to us inside a hand-made fortune cookie, which we later learned they called Wisdom Cookies. And oh, what great wisdom it imparted to two lost souls who were hungry for light and hope and a better way. The paper inside the cookie read, 'What else does this craving, and this helplessness proclaim but that there was once in man a true happiness, of which all that now remains is the empty print and trace? This he tries in vain to fill with everything around him, seeking in things that are not there the help he cannot find in those that are, though none can help, since this infinite abyss can be filled only with an infinite and immutable object; in other words, by God himself.'

"Those words, drawn from Blaise Pascal's, *Pensées Number Seven*, helped us to know that this holy longing was not unique to us, but part of the human condition—a seed planted deep within each soul that waits for the time and circumstance when selfishness gives way to humility, creating space for growth to become possible.

"We are grateful for each of you who've loved us and encouraged us over these past twenty-six years. We are grateful for an angel of a man, Isaac Bingham, who witnessed, first-hand, the direction we were heading and stepped in, as all good Niederbippians are quick to do, to help us avoid a cataclysmic disaster. Most of the greatest joys we know have been on this side of that great divide, and the rest have been enhanced by the understanding of life's purposes we've gained through exercising the keys of joy. Our only regret is that we didn't learn these things earlier so our children might have enjoyed a more stable and secure upbringing. But no matter where one is on life's highway, we've discovered that the keys of joy, when practiced and embraced with humility and sincerity, have the ability to bless and enhance every aspect of life. Though we lived our first nearly-fifty years without them, our grandchildren have grown up with their influence. Our sons each embraced them when they witnessed what they did for Tom and me, and they each found wonderful partners who recognized the moral strength and stability their practice of the keys promoted in each of them."

Emma stood up straight, looking strong and bold and at least ten years younger than most women her age as she smiled at the congregation. She extended her hands to Tom who stood from his front row seat and walked to his wife at the podium.

He wrapped his arm around her waist and kissed her on the cheek before turning to smile at the congregation. "Thank you!" he said. "Thank you for loving and embracing us. Our lives have been blessed by knowing and loving you. If we could live to celebrate another fifty years of marriage, we'd want to do it right here with all of you."

Emma nodded and smiled even broader than before. "I'd be more than happy with twenty more good years."

"Me, too," Tom responded, "but for now, we'd love to have you join us this afternoon for a simple celebration of our inaugural Sourdough Sunday at one o'clock. Jake and Amy Kimball have graciously agreed to help us establish our own Chapter dedicated to the breaking of bread while they're getting their feet back under them after Baby Isaac's arrival. Everyone is welcome; come as you are and bring a friend."

Notes

1. 1 Corinthians 2:14

מייחה צע

CHAPTER 146

מייחה צע

I can see how it might be possible for a man to look down
upon the earth and be an atheist,
but I cannot conceive how a man could look up into the
heavens and say there is no God.
—Abraham Lincoln—

The congregation rose to sing the closing hymn as Tom and Emma made their way back to their seats. Before turning around, Emma glanced at Genevieve, a quick flash of connection registering over her face. After the first verse, Emma looked over her shoulder and offered Genevieve a warm smile. Curious, Genevieve returned the greeting with a smile of her own.

"Are you Genevieve Patterson?" Emma whispered as the congregation sat back down.

Genevieve nodded.

"I think we have some things to talk about, don't we?" Emma winked, turning back around as a middle-aged woman approached the pulpit to offer a benediction.

At the echoed utterance of 'Amen,' Emma turned back again. "I hope you'll come this afternoon. I'd love to catch a minute with you if you're available."

Genevieve turned to Matt, who nodded. "I think we'd like that."

Emma smiled as Tom turned to face them both. "We've been excited to meet you ever since we heard the good news," he managed before the congregation overtook them in a rush of joyful salutations.

"We'll look forward to talking to you later," Emma said over her shoulder as she offered a young woman a side hug.

"We'll be there," Matt assured her.

"Can we come with you?" Holly asked, turning to Matt and Genevieve.

"I hope you will," Matt responded. "It sounds like a cool place that everyone should check out."

"That's what I was thinking," Ephraim said. "I'll go tell the others. I know they were talking about visiting that tree down on the riverbank."

"*On a Sunday?*" Genevieve asked, looking concerned.

"Is that a problem?" asked Ephraim.

"No…not exactly. But I know at least one person who has a standing appointment at the tree, every Sunday after church."

"What time?" asked Greg.

"I'm not sure, but I do know she walks slower than you do. If you hurry, you could probably beat her."

"You guys don't want to come?" asked Holly.

"Oh…uh, sure," Genevieve said after glancing quickly at Matt. "Let's go."

They met the other campers in the courtyard. After bidding farewell to Pops and Ruby, who had reluctantly decided a quiet afternoon would be best for their constitutions, all twelve campers descended the stairs of the courtyard, following close behind Matt and Genevieve as they speed-walked out of town.

"I'm gonna miss this place," Susan said as they approached the highway and were met by the glorious vista of the forested hills on the other side of the river, the first hints of fall colors randomly scattered across the hillside.

"What if we just stayed here?" Josh asked as they crossed the road.

"What do you mean?" Sonja asked.

"Well, you know…what if we just didn't leave at the end of the summer. We could just…I don't know…help Matt and Genevieve on the farm through the winter and then build a commune or something. It would be fun, right?"

"Yeah, it would be super fun," Greg responded as they walked past the Englehart Ebenezer, "but…that's not really why we came."

Many of the campers turned to Greg with sour faces.

"No offense," he responded, holding out his hands as if to protect himself. "I love you guys, and if there was nothing better to do than hang out together in a commune for the rest of our lives, I'd be totally in. But… but we know better than that now, right? We know there's something better than this, don't we?"

Many of them nodded.

"So what if we just got back together every couple of years with our husbands and wives and had a chance to catch up? Maybe go camping, or meet in Europe, or find a kibbutz somewhere and just spend a week loving each other," Josh suggested.

"I really can't believe I'm saying this, but I'm in," James replied, "that is, if Crystal will join me."

"Yeah, I guess you guys are okay," Crystal responded in a whiny

Jersey accent that got them all laughing as they moved together like a twelve-man Chinese dragon, winding their way over the narrow path, Genevieve leading the way.

"Do you think we'll ever be able to make friendships like we have this summer?" Sonja asked.

"I've been wondering the same thing," Greg responded. "It's been amazing to me to watch the twelve of us, who have little more in common than the fact that we're all single, come together to create something unlike anything I've ever experienced before. I want to thank you guys for that. I came here with zero confidence that this was going to be fun and look at us! We're practically family."

"Uh, I don't know what kind of family you came from, but this is way better than my very best family gatherings," Crystal replied.

"Me, too," Susan agreed.

"Me, three," said Josh.

Many of the others nodded as they continued to walk.

"You said that old lady comes all the way out here every Sunday?" Spencer asked doubtfully.

Genevieve laughed, turning around as she continued to walk backwards. "That old lady happens to have a name—Hildegard. And yes, every Sunday, as far as I know."

"Why? It's kind of a long way, especially for a lady as old as she is," responded Sonja.

"I've been thinking about it, and I wonder if her jaunts out here have anything to do with self-discipline," Genevieve responded.

"Self-discipline? Really? Maybe she just likes to go on long walks," Sonja suggested.

"I guess I don't know for sure, but there seems to be a deliberate, thoughtful purpose behind what a lot of folks do around here, right?" Genevieve replied. "Look at Ruby for example. I don't know many people who, at ninety-plus years old, are still as physically active as she is."

"You almost make it sound like you know a lot of nonagenarians," James responded.

"*Nonagenarians*? Bro, you don't have to make up words to make yourself sound smart," Spencer replied.

"Uhh, that's actually a real word, Spencer," Susan retorted. "And it means someone who's in their nineties."

"Oh," Spencer uttered. "My bad."

"No, I guess I don't know many *nonagenarians*," Genevieve continued, smiling at the friendly banter, "but there are several old folks around here, and you don't see any of them buzzing around on electric wheelchairs or scooters, or sitting around, waiting to die."

"I've noticed the same thing," said Rachael. "And you may have also noticed there aren't many chubby folks around here either, and the ones who are usually tourists."

"Yeah, I have noticed that. I've been thinking that might have something to do with the whole self-discipline thing, too," Genevieve replied.

"What's with the self-discipline kick?" asked James.

"Just…finding connections," Genevieve answered.

"What kind of connections?" asked Holly.

"Just small stuff, mostly—stuff you might miss if you weren't paying attention. Hildegard told us herself that this tree is her favorite place to be still. She's in her late nineties and could for sure find stillness much closer to home, but I get the feeling she comes out here very deliberately, and not just because it's beautiful. Ruby still climbs the stairs in the big house at least a couple of times each day, and she and Pops go on walks most afternoons. Very few of the locals around here are carrying around any more than a few extra pounds, and most of those are over sixty. You don't see anyone living in a McMansion, or driving fancy cars, or trying to show off their wealth, if they have any. As far as I can tell, you don't see anyone trying to keep up with the Joneses. I guess I'm just making connections between the keys of joy these people profess to live by and the way they actually live. It seems like these ideas permeate everything they do and the way they live their lives. It's kind of refreshing, don't you think? Even the oldest folks around here are engaged in life. They've got purpose and passion, and they're enjoying life rather than just crossing days off the calendar."

"I've never thought about that, but my grandparents moved to a one-level house in the suburbs when they retired so they wouldn't have to climb stairs," Ephraim reported. "They immediately got a guy to mow their lawn, and it wasn't more than a year later that they bought matching Jazzy scooters and started driving their dog around the block when he needed a walk."

"Pfff, and I'm sure the next thing you're going to say is that they both got fat and died," James responded sarcastically.

Ephraim didn't respond for a moment. "Actually, that's almost exactly what happened. They both ended up with diabetes and were dead before they were even seventy-five."

"*What?*" Josh asked.

"Yeah," Ephraim said, slowing down his pace as he thought about it. "I'm sure there were other things too…I mean they were both heavy smokers when I was a kid, and they definitely drank too much throughout their lives, but…yeah… I can't believe I've never connected these dots before."

"What dots are you talking about?" asked Rachael.

"They stopped climbing stairs, bought a rambler in the suburbs, and not only did they never climb stairs again, they basically stopped walking, stopped cooking, started eating TV dinners, gained some weight, and…and they basically gave up on life."

"Well, kids, just remember, it all starts heading south when you stop climbing stairs," James responded with a little laugh, but no one joined him. Even Crystal rolled her eyes and shook her head.

"We've all heard Pops and Ruby talking about how all their contemporaries are dead," Susan added. "I think there's probably a bigger connection to what Ephraim and Genevieve are saying than any of us have seen. Working the farm all these years has been a lot of hard work for Pops and Ruby, but is there any one of us who hasn't lost weight or inches or both? Is there any one of us who isn't in the best shape of their lives?"

"I'm probably down close to twenty pounds," Sonja admitted, "and that despite the fact that I've been eating bread every day for the last four months."

Rachael nodded, "I've never felt stronger, and none of us has been to the gym in four months. How long do you think that can last when we go home?"

"Did you ever like going to the gym?" Spencer asked.

She shrugged. "Not really, but I felt like I had to go?"

"Why?"

"Because I…I didn't want to get fat. And peer pressure. And it was basically my only social interaction."

Spencer nodded. "So, I've been thinking about all of this for at least a month, but what if it was all a lie?"

"Which part?" asked Holly.

"All of it. Everything! What if our whole lives have just been lies? I doubt if any of us really enjoyed going to the gym or working out, but we did it because we were *afraid*…We worked jobs we didn't enjoy because we were afraid of quitting and following our dreams. We hung out with people we didn't like because we were afraid of loneliness. We for sure all did a long list of things we didn't really want to do just because we were afraid of this or that. And in the meantime, we missed out on doing the things we really wanted to do because we were afraid of failing, or losing, or dying alone. It's almost like we subliminally think that life's supposed to suck, and so we've all bought into this crazy self-fulfilling prophecy to make it suck. And then we come here and everything gets turned on its head, and suddenly our jobs aren't as sexy as we thought they were, and friendships we've endured for years feel suddenly shallow and meaningless, and we eat bread and actually lose weight, and we get around on crappy, antique bicycles with zero suspension, and we're somehow having at least as much fun as we did when we were kids. And it costs us basically nothing, and we're all happy and mentally balanced despite the fact that none of us have been to our therapists for months, and to my knowledge, none of us are on antidepressants. And yet we're still having fun playing shop at the farm stand, where we spend a whole day working to make less than we used to spend on lunch. And somehow we're happier than we've been in years! I'm with Josh. Why don't we just stay here and keep doing more of this?"

Many of the campers nodded, confused by emotions Spencer's words evoked.

"Because that's not why you came," a small but strong voice came from behind them.

They all turned to see Hildegard, leaning on her cane, a crooked smile spread across her face.

"How long have you been here?" Genevieve asked.

"Long enough to know that none of you wants to go home."

"No, why would we? Life's better here," Josh replied.

Hildegard shook her head and walked forward, the campers parting to let her through as she walked right up to Josh and looked up into his surprised face. "You didn't come here to stay. You came here to get yourself ready for the greatest adventure of your life. If you give up now, you'll be wasting all the effort and all the beautiful changes that have come into your lives. You can't give up now, before you even put these truths and changes to the test."

"Why not? What if I've changed my mind? What if I don't really want to get married after all? What if life is better just doing this?"

Hildegard laughed. She shook her head and laughed some more.

"What's so funny?"

"Are you a man or a mouse?"

"Huh?"

"You heard me. Are you a man or a mouse?"

"I'm a man."

"Then stop thinking like a mouse." She pivoted slowly on her cane, peering scrutinizingly at each of them. "Do you really think any of you would truly be happy here?"

"Well, yeah, we're pretty happy here now," Spencer said as several of the campers nodded.

"Of course you are. Why wouldn't you be? Your lives are uncomplicated, you've got minimal responsibilities, you don't have bills or jobs or anything that makes life difficult."

"Right! Why would I want any of that when I could have this, and be happy?" Josh asked.

Hildegard smiled but shook her head. She shuffled forward, the campers making way for her as she continued along the path out ahead of them. The campers looked at each other, wondering what was going on.

"Well, are you coming with me or are you going to stand there like a herd of mice?" Hildegard asked over her shoulder.

"Would you like us to come?" Matt asked.

"You might as well. You've got nothing better to do until one o'clock, and you're talking like your brains have been starved of oxygen."

They followed in silence, glancing at each other contritely as if they'd all been smacked upside the head by the stern hand of reality. She continued on at a surprisingly quick pace for one as old and bent as she was. In another hundred yards, Hildegard turned off the main trail and onto the perpendicular path that led straight into the low-hanging branches of the splendid willow. With the tip of her cane, she parted the dangling branches and entered the canopy, the campers following close behind, silently gazing in awe at their surroundings until the last of them had entered and the veil of branches had closed behind them.

Genevieve took Matt's hand as they watched the campers experiencing the magic of this place for the very first time, their eyes lifted to the dark canopy above, illuminated by the dancing, bedazzled flashes of light reflecting off the river's rippled surface. Like spellbound children, they silently gazed as their eyes adjusted to the vision before them, serenaded by the gentle purr of the river as the draping branches skipped and skittered across her surface.

"What is this place?" Greg whispered reverently, breaking the silence.

"This is Hildegard's temple," Matt responded.

"No," Hildegard said, shaking her head. "This is God's temple. I just come here to check my alignment and discover the answers God is willing to share with me."

"Hey, it says *Be still and know that I am God* here on this branch," James said, looking up from the river's edge.

Hildegard nodded. "That great secret and invitation should be familiar to all of you by now."

Many of them turned toward James, his finger tracing the letters carved into the low branch.

"It's tempting to want to stay here forever, isn't it?" Hildegard asked, her eyes turned to the green canopy, scanning the sacred space.

"Why can't we?" asked Spencer. "What's wrong with wanting to make Niederbipp our home?"

"It's a common question. I'm sure I've heard it every year from campers just like you for the past eighty years. In order to understand why you can't stay, you need to ask yourself, 'Why do I want to stay?'"

"Isn't that obvious? I want to stay because it's peaceful and beautiful, and I feel alive here," Spencer answered.

Hildegard smiled. "Yes, it is indeed all of those things. I'm glad that you see it. Some of you recognized all of that right away. For others of you, it took a little longer. And every week there are tourists who walk around this town moaning and complaining that this is not at all what their friends told them it would be. I don't know what those folks came expecting to see, but it's certainly some other definition of 'peaceful' and 'beautiful'. Most folks see it. But there are still plenty of folks who miss out on the beauty you've all seen because there aren't enough restaurant choices, or the cobblestones aren't as smooth as the pavement back home, or there's not a bar to be found in the whole darn county. Can you imagine missing the beauty of all of this because there's no bar?" She smiled again and shook her head. "Believe it or not, there are places like Niederbipp in every community. Sure, they may not have the same physical charms, but they radiate with the same energy and goodness."

"I've never found anything like this before," Spencer argued. "I've been in at least forty states and I've never…"

"Ahh, but were you looking?" Hildegard asked, cutting him off. "Were you looking into the eyes of the people you encountered? Were you opening your heart to them and allowing yourself to be vulnerable as you've done here this summer? Or were you too busy to see, to watch, to connect? Were you looking for this, or were you looking for a place to numb your senses or fog your brains in an effort to relax or unplug from the unpleasant reality you'd surrounded yourself with?"

She waited a moment for her words to sink in. "Those who stay in Niederbipp never stay without a purpose. That's what makes Niederbipp special."

"I don't understand," James replied.

"No, and you won't until you've come to the joyful place of recognizing that there's more to life than satisfying your own pleasure sensors. You've learned much of that over these last four months, about the joys that come from truly connecting with others when there's nothing more than honest friendship as a reward. If you're honest with yourselves, you'll recognize that too many years of your life have been focused on feeding your egos and the dopamine surges that come from advancing your selfish intentions. I'd wager that what you most love about Niederbipp is that it's been a break from all those things. And the break in the monotony of your lives has allowed the fog to dissipate, allowing you to see clearly—perhaps for the first time in your lives.

"If you're honest with yourself, you'll recognize that before you came here, your life was largely about the meaningless accumulation of everything that the world sees as success. You wanted fancy clothes and cars and vacations. And most of that wasn't just about having it per se. It was about having more of it than your friends and neighbors. But you were never satisfied, were you? It was never enough. It never could be."

Josh nodded. "Why is that?"

"Because there is no *thing* that can possibly enhance the beauty and richness of the soul. You each heard Emma's sermon today. She's spent most of her life guiding individuals and couples through the landmines of life in their quest for happiness and balance. You heard what she said about our selfish natures standing in the way of us coming to an understanding of our best natures."

Many of the campers nodded.

"Over these last four months, you've discovered you need none of those things you left behind in order to be happy. For many of you, you've spent years feathering your nests with things that have only crowded and complicated it, things that add neither happiness nor peace to your lives. And then you come here with little more than a swimsuit and some toiletries. You're handed a small stack of second-hand farm duds, and you spend your days doing physical work you've never done before, completely isolated from your phones and computers and the frantic life you left behind. But instead of being lost, you've actually found yourself. Instead of being distracted by meaningless things, you've never been more focused on the things of great meaning. Instead of feasting on the soulless pleasures of the flesh, you've fed your spirits on the simple, free, beautiful truths that can only be perceived and valued by a meek and humble heart."

"Right, so why wouldn't we want to stay here?" Sonja asked.

"Oh, don't get me wrong, I can understand why you *would* want to stay, but that's not why you came."

"Well, isn't hanging out here at least as meaningful a purpose?" Ephraim asked.

Hildegard smiled but shook her head. "What was it that Emma said about ships?"

The campers looked at each other for the answer until all eyes fell on Matt, who squirmed under their gaze.

He opened his journal to the page where his pen occupied the gutter. "Are you asking about the quote from John Augustus Shedd?"

Hildegard nodded affirmatively.

"I believe it was, 'A ship in harbor is safe, but that is not what ships are built for.'"

"Very good. I'm glad to see at least one of you listened." She smiled warmly at the others. "At the close of every summer, I hear grumblings among the Ruby's campers as they contemplate returning to the lives they left behind. Of course, there is fear of losing this," she said, motioning to the group. "There is fear that it will never be the same."

"Aren't those fears reasonable?" asked Susan.

"Yes, of course they are. Once you leave Niederbipp, it will never be the same."

The campers looked at one another sideways as if they were wondering what bit of bad news was coming next.

"Staying might delay the change for a week or two, but change is as inevitable as the ocean's tides. There've been many campers like yourselves who've tried to extend their summer here, but it never lasts long."

"Why not?" asked Josh.

"Because you can't continue on in anything indefinitely. It's contrary to all the laws of nature. The Good Book says, 'There's a time and a season for every purpose under heaven.'₁ Your season for working the farm on Harmony Hill is quickly coming to a close, but life must go on, and there are plenty of beautiful, lovely seasons yet to come. You wouldn't want to miss out on those—there are far too many good things and good seasons yet to come."

"I don't know if anything can be better than this," Sonja suggested.

Hildegard thought about it for a moment before nodding her head. "Then I would suggest that you're either lacking ambition or imagination."

"Really?" Sonja challenged. "Has every season of your life been better than the one before it?"

Hildegard shook her head. "I'd be lying if I said that it was, but I don't believe every season needs to be better than the one before it in order for it to be good. We need winters to fully appreciate the spring. We need spring to prepare us for summers. And without autumn, winter would be a mighty big shock to the system. We can learn much from watching nature and observing the cycles of life. These observations can prepare us well for the coming season, helping us accept and embrace inevitable changes that come to each of us. This is why I come to this tree often, nine months out of the year, to drink deeply and fill my mental and spiritual canteen with memories I can treasure when the cold and snow prevent me from coming here physically each Sunday."

"I can't imagine this place being anywhere near as beautiful in the winter," James suggested, looking up at the green canopy overhead.

Hildegard nodded. "No, it's not, but then I suppose it's never exactly the same way twice, even from week to week. We must learn from the past so we can fully live in the present while we dream of the future. Your future, the one you've been waiting your whole lives for, the one that brought you here this summer, won't officially begin until you're on your way home and the realities of life rest upon your shoulders once again."

"Uh, yeah, I think that whole weight on our shoulders thing…that's what we're trying to avoid," Spencer reported.

"Ahh yes, avoidance…" She shook her head. "What is it they say about that? Oh, yes, I think it begins with, 'You can run, but reality will always find you'."

"Ughhh," many of the campers groaned in unison.

"Oh, come on, it'll be fun!"

"Easy for you to say. You've spent most of your life here. How come you got to stay?" Rachael asked.

"Well, to make a long story short, I never intended to stay, but this is where God planted me. I came from Germany as a teenager between the two World Wars, one of just a small handful of Jews in a Quaker town. I married a few years later, but my husband was killed in Europe before we could celebrate our first anniversary. I stayed because this was my home. But I've also stayed, very deliberately, because of joy. I stayed because I needed to meet all of you…you and eighty years' worth of campers and tourists who've washed up on the shores of Niederbipp with questions I knew the answers for, or at least, where to find them.

"So...this is your job?" Holly asked.

Hildegard shook her head. "I taught school, full-time, for nearly fifty years. Once you spend fifty years doing anything you love, it's difficult to not find a way to keep doing it in some manner. The subjects are different, but the work is much the same...to help young people—and those whose hearts are young enough to listen and learn. I've discovered that if you're really lucky, and your life is long, and you have no trouble forgetting all the nonsense about minding your own business...then you get to spend your life helping people open their eyes and hearts to the most important truths in life."

"I wouldn't mind doing that...maybe," James said, looking a little uncertain.

"And we all hope you will, in your own way, wherever you land," Hildegard replied.

"But Genevieve and Matt get to stay!" protested Josh.

"Yes, and what a rare case they are! Once every five decades or so, a new matchmaker is chosen to run the farm on Harmony Hill. Genevieve will be only the third matchmaker I've known over my eighty years in Niederbipp."

"But why can't we stay, too?" Crystal asked. "James and I are getting married the week after Genevieve and Matt. Why can't we just find a cozy home right in town somewhere?"

"Uh, Babe, as much as I'd love that," James responded quickly, "I can't imagine there being many folks around here who could afford my hourly fees."

"Okay, but we could...or...but...pfffff."

Hildegard offered Crystal a warm, knowing smile. "Love is why you came here. You were looking for it. Each of you was hungry for it. If you've already found what you're looking for, congratulations! If you haven't, but you've learned to let go of your selfishness, and you leave here practicing the keys of joy, love will certainly find you."

"How can you be sure of that?" Holly asked.

"It's one of the most basic but often forgotten laws of nature. Light is attracted to light. Love is attracted to love. Joy is drawn to joy. If you put those things out into the universe, that's what will come back to you."

"I've heard of that before, but isn't that some sort of New Age Mumbo Jumbo?" James asked.

"Oh, it's been adopted over the years by all sorts of folks who speak 'Mumbo Jumbo' but it was part of the keys of joy for millennia before they found it."

"I'm starting to wonder if the keys of joy hold the promise of solving all the world's problems," Ephraim suggested.

"Surely they do."

"But if that's true, why don't more people know about them?" asked Susan.

"Because most people don't want the answers to be so simple."

"Why not? Isn't that counterintuitive?" asked Rachael.

"Oh, I suppose it is. I believe most people want easy answers, until those answers require them to look inward and remodel their own soul. Most of us would much rather blame others than take an honest look at who we are and mend ourselves. The world has plenty of angry, bitter folks who've pushed the blame of their unhappiness onto the ignorant, incompetent, boorish fools that surround them."

"Uh, yeah, I totally get that," James admitted.

"And what have you learned about that line of thinking over the last four months?"

James took a moment, looking into each of their faces and then down at his own feet before responding. "I guess I've learned that all the world will be ignorant and incompetent until I set aside my own selfishness and open my heart to love."

Hildegard nodded slowly. "Very good. If that's the only thing you learn this summer, your time here will have been well spent. But there's always more light to be accumulated and more love to be shared."

"And that last part…that's what you've been about these last eighty years?" Genevieve asked.

"I'd like to say yes, but it took some time to discover my calling in life. I was a young widow when the war ended. I was a foreigner, a German Jew, and a hot-headed young woman who believed the world owed me something for my troubles. Of course that was foolishness. No matter your lot in life, the world owes you nothing, and joy can never be yours if you're bent on waiting for it to be delivered to you."

Holly nodded thoughtfully. "Because that's against the law of attraction?"

"Yes, but if you think about it, you'll discover it's also contrary to every single one of the keys of joy."

"Because it's selfishness…?" Crystal mused.

"Yes! Do you see it?"

Several of the campers nodded slowly.

"We each have the ability to attract either light or darkness by what we think about and how we act. It's easy to wallow in the mud bogs of selfishness and cover one's self with the dark, cold lather of self-pity. But there are neither answers nor solutions to be found there. I discovered for myself, as all survivors do who find light, that if I wanted joy, I had to step far away from both selfishness and self-pity, and turn my face to the light of hope. That's where it began for me—seeing others who'd experienced pain and loss but who'd somehow found a way to smile and spread light instead of anguish and hopelessness. My life began to change with that realization. Reverence came next for me, enhancing my hope with each step toward the light and awe I experienced in turning my face back to the golden light of God's perfect love. Charity became easy for me after that as I recognized it wasn't enough to simply feel God's love; I needed to share it."

"And patience and self-discipline?" Holly asked.

"Honestly, I'm still working on both, but the more I do, the more I recognize they're both byproducts of one's faithful exercise of the first three keys."

"And the first three..." Matt mused, "...each of them is an antidote to selfishness, aren't they?"

Hildegard smiled and nodded. "The first three help us recognize the purpose and benefit of the journey, while patience and self-discipline help us remember that the work of overcoming selfishness doesn't stop until we've taken our last breath."

"Pfff..." James responded with exasperation.

"Before you allow yourself to get discouraged," Hildegard responded, "I want you each to recognize how far you've come in just four short months. When you arrived, your lives were all about you! You were twelve separate islands surrounded by a prickly reef of self-interest. Over these four months, as you've learned eternal truths and recognized both your weaknesses and your strengths, you've allowed yourselves to gravitate toward each other. In the process, you've developed unity and harmony until that prickly reef of self-interest that separated you has been mostly broken down by friendship and love, and even further evaporated by the bright light of joy. Selfishness has given way to charity."

James nodded. "You're right. We have come a long way. But I really can't imagine ever being like Ruby and Pops."

"No, that's hard to imagine when you're just four months into a new life, isn't it? But remember that fifty-seven summers ago, Pops and Ruby were each struggling to overcome their selfishness and make sense of the keys of joy. Patience is its own key for a reason. It's one of the biggest struggles of human nature, but its rewards are limitless for those who embrace its commitments and continually work on it. And self-discipline...just imagine how refined each of you could become over the course of the next fifty to sixty years if you stick with this and continue to progress toward joy."

"I'm beginning to feel like this whole joy thing is a total lifestyle change for the rest of our lives," Sonja suggested.

"In some ways, I suppose it is."

"Isn't it? In every way?" James asked, looking overwhelmed.

"It all depends on who and where you are when you begin this journey. If selfishness has been your general rule of thumb, you will likely have a few more laps or extra conditioning to get yourself moving in the right direction. But for most of us, it requires only a change in mentality and attitude, at least in the beginning."

"What kind of change?" Crystal asked, looking fearful.

"Oh, don't worry. You've already been immersed in the process and many of you have already initiated the change of heart."

"How can you be sure?" Greg asked.

"Because no one can endure even a month on Harmony Hill without it changing you and your attitudes and pointing you toward the greater paths of joy. It's always a pleasure to watch that change as twelve unique and independent souls begin to move and think with a more expansive consideration of the world and the people around them. They begin to see, as each of you have, the interconnectedness of humanity. Independence becomes far less important or attractive than being a strong and inclusive team player who's willing to be vulnerable and humble for the sake of unity."

"But doesn't that get scary?" Susan asked. "What about losing your identity or forgetting who you are?"

Hildegard nodded. "I suppose, to an extent, you're asking the wrong person. I'm a widow who never had to contend with either my spouse or children to maintain some portions of my independence. But I'm a Jewish woman living in a Christian community. If I was focused on our differences and my need for autonomy, I might have lost my mind in a community as small and tight knit as Niederbipp. But I learned long ago that there's far more that unites me with these and all the people of the earth than there is that divides any of us. I don't know if there's a person on earth who's capable of producing more goodness on her own than she could with a handful of trusted neighbors and friends."

"I guess that's still part of my challenge—trust," Susan admitted. "How are you supposed to get past that?"

"How have *you* gotten past that?"

Susan looked thoughtful for a moment, her face quickly brightening as Genevieve and Holly stood next to her on either side and put their arms around her. She turned to each of them, looking surprised by the emotion their small act of kindness and connection triggered.

"Trust, like most good things in life," Hildegard continued, "grows over time, and often requires us to set aside our fears and biases to allow love to prevail. Some will likely disappoint us, but one of the biggest mistakes in life is trusting no one out of fear of being disappointed or hurt by everyone. I may be naive, but I believe most people have a desire to trust and be trusted—to love and be loved. It's in our nature to want to form trusting, ennobling, loving connections. Without those connections, life, for all but the most introverted, is shallow, unfulfilling and lonely."

"But living by the keys of joy could help with all of those things, right?" Matt asked.

Hildegard smiled as she turned to him. "Can you think of any challenge or problem that could not be helped if not altogether eliminated through the widespread application of the keys of joy?"

The campers looked at each other, but no one spoke, each of them searching their minds unsuccessfully for outliers.

Hildegard shook her head. "You could think about that question all day long and not come up with an answer."

"So why don't more people know about this?" asked Ephraim.

"Oh, I think most people do, they've just forgotten."

"You think so?" Josh responded, looking confused.

Hildegard nodded. "Let me ask you this, were any of the keys completely foreign to you?"

"Uh, yeah, I can't say I'd ever heard of them before coming here."

"Maybe not all together, and they've probably never been individually presented to you as keys to anything before. But didn't they make sense and ring true to you as you learned the name of each one?"

The campers looked at each other, many of them nodding.

"They make sense, but I can't say any of them feel natural to me," Crystal replied.

"They may not feel natural to you at this point in your life, but I've witnessed some portion of each of the five keys in the children I taught in school and the younger children I've watched throughout my life. There is, in the innocence of youth, a more natural propensity toward all of the keys. But things begin to change as innocence is lost and our connections to our better selves become clouded by our egotism and pride. Without an intentional, deliberate effort to maintain the keys and keep them shining bright, they will tarnish and rust and become lost in our ignorant pursuit of counterfeit treasures, immediate gratifications, and other shallowly sparkly things."

"Hmmm...so, when one has lost his connections to the real treasure, how does one go about finding it again?" Spencer asked humbly.

Hildegard nodded, looking up into the grey-green canopy overhead, the river's bedazzling reflections still dancing through the branches. "I suppose we each have to find our own way back, don't we? The timing and the details will be different for everyone, but I've noticed that if I'm going the right direction, there will be Ebenezers to help mark the right path."

"Ebenezers? Are you talking about those stacks of rocks? Like the one we passed on the way here...and one on the farm?" Josh asked, looking confused.

Hildegard nodded. "Yes, but you should know that not all Ebenezers are literally made of rocks."

"What? Sonja asked. "Isn't that what an Ebenezer is? I read in Thomas's book that Ebenezer means *stone of help*. Isn't that why the Engleharts built their Ebenezer...to remind future generations of the faith of the founders of this town?"

"I'm glad to see you've been doing your homework. What else do you know?"

Sonja shrugged. "I don't think I know anything else about it."

"Many beautiful truths are lost over time as practices and fashions change. My people—the people of Judah and Israel—have a long history of preserving, in both written and oral stories, their most valuable truths. The *stone of help* that the Prophet Samuel caused to be raised as a memorial to God has much deeper meaning than the stone itself. To my knowledge, Ebenezer also referred to two people."

"Who?" Susan asked.

"The first was the first woman, Eve, the crowning creation, and helpmeet to the first man, Adam."

"Helpmeet?" James asked.

"That's right. A companion and partner who was neither subordinate, nor superior, but did for man something he could never do for himself—offer, through her partnership, a perpetuation of life."

"And who was the second?" asked Greg.

"YHWH, otherwise known in English as Jehovah."

"And YHWH…Jehovah…that's the Hebrew name of God, right?" Matt asked.

"That's right."

Matt glanced at Genevieve before opening his journal once again, flipping to the first few pages to the crude sketch of a house perched on a rock above billowing waves. "Remember talking about this at dinner, a few months ago?" he asked as the campers gathered around him. Many of them read over his notes about the wise man and the foolish man and the diverse locations of their real estate ventures. At the bottom of the two-page spread, Matt had written in block letters, "Jesus Christ is the rock!"

Matt looked up at Hildegard who met his gaze with a smile and a nod.

"But…you're a Jew, aren't you?" Josh asked.

"Born a Jew, always a Jew," she responded.

"But you also believe in Jesus Christ?" Josh pressed.

She nodded. "You cannot live among good Christians in a town like Niederbipp without them rubbing off on you. There are certainly Jews who'll argue with me and tell me I've lost my way, perhaps call me a Mumar or even a Gentile, but we must each find our truth."

"And you found it in Christianity?" Josh continued.

She nodded, looking closely at his face for a moment. "You look like you could also be a Yehudi, eh?"

Josh smiled. "Half-Yehudi, half-Gentile."

She reached out her hand and took his. "Shalom."

"Shalom aleichem," he replied, offering her a genuine smile.

"Sehr gut!" she responded. "I'm glad you're here."

"Why do you say that?" he asked awkwardly.

"Because a man of your background could use some hope…hope and fertile ground for the seedlings of faith to take root."

He laughed. "You can say that again. Actually, I think I've found quite a lot of that already."

"I'd suspect that you would. You can't spend much time here without it rubbing off on you."

"No…I…I know that's true. Honestly, I never imagined I'd find God at all."

"Why not?"

Josh shrugged. "I've spent a lot of years either cursing God or ignoring him, and the rest of my life pretending to be apathetic about all religion. It just didn't feel like it mattered, and my life was uncomplicated without it, or so I thought."

Hildegard nodded, not taking her eyes off him. "And how do you feel now?"

Josh looked from side to side into the faces of his fellow campers. "And now I realize I wasted a lot of time."

She nodded knowingly. "You found Him, didn't you?"

He nodded. "I think it was actually *He* who found me."

"Oh, yes. Well…He always knew where you were, didn't He?"

Josh looked surprised.

Hildegard nodded. "To Him, we are never lost. It's only we who go wandering down divergent paths, searching for our own ways. But God is never far. I like to imagine Him as a loving parent who recognizes our need to stretch and prove our wings, as He anxiously awaits our return to the paradise and the love we've left behind."

"And this is where this comes in, right?" Matt asked, holding open his journal once again to the sketch of the house on the rock.

Hildegard looked down at the sketch and nodded. "My people have been waiting for the Messiah since the time Abraham left the idolatry of his father's faith and wandered into the wilderness, determined to worship the one true God. Though the Messiah's birth was prophesied by Abraham's children for thousands of years, when He arrived as a vulnerable child, my people rejected Him. They didn't want a child or a peacemaker. They wanted a warrior—a captain of warriors, who would help them overpower and overcome their enemies, and help them reclaim their birthright." She shook her head. "I suppose when you're being governed and taxed by the heavy hand of the Roman Empire, the last thing you want is a peaceful Messiah; one who encourages you to forgive and even pray for your enemies, and to turn the other cheek.

"I suppose my people are not unlike the rest of the world today, who, if they want a God at all, they want him to yield to *their* will, rather than the other way around. But from the time Elohim and JHWH made covenants with Abraham, there remains a birthright and a promise that's available to all of us. If we build upon that rock," she said, pointing her crooked finger at Matt's sketch, "we will not fall when the rains and winds beat upon our houses."

"You believe that?" Josh asked earnestly.

She shook her head. "After more than nine-and-a-half decades, I *know* that. My exercise of reverence has transformed my faith into knowledge."

As Matt looked down at the old woman's finger, firmly planted on the sketch in his notebook, an idea came to him. He looked into her face as she scanned the faces of each of the campers. "You're a..." He hesitated. Hildegard turned and looked at him, giving him her full attention, nodding ever so slightly as if she could see his thoughts and wanted him to continue. "You're an Ebenezer, aren't you?" he said softly.

She offered a gentle smile as all eyes rested upon her. "A stone of help..." She nodded. "I hope so; a very small one, anyway."

"I never considered that it might be possible for a person to be an Ebenezer," Genevieve admitted.

"I think it's only possible for those whose feet are planted firmly on the rock of salvation and desire nothing more than to help others find the same joy."

"Like Ruby and Pops," Holly suggested.

"And Thomas, too," Greg added.

"That's what you were talking about just a minute ago, right?" Susan asked. "That not all Ebenezers are made of rock?"

Hildegard nodded. "But all Ebenezers must be built upon the rock."

Matt nodded, looking down at his open hand as he remembered the Ebenezer on the farm. "It has to begin with reverence, doesn't it?" he asked, touching the tip of this thumb to the tip of each of his other fingers on his left hand.

"There may be other things that bring you to reverence—take hope, for example, or maybe charity. But unless those things are built on the rock of reverence, their ability to inspire, encourage, and change one's life on an eternal scale will be limited. Even then, when your foundation is sure, the winds will continue to howl, and the rains will certainly continue to beat down on your house."

"Does it ever end?" Greg asked, looking concerned.

Hildegard shook her head. "Not in this life, at least not as far as I've been able to tell."

"So, if it's going to suck either way, what's the point of going to all the trouble of building on this rock of faith?" Josh asked.

Hildegard smiled pleasantly at his challenge as if she'd heard it before. "Though it's true that building on the rock does require more work and does not exempt you from the storm, it does limit the storm's power to upset your house. Shingles may fly and water may get in through the cracks, but your house will live to see the sunshine again. Repairs can be made to a house on the rocks, while the house that's built on the sand will be washed away every time."

Matt looked up. "You've all seen the Ebenezer behind the milk barn, right?"

They all nodded.

"Have any of you noticed the word carved into the big rock at the bottom?"

"It's a German word, right?" Greg asked.

"Yes." Matt flipped a couple of pages in his journal, opening to a rough sketch of the tall Ebenezer, the large stone at the bottom marked with block letters: Ehrfurcht. "Genevieve and I looked this up a couple of months ago. It's the German word for reverence."

Hildegard nodded. "That Ebenezer is a fine metaphor, especially if you'll take the time to apply its lessons to your own life."

"What kind of metaphor?" asked Crystal.

"If it's only a pile of rocks that you care to see, then you won't be disappointed. But if you'll look a little deeper and ask questions about why and how, there are much bigger answers to be had."

"I think I read in Thomas's book that those rocks were brought up from the river by the first family who homesteaded on the farm," Sonja suggested.

"That is correct."

"Why would they go to all the trouble of bringing up rocks from the river when there are plenty of rocks on the farm?" Crystal asked, puzzled.

"That's a great *why* question that would be worth pursuing," Hildegard suggested. "And while you're at it, you might take a look at Matt's list of the words he's interpreted so far, asking yourself questions along the way."

"It *all* has meaning, doesn't it?" asked Holly.

Hildegard nodded. "The farm has played host to matchmakers for more than three hundred years. That's a lot of time to stitch meaning and purpose into all things."

"Why don't they just make it easy and tell us the answers up front?" Crystal asked with a little laugh.

"What fun would that be?" Hildegard replied.

"You think wandering around looking for answers is fun?" Crystal challenged.

Hildegard smiled serenely. "It's as fun as you'll allow it to be. There are few things repeated more frequently in scripture than the invitation to ask, seek and knock. This suggests to me that God does not want us to be spoon-fed by others or passive about our own learning. I believe He wants us to be inquisitive and sincerely seek for truth wherever we are. Jesus encouraged us to be like children, humble, meek, honest and filled with questions that can provide opportunities for growth and understanding. Your generation is the first generation to have entire libraries available to you at your fingertips. Instant gratification certainly has its perks, but also its faults and limitations. Just as we cannot gain muscle without work and resistance, the knowledge and wisdom of the soul requires something more of us than simply downloading it and never needing to think about it again."

"Is that why you come here every Sunday?" Matt asked.

"In part," Hildegard responded with a nod. "The walk is always good for my legs and my back. I've learned from watching my friends that once you stop walking, you stop being able to walk. The same is true of many things, including thinking and dreaming and asking questions that really matter. But you also can't beat the beauty of this place, right?"

All the campers nodded.

"There are some junctions in the world where all the elements of joy flow freely. This is one of those for me. I come here to remind myself what I'm looking for; to remind myself where my feet need to be planted; to remind myself of the eternal nature of my soul; and to remind myself that all questions have answers if I have the patience and self-discipline to watch and wait and listen for God's whispers meant only for me."

"Be still and know that I am God," James said softly, pointing over his shoulder to the low-hanging branch.

Hildegard nodded. "Can you think of a more incredible invitation?"

"An invitation? That's the way you see it?" Crystal replied after glancing at the others.

"Is that not the way it was meant to be seen?"

"I...I don't know," admitted Crystal.

"That's the way I've always taken it—as an invitation to know God. And what a beautifully simple way to find him—to separate ourselves from the noise of the world, and the noise in our hearts and heads, and simply be still as we open ourselves to understanding the heart, mind, and the will of the creator of the entire universe."

"That's a beautiful way to think of it," Susan responded thoughtfully.

"Thank you. It's become a beautiful way to live, searching for God and finding Him in every face, every flower, and in every tree."

Notes

1. Ecclesiastes 3:1

CHAPTER 147

Conscientious Partakers

*When we build, let us think that we build forever.
Let it not be for present delight nor for our use alone.
Let it be such work as our descendants will look upon with
praise and thanksgiving in their hearts.*
—John Ruskin—

The campers were mostly silent as they left Hildegard alone at the sacred tree and made their way north, following the river trail. Bright white clouds sailed across the azure sky like a heavenly regatta, casting moving shadows across this valley once carved by the Allegheny. Dragonflies performed aerial stunts for the campers' entertainment, while bright green mayflies took flight from the grasses and shrubbery as they passed by.

They stopped to skip rocks near the fairgrounds where the river was wide and smooth as glass, reflecting the woods and hills on the other side. Old wooden benches lined the top of the riverbank, offering a great view of the natural wonders around them.

They laughed together as they watched Greg trying to teach Holly how to skip rocks, especially when he remembered she was left-handed and had to start with his tutorial again from the beginning. The rest of the campers found their way to the benches, hooting for Holly as she proudly exclaimed, "One in a row!" But Greg was kind and Holly was patient, and her unpolished, single kerplunks slowly improved to two, then three, and eventually six skips.

Thrilled with her quick progress, Holly threw her arms around Greg's neck and hugged him, throwing him off balance. He stumbled, trying to catch himself under her added weight. Before he found his footing he was standing in the water, both pant legs wet above his knees. But Holly had somehow swung her legs high, wrapping them around Greg's waist, avoiding even the slightest drop of water.

The campers went wild, standing and cheering as Greg and Holly both smiled and waved like they'd gracefully stuck an impossible landing in a previously unknown Olympic event. While the other campers rushed to help them, Genevieve tugged Matt's hand, inviting him to sit back down.

"What do you think of them together?" Genevieve asked as they watched Holly loosen her grip from Greg's neck and jump down on the stony shore.

"Are you talking about their performance, or them as a couple?"

"Yes," Genevieve replied.

"Hmm, I'd give them a 9.7 on the routine and a 9.8 on the possibility of them working as a couple."

Genevieve nodded, not taking her eyes off them. "Despite their age difference?"

"You do know they're closer in age than we are, right?" Matt asked with a chuckle.

"Oh, yeah. Hmmm. It's not such a big deal, is it?"

"I think I'd be more concerned about Greg's self-confidence than his age."

"Why?"

"He's come a long way over these last four months—heaven knows we all have. But I don't know if he's aware of how good of a guy he's become."

"Isn't a little humility a good thing?"

"Sure, but is he far enough away from his past to confidently know that he'd never want to go back?"

Genevieve sat silent for a moment. "Are you? Am I?"

Matt nodded slowly. "Fair enough."

"You know I could never go back to what I was," she replied, nudging his arm.

"I know," he said, smiling. He put his arm around her, and they turned to watch the other campers animatedly conversing as they playfully mimicked Holly's moves with spirited exaggeration. "Has it hit you yet that we get to do this for the rest of our lives?"

"I was just thinking the same thing. Do you think we'll be any good at it?"

"I'm ready to do my best, as long as it's with you."

"Yeah, me too." She looked distracted as she watched the rest of the campers interacting with each other. "Well, if Greg and Holly ended up together, that'd make six of us," she said, looking over the campers with an eye of scrutiny.

"You think there's another match among the rest?"

"Well, yeah, of course. That's the point, right?"

Matt watched her, curiously. "You do know it might not work out that way, don't you?"

"What do you mean?"

"That they all might leave here next month without a partner."

"What? I mean, yeah, but…that would suck if anyone spent five months here and went home without a love interest, right?"

"Well, I won't argue with that, but that's not really what this is all about."

"What do you mean?"

"You're kidding me right now, right?" he asked, turning to face her.

"Matt, we…you…you all came to a matchmaking farm. *Ruby's a matchmaker.* I don't understand what you're saying. Isn't that what our job is going to be?"

"Oh, boy," Matt responded, looking concerned. "You thought… wait…really?" He scanned her face as if he were looking for any signs of sarcasm.

"Matt, what have we signed up for?"

"Well, to be matchmakers…kind of."

"What do you mean, *kind of*?"

"You're really serious about this?" he asked, looking concerned.

"Yeah, why? What am I missing?"

"Genevieve…" He smiled and shook his head. "Yes, matches sometimes happen here—in fact they're somewhat common, but none of us came here this summer anticipating we'd be leaving engaged."

"What?!?" Genevieve whispered, visibly shocked.

He shook his head.

"Why did you come then? What about matchmaking? Isn't that what Ruby's job is?"

"Well, sure, I mean…kind of."

"Matt, what are you saying?" she asked, growing visibly distressed.

"Oh my gosh…it was all in the paperwork…the paperwork that you never got. We didn't necessarily come here to get married. We came here to get ourselves *ready to get married*, to figure out where we needed help and what we could do to eventually be better at marriage and family."

"You honestly didn't come here expecting to get married?"

"Uh, I'm a little reluctant to say."

"Why?"

"Because I'm worried about what that means for us. You know you don't have to marry me, or any of the other guys, right?"

"Of course I don't," she replied. "But is it bad that I want to marry you?"

"Really?"

"Matt, you just pulled the rug out from underneath me and you can't answer me?"

"Genevieve, I love you. I want to marry you. I just want to make sure you want to marry me—that you're not thinking that you have to marry me because you have to be married or partnered-off by the end of the summer."

"No, I…Matt, of course not. But what's our job going to be for the next fifty years if it's not to match people up and help get them married?"

"I…it's like I said…to help people get ready for marriage. But people have to ultimately make that decision for themselves. This isn't about arranging marriages without mutual consent."

"Well, no, of course not. That would be illegal or at least…silly. But…" she sat silent for a long moment. "So, you're telling me that Ruby isn't *actually* a matchmaker?"

Matt shrugged. "Did she match us?"

"Well, no, not exactly. But she didn't…" She pinched the bridge of her nose. "Am I the only one who didn't know all of this?"

He rested his hand on her knee, squeezing it softly. "I would assume," he said after a moment, "they all received the same paperwork I did. They'd have to know."

"And what was it exactly that the paperwork said?"

"*Exactly*? Pfff, it's been months since I read it, but it basically said that the commitment of five months on the farm would provide a foundation for each participant to be better prepared for marriage, while increasing our potential for happiness and success with the marriage partner of our choosing."

"And there was no...guarantee or even an implication that you'd be married off at the end of the summer?"

Matt smiled, shaking his head. "You were thinking more along the lines of Yente from *Fiddler on the Roof*?"

She nodded.

"And now that you know the truth, aren't you at least a little bit relieved?"

She didn't answer right away. "Matt...this is...this is...Wait, so, we get to live here and share the keys of joy with people who *want* to be married, *but we don't have to be responsible for getting them together?*"

"Yes, that's right."

She took a deep breath and exhaled loudly. "You're not just messing with me?"

Matt laughed softly. "No. We just have to move them along...you know...help get them ready for the biggest decision of their lives. You wouldn't want to carry the burden of responsibility for twelve huge decisions each summer for the next fifty to sixty years?!"

She shook her head. "Matt, do you have any idea how much time that could free up for me to write? I imagined spending our evenings working out the details of how to create six happy and healthy marriages by the end of every summer. This is—okay, yeah—a little shocking, yes. But this is really good news!"

Matt looked at her for a moment before smiling kindly. "I think I love you more than I did just five minutes ago. Have you really been worrying about getting everyone here matched up before the end of the summer?"

Genevieve sat silent for a moment. "When you put it that way it does seem pretty outrageous, doesn't it?"

He shrugged. "It would be a lot. The paperwork that the rest of us received said something about how this would be the most important and consequential decision of our lives, and that we should begin immediately considering how our personal choices and accountability could ultimately influence the success of the union we will choose and the level of happiness we aspire to within our marriage."

"Are you guys ready? It's almost one o'clock," Spencer hollered from the beach.

"Ready when you are," Matt responded with a nod of his head.

They continued on along the path that ran parallel to the river, Matt and Genevieve falling behind as they quietly watched and listened to the others. After another hundred yards they came to a rusty, old, iron bridge that crossed the river.

"Look," Ephraim said, pointing to the far side where five old cannons were mounted on a fat wooden beam. "Those were probably the cannons we heard on the 4th of July, right?"

"*Remember the keys of liberty!*" Matt shouted.

"That's right! That's what the village people said at the end of the fireworks show when the cannons blasted," Susan remembered.

"I read something about those cannons in Thomas's book just the other night," Sonja replied.

"What about them?" asked Rachael.

"Uh, something about how they were given to the town by the US government in the early 1800's to help protect themselves against Indian attacks."

"Indian attacks? Here?" James asked, doubtfully.

"That's what it said. But the Niederbippians had already made peace with the Indians and had been trading with them for years. The villagers considered melting the cannons down and doing something useful with the brass, but they never came to a consensus. So, after a couple of years the townsfolk decided to just move the cannons across the river and let nature reclaim them. They were basically forgotten for over a hundred years. It wasn't until this bridge was built during The Great Depression, when the Civilian Conservation Corps needed wood for their projects, that the cannons were discovered again. But not long after that, World War II broke out. As conscientious objectors and pacifists, most of the Niederbippians, who'd successfully avoided wars since they'd first arrived, were not the least bit interested in getting involved with the war. But towards the end of the war, six young men, after becoming incensed by the atrocities that were taking place in Europe, left their homes and their wives and joined the Army. They all returned home in caskets less than a year later after a German air raid cut their lives short."

"Those government-issued crosses in the town cemetery…I assume they're probably for them?" James suggested.

"One of them is for Hildegard's husband," Genevieve replied.

"Seriously?" Rachael asked.

Genevieve nodded. "I know she visits his grave at least every Sunday. I get the feeling from talking to her that it was pretty rough for the whole town."

"Yeah, that's what Thomas's book said," Sonja continued. "He said the town leaders of the time were so upset that the war had taken some of the best and brightest sons of Niederbipp that they wanted to create an anti-war memorial that might keep younger generations from glorifying war or ever considering it. Thomas's book said they took the wheels off the cannons and permanently mounted them so they could never be used for destruction. The only time they're actually ever used is on the 4th of July to help Niederbippians remember to never give up their principles and traditions of peace and liberty."

"Remember the keys of liberty," Matt mused.

"We're here; we might as well check them out," Sonja suggested, looking across the river to the mottled brass cylinders shining in the sun. She led out, crossing the narrow bridge, the rest of the campers following close behind.

They found the cannons much as Sonja had described them, permanently mounted on a solid wooden beam, five words carved deep into the beam's face—REMEMBER THE KEYS OF LIBERTY. A brass plaque was bolted to a shorter, upright, perpendicular beam that intersected the larger beam to which the cannons were attached.

As the others examined the cannons, James stood in front of the plaque and read it aloud.

IN MEMORY OF THOSE WHO DIED IN
THE CAUSE OF LIBERTY,
AND THE MANY MORE
WHO HAVE LIVED PEACEFULLY
AND CONSCIENTIOUSLY
IN THE CAUSE OF MORAL LIBERTY
AND ETERNAL JOY.

"WE ARE TOO READY TO RETALIATE,
RATHER THAN FORGIVE, OR GAIN
BY LOVE,
AND YET WE COULD HURT NO MAN
THAT WE BELIEVE LOVES US.
LET US THEN TRY WHAT LOVE
WILL DO:
FOR IF MEN DID ONCE SEE WE LOVE
THEM,
WE SHOULD SOON FIND THEY
WOULD NOT HARM US.
FORCE MAY SUBDUE, BUT LOVE
GAINS:
AND HE THAT FORGIVES FIRST, WINS
THE LAUREL."

"I remember Pops shared that with us a while back," Susan replied.

"Yeah, I remember," James replied. "In this context...with the cannons...it feels a little more real."

Spencer walked next to James and reached out his hand, running his thumb over the raised letters, five lines from the bottom. These words were polished smooth, clean of the tarnish that slightly obscured the others.

LET US THEN TRY WHAT LOVE CAN DO.

"Do you think it's realistic?" Spencer asked thoughtfully.

"That love has the power to win?" James asked.

Spencer nodded.

"I remember the debate I had with Pops a couple of months ago about that very question. I remember arguing that love felt like a weak and implausible answer to the louder and stronger forces in the world.'"

"And now?" Crystal asked, standing next to him, sliding her fingers into his.

James took a deep breath. "I guess now I have to admit that my opinions have changed."

Matt took a step back from the cannons, seeing something he'd missed before. Finding it now, he shook his head and smiled, closing his eyes as he looked up into the sky, the sun warm on his face.

"Hey, I think we probably all missed this," Sonja said, stepping back so she stood next to Matt.

The rest of the campers followed, stepping backwards across the gravel where several benches marked the borders of the memorial, offering a view of the cannons against the backdrop of the town.

"Hey, is that a cross?" Greg asked, looking at the wooden structure with his head turned so his left ear was parallel to the ground.

"Yeah, and look where the other end is planted," Holly said pointing.

They all turned their heads to see that the end of the thick beam was embedded deep into a large natural boulder at the other end of the structure.

"I don't know much about crosses, but aren't they supposed to be upright?" James asked.

"It's been a long time since I've studied any of this at Bible Camp," Susan admitted, "but I remember that a cross laid on its side symbolizes that salvation has been achieved, and that Jesus is risen, no longer burdened by either the cross or the sins of the world. But it's also a reminder to believers to take up their cross daily and follow him."

"Wow!" Matt responded.

"What?" asked Genevieve.

He didn't answer, walking instead back to the cannon closest to the plaque. The others followed, looking over his shoulder as he ran his hand over the tarnished cylinder, stopping at a small symbol engraved on the thick lip of the muzzle.

"Is that a circle with a cross in it?" asked Holly, pointing to the symbol, no bigger than an inch across.

Matt nodded.

The campers turned to the other cannons, finding a small hourglass engraved on the second cannon, an anchor on the third, a scale on the fourth, and a heart with flames on the fifth. Though each of the symbols were obscured by tarnish, they were clearly visible to those who knew what to look for.

"What was that bit about taking up your cross?" Matt asked, turning to Susan.

"Oh, it's a scripture, from the Bible somewhere—maybe in Luke? It says something about if you want to be Christ's disciple, you have to be willing to deny yourself and take up your cross daily and follow him."

"That wouldn't be from Luke 9:23, would it?" Greg asked, pointing to the carving on the stone into which the beam had been inserted. They all gathered around, looking at the small but bold characters carved by a skilled chisel.

Matt opened his journal and wrote down the reference. "This is far from just a stage for the annual pyrotechnics show, isn't it?"

Most of the campers nodded their heads.

"Do you think there's anything around here that doesn't have some kind of deeper meaning?" Holly asked.

"If there is, it seems like the good people of Niederbipp will fix that right away," Rachael responded.

"They're all Ebenezers, aren't they?" asked Josh.

"Are you talking about the people of Niederbipp, or all these places and symbols?" Ephraim asked.

"Maybe both. Aren't they all *stones of help*? Don't they all invite anyone with eyes to see to look a little deeper and ask a few questions that can get us closer to understanding the purpose of life and where we fit in it?"

Many of the campers nodded thoughtfully.

"Who would have guessed that even cannons could be changed from implements of war and destruction into something meaningful and constructive?" Ephraim asked.

"Yeah, to wake people up, and to invite them to remember really important things," Susan offered. "I like this purpose way better."

"The writing's on the wall," James replied, shaking his head as he pointed to the symbol of the hourglass on the lip of the second cannon.

"It all feels like an invitation, doesn't it?" Genevieve suggested.

"What kind of invitation?" Sonja asked.

"To ask, and learn, and think bigger. These cannons, the cross, the carving on the rock…it all feels like an invitation to make connections and fill in the gaps."

"Yeah, almost like a visual parable," Susan suggested.

"What does that mean?" Crystal asked.

"Well, parables are stories with many potential meanings for different people, depending on where they are or what they're looking for. For those who are looking at this as just an anti-war monument, well, it's not a bad-looking monument, right? But for those who want to know and see more, there are answers and even a treasure map to point you in the right direction," Susan said, pointing to the scriptural reference carved into the boulder. "We easily could've missed it had we not already learned to make connections. But it seems like every time we turn around, if we're open to learning and curious enough to ask, the answers are never very far away."

"I like that," Matt replied. "How would each of our lives be better if we looked for God's handwriting, fingerprints, or instructions on everything we encountered?"

"Everything? Pfff, we'd probably turn out to be zealots and fanatics," James suggested cynically.

"Maybe, but considering the people that we've met this summer, I can't think of any of them who could be considered a fanatic, can you?" Matt asked.

Holly shook her head. "It feels like everyone just wants to help us find our way to joy, don't they?"

"I agree," Sonja offered, "but we're all going home in a few weeks—home to the same tidy comfort zones we finally broke free of. How do we keep from slipping back into the same velvet-lined ruts that kept us from growing before we came here?"

"Your question reminds me of that story Pops told us at the beginning of the summer," Ephraim said. "You know, that one about the turkeys who went to flight school to learn to how to soar, and then they landed… and walked home?"

"I thought about that story just yesterday," Josh admitted. "If we can't build a commune and all live together forever, I propose that we at least start a monthly group chat so we can check on each other regularly and make sure we're not backsliding."

"And we could also keep in touch through social media," Holly suggested.

"Ughhh, I've wasted way too much of my life on social media," Rachael responded.

"Well, what if it wasn't a waste? What if we just shared the real stuff, the things we're learning and the progress we're making."

Rachael nodded. "That would be different. It's been really nice not having to compare my crappy life to everyone else's perfectly

Photoshopped, imaginary world. That's one thing I've loved about this experience—that I could be real and vulnerable and not have to worry about how ridiculous I am."

"I think we've all grown to appreciate your brand of ridiculousness," Genevieve responded. "It seems to dovetail nicely with all of ours."

Rachael smiled. "I love you guys. I don't know what I'm going to do without you."

"Hey, let's knock off the funeral talk," Spencer replied. "We still have a whole month together!" He draped one arm over Rachael's shoulder and his other arm over Holly's. Each of the campers followed as they'd done in the past, creating a large, circular hug.

"Promise me we'll all stay close," Holly pleaded.

"I promise," said James.

"Me too," Susan added.

"Me three," said Josh as they each nodded and smiled at each other, unitedly grateful for the most meaningful friendships any of them had ever enjoyed.

CHAPTER 148

The Parkins

*Everybody applauds the repentant man,
but the repentant man saves his applause for the
obedient man.*
—Melbourne Romney III—

"Didn't Thomas say the Parkins' place was just a mile north of town?" Sonja asked as they crossed back over the bridge. "That sounds right," Josh replied, turning to look to the other side of the highway for any signs of human habitation. "We've got to be pretty close, right?"

"Why don't we just take this trail up to the highway and get our bearings," James suggested. He didn't wait for an answer, turning to take the lead. Crystal hurried to catch up, taking a hold of his hand.

A few dozen paces from the end of the bridge, they crossed the deserted two-lane highway and walked along the far shoulder, drawn by the large American flag that waved in the breeze, high above the tops of the trees about a hundred yards to the north.

"This could be it," Sonja suggested as they approached a gravel driveway that ran perpendicular to the blacktop. Two stone towers, on either side of the drive, rose at least ten feet from the ground, each hosting a hammered metal lamp on top with yellow glass.

"I think this is definitely it," Matt suggested, pointing to the tile that was embedded in each of the pillars at about eye level.

"Hey, aren't those the keys of joy?" Rachael asked, stepping closer to examine the bas relief carving, highlighted by the brown, metallic glaze. It looked much like the other joy clusters they'd seen in other places, each of the keys represented in one overlapping symbol.

"I think Jake made those," Matt suggested. "I saw some just like them at the Pottery the night their baby was born."

"You're right. I remember that," Genevieve responded.

"If this is it, let's go. I'm hungry, and I've got a bread-shaped hole in my stomach that could use filling!" Spencer moaned.

"I think I can smell bread," Sonja said, moving past the pillars. A thick grove of trees blocked the view, but the narrow gravel drive cut its way through them, and they followed it, anxious to see what lay beyond. They slowed as they came to the edge of the shadows cast by the trees. There, at the other end of the clearing stood one of the most fabulous houses any of them had ever seen. Completely built of stones that looked like they'd been rounded and tumbled by the river, the house was framed by two turrets which flanked the generous oak door. A colorful, stained-glass transom with a floral pattern shone above the door frame. This looked out over two large boulders that had been carved out to form enormous planters, each of them hosting a miniature tree with vibrant flowers planted around their roots.

The mansion, looking like it had been imported from an estate in Britain, blended elements of both Tudor and Victorian architecture. The roof was shingled with thick, hand-cut shakes, and was framed by tarnished copper gutters. Flower boxes overflowing with colorful geraniums highlighted the diamond-cut leaded windows on both the first and second floors.

They turned together at the sound of a smack and watched a red and white croquet ball roll across the freshly mowed lawn toward an iron wicket. Two little girls in Sunday dresses with matching bows in their hair chased after it, each of them wielding opposite ends of the same croquet mallet over their heads and hopping forward, surprisingly gracefully, on their left feet.

"This looks like a game I need to learn," Susan responded, laughing as they all watched the girls pivot together without their right feet touching the ground. Leaning forward until the tops of their heads touched, they stood over the ball, balancing with their free hands as they worked to position their other hands on the mallet. At the count of three, they swung the mallet hard, smacking the ball back the way it had come. Then, with grace and dexterity, they hopped back, disappearing beyond the edge of the house.

"I think our creativity could use a shot in the arm," James suggested, walking toward the far end of the house where the short grass had been obviously trampled by dozens of feet. The other campers followed close behind, anxious to see what other surprises awaited them.

As they walked along the front of the mansion, they each admired the beauty and variety of the colorful stones that made up her walls. Fruit trees grew between the mansion and the highway, blocking the view and further creating a feeling of seclusion and peace.

"What a cool place," Matt said to Genevieve who walked next to him, her eyes filled with wonder.

"This is a dream," she responded.

Again, the smack of a ball was heard and again the same little girls came hopping around the corner after it.

"What are you playing?" Crystal asked when the girls looked up at them.

"We call it Croquilly," the taller of the two girls said.

"Croquilly? I've never heard of it," James responded.

"That's probably because we only made it up about twenty minutes ago," the girl responded.

"Yeah, it's a little bit like croquet, but it's combined with all the silly things we could think of," the other girl added.

James looked around the corner of the house, surprised not to see any competing teams. "Who are you playing against?"

"Just ourselves. But we're winning!" the tall girl responded.

"What are the rules?" Crystal asked as the campers all looked on, genuinely amused.

"We're still making them up. But really, it's more fun to play games without rules, don't you think?"

"Actually, yes, I feel the same way," Susan replied. "Is there room for another team to play?"

"*You wanna play with us?*" the shorter girl asked, looking quite surprised.

"If you'll teach me and Spencer, here, how it's done."

"Aren't you grown-ups?" The smaller girl asked.

"That's debatable," Spencer responded, stepping forward. "You got a thing against grown-ups?"

"Yeah, most of them are boring. They just want to sit around and talk. Nobody wanted to play with us."

"That's probably because they don't know how much fun it is to play made-up games," Spencer replied.

"Do you?"

"Heck yes, we do!" Spencer responded. "Do you have another one of those giant hammer thingys and an extra ball?"

"Sure, Mister, they're over there by the tree," the tall girl said, pointing over her shoulder.

"Who else wants to play Croquilly?" Spencer asked, stopping to turn back around.

"We do," Crystal said, grabbing James by the arm.

"Grab one for us too," Holly said, nudging Greg forward.

The little girls beamed, turning to each other with bright eyes.

"Maybe you could teach us all how to play," Genevieve suggested.

"Really?" the smaller girl responded, looking either amused or confused, or both.

The others quickly returned with the mallets and balls, handing them out to each of the couples.

"It doesn't look like there's enough for all of us," Genevieve noticed as the implements of the game were handed out. "Would you like us to be the referees?" she asked the little girls as she pointed to Matt.

"No, I don't think we need a referee. And besides, you don't know the rules," the taller girl responded judiciously. "Maybe you could make crowns for the winners instead?"

"Oh, uh, sure," Genevieve replied, looking at Matt.

"Absolutely!" Matt replied, pointing to a patch of dandelions and wildflowers growing just beyond the shorn lawn.

While the girls began teaching the campers the fine points of Croquilly, Matt and Genevieve wandered through the small orchard to the patch of tall grass where the flowers and dandelions had been allowed to grow wild.

As they picked and did their best to braid the flowers into crowns, Matt and Genevieve continued their conversation about the changes in her perceived expectations, further settling her nerves and helping her recognize how much better this plan was. As she vocalized this relief, they spoke of how this would allow them to focus their energies on better understanding the keys of joy while sharing them with the campers who would hopefully continue to apply to spend the summer here.

When they'd assembled a dozen crowns in various sizes and designs, they wandered back to the playing field to better watch the peculiar play. Though the aim of the game was still unclear, what was clear was that this required far more coordination than they'd previously appreciated. Hopping on one foot, chasing a ball, while holding the mallet overhead with a partner not only required personal balance and grace, but also communication, patience and mutual support. It also required on-the-fly alterations demanded by the nuances in the terrain. Allowances had to be made for variations in the height and gait of team members, the distance of their hop, and their ability to hold and swing the mallet together in order to meet the ball with a respectable smack. Most of the campers were still smiling by this point. The rest of them laughed themselves silly as they tried to keep up with the two little girls who'd started it all.

Matt and Genevieve noticed that a small group of spectators had gathered on the far end of the field. They were laughing and cheering as the players crisscrossed the lawn, smacking and chasing the colorful croquet balls with loony, animated antics. An unusually loud smack hit by Greg and Holly sent their ball rocketing up the field toward James and Crystal. The timing couldn't have been better. Just as they jointly pulled back their mallet to strike their own ball, Greg and Holly's ball zoomed right between their legs, smacking their ball with such force that it sent both balls sailing across the lawn. Without a ball for their mallet to hit, James and Crystal were thrown off balance as their mallet swung forward, causing them both to crumple to the ground in a heap of laughter.

The others, exhausted from their exertions, hopped to the middle of the field, collapsing in a jovial puddle of happy expressions. The little girls joined them, obviously spent. The spectators moved forward with additional cheers as Matt and Genevieve crowned each participant with their crudely fashioned wildflower halos.

Since they were all sprawled out on the lawn anyway, and with nowhere in particular to go, they stayed where they were, catching their breaths and watching the clouds blossom and morph as they sailed across the sky.

"This looks like a Sunday afternoon done right," Emma said after five minutes had passed. "I hope you haven't all collapsed from a lack of nourishment."

"No, these are *our* friends, Gran," one of the little girls said, gruffly. "They're the only ones who would play with us."

"Well, that hardly seems right," Emma replied. She walked around the human puddle to her granddaughters and laid out on the ground next to them. "Maybe the others just forgot how much fun this is," she said, looking up into the clouds.

"Yeah, probably. Grownups are dumb," the granddaughter confessed.

"Then you're lucky to find friends who can still remember how much fun it is to be kids," Emma said. "Those are the luckiest friendships of all."

"I'm glad you never forgot, Gran," said the smaller of the two girls.

"It looks like I've missed a whole lot of fun," Tom said, laying down on the grass next to his wife.

"Oh, you did, Gramps! We made up a new game and it's real fun and we found a whole bunch of fun big kids who wanted to play with us," reported the smaller girl.

"Lucky you. These big kids must have been well trained," Tom acknowledged.

"Yeah, pretty much," the girl said, rolling over to look at the campers.

"You've got some great girls here," Susan said, lifting her head off the grass.

"Aren't they the best?" Emma replied. "I'd love to have a dozen more just like them. Millie and Ivy have kept us remembering the simple pleasures of life since before they could even talk. It kills us that we only get to see them a few times a year."

"Yeah, you should move to Seattle with us," the older girl said.

"Nuh uh, you should move to Raleigh so you can be closer to us," the younger girl responded fiercely.

"Or maybe you two could talk your parents into moving closer to us," Tom suggested.

"Yeah, that's an even better idea," the older girl replied.

"Yeah, then we could play every day with these guys, too."

"That would be fun," James said, lifting his head. "But we have to leave at the end of the summer. We have to go back to work and get married so we can have kids like you two."

"Okay, and then you can bring them back here and we can play with them," the younger girl replied.

"Do you think you'll still want to play when you're older?" Crystal asked.

"Yeah, duh!" the girl responded as all the adults laughed.

"Who's ready for some bread?" Emma asked.

Several hands shot up, including those of the little girls.

"We just pulled three more loaves from the oven. They ought to be cool enough now to cut into. Come and join us," Tom suggested as he scrambled to his feet. He reached down, extending a hand to his wife, pulling her from the ground.

The campers responded in kind, getting to their feet and donning the floral crowns they'd been awarded. They followed their hosts around the house and over the path that cut through the woods behind it. The aroma of fresh bread grew stronger with each step and everyone's mouths were watering before they saw the gazebo.

Nestled in a clearing that was only as big as the structure itself, the circular gazebo was a beauty to behold. Its cement foundation, plated with river rocks that matched the home, rose three stone steps off the forest floor. Twelve pillars, set at regular intervals, circled the foundation, holding up the nearly circular roof that was covered with orange-colored, cedar shake shingles. Simple benches lined the perimeter, sheltered by the generous overhang of the roof. The shaded space underneath was illuminated with a thousand tiny lights, offering a glimpse of the intricate timber construction.

"You built this yourselves?" Ephraim asked, awestruck as he took it all in.

"We designed it ourselves, and did much of the work, but we had a lot of help," Emma admitted.

Holly ran her palm over one of the bedazzled, mosaicked pillars that greeted them at the stairs. "This must have taken forever!"

"About three years of fairly steady work," Emma replied. "But, like I said, we had a lot of help."

"Did Jake and Amy help you?" Genevieve asked, running her fingers over a tile that matched the ones on the pillars at the estate's entry.

Emma nodded, smiling at the tile. "We commissioned several pieces, and we were happy when Jake and Amy offered to donate a dozen boxes of pottery shards to the project."

"We never could have guessed it would turn out this well," Jake said, stepping from behind the oven, dusting his floury hands off on his red apron. "It was good to see it go to use rather than be sent to the landfill."

"You mean this is all shards and garbage?" Crystal asked, scanning each of the colorful, whimsical pillars.

Jake shrugged. "One man's garbage can be another man's art if you're capable of looking at things with an open mind."

"There's actually deep symbolism in much of this," Tom added. "We work with twelve couples every week in our marriage reboot sessions. Each of them arrives in various degrees of brokenness, many feeling hopeless and incapable of being repaired."

Greg nodded slowly. "And then you teach them how to turn their broken bits into mosaics?"

"In so many words, yes. There's nothing like a visual like this that can help people see that even brokenness can be beautiful and functional. We actually got the idea from Jake's predecessor," Tom said, turning to the potter.

"From the dishes, right?" Jake asked.

Tom nodded. "It's hard to believe, but that was over twenty-six years ago, not long after we bought this old place. Isaac had us to dinner and served us on a completely mismatched set of dishes he and his predecessors had made over the previous thirty decades."

Emma laughed. "I remember thinking he was crazy. Every single one of the pieces he put on the table that night was broken or flawed, and here he was a potter. It felt like really bad advertising."

"I remember feeling the same way during my first meal in Niederbipp," Jake admitted. "I couldn't believe there were actually three hundred years' worth of broken, junky pots scattered around the whole kitchen. It wasn't until weeks later, when I found that quote from Keats, that I began taking a different look at things."

"What quote are you talking about?" Matt asked.

"We actually liked it so much we had it embossed in our concrete floor over here at the north entry to the gazebo," Tom said, leading them forward. Several of the benches were occupied by friends and visitors who were enjoying both the warm bread and the warm conversation. They nodded and smiled as the campers walked past.

"It may be hard to read in this light," Tom said as he knelt and blew away the light dust from the recessed lettering. He stood again as Emma recited the message she had memorized.

"Don't be discouraged by failure. It can be a positive experience. Failure is, in a sense, the highway to success, inasmuch as every discovery of what is false leads us to seek earnestly after what is true, and every fresh experience points out some form of error which we shall afterwards carefully avoid." — John Keats.

Matt turned and smiled at Genevieve as he opened his journal and quickly scribbled down the thoughtful words.

"So…failure…" Ephraim paused, carefully organizing his thoughts. "Why would you ever want to keep them around?"

"I wondered the same thing," Jake admitted, stepping forward. "And then one night I found this quote rolled up in one of those old pots along with a note from the potter I replaced. It said something about how there was wisdom and experience to be gained from each of the pots on the shelf that might help future potters avoid some of the mistakes made by the potters of the past."

"Wow, I could imagine that could be really helpful," Susan responded.

"Priceless, actually. I've gone back to those pots thousands of times over the last eight years, looking at the glazes, and flaws, and idiosyncrasies of each of the pieces in the collection. I'm sure those observations have saved me thousands of hours and helped me avoid hundreds of mistakes."

"Wow," Greg replied. "Do they have anything like that catalog of broken pots for non-potters who are trying to avoid making mistakes?"

Jake smiled and nodded, turning to Tom before stepping away and returning to the oven.

"The things you've been learning this summer," Tom said, inviting their attention again, "the keys of joy, as they're often called, can help each of you assemble your own library of reference material that might, if studied with any sense of reverence and integrity, help you avoid many of the pitfalls and landmines on life's battlefields."

"It might be difficult for you to grasp how these keys apply to you and your future marriage," Emma suggested, "but take it from us and our nearly one hundred years of combined experience with family counseling; the keys don't only have the ability to bring you joy if you'll put them to work in your life, they also have the ability to set you free."

"Free from the burdens and mistakes so many have made before you," Tom said, pointing from the floor to the mosaicked pillars that flanked the north stairs.

"Some of that looks like it could be china," Genevieve said, stepping forward to take a closer look at the detail of the shattered dishes. She ran her finger across the fine, darkened spiderweb patterns that ran across their surfaces.

"Yes, that's what's left of Josephine Whitmore's fine china. We found buckets worth of shards scattered among the ruins of the old house, along with nearly as many buckets worth of their everyday Spode ware," she said, pointing to the reconstructed pastoral scene of a farmer at work in the still-vibrant cobalt blue.

"Was it all destroyed?" Genevieve asked solemnly.

"Nearly. They must have been grand sets, both of them, complete with soup bowls, salad and bread plates, dinner plates and serving pieces. The only piece that remains whole sits on our mantle. It's a gravy boat that we found wrapped in a ratty old cloth, hiding in the remnants of the chimney."

"My grandmother had a set like this," Sonja said, stepping forward and kneeling in front of a pillar where another scene from a broken plate had been mostly reconstructed and creatively combined with other shards of pottery, bits of colored glass and mirror.

"This is like a library of broken dreams and sad stories," Greg said, stepping forward to touch the pillar.

"You can certainly look at it that way," Emma responded. "But we would much prefer for you to see it as a library of wisdom and experience that can help you bypass many avoidable mistakes."

"Like what?""

"Like the pieces of this mirror," Tom offered, pointing to several dozen shards of thick mirror that encircled the remnants of one of the blue Spode plates.

"Was that also broken in the Whitmore's civil war?" Holly asked.

"No, I actually broke this mirror, as well as two others on the same day, several years ago," Tom admitted.

"Whoa, that's like twenty-one years of bad luck," Rachael replied.

"Yes, and a fair amount of money, and a two-week delay in having mirrors in three of our bathrooms," Tom added.

"What happened?" asked Josh.

"Oh, a mistake I've repeated many times over the course of our marriage. I was impatient. We'd driven up from Pittsburgh, anxious to get these installed. We pulled up to the front door and Emma said she'd be right back after she visited the little girl's room. Well, I waited as long as I wanted to, and then I took matters into my own hands. This was the result," he said, pointing.

"You dropped them?" Ephraim asked.

"No, it was much more epic than that. I thought I'd speed things up by carrying all three at a time. They were wrapped up in a blanket to keep them safe, but mirrors and stairs and clumsy men are a bad combination."

"It was the perfect storm," Emma said with a wink. "The trifecta of the manly man."

"Hmmm, let me guess," Spencer mused. "Was it brawn before brains, pride before grace, and restlessness before patience?"

Tom laughed. "You talk like a man who's gained some wisdom yourself."

"I'm not so sure about that, but at least I know what to call it," Spencer admitted.

"Yes, well...you're right on all points," Tom confessed.

"I watched the whole thing and could repeat it all play by play," Emma teased, "but to make a long story short, Tom missed the top stair, tripped on a corner of the blanket when he tried to catch himself, and somehow rode the whole bundle down the stairs, breaking all three mirrors and narrowly avoiding a self-castration of epic proportions."

"Guilty as charged," Tom said, and I've got a great scar on my backside to prove it."

"So, these mirrors...here...they're part of your personal library?" Greg suggested.

"Yes, but hopefully not mine only. I put them here for others to see and learn from them, too. It would be a shame to waste a story with a lesson like that, don't you think? And all because I couldn't wait three more minutes!" He shook his head and smiled. "Many of the biggest problems we face in life come as a result of being impatient; from somehow believing that our timing is better than God's timing. Some people never learn the lesson of patience, forcing this thing or that person to fit their will rather than stepping back when they're frustrated and taking in the big picture. There were at least a dozen other things I could have busied myself with while I waited for Emma that day, but I couldn't see any of them because I was focused entirely on the stupid mirrors."

"And you're okay sharing that story with other people?" James asked, looking surprised.

Tom smiled kindly and nodded. "I've got nothing more to lose. I lost three mirrors, a little pride and nearly my manhood. If I can help others avoid any of that, it feels like it could be a great gift."

"Yeah, well, thanks, but I'm one of those guys who tends to blow through caution signs and fly off the edge of the cliff, determined to make my own mistakes," James reported.

Tom nodded. "In our natural state, I think most of us are proud to one degree or another. We don't like either strangers or those closest to us telling us what to do or how to think."

"So, if you're naturally that way, what chance do you have of changing?" Greg asked thoughtfully.

"Oh, quite a good chance, I'd say," Emma responded. "Every choice you made today was yours, from getting out of bed, to riding your bike to church, to coming out here for a slice of bread, and choosing to be detoured by my granddaughters and two old birds who've been married longer than you've been alive. Your endless number of daily choices each have power and consequences for both good and ill. One choice leads to another and another and another as you've all experienced in just the last few hours. Those choices and consequences have brought you here today, at the inaugural event of this gazebo dedicated to the God of joy and the keys of liberty and happiness he's shared with humankind from the beginning of creation.

"'What chance do you have of changing your natural inclinations?' you ask," Emma continued. "By yourself, probably far less than you would like to admit. But with the help of God, we believe your chance expands exponentially, one hundred percent or better. And the keys you've been learning all summer can help you to multiply and magnify your potential for honest change and real success."

"What did that change look like for you, specifically with the mirrors?" James challenged.

Tom smiled. "With those three mirrors, very little, other than hanging onto the memory and putting the shards to work in a place that could help me remember. I've never been much of a patient guy. I don't like waiting for anyone or anything, but that day on the stairs made me want to change. It made me face the reality of my weakness and take an inventory of where I was. I realized in that inventory that I'd been trying to tackle my patience on my own." He opened his left palm and wiggled his index finger, trying and failing to make it close completely into his palm.

"The keys are each powerful in their own way, but when one consciously begins combining each of the keys, the power of each one is multiplied. Four fingers are obviously far stronger than one, but they are exponentially stronger and more sure when the thumb of reverence is combined with any and all of them. That thumb and the reverence it represents has the power to help you overcome your natural tendencies in ways that nothing else can. It's *opposed* to all that is natural within us, inviting us to become new creatures through the power of Christ's redeeming sacrifice. Until that becomes part of who we are, everything else is window dressing and bedazzled dead ends, limited in their ability to lift or change or become all that we have the potential to become."

"Tom and I spent the first half of our career trying to lift individuals and marriages where they were, but we were always frustrated by the results. It wasn't until we came here and learned the keys of joy that we began to recognize how limited our work had been," Emma said. "When we began to understand the key of reverence, all the challenges we'd faced in our own marriage suddenly began to have solutions. And by exercising the other keys, especially patience and charity toward each other, the pace of positive change picked up immediately. We began to truly see each other as teammates rather than competitors. We encouraged each other in ways we never had been able to before. For the first time in our marriage, we began feeling equally yoked in our work and in all that we did."

"And you tie all of that change to living the keys of joy?" Susan asked.

Emma nodded. "We'd tried dozens of other ideas, techniques and philosophies. Some of them improved things for a minute, but things couldn't fully change until our hearts were changed."

"Judging from your sermon today, it sounds like you had to come to a place of near destruction before you were willing to change your hearts," Matt suggested.

"Obliteration would probably be the better word," Emma replied. "Had it not been for Isaac and the things he taught us that fateful day when he found us down by the river, ready to kill each other, nothing you see here today would have happened. Our marriage, our family, our dreams—they would all have gone in a very different direction. And we would have missed out on these past two-and-a-half decades of joy and hope. Our children, their marriages, our grandchildren, our work helping other marriages succeed—it all would have been very different."

"Okay, not to play the devil's advocate, but could the other direction not also be good?" James asked.

Emma and Tom looked at each other, stepping closer and resting their arms around each other.

"We talk about this question from time to time," Tom admitted. "The work we've done together on our marriage over these last two-and-a-half decades has been difficult at times. It has stretched us in places we weren't really comfortable stretching. It's caused us to look deep into our heads and hearts and better understand our personal weaknesses. Could we possibly be happy had we gone our separate ways? The answer's an obvious 'yes'. People get divorced and remarried every day. But in our business, we know that happiness does not generally follow those who avoid facing the hard questions of working their way through their own weaknesses in their search for solutions."

"The idea of living happily ever after without a whole lot of work is as improbable as finding gold bars washed up on the shore of your favorite beach," Emma added. "It just doesn't work out that way. In our own experience, and after years of counseling with thousands of other couples, we recognize that those marriages that work out are the ones where partners consistently work together while practicing charity and patience toward each other. But the ones that thrive, that are joyful and full of love, they all have at least one thing in common."

Tom nodded. "They've all invited God to be a partner in their companionship and union."

Matt looked to the left where an antique yoke was suspended from one of the gazebo's outside beams. "We have one of those hanging in our dining hall, to remind us of that truth."

Emma turned and nodded. "Yes, we were introduced to the concept of the yoke during our first visit to the farm on Harmony Hill. We now use it every week in our sessions to help couples recognize the power that comes from working side by side in a union that invites God to be a participant."

"And what about the saw?" Ephraim asked. "Does that have meaning too?"

"You bet it does," Tom responded. He took Emma by the hand and led them all to the opening between the pillars next to the yoke. There, hanging from the wooden handles was a rusted out, toothy piece of metal, a wooden handle on each end.

"That's a logging saw, isn't it?" Josh asked.

"Yes. We found it in the remnants of an outbuilding not far from here," Tom replied. "It quickly turned into a symbol of marriage for us."

"Because it takes two people to use it?" asked Crystal.

"Yes, but there's more to it than that," Emma responded. "Mr. Whitmore, the fellow who originally built our home, was a lumberman. He made his fortune harvesting the old growth trees that grew up and down this river. He probably didn't do much of the felling of trees himself, but he surely would have known from watching his men work the value of teamwork, the alternating push and pull required to get things done."

"We use a similar saw to teach many different principles in our sessions," Tom explained. "We make it a little easier for our participants by laying a log across two sawhorses and inviting each couple to take hold of opposite sides of a saw and cut through the log. Every week it seems we have at least one partner in a marriage who arrives thinking he can somehow force the saw through the log on his own, only to quickly discover that he's helpless without someone on the other side."

"It's almost like our washing machine, and the flour mill," Susan responded.

"That's what we understand," said Emma. "It's too bad that more couples don't have a chance to learn these basic truths before they marry. We've admired the work Ruby and Lorenzo do as we've observed and interacted with kids like you over the years. So many marital challenges could be avoided if more people could appreciate the importance of balance and teamwork. You kids have a head start on important lessons that many couples never learn."

Matt looked around the circular structure under which they stood, recognizing that only the space between these three pillars were occupied by hanging implements. "There must be a symbolic reason to hang these next to each other," he suggested.

"Why do you say that?" James asked.

"I was just noticing that, too," Genevieve said. "And look, there's the symbol of the scales up there." She pointed to a stylized mosaic of a pair of balance scales at the top of the center pillar.

"I'm glad to see you're recognizing the symbols you've been taught," Emma replied. "We've spent a lot of time talking about the meaning behind the symbol of the scales and how they relate to the choices we make in marriage. Learning the balance and communication required to effectively use a saw can go a long way to creating harmony in a marriage, but it will always be lacking something more."

"The saw might actually be a better symbol for dating than it is for marriage," Tom suggested.

"Mmm, because you can simply walk away from your side of the saw, right?" Holly replied.

"Exactly," Tom said with a nod. "You probably all know marriages that have been treated like that, that when the saw gets stuck or things don't run smoothly, instead of working together to get things moving again, one or both parties simply walk away."

Many of the campers nodded.

"The symbol of the yoke is a lot different, isn't it?" Holly asked as they all turned to look at it a little more closely.

"What do you see that is different?" Emma asked.

"Well, each of the collars suggest a real commitment, not just something you can walk away from without thinking about it," Crystal replied.

Emma nodded.

"We know how a yoke works from working on the planters and harrowers that first week," Josh added. "Unless we were working together, talking and listening and communicating with each other, we were either going crooked or headed for the rocks."

"I wish we had time each week to share the beautiful lessons of the farm on Harmony Hill," Emma admitted. "We have to condense so much to fit it into one short week. We've often felt envious of the five months Pops and Ruby have to spend with you."

Matt walked forward, reaching up to take hold of the stout iron ring that hung between the yoke's two collars. "This is ultimately the difference between what you want most, and what you want now, isn't it."

"Didn't Pops and Ruby suggest that that ring represents the love of God?" Holly asked.

Matt nodded, turning around to the others. "A ring is a symbol, of course, of eternity, right?"

They all nodded.

"Are my eyes playing tricks on me, or is there something inscribed on that ring?" Greg asked, stepping forward. The others moved forward, looking over his shoulder.

"The writing is always on the wall, isn't it?" Emma asked as she and Tom stepped aside to make room.

"It says, 'for my yoke is easy, and my burden is light. Matthew 11:30.'"

"It doesn't look so light to me," Crystal said.

"Maybe not, but you don't have to carry it alone, do you?" Genevieve responded.

"Not if you and your spouse remain committed, both to each other and to God," Emma replied. "We each get to decide the level of our commitment to both our marriage partner and to God, but we rarely get to choose the consequences if our choices lead us away from our commitments to either one."

"In a world that's growing increasingly secular, the love and power of God is often not even mentioned at weddings anymore," Tom lamented. "Many folks simply don't want to be bothered by a connection to deity. And so they head out on their own, determined to fend for themselves, or die trying."

"But many don't know what they're missing until it's too late, when one or both partners have walked away from what should be considered the biggest commitment of a lifetime," Emma added.

"How do you help people in that situation?" Rachael asked.

Tom looked at Emma and shook his head. "I don't know if there's a marriage counselor in the world who can help salvage a marriage when partners are uncommitted and lack an honest desire for reconciliation."

"So…who are your clients?" asked Genevieve.

"Mostly folks who've been married long enough to know that it's not as easy as they thought it would be and are humble enough to want to work on themselves so they can enjoy the blessings that come from a more holy and inspired unity," Tom explained.

"By the time they get to us, most couples are battle worn and weary," Emma added.

"So, they come here as their last-ditch effort to fix things?" James asked.

"In many cases, yes," Emma admitted. "Most of our clients have been married between twenty and thirty years. Their oldest kids have mostly moved out and they find themselves looking at each other and wondering if they even remember the person they married decades earlier when life was easy and the world was their oyster."

"And how do you help them?" Holly asked. "That seems like a lot of work."

Emma nodded. "It is work, but the work is theirs to do. Our job, as we've discovered it, is to teach them true principles that have the power to bring back the magic they once knew."

"You don't often regain magic of any kind without honest effort," Tom added. "We have only six full days with them. The rest is up to them."

"So, let me get this straight…you teach them all five keys of joy *in six days*?" James asked dubiously.

"Well, yes and no. They learn what the keys are in those six days, yes. But we let them know up front that it will likely take them the rest of their lives to truly know them," Emma admitted.

"My parents are still working on the things they learned here eight summers ago," said a voice from behind them.

They all turned to see the red-headed Madonna; a small living bundle swaddled in her arms.

"Amy's parents came to us after, what, thirty-five years of marriage?" Tom asked.

"Thirty-seven," she said, shifting the bundle in her arms. "They just celebrated their forty-fifth anniversary, thanks in large part to the things they learned here that week."

"Would you like me to hold him?" Genevieve asked, stepping forward.

"Oh, uh, sure," Amy replied, looking a little nervous as she handed over her baby. Many of the women and a couple of the men looked over

Genevieve's shoulder to smile at the milk-drunk baby who was teetering on the edge of sleep.

"Forty-five years of marriage!" Tom responded, shaking his head. "That's pretty impressive, especially these days. I've said it before, but I think the only reason your parents have made it this far is because your dad finally recognized how much of a saint your mother is."

Amy laughed. "I'm not sure if he's completely admitted that yet, but he's come a long way, thanks to the two of you."

"It was good to see your mom a few weeks back," Emma replied.

"Oh, she dropped by then?" Amy asked, looking surprised.

"Yes, just to say a quick hello on her way back from a jog. She seems happy."

"I think she finally is. Jake and I were both a bit worried when she told us she was coming to help, but I think she's finally ready to accept the fact that we're artists and we're happy."

Emma nodded. "Did she happen to tell you why she'd come to that point?"

"No." Amy looked confused. "Why?"

"She…we don't normally share anything that any particular client shares with us, but considering that it's been over eight years since your parents spent time here, I'm don't feel like I'm betraying any trust in saying that your parents are both pleased and surprised by the strength of your marriage and the level of happiness you and Jake share," Emma reported.

"She said that?" Amy asked, looking surprised.

"She did," Tom confirmed.

Amy smiled. "The closest she got to telling us any of that is that she was happy we'd found our people."

"Well, then I'd say Cathy Eckstein has made a lot of progress, and maybe has a little more to go," Tom replied.

"You call that progress?" Rachael asked, looking up from the baby.

Tom nodded. "Considering where they were when they arrived, yes,

I'd call that great progress. We're all in a different place, fighting our own battles, working our way through our myriad challenges."

"Accepting the choices of others, especially one's own children, can be some of the most difficult challenges couples can face together," Emma added. "Applying the keys of hope, charity and patience can alleviate much of that angst."

"I'd argue that self-discipline and reverence would also go a long way," Tom added.

Emma nodded thoughtfully. "The tools you kids have begun learning this summer have the ability to scatter joy, hope and happiness far more broadly than you ever could imagine. To date, after twenty-six years of knowing them and sharing them with our clients, we have yet to identify even one challenge that couldn't be altered, fixed, or improved by the application of one or more of the keys."

"What can you tell us about your benches?" Josh asked.

"What would you like to know?" asked Emma.

"I noticed there are words carved into the faces of each of them, but none of them are the names of the keys of joy."

"Good eye," Tom responded. "'We've noticed over the years that for many, the keys of joy can feel overwhelming, like unattainable goals. The words and values on the benches have been identified as smaller, accessible virtues that are building blocks, bringing those who follow them closer to a comprehensive understanding of each of the keys."

"Tell me about this one," Josh said, pointing to the bench at his right.

"Obedience? Yes, what can I tell you?"

"I guess I've just never connected obedience to joy," Josh admitted.

Tom nodded thoughtfully. "There aren't many people who do in our world today."

"So how do you know it's important?" asked James.

"People have been asking the same question throughout the long and crooked history of mankind. But the simple truth is that there is no road that leads to either happiness or joy that bypasses the need to honor and obey the commandments of God."

"It's like that quote from C.S. Lewis that Pops shared with us early on, right?" Holly asked.

Matt nodded, flipping through several pages in his journal before looking up. "I think this is what you were referring to. 'What Satan put into the heads of our remote ancestors was the idea that they could "be like gods"—could set up on their own as if they had created themselves—be their own masters—invent some sort of happiness for themselves outside God, apart from God. And out of that hopeless attempt has come nearly all that we call human history—money, poverty, ambition, war, prostitution, classes, empires, slavery—the long terrible story of man trying to find something other than God which will make him happy.'"

"It seems you've been a good student," Tom suggested. "Did you happen to copy the second half of that quote?"

Matt nodded, looking back down at his journal. "'God made us: invented us as a man invents an engine. A car is made to run on petrol, and it would not run properly on anything else. Now God designed the human machine to run on Himself. He Himself is the fuel our spirits were designed to burn, or the food our spirits were designed to feed on. There is no other. That is why it is just no good asking God to make us happy in our own way without bothering about religion. God cannot give us a happiness and peace apart from Himself, because it is not there. There is no such thing.'"

Tom nodded. "You may not think about the importance of the ten commandments when you're young; after all, they are thousands of years old. But Emma and I have observed that most of the personal and marital challenges people face in life come from disobedience to God's laws. Those ten basic laws have created the foundation for governments and justice systems throughout the Judeo-Christian world, and beyond. Much of what we call civilization depends on the honoring of these laws. Without them, chaos ensues, and lives and relationships are ruined."

"Obedience is the foundation of many important things in life," Emma added. "It's the cornerstone against which all genuine progress is measured. Without a basic level of righteousness that comes through obedience, anything one builds in life is doomed to be crooked or inferior."

"Except the Lord build the house, they labor in vain that build it," Susan mused.

"Exactly," Emma replied. "Like Tom suggested, there are no shortcuts or bypasses that allow us to find joy without obedience."

"If that's true, why isn't obedience one of the keys of joy?" Ephraim asked.

"We believe obedience plays an important role in many of the keys," Emma responded. "You can't be truly reverent without being obedient. The same is true of charity and self-discipline."

Matt looked around at the pillars on which the gazebo rested. "Is there a significance to the twelve pillars?"

Tom nodded. "We spent a lot of time thinking and planning this structure. We wanted everything to not only make structural sense, but to have significance and meaning as well. The four central pillars between each of the four sets of stairs represent the keys of patience, hope, self-discipline and charity."

The campers turned and looked around, recognizing the mosaicked symbols of each key high on the middle pillars of each quadrant.

"The four sets of stairs..." Matt said, turning all the way around as he considered his question. "They appear to be marking the four cardinal directions."

Emma smiled. "They do indeed."

"So, like a compass?" Ephraim observed.

"You're seeing it now," Tom confirmed.

"And, if this is a compass, that would mean that the oven is the center," Josh said, turning around and walking to the shallow, circular, mosaicked countertop that surrounded the domed oven, the mouth of which faced north. All of the campers followed, feeling the heat increase slightly with every step. They followed Josh's eyes as he looked up at the round iron ring through which passed the oven's brick chimney. Like the center of a pinwheel, all twelve rough-hewn wooden beams tied into this iron ring with mammoth bolts, extending out to rest atop each of the twelve mosaicked pillars.

Jake stepped back from the oven, making room for the campers to circumnavigate this central structure.

Four circular tiles were positioned on the chimney at intervals that mimicked the cardinal positioning of the stairs. These tiles, glazed in four colors; white, black, red and yellow, were nearly the size of dinner plates, each with a chubby rim. Four spokes extended from the middle of each plate, dividing each of them into four quadrants.

"Reverence," Matt mused, smiling. "It's the center of it all, isn't it?"

Emma smiled and nodded.

"Give us this day our daily bread," Holly read slowly as she circled the oven, reading from the tiles that formed a band halfway up the chimney.

"Those were some of the tiles we commissioned from Jake," Tom replied.

"I was happy to be a small part of this," Jake responded.

"What do each of the colors represent?" Sonja asked, looking up at the circular tiles connected to the chimney.

"I wondered the same thing when Emma and Tom ordered them," Jake admitted.

"And do you remember what we told you?" Emma asked.

Jake nodded. "I remember you saying that the circle with the cross in it is one of the most universal symbols in the world, and that the four colors represent the four races of the earth."

"So, it's like the Native American Medicine Wheel, or their Circle of Life?" Matt asked.

"It's a nod to both of those things, and many others," Emma acknowledged. "Once you begin looking at ancient symbols, you begin to recognize that many different cultures have been influenced by each other. The cross, of course, is a symbol of Christianity, but this symbol was used by ancient people since at least 4,000 years before Christ was born. It's also a symbol of unity, the four seasons of the year, the four elements of matter, the four states of being, the four cardinal directions, and the four stages of life. And though each of these meanings vary, all of them invite reverence to one degree or another."

Tom nodded. "When we began planning for this gazebo, we began an in-depth study of the symbols associated with the keys of joy. So many of them have been used for centuries, if not millennia, to tell stories and offer meaning before much of the world was literate. Now that most of the world reads, much of the meaning behind important symbols has been lost."

"Did you build this to help preserve that meaning?" Matt asked as he turned his head, looking over the impressive structure.

Emma and Tom both nodded. "We'll both be seventy-four later this year," Emma explained. "We don't know how much longer we'll be able to host our weeklong sessions. But we hope that when our time is up, there'll be a couple who'll want to keep this work going…who'll want to keep sharing the keys of joy with couples who are desperately looking for answers to life's most persistent and challenging questions."

"You'd really walk away from all you've created here?" Sonja asked.

Emma smiled. "We all have to walk away at some point, and the only things we get to take with us are the love and joy we've accumulated along the way. The house and this estate have only been some of our life's work. And though they've given us meaning and joy, it pales in comparison to the joys we've derived from our friendship and love for each other and our family."

"We were this close to missing out on all of this," Tom said, holding up his thumb and index finger with very little space between them. "If it hadn't been for learning the keys of joy at that critical time, all would certainly have been lost to the ravenous ego monsters of selfishness and discontent."

"*The ravenous ego monsters of selfishness and discontent,*" Spencer repeated thoughtfully. "I'm pretty sure I've been wrestling with those monsters all my life."

"We all do until we put away the natural man and make room in our hearts for joy," Tom offered.

"Even then, the struggle is real," Emma replied.

"Yes," Tom acknowledged, "but with God on your side, the struggle is surmountable, and the path is filled with purpose and meaning."

"And if you're lucky, there'll be bread at the end of the day," Jake said, lifting a still-warm round loaf of sourdough bread, a deep cross scored into its top crust.

CHAPTER 149

The Gazebo

*Retire into yourself as much as possible.
Associate with people who are likely to improve you.
Welcome those whom you are capable of improving.
The process is a mutual one. People learn as they teach.*
—Seneca the Younger—

While the campers enjoyed slices of warm bread slathered in butter and homemade jams, many of them walked alongside Matt who'd busied himself exploring the details of the gazebo, writing down the words that had been carved into each of the sixteen benches that stood between each of the pillars and the stairs. The exploration was slowed by the other guests who occupied many of these benches, some of them completely unaware that their bench bore the name of an important virtue.

The words REPENTANCE and FORGIVENESS were carved into the benches that stood on either side of the pillar bearing the symbol of the burning heart of charity. MERCY and LOVE were carved into the benches on either side of these.

On the benches near the pillar bearing the symbol of the hourglass of patience, the words UNSELFISHNESS, GRATITUDE, MEEKNESS and HUMILITY had been carved.

They moved on to the pillar bearing the anchor of hope. Here, the benches read WHOLEHEARTEDNESS, KINDNESS, GENTLENESS, and SERVICE.

Returning to the mosaicked balance scales, next to the bench bearing the word OBEDIENCE, they discovered the words ACCOUNTABILITY, MODERATION, and VIRTUE.

With these words jotted down in Matt's journal, the campers gathered around a recently vacated bench to enjoy another slice of bread and discuss the newly discovered virtues. They quickly recognized that many of the virtues had applications to more than one of the keys of joy, while all of them could be enhanced and complemented by the application of the key of reverence.

"There was something else we hoped to talk to Genevieve and Matt about," Emma said, interrupting the thoughtful and lively discussion. Tom stood by her side and nodded.

"What can we do for you?" Matt asked as he and Genevieve joined them, a few paces away.

"Are the rumors true that you two will be joining the Niederbipp community permanently and taking over the farm on Harmony Hill?" Emma asked.

Genevieve and Matt both nodded.

"We plan to marry on October 1st," Matt replied.

Emma turned to her husband and smiled before turning back to them. "We're thrilled for both of you, and we'd like to offer our assistance if we can ever be helpful."

"Thank you," Genevieve replied.

"Yes, we're glad the magical work that takes place on Harmony Hill will continue for at least another generation," Tom added. "Ruby and Lorenzo have at least twenty years on us, and they've been great examples of longevity and passion. They've inspired us in ways far too numerous to even begin mentioning."

"I think we know what you mean," Matt suggested as Genevieve nodded.

"We'd like to run an idea past you to consider in the coming years," said Tom.

"Oh, uh, sure. What's up?"

"As we've contemplated cutting back our weekly session schedule to spend more time with the grandkids while they still think we're cool, we think we'd like to open our home to alums from Harmony Hill for reunions," Emma suggested.

"Seriously?" Genevieve asked.

"Well, yes, unless you don't think anyone would be interested," Emma replied.

"Actually, we *know* people would be interested. We've all just been talking about finding a place to have reunions. This would be amazing!" Genevieve responded.

"Absolutely," Matt added. "What are you thinking about timing?"

Emma and Tom looked at each other, each of them shrugging.

"We're not really sure," Tom admitted. "We'd probably like to slowly drop a week each year, opening the possibility for there to be at least a few reunions throughout the year. We thought it might help people who've learned the keys of joy, to keep them fresh in their minds as they move forward with life. We know you could do that on the farm, but we know it would be far more comfortable for each of the couples to have their own rooms and bathrooms rather than cramming into the bunkhouses during the offseason when it's cold. Our home has room for as many as twelve couples."

"Wow, that's really generous. What do you anticipate something like that would cost?" Matt asked.

"We've discussed that, and it feels funny charging anything. After all, we've had the success we've had because of the things we've learned from Ruby and Lorenzo. If we could just cover the costs of food and cleaning, we'd feel good about that," Emma offered.

"That sounds more than generous," Genevieve replied. "Thank you. I'd guess many of the alums would surely be interested, including our group."

"Good. We'd love to see our home being used to perpetuate the light of joy, even when we're not using it," said Tom.

"That's very Protopian of you," Matt responded, reaching out his hand to Tom and Emma.

"Yes, thank you," Genevieve replied. "That's very kind."

"Our pleasure," assured Emma. "It just occurred to me that you two may be in need of a reception hall."

Matt and Genevieve glanced at each other.

"Our wedding will be at the church in Niederbipp," Genevieve explained, "and we planned to keep things simple. We're both from small families and don't anticipate many friends making the journey."

"Mmm. Well, if you change your mind and would like a place to gather, you're welcome to use the gazebo, free of charge." Emma offered.

"Honestly?" Genevieve asked, looking shocked.

"Absolutely," Tom affirmed. "We had weddings and parties in mind when we built this place. The closest thing to offering this kind of space is the Elks Club up in Tionesta, but folks say it smells funny and it's less than charming. We'd be honored to have yours be the first wedding party we host."

"You're serious?" Genevieve asked.

"Of course," Emma responded with a warm smile. "We'd be honored to host you."

Genevieve let out a nearly inaudible squeal as she wrapped her arms around Matt, looking up into his face. "I know we wanted to keep it simple, but what if we all came here for dancing and refreshments?"

Matt laughed, shaking his head. "You want me to dance?"

"Well, okay, maybe not dancing, but mingling then, and cookies—maybe eclairs."

Matt laughed again. "You had me at eclairs."

Genevieve nodded, turning back to the Parkins. "If you're serious, we'd be delighted to celebrate our marriage here."

"Then it's a done deal. We'll have guests here that weekend, but we'll reserve this space for you and your party. The facilities are a little primitive, but there's a water pump over there and a luxurious outhouse about twenty yards from the west steps," Tom said, pointing.

"It's perfect," Genevieve said, her eyes full of light.

"You two will make it perfect," Emma responded. "We're happy for you, and even happier that we get to keep you around for the near future."

"Thank you, again," Matt replied.

"You're very welcome," Tom said. Both he and Emma moved forward, offering them each a generous hug.

"You two are going to be great additions to Niederbipp," Emma said. "I can feel it."

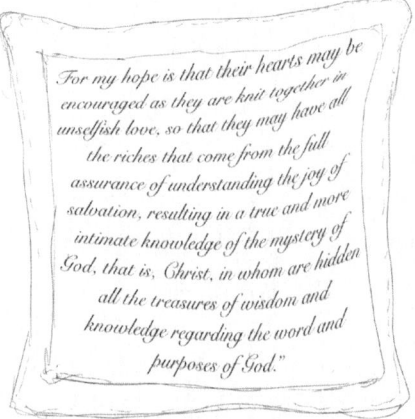

For my hope is that their hearts may be encouraged as they are knit together in unselfish love, so that they may have all the riches that come from the full assurance of understanding the joy of salvation, resulting in a true and more intimate knowledge of the mystery of God, that is, Christ, in whom are hidden all the treasures of wisdom and knowledge regarding the word and purposes of God."

CHAPTER 150

The Work of Joy

Live according to your highest light and more light will be given.
—Peace Pilgrim—

The excitement of the announcement that there would be a reunion carried all of them joyfully back the way they'd come. Afternoon had turned to early evening before they made it back to the farm. The discussion they'd enjoyed on their way home regarding the virtues carved into the benches continued after evening chores when they crowded into the kitchen to prepare dinner. Salad greens, tomatoes, cucumbers and peppers were picked fresh from the garden, eggs were boiled, and cheese was cut and cubed to create a giant salad.

As they gathered around the table to eat, the campers shared with Pops and Ruby the things they'd learned from their walk by the river and their time with the Parkins. Despite her joyful expressions, none of them could deny that Ruby looked weak and pale.

After cleaning up the kitchen, they all gathered on the porch to enjoy the golden hour, the sky on fire with yellow, orange and red streaks that painted everything on the farm in warm, inviting hues. Holly drew a random card from the game file and invited everyone to gather around to hear the details.

"Spud-o-riffic is a timed relay race played with spoons and spuds. Each team has two players, and each player holds a spoon handle in their teeth. Each team is given a small, red spud, not much bigger than the spoon. Team members stand on opposite sides of the porch to begin. Balancing the spud on the first player's spoon, he moves across the porch and transfers the potato onto the spoon of his partner without either player using their hands. The one receiving the potato then turns around seven times before walking the potato back across the porch and around a chair before returning to his or her partner and transferring the potato back to his or her partner's spoon and the process begins again. This is repeated as many times as possible in three minutes. Each successful transfer is worth ten points. Dropping a potato will cost you five points."

"This is ridiculous," James responded.

"No more than any of the other games, and they've all been fun," Spencer argued, getting to his feet.

"There's more," Holly said, turning over the card. "'The team with the most successful transfers and points wins the potato and bragging rights. Any team who laughs enough to create visible snot bubbles shall be awarded twenty bonus points for each bubble."

"I'll go get the spoons and a couple of spuds," Spencer said with a laugh.

When he returned, the furniture had been pushed back, leaving a clear path in the middle of the deck with enough clearance around the chair that it could be circumnavigated without much trouble.

James and Crystal went first and immediately fumbled the potato in the first transfer attempt. They made up for it quickly, however, when Crystal grabbed hold of James's belt on her return from her trip around the chair, pulling him in close before even attempting to transfer the potato to his spoon. They ended with a respectable twenty-five points.

Holly and Greg surprised everyone with a quick lead, due in large part to Holly's aggressive finessing. As Greg first approached her, Holly reached up and took hold of both sides of his face, pulling him down to her level and controlling his movements as she fluidly scooped her spoon under the potato precariously balanced on his spoon. When the timer rang, ending their play, they'd scored a whopping seventy points.

The campers laughed out loud as they watched the unique antics of each team, and laughed some more at the silly grunts and noises they each made and hilarious faces they each pulled as they all went cross-eyed in their up-close-and-personal attempts to transfer the small spud from player to player.

Ruby and Lorenzo opted out of the evening's contest, content to simply laugh and enjoy the comical shenanigans. In the end, it was Sonja and Josh who won the tournament with an impressive ninety points, though this was largely due to the fact that Sonja was suffering from some allergies and succeeded in blowing not one, not two, but three stellar snot bubbles. This, of course, got everyone laughing, making it difficult for all subsequent contestants to score anything above a thirty.

"Oh, it's good for my soul to laugh," Ruby said with bright eyes when the contest had been declared and the prizes had been awarded. They moved the furniture back into place and sat back down, their faces sore from the constant smiles and laughter.

"It's hard to believe how fast this summer's flown by," Ruby said, looking into each of their faces with her kind, steel blue eyes. "We'll be bidding you all farewell in just over a month."

Her words caused them each to stop their joviality.

She took a deep breath and let it out slowly in almost a whistle. "This last month will be the busiest one yet as the majority of the harvest is ahead of us. The pears and apples will need to be picked, and either sold, or pressed or bottled. The best part of the tomatoes are still on the vine. The farm stand will be busier than ever as home canners will be looking for fruits to fill their pantries. The yarn we made months ago still needs to be dyed and made ready for socks."

"Are you going to be teaching Genevieve how to knit socks?" Crystal asked.

"I will if she wants to, but that skill may die with me."

The campers glanced at each other sideways, not at all comfortable with this fatalistic talk.

"Actually, if you don't mind, I think I would like to learn how to knit," Genevieve replied.

"Well, we'll see what we can do," Ruby replied. "There's much to do, and only a few weeks to do it all. Remember you'll be married in less than a month, and your time with me is a whole week shorter than it is with these other kids."

"But we'll have…after," Genevieve replied, sounding almost desperate.

"We shall see. I'm tired, dear ones," Ruby said with a gentle smile. "I've been working hard to keep my energy going, but I'm reluctantly slowing down, despite my best efforts. I'm pacing myself to make it through the finish line on October 8th. I'll need your help."

"Of course," Susan said. "We all want to support you. How can we be more helpful?"

"Keep asking questions. Keep learning. Keep striving to live up to truths you've adopted."

"I don't understand. How does that help you?" asked James.

"It fills me with hope that the years we've spent on this farm have been worthwhile. It gives us a sense of purpose, knowing that if you choose to live the truths you've been taught, you'll each find the joy we've been promising you."

Josh looked at the others before responding. "I think we've already found that joy."

Ruby smiled. "I'm glad you feel that way, but the joy you've experienced can't be more than a small sampling of the great joys that lie ahead for each of you. You won't know the fullness of those joys for some time yet—till you see them working in the lives of your children and your children's children. You won't know the full power behind that joy until you and your spouse have lived and loved according to the keys of joy for some time…maybe decades. And then one day, when all is said and done, you'll sit down next to each other on a quiet bench somewhere and you'll count your blessings and you'll be overwhelmed by the long list and the hand of grace that's followed you over the time you've been striving to live by the keys."

"Is that what you've been doing this afternoon?" Genevieve asked, thoughtfully.

Ruby nodded. "Pops and I spend a lot of time doing that these days. Our heads and hearts are overflowing with memories of campers like each of you and the countless blessings we've enjoyed as we've witnessed the miracles of hearts and minds changing and growing and turning to the one true source of all joy."

"That reminds me of the pillow in the library," Holly replied.

Ruby smiled and nodded.

"What pillow are you talking about?" asked Crystal.

"The one on the couch, with the cross stitching."

Many of the campers looked confused.

"I'll go get it," Holly said, jumping to her feet. She returned a moment later, carrying the throw pillow in her hands. "Did you really never see this?"

They all turned to her, standing at the edge of the circle of chairs. The colorful batik fabric on the back of the pillow looked familiar, but it was clear when she turned it around that they all had missed it.

"What does it say?" Sonja asked.

Holly turned the pillow back around and held it close to her face so she could read it in the low light. "For my hope is that their hearts may be encouraged as they are knit together in unselfish love, so that they may have all the riches that come from the full assurance of understanding the joy of salvation, resulting in a true and more intimate knowledge of the mystery of God, that is, Christ, in whom are hidden all the treasures of wisdom and knowledge regarding the word and purposes of God."

"Whoa, where does that come from?" Josh asked.

Holly looked back down at the pillow. "It says Colossians 2:2-3."

"Please read it again," Matt asked.

She read it a second time, a little slower than before.

"Hearts knit together in unselfish love..." Rachael mused. "That sounds like what's happened to us."

Many of the campers nodded affirmatively.

"That's beautiful," Matt responded. "What was the part about riches again?"

Holly turned back to the pillow. "...so that they may have all the riches that come from the full assurance of understanding the joy of salvation..."

The campers sat in silence for a moment.

"And that joy of salvation..." Greg said, reaching for the pillow, which Holly was quick to share. "...that only comes through the knowledge of God and Christ."

The campers sat quietly, each working through their own thoughts.

"That's what this whole summer's been about, hasn't it?" Susan asked.

"I was just thinking that this is what this whole farm is about," Sonja replied.

"And maybe the whole town of Niederbipp," Ephraim added.

"You're all right," Pops replied.

Genevieve shook her head, looking over Greg's shoulder. "And that pillow's been in the library all summer?"

Ruby smiled. "That pillow's been in the library for over thirty years.

I made it to replace the one that had been here when we arrived and had been nearly loved to death."

"How many more truths have we missed?" asked Holly.

Ruby and Pops smiled.

"There are truths to be found everywhere if your eyes, head and heart are open to see them," Ruby said.

"We've shared Winston Churchill's wisdom before, but it's a good one," Pops suggested. "'Man will occasionally stumble over the truth, but most times he will pick himself up and hurry off as if nothing had happened.'"

"So how do we avoid doing that when we leave here?" Greg asked as many of the campers nodded, sharing the concern.

"It's a common question each year as our campers reach this point and begin contemplating their return to lives that will soon be complicated by so many distractions," Ruby replied.

"And what do you tell them?" James asked.

"The same thing Moses shared with the children of Israel in his farewell address before they finally entered into the promised land," Pops replied.

"Moses? Like a million years ago? That Moses?" Spencer asked.

Pops chuckled. "That's the one."

"How could that be relevant to us?" James challenged.

"That's a critical question in understanding all truth," Pops explained. "Patience and self-discipline will each play a determinant role in the answers you receive, especially as they relate to attitude."

James smiled, shaking his head. "I'm still working on that. Sorry if I sounded ignorant and impatient."

Pops smiled and winked at James. "So much of the truth we are able to perceive and accept is determined by the sincerity of our hearts and the authenticity of our intent. We should never expect to receive more light until we've honestly implemented the light we have. Flirting with any truth on the periphery rarely if ever yields anything more than disappointment and disengagement. We hope you've each learned over the course of this summer that if you want anything worth having, you have to throw yourself wholeheartedly into it."

Spencer nodded humbly. "You have to be all in."

"That's right," Pops affirmed. "Truth can sense your level of commitment from a long distance away, and will either open or close its doors to you as it sniffs you out and determines your earnestness. This is as true today as it was in Moses' time. Those children of Israel who miraculously escaped the tyranny of the Egyptians and walked through the Red Sea on dry ground were still unprepared for the work God had for them to do. Their sincerity was limited. They were easily distracted. Despite the many miracles they witnessed and experienced, being faithfully fed and directed and nourished, they whined and bellyached until, over the course of forty years, the last of the old guard died, and the next generation was more willing to obey God's commands.

"Moses, in one of his final sermons, called the children of Israel together and commanded them once again to love God with all their hearts, souls, and strength, and to carry that love in their hearts. He commanded them to diligently teach that love of God to their children, to speak of God in their homes and in their daily work, and to think of God at both the beginning and the end of the day in prayer."

"So, basically always," Greg suggested.

Pops nodded.

"That almost feels oppressive," James whined.

"I can see how you might feel that way, but remember that the children of Israel didn't exactly have a stellar record of governing themselves. They'd lost their freedom to the Egyptians as a consequence of sin and disobeying God. It wasn't the first time, and it was far from the last that Israel's choices and egos would lead them away from God where they would crash and burn and spend time in captivity before they would humble themselves and return to a place of liberty and joy."

"It sounds like that quote from Greg's Wisdom Cookie a few weeks back," Matt said.

"Only you would remember something from Josh's Wisdom Cookie from weeks ago," James teased.

"Actually, I think I remember it, too," Greg responded. "I've thought about it many times since then."

"What was the quote?" Susan asked.

Greg turned to Matt. "It was the one from William Penn, right?"

Matt nodded. "Men must be governed by God…"

"…or they will be ruled by tyrants," Greg said, finishing the quote.

"I'm curious what's kept you thinking about that quote," Holly asked, leaning forward to look at Greg.

"I guess it's helped me recognize that tyrants come in many forms. For me, the biggest tyrants I've faced in life are my own addictions and weaknesses. It really wasn't until AA that I found God for the first time in my life and started working my way to freedom."

"But your mom was here," Sonja argued. "Surely she must have taught you the keys of joy. Didn't any of that stick?"

Greg smiled good-naturedly. "My mother taught me those very words when I was teenager, but I didn't want what she had to offer. It wasn't cool to be good and do good. I understand why Moses would encourage the Israelites to teach the love of God to their children, but some of us stubborn ones still have to figure it out on our own. I know it's cliche, but I had to be broken beyond what I thought drugs and alcohol could fix before I could see that my only hope was returning to the basics my mother had tried so hard to teach me."

"There's got to be a better way," Crystal replied.

Pops and Ruby both smiled and nodded their heads.

"You might have heard of the keys of liberty?" Ruby said with a sly smile.

"Okay, but…how do you keep your kids from wandering?" Crystal replied. "It's great to know the keys and the answers, but if they don't care…if they choose their own path that leads to captivity and suffering… it just feels so hard."

"Yes, it will undoubtedly be gut-wrenching for each of you to watch as your children make choices that will lead to captivity and addictions and heartache," Ruby acknowledged.

"How do you avoid that heartache?" Holly asked.

"Well, I can think of at least a few ways," Ruby said. "The first is to dig yourself a happy little hole in the dirt somewhere, never marry or have children, and live a no-nonsense life all by your lonesome."

"That's not very attractive either," Ephraim responded.

"No. But it's likely the only foolproof way of avoiding the sorrow of errant children," Pops replied.

"Is there no other way?" Rachael asked.

"Foolproof? I don't think so," Pops replied. "Moral agency is one of the greatest gifts of life. If we're lucky, our parents and our consciences will help us navigate through the early years as we learn to discern truth from error. Moses' invitation and command to diligently teach your children how to love God in all that you do, from sunup to sundown, wasn't made, I believe, because it sounded like a nice idea. He'd raised his own children and watched the behavior of at least a few generations as they'd wobbled and wandered, and made choices that brought them either closer to liberty or drove them far from it."

"Why can't we just withhold the ability to make choices from our kids until they're twenty-one?" James asked, as all the campers laughed.

"Why stop at twenty-one?" Pops answered. "Why not twenty-eight or forty?"

The laughter quickly died.

"Because we each have to learn from making mistakes, don't we?" Holly responded ruefully.

Ruby nodded. "Because, as Emma suggested in her sermon this morning, if we never know the bitter, we have little appreciation for the sweet. Your kids will take their turns alternating between breaking your hearts and filling you with joy. And you will likely have little control over the timing of either one."

"Uh, yeah, you're making parenting sound really amazing," spewed Crystal.

"If it were easy, everyone would do it," Pops replied. "Hard isn't bad. Hard is just hard. And the hard times pass, and the sun comes out, and life moves on, and if you're mindful about the experience, you learn and take notes for the next time around."

"And if you're not mindful and you're a slow learner?" Greg asked.

"Well, then you may have a few more tries before you recognize any progress," Ruby explained. "As you've learned, Greg, until you have at least a little humility, progress with understanding anything spiritual— including yourself— will be slow."

"And I suppose that's the reason for Moses commanding his people to love God and to teach that love to their children?" Matt suggested.

"I think you must be right," Pops affirmed. "Because the children of Israel were not humble and showed no loyalty to the God who offered them liberty from their oppressors, their progress was quite literally dammed. They were halted. And they spent the next forty years aimlessly wandering in circles in the desert until their hearts had been softened enough that they could move forward and inherit the land they'd been promised for decades."

"So, what does loving God look like?" James asked.

"Excellent question," Pops replied. "Any thoughts?"

"Well, Tom and Emma suggested this afternoon that obedience plays a role in that," said Holly.

"Obedience is always a great place to begin," Ruby replied. "Jesus himself said, 'If you love me, keep my commandments.'$_2$ And He later stated, as we've discussed before, that the most important commandments are to love God and to love your neighbor as yourself."

"Reverence and charity," Ephraim said, lifting his hand and touching his thumb to his pinky. "The first and the last commandments."

"Exactly," Pops replied. "We spoke of this briefly some time back, but Moses taught the Israelites that they should tie these commandments as symbols to their hands and wear them on their foreheads, and to even write them on their door frames and on their gates to help remind them always of their promises to love, honor, and remember God."$_3$

"Is God really so insecure that he can't handle people thinking about anything else?" James asked.

Pops smiled but shook his head. "James, what happens when we forget that each of us is a son or daughter of God?"

James looked uncomfortable. "I...I guess we treat each other differently, don't we?"

Many of the campers nodded.

"It's a lot easier to be rude or unkind if you look at everyone as if they're just a schmuck or a jerk," Ephraim responded.

"And where does that lead?" Pops pressed.

They all sat silent for a moment as they considered the question.

"It basically leads to the world we have now," Genevieve responded. "There's no trust, no love, no peace...and not much joy."

Pops nodded. "And if you contrast that with what you've experienced in Niederbipp and on the farm where the keys of joy are symbolically written on everyone's hand, and the people talk openly of the love of God, and the symbols of joy adorn the homes and gates and hearts of the people?"

"We saw those symbols today at Tom and Emma's. They were all over the place, from the front gate to the Gazebo," Holly reported.

"Yes, the Parkins have taken this charge to heart and have been determined to share the powerful truths they've learned with others," Pops replied.

Ruby nodded. "The founders of this farm recognized the pivotal position young people were in as they approached marriage. They believed that if they could help individuals and couples learn the keys of joy before marriage, they could potentially multiply their efforts when marriages and families were formed and expanded."

"You kids have baked enough bread this summer to know the power of both yeast and salt," Pops continued. "It doesn't take much of either one to change the quality and improve the taste of the bread, and yet without it, the results are always less than pleasing."

The campers, recognizing this truth from firsthand experience, nodded with understanding.

"The early founders of this town recognized the direction the world was turning. They'd joined the Quaker church in Southern Germany and Switzerland and immigrated to the new world in the early 1700s with a hope of enjoying a peaceful and prosperous community of like-minded believers," Pops explained. "Had they arrived forty years earlier, when William Penn first established his colony as the site of his Holy Experiment, they might have stayed in Philadelphia and helped perpetuate Penn's ideals of his city of brotherly love.

"But sadly, by the time the Niederbippians arrived, Penn's Philadelphia had already given way to a very different air. Brotherly love was quickly being overrun by greed and selfishness. They knew they could not both maintain the integrity their faith had inspired and remain among the Philadelphians."

"That's why they came here, right?" Sonja replied. "I read about this in Thomas's book."

"That's right," Pops affirmed. "Separating themselves from the world helped maintain the beauty and simplicity of their faith. They were able to put down roots and build solid foundations, both spiritually and physically, that still serve the community today. But they also recognized from the very beginning that it would be impossible for the entire loaf to rise if all the faithful leaven was concentrated in one location. The keys of joy, they knew, needed to be shared. This farm was established in part to help spread the leaven of hope and love and joy to places both far and near."

"And that's what you hope we become? Leaven to our families and communities?" Rachael asked.

Ruby nodded. "Hope is a beautiful, sustaining, ennobling power. Hope has kept us going these past fifty-six years. It's given us grit to continue in the face of discouragement and helped us recognize our purpose and ambitions in sharing the treasures of joy. It may not be incredibly efficient, but it's a beautiful design, don't you think?"

"What? That we get a taste of paradise, and then have to be cruelly dumped back into the real world?" Crystal chided. "Forgive me, but I'm not seeing the beauty of that design at all. It just feels cruel and inhumane."

Ruby pursed her lips, nodding slightly. "We hear similar grumblings every year."

"Then why can't something be changed? Why can't we expand the borders of Niederbipp so everyone who wants to live here can come and stay like you have? Like Matt and Genevieve get to?"

Ruby nodded as all eyes turned to her. "There may come a time when the famine of hope and joy is so profound that people will come running back to places like Niederbipp to find those who are anxiously engaged in living by the keys of joy. But for the time being, Pops and I are still convinced that the pattern established by our predecessors is both wise and prudent. Every summer, twelve individuals leave Harmony Hill with the potential to establish colonies of joy in places all over the country and the world. If you will remember the symbols of joy written on your hands, and carry the truths you've learned in your hearts, and regularly recall the things you've learned here, teaching them to your children and your families, joy will be your companion wherever you go.

"We believe Harmony Hill and Niederbipp will always serve as a repository for the keys and the truths of joy, but they were never meant to stay here. Some men and women will answer the call to keep the flames of joy burning bright and stoke the fires of faith. But the world is big and ever in need of light and hope and leavening and salt. I don't know if it matters much where you are called to stoke or fan the flames of hope and joy. I think it really only matters how you respond to the call, what you do with the light you've been given, and how you share it and encourage others to spread the joy. Paradise isn't necessarily a place, Crystal. Paradise is a way of living and loving that selflessly improves life for those around you, elevating and ennobling everyone within your reach. Equipped with even a basic understanding of the keys of joy, you each have the ability to lift and love and add value to every interaction, every community, every congregation and gathering and society."

Crystal nodded humbly.

"Jesus spoke to his early followers at the sermon on the mount and invited them all to let their lights shine so people could see their good works and develop within themselves a desire to know and understand their Father in Heaven,"[4] Pops continued. "The gifts of light and understanding you've been given this summer were never intended to serve you alone. You've been entrusted with these truths with the hope that you will share and invite and inspire all with whom you will interact for the rest of your lives."

"Colonies of joy, huh?" Greg replied pensively.

Pops and Ruby both smiled and nodded.

"Imagine how the level of hope and light might change across the world if every community were blessed by a colony of joy that invited everyone of all faiths, ethnicities and persuasions to unite in the work of joy," Ruby added.

"I don't think we have to imagine what it would be like," Susan replied. "We've been enveloped in a community like that all summer."

Ruby nodded. "Yes, you each have tasted the fruits of a community built on the foundation of joy. Our invitation to you is to go and build a life that will invite others to do the same."

Notes
1. Amplified Bible
2. John 14:15
3. Deuteronomy 6: 8-9
4. Matthew 5:16

CHAPTER 151

Of Socks and Green Tomatoes

The most satisfying thing in life is to have been able to give a large part of one's self to others.
—Pierre Teilhard de Chardin—

Despite the fact that they knew the end of their time on Harmony Hill was quickly drawing to a close, the explanation Pops and Ruby gave the campers that night changed all future discussions about their impending departure from one of somberness to one of hope and excitement. The tools and keys they'd learned had opened their hearts and minds to far greater potentials than any of them had ever imagined prior to arriving on Harmony Hill at the beginning of the summer.

The passage of time increased dramatically over the next few weeks as the orchard was stripped of its fruit and the kitchen remained constantly busy with the processing and bottling of the hundreds of bottles of applesauce, pie filling and halved pears. The rest of the fruit was sold by the bushel or the bag at the fruit stand, slowly filling the farm's meager coffers for the anticipated tax assessment, gas for the truck, animal feed, and the few sundry necessities that couldn't be produced on the farm.

In the afternoons, or whenever they could get away, Matt and Genevieve continued their wedding plans. On one afternoon they ordered flowers from The Dandelion Cottage, Joseph and Gloria's shop. When the florists asked about their honeymoon plans, Matt and Genevieve were surprised and thrilled when Joseph offered them the use of their Volkswagen Westfalia van for a week—an offer that felt too generous to refuse outright. Instead, they left it on the table until they could discuss it.

Since they had no other pressing matters that afternoon, Matt and Genevieve walked down the street to Mancini's Ice Cafe where they spent the next hour discussing a wide range of possibilities over two large bowls of ice cream. Considering Ruby's health and the need to wrap up the season with the rest of the campers, they decided they really shouldn't be gone for more than five or six days. That would be too short for a European honeymoon, but long enough for a New England road trip. Feeling a little sheepish, they returned to the flower shop and accepted Joseph's offer with a handshake and the promise of many dinner invitations to the farm on Harmony Hill over the coming years.

While in the neighborhood, they made a visit to Albert and Lin's tailor shop to try on their wedding attire and make decisions on the length of the hems. They left the shop feeling a little overwhelmed with the reality that they were getting married in just a couple of weeks. But the stress was short-lived, falling away as they left the shop and Matt took Genevieve's hand in his and they walked back to their bikes.

The overtime work on the farm and the regular chore rotations helped keep the wedding stress levels low. They simply didn't have time to worry about any of it. Having told their parents about their plans to marry and keep it all simple, neither Matt nor Genevieve spent much time working on guest lists or plans to entertain anyone. Because they were both only children whose grandparents had passed away, their closest family members were cousins and a few scattered aunts and uncles. This felt like a great relief, knowing expectations and preparations for the wedding would be minimal. There were no appointments with stationers, no visits with party planners, no choosing of colors and linens for the after party, and absolutely no flexing of wallets or egos. It was going to be a no-frills wedding, and that suited both Matt and the *new* Genevieve Patterson quite well.

Several letters arrived over the course of the next several days from their parents. Genevieve's folks offered to host a wedding party at their country club, while Matt's mom and dad offered to pay for tuxedos and flowers. Matt knew that meant that his mom would be scrimping, and his father would be shirking. They both climbed the drive to use the payphone several times that week, thanking their parents for the kind and thoughtful offers, but turning them down for reasons of simplicity and optics. This, they explained, would not be a tuxedo wedding. And traveling back to Boston to attend a fancy party in their honor was not something either of them felt would be a good use of their few days away. Instead, they promised to spend a night at Genevieve's parents' home and invite them to the farm over Christmas, as long as they'd help with the chores.

A certified letter arrived in the mail the next day from Genevieve's parents, along with a check for $30,000 and a short explanation from her father saying that it was the minimum he'd expected to pay for his only daughter's wedding party at the country club. An attached letter from her mother assured her that they'd be willing to pay up to $20,000 more if they needed it, which she admitted was still far less money than some of the wedding parties they'd attended in recent years. She offered her help with wedding planning but recognized that Genevieve was a fully liberated woman and did not want to step on her toes or get in her way.

They admitted that they'd spent some time earlier that summer surfing the internet for any references to "Neiderboops", but they'd been unable to discover much from their apartment in Paris. A closer examination of the spelling from one of Genevieve's earlier letters led them to discover exactly 12 links to business websites in Niederbipp, including a grocery store, a car dealership, the regional hospital, and a few bed-and-breakfasts. Reading between the lines, there was an implicit and underlying sense of worry that the only daughter of a small-time tycoon was choosing such an alternative path for her life and future. They expressed hope that she knew what she was doing but trusted that her superior genetics and inherited intellect would enable her to choose the best path for her future.

As a side note, they expressed gratitude that the timing of her wedding would not interfere with their attendance at either the Bostonian Masquerade Ball or the annual Prix de l'Arc de Triomphe. They admitted they'd have to leave for Paris immediately following the wedding and hoped that wouldn't sound too insensitive, but it was, after all, the most important horse race in the world and one they hadn't missed since Genevieve had left for college, twelve years earlier.

For Matt, the whole thing felt cold and strange. Not that his family was in any way a flawless model of love and support—it most certainly wasn't. But the idea of being thrilled that the wedding of their only child squeezed seamlessly in between their society events and an international horse race felt somehow shallow and insensitive. He wondered what might have happened had their wedding conflicted with any of the events on their calendar.

On a walk that afternoon, they talked about the priorities of their own future family, recognizing that the farm and the seasonal campers would certainly influence the time and commitment to their own children. Though they had no illusions that the balance would be easy, they committed to make each other and their future children their first and second priorities. Matt also promised Genevieve that he'd take her on a date at least once a week, even if that date consisted of nothing more than a walk to the end of the road and back.

Returning from their walk to find her father's check and the pledge of more if it were needed, Genevieve and Matt took the question of what to do with it to their fellow campers. A discussion held at the dinner table opened the eyes of each of them. Though they each knew of weddings costing considerably more, the idea of blowing even half of the check for a wedding party now felt indulgent, even gluttonous. Having been almost completely removed from money for the last several months other than their weekly assignment at the farm stand, the conversation triggered an acute recognition that their financial opinions had been forever altered. Even Crystal, who'd struggled with money and fairness issues her whole life, admitted that she felt unprepared to return to the outside world where comparisons and keeping up with the Joneses had blinded her to the small and simple joys that had so profoundly changed her outlook since coming to the farm, many of which cost nothing or very little.

While each of the campers considered the truth of Crystal's experience, Pops shared the sad story of their late friend, Robert Allen. Bob had grown up in Niederbipp, but had always dreamt of living a bigger, more grandiose life. He and his wife had left to chase his dreams, teaming up with a couple of friends in Colorado to found a new ski town they called Vail. Bob had later served multiple terms as the town's mayor, staying on long after his wife and children had chosen to return to Niederbipp to be closer to family. He'd worked hard, made his fortune, and planned well for retirement. But only three months after he retired and moved home, his wife of forty years passed away. In the months and years that followed, Pops explained how Bob recognized that he'd traded diamonds for common stones, giving up his children's childhood for the pride and money of a high-profile career. With his wife's death, the glue that held the family together faded away quickly, leaving Bob with a lot of time to think about his life's choices.

Ruby shared that Bob didn't even know the birthdays or phone numbers of his own children, having neglected to ever make them a priority. Filled with regrets and loneliness, he'd spent the last twenty-eight years of his life walking the riverbanks, collecting pretty rocks and bottle caps which he shared with everyone he encountered in the hopes of helping them find joy in the small things, while avoiding the same mistakes he'd made.

With these lessons in mind, Greg suggested saving the money to buy a used pickup truck when the old farm truck finally died. They all agreed that the suggestion was far more practical than blowing it all on a wedding. Instead, Matt and Genevieve made a trip to the bank the next day, opened an account, and deposited the check, deciding they'd use whatever funds they needed to pay for the wedding expenses and set the rest aside for a rainy day.

With the generous offer of using the Parkin's gazebo as a gathering place for their wedding party, Matt and Genevieve enlisted the help of each of the campers over the course of a week's worth of afternoons to "taste test" several kinds of cookies until they'd settled on five varieties everyone seemed to enjoy. Snickerdoodles, chocolate chip, molasses, oatmeal raisin and pumpkin chocolate chip each made the list. Enough dough to bake several dozen of each variety was made and frozen so the cookies could be baked fresh the day before the wedding.

On another afternoon, Matt and Genevieve visited with Jake and Amy to learn more about their wedding. With Genevieve being a very lapsed Catholic and Matt having grown up in a tangled conglomerate of Protestant practices, it was really only their new-found spiritualism and faith in God that united their spiritual lives. They found that Jake and Amy shared many of their basic tenets, and they were happy to hear more about the traditional Quaker wedding that had united them.

They learned that because there is no paid ministry in a Quaker church, and no priesthood or clergy to officiate, a Quaker wedding is considered *self-uniting,* and all the guests are invited to participate as witnesses to the union, even signing their names to the marriage certificate. The ceremony, other than the reading of the vows, they learned, is often silent. Participants and guests are invited to say a few, brief words as directed by the Holy Spirit, but because silence is considered the Quaker's sacrament, guests are urged to speak only if it improves on the silence.

They also learned from Amy and Jake that nearly all of the old-timers in town were married in the church after the Quaker tradition, and that many of the campers from Harmony Hill, including Pops and Ruby, had been married in self-uniting ceremonies.

The porch discussion that evening centered around marriage ceremonies. James and Crystal admitted they had looked at the Quaker ceremony but had opted to have James's good friend, Bryan, marry them. Having recently received his credentials from the internet, Bryan had been soliciting his single friends for opportunities to practice. And considering that neither of them had any strong religious ties, it felt like the right thing to do.

After listening to Ruby and Pops share their story, it was also clear to Matt and Genevieve what they should do. Pops spoke of the solemnity of their wedding day, the small assemblage of friends and family gathered in the Niederbipp chapel, and the sense of peace and dignity that filled the hall. Pops excused himself for a moment, returning with the framed wedding certificate that had been hanging in their bedroom for more than five-and-a-half decades. The certificate, beautifully hand-drawn in fancy calligraphy and embellished with watercolor flourishes, had yellowed over time. But they all listened to their elderly hosts speak of that glorious evening as if it had been yesterday. They both spoke of the sense that God and his angels had smiled on their union, when, as they'd gathered in the church courtyard to enjoy a simple cake with their guests, a glorious evening light had saturated the valley like a benediction.

Only eighteen people had signed their names to the certificate that day as witnesses to their union. As Pops read the names of those who'd been there, they both got a little teary, recognizing that every one of them were now dead and gone. Even with a porch full of people who loved and admired Pops and Ruby, there was an undeniable sense of loneliness that those with whom life's greatest bonds had been forged, had, in the interlude, been taken from them.

Matt and Genevieve took a long walk that evening after the gathering on the porch. They walked up the drive and kept walking, down past the Cartwright farm and to the end of the road where the forest trail began. They held hands as they walked and talked, shaking off the last bits of melancholy from Pops and Ruby's shuffle down memory lane. They both acknowledged how fifty-six years had felt like a long time prior to that evening, but as they had watched their elderly hosts fondly sharing memories, fifty-six years had somehow felt far too short. They recognized, however, that in that same amount of time, Matt would be a hundred years old, and that they could potentially be great-grandparents.

The talk of old age and future posterity brought with it its own sense of mortality. By the time they made it back to the farm's drive, they still weren't ready for bed. Instead, they wandered past the phone booth and took a seat on the bench that overlooked the valley. Only a few lights shone from the town, but the small sliver of a moon allowed the night's myriad stars to shine bright. Matt and Genevieve sat in silent awe for a long time, snuggling with each other against the chill of the night. They spoke of change; change of perspective, change of dreams, change of expectations, and the dozens of other changes that had brought each of them to a place where they looked forward to welcoming twelve campers to the farm each summer for the foreseeable future. They spoke of hope and love and the keys of joy which they acknowledged had been the catalyst for much of the growth and progress they'd experienced. They spoke of sharing those truths with others and living them more completely in a way that might allow them to shine in the same way as Pops and Ruby, and Tom and Emma, Hildedgard and Thomas, and Jake and Amy, and so many other Niederbippians did.

When they ran out of things to say, they walked to the top of the drive, looking down over the starlit pond, the garden, and the farmhouse. What had felt overwhelming just weeks before somehow had begun to feel tenable. They held each other close, silently comforted by the fact that they were doing all of this together. As they walked down the rutted drive, hand in hand, there was no place for fear or uncertainty. The light of hope had chased out all darkness, making room for optimism and love to grow unencumbered.

Matt walked Genevieve to her door. Even without a watch, they still knew it was well after one o'clock in the morning, and that the rooster would soon be rousing the farm from its slumber, but neither of them wanted to let go or say goodnight. Instead, they held onto each other, warmed by the physical, emotional, and spiritual connection they shared. Without a need for words or any additional physical expressions, they silently relished the sense of pure connection.

Something changed that night for both of them, and it wasn't long before the others recognized it as well. There was an undeniable sense of sexual tension between Matt and Genevieve, but it was Holly who identified and coined the term *Comprehensive Aggregate Attraction* to best describe what she and the other women were witnessing. Comprehensive Aggregate Attraction, as Holly defined it, was the uncommon connection where the limited ability to pursue physical romance focused the senses to more fully appreciate the often less-conspicuous qualities of an individual. Whatever it was or how it was described, no one could deny that it was inspiring to witness love growing in such a pure and unadulterated manner.

One afternoon, about a week after the bottling of the apples and pears had been completed and the pigs had grown fat on the scraps from the kitchen, Pops led four of the men to the pig pen for the annual culling of the swineherd. The piglets that had been born a month before the campers arrived had grown exponentially larger over the course of the summer, each of them now weighing well over two hundred pounds. Of the nine hogs, six were selected for auction, while three were slated for the butcher. After the commotion of the sorting, the giant sow found her place in the shade of the awning and took a nap, seemingly unaware or unconcerned for the fate of her children.

Pop explained that this was always one of his least favorite annual tasks, but that the auction in Warren always paid top dollar for the hogs from Harmony Hill. Even in years when the market was more saturated than others, Pops's pigs had often fetched five hundred dollars a head, sometimes even more. Being no fan of butchering, he had long employed the Amish brothers, Ezra and Tobias Stoltzfuss to do the unsavory job for him. The brothers, who ran a butchery service from their uncle's farm, offered fair prices and produced the best hickory-smoked bacon in the whole county.

A horse trailer, borrowed from the Cartwrights, was brought around to the swine yard and the six hogs were cajoled inside with a bucket of wormy apples. Recognizing this all would soon be his responsibility, Matt joined Pops and Ephraim on the two-hour round trip to Warren, while Spencer and James washed the remaining hogs for both their debut and final performance with the butchers. Though the men had all taken their turns feeding the pigs and had watched them grow with this purpose ultimately in mind, the reality that an animal would have to die so that next year's campers could enjoy bacon left all of them far more subdued than normal. Upon the return of the pickup, the last three hogs were loaded into the trailer, and all four of the men accompanied Pops to the Stoltzfuss farm.

The barn they had all helped build on a single Saturday several months earlier was now occupied with the impressive energy of a two-hundred-head dairy operation. They drove past the barn and around to the east end of the farm where the Amish brothers had set up their shop in the larger half of a tack barn. Both men came out to meet them wearing aprons smeared with blood. Pops introduced the campers to Tobias and Ezra, explaining to the brothers that Matt would soon be taking over the farm on Harmony Hill. The men seemed to understand without any need for explanation, but for Matt, the reality of what this meant hung on him like a heavy stone. That feeling remained while Pops placed his order. Matt tried to make mental notes of everything he was hearing, but he knew he'd have to rely on these men to help him learn the ropes for the next several years. Chops, sausage, roasts, bacon, hocks and hams were listed on the order while the pigs were turned loose in a small holding pen where they would wait their turn at the processing.

The burden Matt had felt continued as the men climbed back into the truck. Taking his turn to ride in the pickup bed, Matt watched silently as the butcher shed disappeared behind the mammoth barn. As they drove out on the farm's gravel drive, Matt looked up to see the keys dangling from the rooster weathervane. Surprised by the sudden surge of hope that came at seeing those keys, Matt focused his eyes on them until long after they'd faded into the background.

The relatively quick ride back to Harmony Hill helped clear his head. Driving past the farmstand and finding it closed meant that Josh and Genevieve had sold out early and were on their way back to the farm by now. As the truck labored to climb the hill, Matt found himself feeling anxious to share his thoughts with Genevieve. But by the time they returned the trailer and pulled into the farmyard, it was clear from the gathering on the porch that he would have to wait.

Ruby, her energy having continued to fade, had spent many afternoons napping, but things were different today. All the women and the remaining men had gathered on the front porch around a strange-looking contraption. A hand crank, connected to a few cogs, sent a shuttle clicking around a three-inch diameter orifice that was lined with six dozen silver hooked needles. Colorful yarn looped up and over the whole contraption through tension rods. With the movement of the shuttle and the crank, yarn was automatically pulled from the skeins and fed into the machine's toothy orifice.

With great curiosity, Ephraim examined the sock knitting machine as Ruby continued to make small adjustments on the tension setters, doing her best to answer questions while explaining what she was doing and why. The sock machine, they learned, had been purchased by a former camper at a flea market several decades earlier and had been sent to the farm as a time-saving gift for Ruby and Pops. This machine, Ruby explained, had been invented during the First World War to allow the public to produce socks for the soldiers in the soggy trenches of Europe.

Ruby admitted she'd never much enjoyed the machine, still preferring to hand-knit every pair of socks she made. But Pops had taken a liking to the contraption that had helped him feel productive, also, on the evenings Ruby that passed knitting on the porch or in the library. With a little practice, Pops explained, he'd been able to produce about one pair of socks each hour compared with Ruby's one pair of socks each day. He admitted his socks weren't as much fun or as intricate as Ruby's designs, but his socks still sold well while also offering him a creative outlet.

After a basic tutorial, the sock-knitting machine quickly became a gathering point for the campers over the next week. This was especially true after Ruby helped expand their creative pallets by teaching the campers how to dye wool. After a quick trip to town to buy Kool-aid in a variety of colors, gallons of different flavors were mixed, and the skeins of yarn were dyed and then dried to create a rainbow of colors. A few of the campers who'd had some experience with tie-dye played around with the skeins and colors, producing a dozen skeins that combined all the colors of the rainbow in uncommon patterns and orders, each one unique.

And despite the fact that summer was running out and the chores kept them busy for many hours each day, the campers did all they could to make time to hang out together. Evening games continued to be played and invented, including a new game called *The Ugliest Pair*, in which the campers took turns being blindfolded and selecting yarn only according to touch. These would be handed to a blindfolded teammate sitting at the knitting machine, who would do their best to use the hand crank to create designs in the socks according to the calls and instructions given by their seeing teammates.

Over the course of an hour, they created a pair of socks that was almost beyond description. Areas of camouflage butted up against polka dots and stripes. Colors ran this way and that. One sock looked like it had two heels, while the other was at least four inches longer than its "mate." And though each sock was ugly by itself, the fact that they had an equally ugly mate somehow made the combination fun, even strangely attractive.

The discussion that evening naturally circled around the odd pairs the campers and their elderly hosts had witnessed over the years. Pops shared the story of JoAnn Johnson and Robert Bricky, a couple who'd met on the farm a dozen years earlier. They'd each come to the farm in their late thirties, each of them individually agreeing to give the possibility of marriage one last chance, though they each had come close to swearing off marriage altogether. JoAnn, who stood over six-foot-four, had significantly narrowed her search for a companion by spending her adult life looking only for marriage partners who were six-foot-five or better. Robert, on the other hand, though tall in spirit, stood only five-foot-six. He'd been constantly turned down for dates by women who didn't want to waste their time with a man who was physically the opposite of most everything they wanted. Because they knew they wouldn't be physically attracted to each other for obvious reasons, they decided early on to become friends. But as that summer had passed, their friendship evolved into love, making room for important possibilities that might have been overlooked had love not had time to grow.

Ruby went on to explain that differences in things like age, weight and height were probably far less important than differences in things like patience, dreams, or spirituality and religion. A good marriage, she maintained, was not based on similarities, but on the ability of two individuals to give and take while remaining true to core correct principles. Differences regarding money, sexual drives, communication and a hundred other things could be sorted out, she insisted, if marriage partners consciously and repeatedly chose to exercise the keys of joy in both their personal lives and their marriage.

This concept was no longer new to any of them. For months they'd been discussing, learning, and even practicing the keys of joy. But with the number of days left on the farm growing increasingly smaller, the meat of what they'd been learning grew increasingly significant as they each considered the life-changing truths and practices they'd be taking home.

While the campers worked their way through their own headspace, the work on the farm continued at a frenzied pace. The threat of the first frost sent the campers to the garden late one afternoon to collect the remaining tomatoes, peppers, cucumbers and zucchini, covering the kitchen island with the harvest. The red tomatoes were either eaten or bottled while the green ones, save for twenty large beefsteaks, were individually wrapped in newspaper and stored in the cellar to ripen over time. With the last of the green tomatoes, Ruby taught the campers the art of mincemeat and fried green tomatoes.

The mincemeat recipe had been passed down through the matchmakers for at least a couple of generations, along with a fabled story of frugality and letting nothing go to waste. As the story went, an early frost had shortened the growing season by several weeks, leaving hundreds of green tomatoes piled up in the kitchen. Knowing these would all go to compost if a productive use was not found for them, Lucy Goldstein got busy, and with what she considered divine help, concocted a vegetarian mincemeat formula that still wins pie contests across the county. The pie filling, consisting mainly of apples, green tomatoes and raisins, had been bottled and stored in the cellar every fall since then, awaiting the holidays and other times to help remember the goodness and mercy of God who made it possible for even green tomatoes to have a purpose.

Many of the campers expressed their doubts that green tomatoes could be reasonably baked into a pie that would be worth eating. But they all had to eat their doubts that evening when Ruby pulled three beautiful pies from the oven and served them warm with dollops of fresh whipped cream.

Nothing went to waste. The last of the cucumbers were bottled for pickles, peppers were eaten fresh, and the zucchini was grated and baked into zucchini bread or frozen for the zucchini breads of the future.

Many of the campers, after trying the zucchini bread, regretted floating so many zucchinis down the river during the Annual Zucchini Regatta.

On the same day that Pops walked the campers to the fields to watch the combine harvesting the wheat, oats and rye that they'd planted in the spring, they also participated in the harvest of the honey. With only three bee suits available, Pops handed the other two hoods and sets of gloves to Matt and Genevieve while the rest of the campers stood back and watched from a safe distance. While Genevieve puffed white smoke from the bellowed smoker, Pops and Matt moved quickly and carefully to sort through the honey-laden frames in the upper boxes, moving the heaviest of them into the waiting wheelbarrows. Tens of thousands of bees poured out of the four hives, buzzing all about in an effort to secure their golden treasure. While the unprotected campers watched, Pops and Matt, their faces obscured by their beekeeping hoods, wheeled the frames away, the trailing clouds of bees growing thinner with each step from their homes.

The campers followed behind from a distance, staying just in front of Genevieve who continued to puff the smoker as she walked backwards. Before they reached the milking barn, the bees had all returned to their hive, leaving the campers to the stolen loot. Pops was patient as he instructed the campers in the work of honey extraction. A hot knife cut the wax from the capped honeycomb, exposing the golden nectar inside. When both sides of the frame had been cleared of wax, the frames were lined up in the stainless steel centrifuge and the campers took turns spinning the carousel until all the honey had been removed. A spigot at the bottom of the centrifuge allowed the honey to flow through a filter and into the waiting bottles. In little more than two hours, the year's haul of sixty-eight quarts of Harmony Hill honey had been processed and moved to the cellar.

Deep-fried scones were served with dinner that night, helping each of the campers appreciate the fine work of their apiarian friends. While they enjoyed the honey, Pops and Ruby shared some of the fun facts they knew about bees. A worker bee, for example, lives only thirty to sixty days, over which time they may contribute as much as 1/12 of a tablespoon of honey. They learned that all worker bees are female, the slightly larger and beady-eyed males serving only one function—to tango with the queen who mates only once in her lifetime, thereafter laying up to two thousand eggs a day, or one-and-half-million eggs over her life span of up to two years. Flying up to several miles to collect pollen, bees work together to produce their nectar, fanning their wings to reduce the water content to between eight and ten percent before the honeycomb cells are capped with wax to preserve it in a way that could keep for millennia.

But the fact that Ruby was most passionate about was the making of a queen. When the workers begin to recognize that their queen is slowing down or growing old, they will begin to feed a larva copious amounts of royal jelly. Though each larva is fed royal jelly, the difference between royalty and the worker is the amount and quality of the food she is given. Five to seven days after the new queen is born, she flies from the hive, mates, and returns to serve her colony for the rest of her life. "Like all the bees in the hive," Ruby stressed, "each of us have the potential to be monarchs. Royalty is determined not by birth, but by what we take into our bodies, minds, and souls, and from the level of respect we demand through the way we live and conduct our lives."

For Genevieve, the talk of nobility being more about character and service than about beauty and privilege was thought-provoking, further strengthening her resolve to stay and dedicate her life to the truths to which Harmony Hill and the town of Niederbipp had exposed her. This simple truth, lived by bees, proved to be a revelation for all the women and many of the men. The rise of physically-beautiful-but-otherwise-shallow men and women in the media made them all a little crazy. Genevieve knew this phenomenon more than most, her work over the last seven years having been focused on the promotion and economics of beauty culture. But she had seen firsthand how short-lived and short-sighted that way of living was. She'd already known too many models who'd given up the best years of their lives to promote the unsustainable and excessive, often neglecting their health and psychological well-being in the process.

A consensus rose from the women the next evening as they chatted late into the night in their bunkhouse. They recognized how much time and treasure they'd wasted being concerned about things that didn't matter. Holly, who'd spent time on a committee her senior year to promote the increase of respect for coeds, shared a couple of the campaigns they'd publicized. Hundreds of T-shirts emblazoned with the words, 'You don't need bigger boobs, you need to read better books,' had been sold and distributed across campus to encourage fellow women to recognize that the source of true beauty and value runs far deeper than many had allowed themselves to believe.

That same evening, in the adjacent bunkhouse, a complementary discussion took place among the men, in which they identified the values of confidence, spiritual sensitivity, modesty and unpretentiousness to be far more important, both in themselves and the women they dated, than had ever been the case before. Physical beauty, they recognized, was an ever-fading asset, while the more noble characteristics they identified grew brighter and more profoundly beautiful with time and maturity. Men like Spencer and James who'd previously made dating decisions almost solely on physical appearances openly recognized how profoundly insufficient and limited their views had been. They each recognized how working intimately with quality women whose natural beauty and confidence grew day by day had changed all of them over the course of the summer. The shallowness of their previous desires had been replaced with their new found ability to see clearly, converse authentically, listen genuinely, and discover the profoundly great fortune of finding these values in others.

Nobility, they learned together in subsequent discussion over meals, work, or gatherings on the porch, had little to do with personal wealth or accumulated stuff, and everything to do with the quality and integrity of the soul.

CHAPTER 152

17927

Without self-knowledge, without understanding the working and functions of his machine, man cannot be free, he cannot govern himself and he will always remain a slave.
—George Gurdjieff—

The sermon at church the next Sunday offered the campers additional food for thought. Cindy McLaughlin, a poised redhead who'd grown up in Niederbipp and had returned with her husband, George, after they'd retired, walked to the pulpit after the invocation. She was dressed smartly in a plaid, pleated skirt and a complementary green, felted jacket that highlighted her graying red hair. As she smiled at the congregation, Matt and Genevieve remembered the rock and the lemon drops that had marked their first interaction with the couple, the night Isaac Kimball had been born. But the words that came from Cindy's mouth made them quickly realize there was far more to her than the quirks and idiosyncrasies that had originally made them wonder.

"As Thomas mentioned, we had the good fortune, seven years ago, of moving back to the home I grew up in after being away for nearly fifty years. Mom had passed away nearly thirty years earlier, and Daddy... well, you all remember Daddy..."

Many in the congregation nodded, not hiding their broad smiles.

"Daddy, as you'll recall, was a collector. One of the beautiful things of having a parent who is a collector is that his house became a time capsule, preserving the history of the past. It's taken George and me the better part of the last seven years to liberate my father's rock collection, returning the largest of them to the riverbanks, while continuing his legacy and dying wish that we share the best of his treasures with the good people of Niederbipp. Thank you for loving and caring for him in those last two decades when he was dearly missing my mother and struggling with his dementia. Within that time capsule that is my childhood home, George and I found this hanging on the wall under a rather thick layer of dust and cobwebs."

She held aloft an eight-inch square wooden frame with a few simple lines of needlepoint preserved beneath the glass. "I don't recall my mother making this—it must have been done before my birth, but as I dusted it off and read its truth, I found myself feeling grateful for the faith and dedication of that noble woman. The words she eternalized in embroidery floss are from the Psalmist who said, 'Train up a child in the way he should go: and when he is old, he will not depart from it.'

"It took me a few years after leaving home to recognize the value of that truth. Every Sunday morning, rain or shine, my mother got us kids out of bed and marched us up the hill to church where we sat on the fourth row, in front of the Goldsteins and behind the Shreyers. We knew this is where we belonged every Sunday morning, and none of us ever doubted it. I've wondered from time to time if it wasn't my mother's way of making sure my brothers and I had a community of fellow believers to draw strength from. It worked. My brothers and I are all grateful for the firm foundation our faith has offered each of us. With Daddy away on business more often than he was at home, I remember many of the good men and women of our congregation looking after me and my brothers and checking in on Mom.

"Even though Daddy's business kept him away for weeks and even months at a time, we knew we were loved, not only by our parents, but by the good people of Niederbipp who looked after us as if we were their own children. All of us have taken our turn with faith crises and tangents along our journeys, but the foundation we gained in our home and on the fourth row of the Niederbipp church has continued to offer us a foundation of hope while reminding us of those great keys that promise joy.

"I was only ten back in 1962 when my mother read to us the story of a fire that started in the mining town of Centralia, Pennsylvania, about a hundred miles from here. The city dump, located in the crater of an abandoned strip mine, had filled up with garbage. Members of the volunteer fire department were hired to reduce the bulk of the garbage by burning it. This wasn't anything new. The dump had been burned many times before, as was standard in those days. By code, layers of local clay had been used for decades to provide fire resistance between the layers. But something was different about the fire of '62. No one knows for certain how it happened, but one way or another, hot coals found their way into the abandoned labyrinth of mine shafts beneath the pit.

"Some firefighters suggested the mine should be flooded with water immediately to ensure the fire would be extinguished, but the majority of their colleagues and townspeople felt like it was a waste of time and resources, believing the fire would go out of its own accord. But as you might guess, the fire did not go out. Among my parent's collection, George and I found this scrapbook filled with decades of articles about the Centralia fire that continues to burn underground to this day." She hefted the old binder, making the yellowed sheets of newsprint visible to all who cared to see.

"I remember my mother reading many of these articles to me and my brothers through the 60s and into the 70s. And from time to time, she would call us on the phone after we'd left home to read portions of articles regarding Centralia's growing problem.

"The articles often spoke of the many residents who simply ignored the wisps of smoke that escaped from the ground, but others sounded the alarm, demanding something be done. Over time, the town was divided into several different factions, each with their own ideas about what should be done. But as is often the case when too many disparate voices demand that their concerns be heard, nothing was done at all, and the fire continued to spread through the underground labyrinth.

"In an article from 1979, we learned that a local gas station owner went out to check the level of his underground tanks and was shocked when the dipstick he used came out hot. A thermometer lowered into the tank recorded a temperature of over 170° Fahrenheit. Two years later, a 12-year-old boy fell into a sinkhole, 4 feet wide and 150 feet deep that collapsed beneath his feet when he was out playing in his own yard. Had it not been for his cousin and a tree root, the boy would have fallen to his death. By then, any hopes of controlling the fire had been extinguished, no pun intended. One by one, lifetime residents of Centralia began to move away, and as they did, the county and state government razed their abandoned houses, further encouraging people to leave.

"In 1992, the governor invoked a claim of eminent domain to try to force people out. Articles in the scrapbook tell of many residents fighting the evictions, but even the best fighters have their limits. After a steady decline in population, Centralia, Pennsylvania is a ghost town today. Highway 61, which once cut through town, has been bypassed. For years, this stretch of abandoned highway that had been blocked by earthen berms became a colorful, mile-long canvas for graffiti artists, but it's since been covered with earth and reclaimed by nature. A once thriving town of fifteen-hundred residents, homes, businesses and farms has been reduced to a smoldering mess of abandonment. Families have been uprooted. Lifestyles have been forever altered. Inheritances have been lost. Hope has been forsaken. And for what purpose?

"As I've studied these articles, it's not difficult to pinpoint the times and places where all of this could have been amended and disasters could have been averted. Hindsight, as they say, is generally 20/20. But unfortunately, by the time clarity is gained, we are often too far away to change the past, and not far enough away to have learned the lessons. Consequences tend to find us whether we're ready or not. And procrastination, though it may help us avoid unpleasantries in the short-term, nearly always leaves us wanting and wishing we'd been more diligent and thoughtful.

"I'm reminded of an old proverb about a nail that says, 'For want of a nail the shoe was lost. For want of a shoe the horse was lost. For want of a horse the rider was lost. For want of a rider the message was lost. For want of a message the battle was lost. For want of a battle the kingdom was lost. And all for the want of a horseshoe nail.'"

"I suppose there are dozens of lessons that could be learned from this proverb, but I'd like to focus my thoughts today around how the equivalent of a horseshoe nail changed the life of an entire community in a very real and fatal way.

"It's not very often that we get to see the long story and recognize key points where ignorant, short-sighted choices led to additional ignorant and short-sighted choices. In fact, this entire scrapbook contains the sad history of kicking the proverbial can down the road until the very road collapsed and fell into oblivion.

"Curious why my mother and then my father went to the trouble of compiling this scrapbook on Centralia, I learned from my oldest brother of my mother's connection to the doomed town. In the last few years, we've learned that my mother's grandfather, William Clyde Barnes, was one of the early settlers of Centralia and served for more than twenty years as the town's postmaster. Our direct line had moved away before my mother was born, but Mom had cousins who remained in the community until the mid-80's when their home was condemned and bulldozed.

"As I've reviewed the articles in this scrapbook over the years, I can't help but think of the power of choices and the tendencies we probably all have to delay the mending of our ways. As we've watched our children and grandchildren exercise their agency, or looked back on some of our own choices, I often find myself thinking of Centralia. In fact, a couple of years ago, I dusted off my mother's old needlepoint basket and cross stitched this." She held up another small frame with five block numbers stitched with colorful embroidery floss to a muslin background and protected under glass.

"17927," she read aloud. "If it sounds like some kind of a code, it's because it is—a code known as a *Zone Improvement Plan Code*, or zip code for short. It may be difficult to imagine the U.S. mail system functioning without the use of zip codes, but until 1963, it did. 17927 was the zip code assigned to Centralia, or at least it was until about twenty years ago when the zip code was discontinued, and the post office was plowed into the dirt. It may seem like a silly thing to go to all the trouble to cross stitch the numbers of a dead zip code and hang it in our home, but for me, the decision was very deliberate. And I hope that someday, when our children and grandchildren sort through the time capsule that is our home, they will ask themselves what this is all about.

"It's been said that most of us must suffer our way to wisdom. In my own quest for wisdom, I've learned that we, too, often choose the paths of least resistance when it's hard work and integrity that are called for. We too often neglect our duties and postpone rectifying our mistakes, leaving our paths strewn with the skeletons of our errors as we motor on. Sometimes, like in the case of the Centralia mine fire, the evidence of those errors lay hidden for years, even decades, ignored until the consequences run their course and eventually catch up. And as far as I've been able to tell, the consequences—both good and bad—though they may be delayed for a season, *always* eventually catch up. I am grateful for the keys of joy and the principle of self-discipline that teach us, if we're open to it, the virtues of moderation and the endless advantages that come as a consequence of hard work and by avoiding our natural tendencies for procrastination. This is what 17927 means to me.

"Just a stone's throw from our home stands a monument called the Englehart Ebenezer. I'm sure many of you know it. It was built nearly three hundred years ago to mark the place where the early settlers built a ferry and moved their company from the east to the west side of the river, saving their mortal lives from the river's destructive floods, and their souls from the corruption of degenerate humanity. Our community has many monuments that have been built to encourage and extend the memory of sacred and important things. I am grateful for these, and for the virtues they inspire. And I find myself wondering from time to time what I will leave behind to serve my family and community as a marker or a monument to some valuable or memorable wisdom we've been blessed to acquire through both heartache and inspiration. I wish there were better ways of passing wisdom from one generation to another. But most of us come only to the straight and narrow paths of light and wisdom after first wandering the crooked paths of indulgence and deception. We often find the truth only after we've trudged our way down to the beach and back a hundred times to build and rebuild our dream homes on foundations completely incapable of supporting them. Few of us are capable of seeing the virtues gained through the experience of others until we've been burned by our own errant, delinquent fires.

"The wise prophet, Confucius, taught that 'By three methods we may learn wisdom: First, by reflection, which is noblest; second, by imitation, which is easiest; and third by experience, which is the bitterest.' I hope someday that this cross stitch will serve as a reminder to my children and grandchildren of lessons learned. I hope it might remind them, as it has me, to extinguish the fires of disharmony and discontent early before they are allowed to grow and become destructive. I hope they will avoid procrastinating the changes necessary to bring peace to their marriages and family relationships. I hope they will act early and often to restore and forgive when they've wronged or been wronged. I hope they will see the big picture and recognize their small but critical role in it.

"As a child, I remember learning from this very pulpit of the Iroquois philosophy that the decisions we make today will be felt seven generations in the future. Wondering what that meant in relatable terms, I turned to my family tree recorded in an old family bible. Seven generations back I discovered my maternal great-great-great-great-grandparents, Solomon Zwahlen and Catharina Frautschi, both born in Saanen, Switzerland at the turn of the 17th century. They were brought to Niederbipp by their parents who'd joined the Quaker church and were looking for religious freedom. Their choices to marry each other and maintain the faith of their childhood not only made it possible for me to do the same, but for my children and grandchildren to grow up with an understanding of the keys of joy. I'm under no illusion that my distant relatives had any inkling of me or my children, but I'm grateful that they kept the faith, that they lived and died holding tight to the truths that inspired their parents, and that they thought enough of those truths to share them with their own children.

"You don't have to look very hard to find examples of poor choices derailing people from positive courses. But there are also to be found, for those who care to see, people making choices that lead away from ignoble paths and into brighter futures, stepping away from histories of abuse, addictions and false gods. I'm grateful for hopeful places like Niederbipp where people are eager to share the hope and the light they've accumulated. I'm grateful for the faith of my ancestors who preserved that faith and passed it down by keeping it vibrant and growing in the way they lived it.

"Faith, I learned from watching my mother, is about far more than simply avoiding the darkness. Faith, ultimately, is about fully embracing the light, allowing it to illuminate every cell of your body until you no longer have any desire to choose the paths of least resistance, but to be good by doing good every hour of every day. It's taken me a lifetime to fully appreciate the example of my mother and the good people who taught me the value and power of joy by letting it shine in the lives they lived.

"I grew up visiting the graves of my grandparents most Sundays after church. We continued that tradition when we moved home. I know I'm undoubtedly biased, but the inscription carved into my grandparents' headstone has become increasingly meaningful to me. It simply says, 'If you miss the joy, you miss it all.' We've done our best to teach the keys of joy to our children and our grandchildren. We pray they'll remember them and deliberately choose to live by them. And we hope that when they stray from the path of joy or forget the keys that can set them free, that they'll find their way back quickly.

"I learned several years ago that my great-grandfather, William Clyde Barnes, left Centralia and moved west in search of a better life. Though the town of Centralia had offered his family an income and some level of security, William and his wife, Mary, believed there had to be something better than the hardscrabble life of a three-saloon mining town. Their daughter, my grandmother, Hannah, came to Niederbipp as a traveling nurse. She learned the keys of joy from her landlady, who later became her mother-in-law when she married my grandfather, Jakob Blümgarten, the local schoolmaster.

"Joy, I've learned, is a choice—a choice that requires the application of our best selves, and a choice that needs to be made every day. It's not easy, especially in the beginning when the exercise of the keys requires a change in practices and attitudes. My grandmother, Hannah Blümgarten, not only learned these lessons herself from my grandfather and his mother, but she took them back to her parents in Starbrick and shared them, changing the lives and perspectives of her whole family in both generational directions. Joy, as it turns out, is power. Joy is light, and the more one has of it, the more one desires to not only acquire more of it, but to share it with anyone who'll listen and accept it. Joy encourages us to stretch, to expand our borders, to think and act beyond our natural abilities. To stretch the Centralia metaphor even further, joy teaches us the importance of putting out fires quickly so we can get on with living and growing and becoming stronger, focusing our efforts on that which matters most.

"The most recent article I added to our Centralia scrapbook was from nearly six months ago. It was written by a fire and ecology scientist, who, after an extensive study of the maps of the labyrinth of tunnels in the fourteen different mines below the ghost town, suggests that the fire will likely burn itself out in the next 250 to 300 years, or in other words, approximately seven generations from that day in 1962 when the fire began and no one did anything about it.

"Meanwhile, a hundred miles to the northwest as the crow flies, seven generations have been raised in our small town. We've had our own share of trials and heartache, but joy has prevailed again and again thanks to the integrity and convictions of those who've kept the light of joy burning brightly in their hearts. Every generation and every person who learns the keys of joy must ask themselves what they'll do with the joy they gain. Will joy be lived? Will it be shared? Or will it fall away and be forgotten in the pursuit of other treasures? We each have to decide our answers. We each get to choose how far the joy will stretch and for how long it will burn in our hearts. We each get to decide how we will care for the truths which have been entrusted to our keeping. Will we make them part of our lives and teach them to our children, or will we forget about them and let them atrophy and die? We cannot determine what future generations will do with the truths we pass on to them, but if we do nothing to carry these truths from those who've come before us to those who will follow us, the links will be broken, and the chain will be lost.

"Many well-intentioned people naively believe that progress can only be accomplished by tossing out the old and moving forward into new territory. Perhaps we all pass through that ideology—anxious to escape the ignorance of our parents' generation, not wanting to be burdened by the limitations and mistakes of the past. But I'm reminded of the archeological findings from ancient civilizations that show evidence of advanced knowledge and understanding. Intricate surgeries, impressive art, architecture and craftsmanship, and vast libraries of learning have all been burned, destroyed, or forgotten by the more *advanced* civilizations that followed. So much beauty, wisdom and know-how has been stamped out and pulverized under the unsympathetic wheels of progress.

"I used to believe that truth was to be found somewhere in the happy space between the extremes of staunch conservatism and resolute progressivism. But ever since deciding to live by the keys of joy, I've come to a very different understanding of truth. Truth, and the joys that come through adhering to it, have never been dependent on or beholden to the ever-changing opinions of mankind. And truth remains truth even if it's in opposition to the attitudes and practices of mankind. Only the truth has the power to truly set us free and inspire our hearts and minds to produce honorable fruits of light and goodness. Jesus himself taught that wolves may come dressed in sheep's clothing, but that we can know any truth by carefully observing the fruits that come from their actions. Indeed, the preaching of any supposed truth is best understood and appreciated not by studying the words, but by carefully observing the lives of those who accept it. So much of my appreciation for the truths of the keys of joy have come from watching so many of you over the course of my lifetime. I am aware that the keys of joy have made none of us perfect, but I believe they've endowed each of us with unquenchable desires to reach and stretch and become better and stronger in our resolve to live our best lives and come closer to God. To my knowledge, it's only the truth that comes from God that can inspire those things.

"George and I have spent enough time away from Niederbipp to know that the truths that are lived and shared in this community are quite unique. We've recognized that the keys of joy are simple and easily understood, yet they offer a way of life that eliminates so many of the common diversions and distractions from the pursuit of happiness.

Reverence allows us to understand that we are children of God. Practicing charity teaches us to love and respect our fellow human beings. Hope has taught us where we can put our trust and filled us with optimism. Self-discipline continues to teach us every day to be better stewards of our time, talents, and gifts, inviting us to be constantly stretching and growing and becoming something more than we might naturally be. Self-discipline has also kept us free of habits and addictions, keeping us happy and healthy and cognizant of the ever-changing, beautiful world around us. And patience…pfff…"

Many of the congregants laughed softly at the silly expression Cindy wore on her face.

"Patience, I fear, will be something I'll be working on for the rest of my life…"

Again, many of the congregants laughed.

"I'll admit that the assignment of patience as one of the keys of joy has never been very comforting to me. It's a battle I fight within myself all the time. In recent years I've come to appreciate it more, not because I've become much better at it, but because I recognize the value and virtue of aligning my will with the will and timing of God's greater vision. I am learning to breathe…learning to listen…learning to wait and watch and see the glorious hand of God in our lives. Patience has taught me to recognize the value of each of the other four keys, keeping me going through my challenges and weaknesses when I have difficulties seeing the big picture. As we've worked on ourselves, doing our best to live by the keys of joy, our lives have been blessed with clarity and purpose. We've recognized our responsibilities as members of a global community to lift and love and offer hope. And through our exercise of the keys, we've been blessed to find the promised joys.

"Today, two communities, separated by a hundred miles of forest and farms, stand in sharp juxtaposition to each other. The first is thriving, focused on eternal truths. It is filled with people who know and love each other and are diligently seeking to live lives filled with purpose and conviction. The second, having long neglected the destructive fires that burned in her forgotten caverns, has given up hope. Nature has reclaimed her, and the world will likely soon forget her, leaving little but ashes and regrets behind.

"As far as I know, we only get one chance at mortality. For most of us that means 75 to 90 years to seek our treasure, find our purpose, and live out our dreams. As the number of days ahead of us continually grows smaller, George and I are grateful that we've found our purpose, are living our convictions, and are experiencing joy every day. We're grateful we still have plenty to do as we continue to learn and grow and work to overcome our weaknesses. Life and God continue to teach us as we strive to live the keys that have provided us and our family with all of the greatest joys we've ever known.

"Thank you! Thank you for being our community, for loving us and encouraging us and teaching us how to live fuller, richer, more deliberate lives. May God bless us all in our efforts to become our best selves as we labor together to live according to the laws of liberty and joy."

Notes
1. Psalms 22: 6

CHAPTER 153

Success in Circuit Lies

Adversity has the effect of eliciting talents which, in prosperous circumstances, would have lain dormant.
—Horace, Roman Poet—

Genevieve smiled as she looked down at Matt's notes, basking in the light of affirmation that her decision to stay here and marry Matt was a good one.

After the hymn and benediction, the campers made their way to the courtyard. With Cindy's sermon, the sad story of Centralia, and the seven-generation principle still fresh in their minds, the campers continued the conversation under the shade of the courtyard's yellowing trees. With the cooler winds of early autumn summoning them to enjoy the afternoon, they rode their bikes back to the farm to make a picnic before walking together to the orchard.

They wandered through the now-empty fruit trees to the benches that circled the fire ring where, months earlier, they'd gathered here one evening for a bonfire. Though all of the campers had spent time here over the last couple of months, this was the first time they'd returned together. The nearly circular bench that encompassed the fire pit was covered with at least sixty years of carvings, scribbles and musings in a wide range of legibility. Some of these looked as though they'd been recently added, while the majority appeared to be little more than worm trails or glyphs from a long-forgotten archeological site. Only one carving stood out boldly. Its message covered much of the top of one of the boards.

"Who carved this out?" Susan asked as they approached.

"I did," Greg admitted. "It felt like the right thing to do. It was so faint that the message was almost lost."

"Well, it's definitely easier to read now," Ephraim responded. "It was almost illegible before."

Greg nodded. "It felt like an important one to remember. It was actually cathartic, memorizing the words as I was cutting out the letters."

"'The unexamined life is not worth living'," Crystal read aloud, standing in front of the carved bench. "Examining our lives...we've done a whole lot of that this summer, haven't we?"

Many of the campers nodded, standing next to her, looking down on the freshly cut lines in the gray, weathered wood.

"What did this mean to you?" Matt asked, turning to Greg.

Greg nodded, looking anxious to share. "I guess for me, it caused me to reflect on what I've been doing for the last few years—and the last twenty years. I don't remember ever thinking about the purpose of life in those crazy years when I was struggling to find myself. I was lost and looking anywhere but inward. I don't know if I even had the capacity to examine my life at that time. I was too busy being angry, raging against anything and everything that felt like a limitation. I thought I'd figured a lot of things out before I came here, and I'm sure I had, but having this time to really take an honest look at where I've been and where I hope to be...it's pretty much changed everything for me."

"Me, too," Holly said, putting her arm around Greg's waist. She looked at him as the others turned to face her. "I know all of our stories are very different, but this idea of examining our lives and constantly working to improve ourselves...it's really a beautiful idea. I'm sure I've thought about it a hundred times since the bonfire. I keep seeing ways that the keys of joy tie into this concept. It feels like maybe Socrates understood some pretty important stuff about life and happiness."

"I can't say I've thought about it every day, but I've been thinking a lot about that quote, too," Spencer admitted. "Socrates had it right. My life was pretty shallow before I started taking a real, honest look about where I was going and what made me happy. I was such a jerk. It was all about me."

Genevieve draped her arm over Spencer's shoulder. "We've all come a long way, haven't we?"

Spencer nodded.

"I keep thinking about what Thomas shared with us the night we were all here for the fire," Rachael admitted.

"Which part?" asked Susan.

"That part about the difference between self-discipline and self-mastery."

"Oh, right, that discipline and discipleship are different from self-mastery in that they require a connection to God," Matt suggested.

"I...I think I might have missed that part," James admitted.

"Yeah, if I remember right, Thomas suggested that it's a big deal to be able to master yourself, but that a disciple of God has no ceiling or limits in his ability to learn and grow in virtue, understanding and grace."

"I remember Thomas saying that it's one thing to answer to ourselves, but quite another thing to know we're also accountable to God," Ephraim said. "In my heart it feels like I've always known that, but I spent way too many years forgetting it. This summer has changed everything for me. It's hard to think about going back."

"I don't think we ever can go back," Susan replied. "We've come too far to ever go back to the way things were."

Ephraim nodded. "I hope you're right."

"Look at where we're standing, guys," Josh replied, taking a step back and turning all the way around. "Doesn't it feel symbolic? We're encircled by the keys of joy…"

"But this time, we're the fire," Sonja suggested. "I thought about that a few weeks ago when Josh and I came down here and discovered the symbols on each of the benches.

"Symbols? Here? Seriously? Where?" James asked.

Sonja nodded, walking to the center of the nearest bench where an hourglass had been carved into the narrow face of the board.

"Look, there's one here too," Holly said, pointing to the face of the board closest to her where a circular cross was discernible to any eye that was looking for it.

"Yeah, there's one on each of the boards," Josh replied as they all turned to look for the symbols.

"Man, how much more have we missed?" Susan asked.

"I don't know," Genevieve mused, "but it feels like maybe we can't get to that point of really seeing anything until we're humble enough to ask and to seek. I mean, sure, it's been here all along, but none of us saw it until we wanted to see it. We had to look. We had to be curious enough to go searching for it. Hasn't it been that way for all of us?"

"'The truth must dazzle gradually, or every man be blind'," Matt mused.

"That's profound," Josh admitted. "You just came up with that on the spot?"

Matt smiled and shook his head. "No, that's Emily Dickinson."

"And you just happened to be saving that in your head for a time like this?" Susan asked dubiously.

Many of the campers laughed.

Matt smiled good-naturedly. "It's that last part of the poem from that cross stitch that's hanging in the music room."

"The one behind the piano?" Holly asked.

Matt nodded.

"There's a cross stitch on the wall by the piano?" James asked.

"Is it the one with all the little blue flowers around the borders?" asked Sonja.

Matt nodded again.

"And you probably have the whole thing memorized already, right?" James asked.

Matt shrugged. "It seemed important."

"What does it say?" Genevieve asked, the rest of the campers curiously looking on.

Matt smiled. "You guys are all going to think I'm a nerd."

"Uhh, yeah, it's way too late for that," Spencer teased. "But I think we're all grateful for your nerdiness. It's at least mildly contagious."

Many of the campers nodded.

Matt shook his head but smiled. "I wrote it down in my journal a few months ago, but I think I probably have most of it memorized. It says:

Tell all the truth but tell it slant —

Success in Circuit lies

Too bright for our infirm Delight

The Truth's superb surprise

As Lightning to the Children eased

With explanation kind

The Truth must dazzle gradually

Or every man be blind."

"Can you say that again?" Holly asked, taking a seat on the circular bench.

One by one, each of the campers moved to the edge of the circle and sat down, looking to Matt as they focused their senses on what he was about to say. He repeated the poem a little slower than before, all of the campers hanging onto each of Dickinson's poetic words.

"That's the way it's been for all of us this summer, right?" Genevieve asked.

"Could you repeat that one more time?" James asked, leaning forward, his elbows on his knees.

Matt looked uncomfortably self-conscious with all eyes on him, but he repeated the poem one more time.

"This is the circuit, isn't it?" Holly said, sitting up straight as she looked around the circle, her arms outstretched in both directions as if she were taking them all into a hug. "This is the circuit that has allowed us to learn the things we've learned."

"Are you saying the keys are the circuit?" Ephraim asked.

"I...I think they could be, right?" Holly suggested.

"I'm not sure I know what a circuit is?" Crystal replied.

"Well, I'm thinking of it in terms of electricity, but I'd guess it's basically the same with anything. A circuit is a loop or a circular path that begins and finishes at the same place," explained Ephraim.

Josh looked around the circular bench. "Success in circuit lies..." he said thoughtfully.

"Remember that explanation Pops gave us of the circle...the first and the last?" Holly asked, drawing a circle from the tip of her thumb, over the top of her fingers, around the bottom of her palm, and back to the tip of her thumb. "Is that not a circuit?"

"I think that qualifies exactly," Ephraim replied.

Matt looked up from his own hand, staring across the circle. "Sonja, what symbol are you sitting on?"

She moved to the side, exposing the circular cross. "Reverence."

Matt smiled and nodded. "So, if this were to play out all the things we've learned this summer as if it were a circuit, and the symbol James would be sitting on is the hourglass of patience, and Greg would be sitting on the anchor of hope. Susan would find the scales of self-discipline under her left hand..." He paused, glancing back down at his hand before looking up at the last side of the circular bench, "And the flaming heart of charity would be found between Josh and Holly."

Each of those mentioned turned to look; each of them confirmed that Matt was correct.

"It's a map, isn't it?" Josh asked, looking up from his own hand.

Matt nodded. "It feels like it, doesn't it? A very circular map that brings us back around, again and again, helping us learn the things we missed the last time around."

Ephraim stood. "But it's not exactly a circle, is it?" He jumped up on the bench, allowing the additional twenty inches of height to improve his bird's eye view. "It's a pentagram."

"Uhh, I thought the pentagram was a Wiccan symbol that's supposed to be evil?" Sonja suggested.

"That's true—today, but that's not the way it started out," Ephraim replied. "I think the Wiccans borrowed it only in the last hundred years or so. It's actually a Christian symbol, but it was also used by the Egyptians and even the Mesopotamians almost four-thousand-years before Christ."

"How do you know this?" James challenged. "How do you know we've not all been indoctrinated in some crazy cult?"

Many of the campers rolled their eyes.

"It's a fair question," Ephraim said, jumping from the bench and sitting back down. "I think my first answer to that question would have to be that the fruits of what we've learned here this summer have nothing to do with evil and everything to do with light and hope."

James nodded, acknowledging Ephraim's truth.

"I feel like I remember something about the pentagram being hijacked by Hollywood and the occult," Sonja replied. "Wasn't it an early Christian symbol? It seems like there was a tie to the five wounds of Christ."

Ephraim nodded. "Yes, and before that, the ancient Greek philosopher, Pythagorus, used the pentagram as a symbol of physical and mental harmony."

"Harmony?" Matt said softly.

"It's been a couple of years, but I seem to remember from my Astronomy 101 class that the planet Venus's unusual orbit around the sun actually forms a pentagram as it moves closer to earth," Holly reported.

"Seriously?" Susan asked.

"That's what I remember. My professor also said that Venus is known as both the Evening and Morning Star—that because of its brightness it's often the first star to appear at night and the last star to disappear in the morning."

"The first and the last…" Matt said, reflectively, almost a whisper.

"What was that?" Josh asked.

Matt shook his head, but he wore a smile on his lips. "The first and the last. That's what Pops called reverence and charity, right?"

"Yes, but isn't that also another name for Jesus Christ?" Sonja suggested. "Alpha and Omega, right? The first and last letters of the Greek alphabet?"

Matt nodded thoughtfully. "So…assuming all of this is tied together…if Jesus is the first and the last…and Venus is the first and last…and the pentagram is a symbol of Venus and harmony, does that not then tie the pentagram to Jesus?"

Many of the campers nodded thoughtfully as the others pondered.

"I think we may have missed something else," Greg said after surveying their surroundings.

They all turned to him in anticipation of what insights he might have.

He looked over his shoulder, orienting himself. "East," he said, pointing to his right. "West." He nodded to his left. "South is behind me, which means north is there!" he said, pointing to the position on the pentagram where the boards marked with the symbols of reverence and charity came together.

"Unbelievable," Matt replied, looking at the four cardinal directions again. "They've thought of everything, and we've missed it all."

"I think we missed something else, too," Genevieve admitted, moving from her seat on Matt's left to the other side of Greg. "If that's north, or the top, and this was south or the bottom, what would this pentagram look like if we stood it up on its end?"

"It would look like...a house," Crystal replied after a moment's thought.

Genevieve nodded. "And do you remember what the first lesson of the farm was?"

Greg shook his head as tears filled his eyes. "Except the Lord build the house, they labor in vain that build it."

The campers sat silent for a moment, recognizing the divine interconnectedness of all the things they'd learned over the course of the summer. It wasn't just the evidence that things had been thought out and considered over the space of many years; it was that there was something sacred here. Everything seemed to have a tie to something else. Astronomy and geometry. Geometry and theology. Theology and community. Community and rectitude. Rectitude and harmony. Harmony. *Harmony.*

Matt shook his head. "We missed it, guys. We've been so overwhelmed with the minutiae that we missed the big picture. We've spent the better part of the last five months on *Harmony* Hill, and I feel like we're just beginning to connect the dots."

"Could we have seen it any earlier?" Susan asked.

All the campers silently considered Susan's question.

Genevieve finally broke the silence. "Susan, tell us more...what are you thinking?

"I'm just going back to Matt's poem...that last part about the need for truth to come gradually so it doesn't leave us all blind. We couldn't have been here before this...we couldn't have seen it even a month ago. Everything that's happened...everything we've seen and felt and experienced...tit's all prepared us for this moment. And today...if we let it...it'll prepare us for what's next, right? Isn't that what we've learned? That there's a pattern for progression?"

"Success in circuit lies..." Ephraim replied. "We've had to come back around to the same lessons and the same ideas again and again before we could see the truths and the answers that God and the universe seem anxious to share with us."

"I guess that's the argument for the key of patience," Holly suggested.

"I agree, but are you talking about our patience, *or God's*?" Sonja asked. "All of this has been right in front of our faces all along, and we missed it."

"We weren't ready to see it, were we?" Susan replied.

"Do you think it's the same everywhere in the world? Do you think God is anxious to help everyone make these connections?" Holly asked.

The campers looked around at each other for a moment, no one responding.

"I have to say yes," Greg responded. "None of us are particularly special, are we?"

Many of the campers shook their heads.

"Isn't it thinking that we're somehow special that gets us into trouble?" Greg continued. "Isn't it that mentality that makes us proud and allows us to think we're somehow better than God or our fellow humans? That we're too smart or too cool or too entitled to have to follow the rules or keep the commandments? And doesn't that lead to most of the problems in the world—stepping away from the path of light and hope, and following our own selfish roads that only lead us further away from joy and basically everything we've learned here this summer?"

The campers sat silent as they considered Greg's questions.

"I guess we really only have one question as we move forward, right?" Holly asked.

"Is it what we plan to do with the truths we've learned this summer?" Susan asked.

"That's what I was thinking," Holly replied. "I'm sure we each have lots of other questions as we look to the future and the fact that we're all going in different directions in another few days and we won't be there to have these same discussions, day after day. But it seems like the one question that's going to matter to each of us is, 'Now what?' How do we keep it alive?"

"I think Ruby gave us the answer to that a while back," Matt suggested. "We have to move the truths we've gathered from our heads to our hearts."

"And we have to replace our fears with love," Holly added.

"You make it sound so easy," Susan replied with a shake of her head.

Ephraim moved closer to Susan, putting his arm around her. "I know we'll all be busy, but we'll all keep in touch, won't we?"

"Yeah, of course," Sonja replied. "And we'll all start our own Keys of Joy chapters, right? People need this stuff. I have to believe they'll want it."

"Yeah, okay, but where do we even start?" asked James. "I don't think it's going to be as easy as we think it is?"

"I think we start with reverence," Josh replied. "That's the way it was for us."

"Yeah, okay, but…come on…*reverence*?" James continued. "I think you've been away so long that you've forgotten how cynical and godless the world is beyond the Niederbipp Valley."

Josh nodded thoughtfully. "But look at us…we found what we were looking for…even if we didn't know exactly what that was when we went looking for it. I think most people eventually find what they're looking for—unless they give up. But I know what I want, and for the first time in my life I know it has a name—joy. And thanks to the things we've learned this summer, we each know that joy has a very distinct recipe."

"And we've each been given the roadmap to get there if we ever get lost," Rachael added, holding up her left hand.

"And if you subscribe to my magazine, I'll send you monthly reminders," Genevieve teased.

Many of the campers laughed.

"I don't know how you're going to find time for writing with everything else you have to do around here," Crystal responded dubiously.

"Love will find a way," Genevieve responded. "It seems like it always does if we'll give it a chance. And besides, I'll have all of you send me ideas as you get married and raise your kids and apply all the good stuff we've learned here."

Matt nodded. "And don't forget that she'll have me to pick up the slack and be constantly encouraging her to keep the good news flowing from Harmony Hill."

CHAPTER 154

Confessions

True love is that which ennobles the personality, fortifies the heart, and sanctifies the existence.
—Henri Frederic Amiel—

The campers woke the next morning to the harsh reality that autumn had arrived. Frost covered the grass where they met for chores, and a thin layer of ice was found on the water trough at the cow shed.

The cooler weather continued through the first part of the week, prompting the colors on the trees to continue to change. On Thursday after they'd managed the farm stand and sold out of their meager offerings early, Matt and Genevieve rode their bikes eight miles north of town to purchase two wedding rings at Castleton's Fine Jewelry. Having been impressed with the meaning and symbolism behind Jake's and Amy's traditional Irish wedding rings, they went looking for something similar. The Claddagh rings, they'd learned, with its two hands clasping a crowned heart, represented friendship, love and loyalty. And though Mr. Castleton tried to steer them in a different direction, specifically to the gold and diamonds, Matt and Genevieve were each thrilled with their selection of two silver Claddagh rings.

They dropped by the Pottery on their way back to the farm and spent an hour talking to Jake and Amy. Genevieve, recognizing the possibility of babies being part of her future, took the opportunity to hold and interact with Baby Isaac, who'd just finished nursing and was pleasantly taking in his environment, staring at the colors and shapes of the pottery and the paintings. While Genevieve and Amy discussed the wedding, Matt learned that Jake had continued to use some of the old tile molds he'd found deep in the cellar to recreate many of the tiles that had been designed and created to adorn the buildings and benches throughout the town. Tile molds representing each of the five keys had been found, and Jake had made many additional molds, including dozens of joy clusters based on the stained-glass piece in Ruby and Pops' library. These, along with hundreds of tiles similar to those embedded in the benches around town, had been sold to the tourists over the years. Not knowing for sure what he'd do with them, Matt purchased several of the small, assorted tiles, knowing he'd come up with something that might help spread the keys of joy to a broader audience.

On their way out of town, Matt and Genevieve reluctantly stopped by Dr. Cummings' office to explain their change of plans. To their relief, the Cummings had heard that Matt and Genevieve had accepted Ruby's offer to be the next matchmakers in Niederbipp, and they knew what that meant for their hopes of passing on the dental practice. They were very understanding, recognizing that it would be far easier to find a dentist to replace them than it would be to find a set of matchmakers to replace Pops and Ruby. Instead of being upset, the old dentist and his wife were supportive of them moving forward without regrets, even extending to them their blessings for a future filled with purpose and happiness.

Friday morning also started out chilly, but quickly warmed up when Matt and Crystal were assigned to milk and cheese duty with Genevieve and James. Though the morning was still cool, the sun had melted most of the frost before the milking was done. After breakfast the four of them returned to the milk barn to make the day's cheese.

The need to replenish the rennet sent all four of them to the nettle patch wearing long, rubber gloves. The nettles had been cut back many times over the course of the summer, but they continued to grow tall and straight, their leaves still damp from the melted frost.

They carefully harvested as many leaves as they could reach, taking care not to brush against the stinging plants. While they waited for these to boil in the big copper kettle, James and Crystal asked Matt and Genevieve to share what they'd learned about the old Ebenezer behind the shed. They went back outside and circled the improbably stacked rocks, Matt pointing to the German words that had been carved into the surface of each of the rocks. Höffnung. Demut. Nächstenliebe, Geduld, Tugend and Barmherzigkeit were easy to read, but some of the others required more work to discern. Matt and Genevieve did their best to remember the English translations for each of the words but recognized they needed to spend more time understanding each of the virtues.

They were all surprised when James admitted he was a little bit jealous, both of the opportunity Matt and Genevieve had to spend the foreseeable future on the farm, and of the greater depth of understanding they would undoubtedly gain over the coming years. In a rare moment of candid honesty, James acknowledged how much he'd learned about himself, love, and so many important aspects of life over the previous five months. As he cuddled with Crystal on the bench next to Matt and Genevieve, he openly acknowledged how his priorities had changed from a headlong pursuit of wealth to a more mindful pursuit of joy, and how, in that shift, he'd begun to see a broader, more sacred and more meaningful purpose to life. He further surprised Genevieve by asking her to not neglect to use her talent and platform to expand the opportunity for others to learn the enriching truths they'd all learned to appreciate that summer. He rather humbly invited her to share his story if she thought it might help others avoid spending time wandering the fruitless paths of selfishness. Crystal offered up her own story as well, hoping her experiences of getting out of debt, taming her tongue, and learning to work and play well with others might enable future campers, or those who read Genevieve's articles, to avoid the habits and patterns which had kept her from joy.

James and Crystal surprised both Genevieve and Matt when they sincerely thanked them for their examples in both their actions and attitudes. They admitted that they'd anticipated that the weeks of their engagement would be brutal, being unable to express themselves more physically than their contracts allowed. But the fact that the four of them had all been in the same boat, having to deal with regular partner rotations when they'd much rather be together, had helped them to know that they could do it and kept them from whining or complaining. Patiently waiting for anything, James and Crystal confessed, had never been part of either of their skill sets, but the keys of self-discipline and patience had given both of them the motivation to commit themselves to a more thoughtful, reflective and restrained experience.

While they strained the leaves from the fresh rennet, Matt and Genevieve talked about their own experience. It was really the first time they'd openly discussed their personal challenges of keeping things on the up-and-up since the day of that forbidden kiss on the backstreets of Niederbipp. Though they neglected to mention the kiss to James and Crystal, what they did choose to share was adequate proof that their sexual desires, though controlled for the moment, would be plenty strong enough to keep them from worrying that they wouldn't figure out the bedroom piece of their friendship and marriage.

For James and Crystal, who'd each sampled the goods offered them in previous relationships, they openly acknowledged how difficult yet refreshing the experience had been to exercise restraint and discipline and keep their commitments to Ruby. The focus on friendship and love had removed the trappings and distractions of lust, allowing them each to focus on truly seeing, understanding, and loving each other without worrying about the pressures and distractions of sex. The result was not only confidence in their ability to be self-disciplined, but a reverence and respect for each other that they had never felt toward any other human.

As they listened, Matt and Genevieve recognized the occurrence and presence of the same feelings and truths in their own relationship. As they continued working together on the cheese, cutting and pressing the curd, the discussion focused on how each of the keys had opened their hearts and minds to possibilities, hopes and ideas they'd never considered prior to coming to Niederbipp. Reverence for God had led each of them to the recognition that there was some greater meaning and purpose to everything in their lives, just waiting to be discovered. But the keys had built on that meaning and purpose, offering each of them a new, multi-dimensional understanding of life, allowing them to see, feel, and experience things in ways they'd never known before. They each recognized that they were seeing things in technicolor that they'd never before even perceived, producing a desire to stretch, connect with others, and share the things they'd learned over the summer with everyone they encountered. It didn't feel right to keep the joy to themselves. Joy, they'd recognized, wanted to be shared in meaningful, personal ways.

They had just finished brining the cheese in the cheese cave when they heard voices upstairs. They finished logging and stowing the new wheels on the shelf before making their way back into the light of day.

"Oh, hello," Crystal said, looking up as she reached the last step out of the underground cave.

"Good morning," responded the woman dressed in jeans, a flannel shirt and cowboy boots, standing next to Pops. Her hair was done up in braids similar to the way the women at the camp had been wearing their hair all summer, but this woman was obviously different. She wore mascara and lipstick, and the normally strong scent of cows and farm was laced with the fragrance of Chanel No. 5.

Crystal nodded, eyeing her suspiciously. She glanced quickly at Pops, looking for any clues.

The others followed Crystal up the stairs, Genevieve reaching the ground floor last, unaware of the guest, or that the other three campers were staring at her.

"Julia!?" Genevieve said, staring at her boss for a moment before rushing to embrace her. "When did you get here?"

"Just a few minutes ago. Pops told me you were down here on cheese duty, and I wanted to see you right away. You look well." She held Genevieve's elbows at arm's-length and looked her over. "You look more like a woman of Niederbipp than a woman of Manhattan," she said with a smile.

"Is that good or bad?"

"It's beautiful, in a perfectly natural way," Julia replied. "There are few things more beautiful than a woman who has found herself and is comfortable in her own skin. I tried to imagine what I would find when I arrived, but your sun-kissed nose…" she smiled and shook her head as she moved her hands from Genevieve's elbows to the tips of her fingers, smiling again at the lack of polish. Julia turned Genevieve's hands over, looking at her calloused palms. She smiled even more broadly than before looking up into her face. "It looks like it's been a fabulous summer," she said, letting go of her hands and bringing her in for another embrace.

"Who's this?" James asked, standing next to Pops.

"This is Ms. Julia Marie Sommerset Galiveto, one of our all-time most favorite campers," Pops said without hesitation. "She's also Genevieve's boss."

Matt nodded, looking on. "Then I'd like to thank you," Matt said, extending his hand to Julia.

She turned and looked up into Matt's face. "Am I safe to assume that you're Matt Owens?"

"Yes."

"I've tried to imagine what you looked like ever since we spoke on the phone a while back, and I've heard a lot about you from Ruby," she said, taking his hand firmly with both of hers.

"I want to thank you for sending Genevieve to Harmony Hill this summer," Matt said.

Julia nodded. "You think it was a good idea, do you?"

Matt nodded, smiling. "I know I'm biased, and I'm sure you have plenty of good ideas, but as far as I'm concerned, I think that's one of the best ideas I've ever heard."

Julia chuckled. "I'm beginning to see why you've fallen for this guy," she said, turning back to Genevieve. "As I've reviewed the photos taken by Patrick O'Brien, I've tried to guess which of the men might have caught your eye, but..."

She turned back to Matt, sliding him closer to Genevieve until their shoulders touched. "Wow! What a handsome couple you two make. I've tried to imagine what you'd look like together, but I have to admit my imagination is no match for the reality that stands before me."

Matt draped his arm across Genevieve's shoulders, and she put her arm around his waist.

"You're early," Genevieve replied. "We weren't expecting you until tomorrow."

"I know. Lawrence and I thought we'd surprise you. We arrived last night and we're staying at the old Clarkston Mansion B-&-B in town. We would have arrived earlier, but we stopped by to pick up some paintings we commissioned from your friend, Amy Kimball. And I hope you don't mind, but while we were in town, we ran into Albert and Lin Schreyer. When they heard we were heading to the farm, they asked us to bring your gown and suit. I figured it was safe to assume it would be better for us to bring them than for you to have to wrestle with fitting them into your bike basket."

"Oh, thanks...I forgot that you know the Schreyers, too, but I don't think I know how or why," Genevieve replied.

"Lin also made my wedding gown, and we've occasionally rented their Airbnb over the last few years when we've come to visit. They're a great couple and skilled tailors. Lawrence refuses to buy a suit anywhere else. He must have a dozen of Albert's suits. When he saw yours, Matt, he had to have one made in the same fabric. Great taste, by the way."

"Oh, uh, thanks. Genevieve helped me pick it out."

"I thought that might be the case. It's hard to go wrong with a classic herringbone. And your dress looked lovely, too, Genevieve. I'm sure you'll be pleased with Patrick O' Brien's work. He'll be arriving later this afternoon to take the final photos of the farm before shooting your wedding on Sunday."

"Uh, sorry to interrupt, but do you mind? We better take care of this," James said, pointing to the cleanup work that still needed to be done.

"Actually, that's why I'm here," Julia said, rolling up her sleeves. "I regret I'm late. I haven't made cheese since I left the farm twenty-six years ago. Can I help with the clean up?"

"You'll probably chip your nails," Crystal replied as if she doubted her sincerity.

Julia shook her head, extending her unpainted fingernails for Crystal to see. "I may be one of the few executive women in New York who doesn't have a regular appointment with her manicurist. Would you like me to haul the whey to the pigs or rinse the cheesecloths and mop the floor?"

Crystal smiled. "You know what you're doing?"

"I spent five months making cheese and milking cows once a week just as you have. That may have been a few years ago, but not much changes around here. I think I can probably handle anything you throw at me."

"Okay, then why don't you take the whey to the pig. The rest of the piglets are probably on their way to becoming bacon by now."

"Stoltzfus bacon?" Julia asked with wide eyes.

"Of course. Why would we go anywhere else?" Pops asked.

"I don't suppose there are any tomatoes left to go with some of that bacon, are there?"

"You're in luck," Pops responded. "We still have a few dozen tomatoes ripening in the cellar. I'll let the kitchen crew know we have a request for lunch."

"Oh, well, only if it's not too much trouble," Julia replied.

"Not at all. I'm sure some of the lettuce has survived the frost as well. BLTs coming right up! And Matt, perhaps you and Julia could take the whey to the sow. Julia was hoping to catch a private moment with you."

"Oh, uh, sure," Matt said, glancing at Genevieve. She nodded, encouraging him.

Without the need for instruction, Julia worked alongside Matt to empty the whey from the caldron into the galvanized milk can. They added the whey that had been expelled by the presses and clamped on the lid before loading the heavy can onto the flatbed cart waiting just out the back door. Matt was surprised by Julia's strength; she looked like she couldn't be more than five-foot-seven and weigh any more than a buck thirty. While Matt provided the power to propel the cart, Julia knew either instinctively or from experience that it was her duty to stabilize the can, which she did expertly, anticipating the rocking and jostling according to the terrain ahead of them.

The giant sow was standing by the trough as if the delivery of the still-warm whey was past due. She began drinking immediately, not waiting for the can to be emptied.

"Ruby speaks very highly of you, Matt," Julia said when they'd returned the can to the cart.

"I think Ruby speaks highly of everybody," Matt said with a shrug. "She's got a talent for that."

"Isn't that the truth? I've always admired her ability to see people—to read them and understand them from the very beginning."

Matt nodded.

"She tells me that she and Pops felt something was different about you from the moment they read your application back in January."

"They did?"

"Yes. I know a little bit about the application process, both from the side of being an applicant myself, but also when I lived with them during the winter of '93 and watched closely as they received applications from potential campers. This isn't an easy process, Matt. I'm sure you know that you were one of more than 800 applicants."

"Yes, I feel honored and humbled to have been chosen."

"I'm glad to hear that. Humility, as I'm sure you're aware, is going to have to play a major role in your work here."

"You almost sound like you're concerned about that?"

Julia nodded thoughtfully. "Do you have a minute?"

"Uh, sure. What's up?"

She sat down on the corner of the cart and patted the place next to her, encouraging him to sit.

"I'm sure you're already aware," she began as soon as he'd sat down, "that this an unusual place. I understand you're well-traveled, as am I, and I would bet that in all your experiences, never have you been surrounded by so many people who are interested in sharing love, light and truth."

"No, that's right," he replied immediately.

She nodded, but then hesitated, pausing for a moment longer than what felt either natural or comfortable. "I need to ask you to forgive me," she said when she finally spoke again.

"For what?"

"For not giving you the benefit of the doubt."

"What do you mean?"

"When Ruby told me that you and Genevieve planned to marry and had accepted her invitation to run the farm and continue the work of matchmaking, I…I have to admit I freaked out a little bit."

"I was under the impression that you were excited about it."

"I am now, but it took me a minute. You'll be happy to know that the FBI, CIA and Interpol all give you a clean bill of health."

"Wait, what?"

"Let's just say I know people."

"You're serious? You had me checked out?"

"You bet I did. But as it turns out, as my friends in high places have suggested, you're a squeaky-clean dentist who's never had a record for anything more than a parking ticket and likes to do humanitarian work for fun. Your last six next-door neighbors all say you were kind and friendly. Your former employers all gave you glowing reviews. Even your junior high school teachers report that you were memorable for your maturity and compassion—said they could always seat the new kid next to you and you'd make them feel like they had a friend."

"Wait, you have a friend that got you all that information?"

"Well, to be perfectly honest, he's actually more of a contract employee. He's a private investigator. A really good one."

"Seriously?"

She nodded. "We've hired him at least a dozen times over the years and he always digs up some skeletons, but not on you. In fact, the only person who shared anything that even came close to less than a glowing review was a woman named Naomi McFadden."

Matt blinked several times. "Do you mean *Naomi Richardson*?"

"That was her name when you knew her, yes. I understand you two were co-workers at a dental office in Knoxville?"

"Yeah, we were. How did you find her? I've been wondering about her for at least fifteen years."

"Funny, she said the same thing about you, but I believe it was seventeen years."

"She's right. She changed her name? McFadden? I assume she got married?"

"Yes. Her husband is a structural engineer. They have four kids and live just outside of Knoxville. Their oldest, you might be interested to know—a fifteen-year-old boy—she named Matthew, after the man who made her believe there were still good guys left in the world, but who ended up breaking her heart nonetheless. She said it's a good thing her father-in-law's name is also Matthew, otherwise it might be weird."

Matt closed his eyes and took a deep breath. "Is she happy?"

"The investigator reported to me that she's the president of the PTA, is the quintessential soccer mom, drives a minivan with fuzzy dice hanging from the rearview mirror, and attends her local Baptist congregation every Sunday where she organizes the annual bake sale and sings in the choir. And, in case you're wondering, yes, she does have a white picket fence around her yard, though her eight-year-old has been grounded indefinitely for breaking several of the said pickets with his soccer ball."

Matt laughed. "Good for her. I...I've always hoped that she'd be happy, but boy, I really screwed up on that one."

Julia nodded thoughtfully. "Am I safe in assuming she was the first girl you ever truly loved?"

Matt nodded. "Before Genevieve, she was the *only* girl I ever loved."

"That's exactly what the investigator suggested."

"What? Seriously?"

"Yep. Like I said, his report was that you were squeaky clean. He even said that you're the kind of guy that any father would be thrilled for his daughter to bring home."

"Well, that was nice of him!" Matt responded with a laugh. "I...I'm really happy for her."

"But?"

"Pfff." He looked like he'd been punched in the gut. "I...I've spent most of the last seventeen years chasing ghosts, wondering what might have been, wishing I'd done something more to secure a future with her."

Julia put her hand on Matt's shoulder. "She was the first girl you ever loved. She'll always hold a place in your heart."

"Isn't that...I don't know...bad? How do I love Genevieve with all my heart if Naomi still has a piece of it out there somewhere?"

"The first cut is always the deepest," she said, her eyes filled with compassion. "She named her son after you. The first cut was the deepest for her, too."

"This isn't something I ever thought I'd still be thinking about on the eve of my wedding," he admitted.

Julia nodded solemnly. "It may sound strange, but that actually gives me hope for you and Genevieve."

"Why?"

"Are you familiar with the Greek playwright, Euripides?"

"Vaguely."

"He has many famous one-liners, but my favorite will always be, 'He is not a lover who does not love forever.' You discovered what love is with Naomi, and that discovery convinced you that you'd never be happy without it. Yes, she will always own a piece of your heart, just as you will always own a piece of hers. I don't know anyone who doesn't have a regret or two, especially when it comes to love. But one woman's loss is another woman's gain. Your presence here this summer could not have happened had you married Naomi. Sure, those pickets might have been yours to repair, but instead you're here, at the intersection of love, time and opportunity, not as a broken soul, but as one who has learned and grown and gained understanding that will not only benefit you, but the millions of souls that you and Genevieve have the potential of influencing."

Matt nodded solemnly. "I guess I've never considered that my circuitous path and flubbed experiences could ever be considered an asset."

Julia smiled warmly. "Who of us has ever traveled a road of any length without flubbed experiences and unexpected detours? No, Matt, power seldom lies in one's flawlessness, but in one's humility and recognition of his countless imperfections."

"Then here am I," Matt said with a laugh. "The most powerful man in the world!"

Julia smiled, looking off into the distant farmyard. "Ruby told me she couldn't have picked a better man to replace Pops. I'll admit that I've worried that her age and illness were causing her to make choices out of desperation rather than inspiration, but I see I didn't need to worry."

"No?"

She shook her head. "One of our reasons for arriving early was to do a little additional research."

"Research?"

"Yes, on the two of you."

"What did you learn? Did we pass?"

She shook her head again. "To simply pass implies something that is unremarkable or average. You didn't pass—you and Genevieve have far exceeded even my greatest hopes. Hildegard, Thomas, Jake and Amy, Susan and Paul, even Lin and Albert—they all endorsed you and Genevieve and expressed great confidence in you."

"You really set all of this up?" he asked as if he were looking for a punchline.

"I wish. I couldn't have planned any of this better myself if I'd been working on it for fifty years. I don't know if you're aware of it, but Ruby and Pops have been praying for this day for many years."

"Yes, they've mentioned that a couple of times."

Julia nodded. "They knew this would all come to an end at some point. They knew they'd have to choose new stewards for the farm if it were to continue. I was there twenty-five years ago when they began receiving applications, watching and listening as they poured over each and every one of the applicants. They prayed every day for God to send them people who would be able to use what they could learn here to improve their lives and keep the light of the keys shining bright in a world that was growing increasingly dim. You are here—each of you is here because you've been prayed over and invited only after answers have come."

Matt nodded reverently. "I was praying, too."

"Of course, you were. Things don't come together like this without prayer and the blessings of God. A willing heart is rarely enough to produce miracles in and of itself. It must be met with the hand of Providence and encouraged and nurtured by the convincing and fortifying power of work and effort. You learned for yourself this summer that a seed rarely sprouts until it's planted. And unless it's tended and nurtured and kept free of weeds, it has little hope of producing much to write home about."

"Are you speaking literally or figuratively?"

"Both. The same is certainly true of love. And from what I've heard from Ruby and Pops and the townies, you and Genevieve have learned how to nurture and grow your love in ways that invite the companionship of Providence."

"I hope so. We're still new at it, but it feels right."

"It feels right to me, too. Even before the investigator got back to us, we knew from talking to our friends in town that something was unique about what you and Genevieve share."

"They've been spying on us?"

She nodded. "Even down to that forbidden kiss that afternoon on Pilatusstrasse, what was it…six weeks ago?"

"Wait, what? You know about that?"

"Who could blame you, really? I understand it was respectful enough to keep you out of trouble with Pops and Ruby, but saucy enough to know you're compatible."

Matt smiled, shaking his head. "Hildegard?"

"The best informant money doesn't need to buy," she responded with a laugh. "I'm sorry to pull you away from Genevieve and your chores, but I wanted you to know that you have my confidence, and as far as it counts for anything, my blessing."

"Thank you," Matt said, humbly.

"No, thank you! Genevieve is one of the brightest and most talented writers we have ever hired, but the problem was that she knew it. I knew this assignment would stretch her and humble her, but I had no idea to what extent. I know your friendship and love for her have been a catalyst for development in areas she might not have ever explored without you. Amy said she couldn't believe the dramatic changes in Genevieve since she knew her in college. I know we all change over time, but not always in a positive way. From what I hear from Ruby, between the wasps, Carlos the sheep, and your mellowing influence, Genevieve has changed her tune from one of aggression and arrogance to someone much more capable of playing the role of Matchmaker-In-Chief. I'll be the first to admit that when I heard that Ruby had offered Genevieve the farm's top job, I worried that Ruby had lost her marbles. Coming to the farm for the summer was a huge stretch. Staying for the next several decades…I couldn't have guessed that if I had all the guesses in the world."

"And now?"

Julia shook her head slightly before turning to face him. "I promised I'd reserve my judgment until I had a chance to see things myself, but I have to say I don't remember the last time I've prayed with a greater hope that everything will work out."

"I've been praying, too. We both have. I know I'm going into much of this with only an inkling of what lies ahead, but…it feels right."

Julia nodded. "I'll agree with that. Lawrence and I were talking last night about how naive we were when we got married and headed off to follow our dreams. If you wait to get married and follow your dreams until you know it all, you may never make it off the couch."

"Do you think I'm dumb to commit my life to this?"

Julia looked pensive as she rolled the question around in her head. "No," she finally said. "I have no doubt this will be the most difficult thing you'll ever do, but the influence you'll have for good for generations to come…there's nothing dumb about that. There will undoubtedly be days and maybe weeks that will feel impossibly long and painful, but the rewards will undoubtedly also be great." Julia paused. "I don't know exactly what this is going to look like for Genevieve—to be writing about the farm and the thousands of truths and lessons that flow from Harmony Hill and the town of Niederbipp, but I have no doubt you'll be a partner with her in all of it. Perhaps you'll also create some collaborative work."

Matt nodded.

"Whatever the future holds, Matt, I hope you'll consider me a friend and an ally. I know Lawrence and I share great hopes that this farm and the values it breathes into the lives of all who come here will live on for many generations to come."

"I hope so, too," Matt replied. "I hope so, too."

CHAPTER 155

Buttercup

Gratitude unlocks the fullness of life. It turns what we have into enough, and more. It turns denial into acceptance, chaos to order, confusion to clarity. It can turn a meal into a feast, a house into a home, a stranger into a friend. Gratitude makes sense of our past, brings peace for today and creates a vision for tomorrow.
—Melody Beattie—

"Do you mind if the four of us go for a walk?" Julia asked Ruby after a lunch of BLTs had been served in the dining hall.

"Not at all," Ruby replied. "I trust you'll be back in time for dinner and porch games?"

"Of course. We wouldn't miss that," Lawrence answered.

Matt and Genevieve led the way, hand in hand, up the steep, rutted drive; Lawrence and Julia followed close behind.

"You've got a magical place here. I hope you two know that," Lawrence said.

Matt and Genevieve turned and smiled at each other.

"I...we...we still have to pinch ourselves, knowing all of this will soon be in our care," Genevieve replied.

Lawrence and Julia turned and looked over the bucolic setting of the farm.

"I don't know if I've ever considered what the Garden of Eden looked like, but I'd like to imagine it being someplace quite like Harmony Hill," Lawrence suggested.

"You've always had a soft spot for this place," Julia replied.

"It's hard not to. The best question I ever asked and the most influential answer I ever received took place on the same day on the other side of that phone booth," he said, pointing over his shoulder.

"You proposed on Harmony Hill?" Matt asked.

"Can you think of a better place?" Lawrence replied.

"Mmm, probably not."

"Yep, I came out to visit Julia after my kid brother had brought her home for Christmas. Poor guy. I knew I was going to marry her the moment she walked through the front door, all wrapped up in that oversized sweater. She was the most beautiful woman I'd ever seen, until this morning." He put his arms around her and kissed her forehead. "It's hard to keep up with a woman who becomes more beautiful every day."

"It's been a good run, babe," Julia answered. "I'm glad you asked."

"I'm glad you said yes, and that you've kept saying yes every day."

She kissed him softly as Matt and Genevieve smiled. Julia pointed down the road, and taking Lawrence's hand, began walking. Matt and Genevieve walked next to them down the middle of the deserted country lane.

"I'm sure we had no idea what this would mean to us when Julia began teaching me about the keys of joy. They felt so familiar, yet new, as we began putting them into action," Lawrence reported. "I'm sure the experience of applying the keys is a lot different for those of you who are lucky enough to learn them every day over the course of five months, but for me, learning the keys opened my mind and heart to the possibility of a new and deeper purpose to life. Watching the keys in action in Julia's life, seeing how they encouraged her to become the best version of herself…I knew I had to jump aboard the joy train, or I'd be left behind."

"You felt that right away?" Matt asked. "That you needed to up your game?"

"Absolutely. I'd seen what spending the summer here did for my brother, Calvin. He's always had a good heart, but he was a man without a plan when he left home that summer, twenty-six years ago. He'd had trouble holding a job, couldn't commit to relationships, and struggled with making decisions."

"He was basically adrift on the open sea," Julia mused. "For me, watching Calvin grow and change into a man of direction and integrity as he learned and began practicing the keys—that was all the proof I needed that the values the keys espoused had the power to improve the world. Of course, they did the same for me, too. But sometimes we don't see the changes in our own lives as clearly as we see them in others."

"Calvin came home a completely different human," Lawrence continued. "He got up in the morning, he was patient with himself and others, there was a drive to do better and be better that had never been there before. I was shocked when I heard that he was attending church on Sundays and finding places to serve. Service—charity, that was never anything our family had found any interest in. Our father was a successful businessman and our parents both raised us to be above the fray. I'm afraid it developed within all of us a sense of snobbery and entitlement. And then Calvin comes home and he's signing up to work at homeless shelters and food pantries, and he becomes a regular at church and is making donations to local charities. But the thing that shocked me most was that he was happy. He was finding joy in the things he was doing. Contrary to how he'd been before, he never sat around, waiting for things to happen. For the first time in his life he was out *making* them happen. I figured it would wear off after a couple of weeks, but it just kept going. He shared with me some of the basic tenets of the keys of joy and I began to see there was something more to life than I'd been able to see."

"Lawrence had finished school and was well on his way in building his own business," Julia explained. "He was four years older than Calvin and was dating a woman to whom he was nearly engaged."

"Yep, Christine Aberystwyth. I was just getting ready to buy an engagement ring but had put everything on hold until after the holidays. And then the day before Christmas, this beautiful woman shows up to join my brother and our family for Christmas, and my whole life changed."

"What did that change look like for you?" Matt asked.

Lawrence looked at Julia. "I guess it quickly became clear that I was looking for the wrong things in life, and in the wrong order."

"The wrong order?" Genevieve asked.

"Yes. Christine and I attended Midnight Mass with Calvin and Julia. It was the first time I'd been to church in at least a decade. Christine quickly grew bored, but I felt something as I listened to the music and participated in the singing with others in the congregation. I didn't sleep that night, tossing and turning as I considered my life. My path had looked so attractive just the day before. I was making good money and living the good life, but something was missing. I heard Julia get up early and wander into the kitchen as I was sleeping on the couch. I got up and followed her, anxious to get to know this charming woman with whom my brother was so enamored. As we sat there and drank peppermint tea that Christmas morning when everyone else in the house was still asleep, my interest in her quickly developed from curiosity and infatuation to complete admiration. By the time the others woke up, I was more in love with Julia than I'd ever loved anyone before. I wanted to know everything about her. I remember being completely swallowed up in everything she had to say about the keys of joy, and everything else for that matter."

"And you felt the same way?" Matt asked, looking at Julia.

"No, not exactly. I remember thinking Lawrence was really charming, but Calvin and I had been writing for a couple of months. We'd both expressed a desire to get to know each other better and see where it went. That was my main reason for coming to meet his family. And then there was this handsome older brother who couldn't leave us alone." Julia smiled and shook her head. "Even when his girlfriend was around over the next week, he basically ignored her and just wanted to know more about the keys of joy and our experience on the farm and the direction I was going with my writing. Before New Year's, Lawrence's girlfriend suggested they take a break, and I'd come to the conclusion that I definitely wanted to marry one of the Galiveto boys, I was just confused which one."

"That's an awkward situation," Genevieve responded.

"Yeah, you have no idea. What made matters even worse was that Lawrence asked me in front of Calvin if he could write to me."

"Ouch! What did you say?" Genevieve asked.

"I told him I wasn't interested in coming between brothers, but that I was open to pen pals. What I'd felt for Calvin, I realized on my way back to Harmony Hill, was, yes, love, but it was more of a love that had grown from a deep connection and friendship. Over the course of the next few days, what I felt for Lawrence, in his absence, was something even more profound. His first letter arrived three days later and I'm sure I read it a dozen times in the first hour. Of course, I wrote back right away. And the next day I received another letter from Lawrence. I think he sent me five letters that week."

"Eight actually, but several of them were delayed," Lawrence replied.

"I was going crazy. I wanted to know more about her. I wanted to learn more about these mystical keys that made her so different. I wanted to figure out a way to be near her."

"But weren't you basically engaged already?" Matt asked.

Lawrence smiled. "That didn't last more than two days into the new year. Christine had recognized that I was in love with my brother's girlfriend before I recognized it myself. About a week later, she suggested we should define our relationship a little bit better in order to avoid confusion. Of course, by that time Julia and I had exchanged at least twenty letters and my heart was in a very different space. I'm afraid our correspondence hurt two people quite badly, but it's all worked out for the best."

"That's right. Ruby told me that your brother married one of Julia's roommates," Genevieve replied.

"Yes. Felicity Merrill," Julia replied. "She was one of my bridesmaids at our wedding and she and Calvin hit it off. They were married six months later. We see each other at least a few times a year and talk regularly."

"You're still close then?" Genevieve asked, looking surprised.

"Of course. Calvin was awkward at the wedding, but he was happy for both of us. And when he and Felicity began dating, we often doubled with them," Julia replied. "It's been a big win for all of us, and having the keys of joy in common has given us and our children a whole lot of strength and an easy community of like-minded family."

"And what happened to your former girlfriend?" Genevieve asked Lawrence.

"Ahh, yes, Christine. She married the summer after we did. We lost touch for several years, but we began exchanging Christmas cards a few years back. She and her family live in Minneapolis where her husband works as a chemical engineer, and she manages a law office. They have three children and are living their own happily ever after."

"Sounds like it all worked out," Matt suggested.

"It has so far," Julia replied.

"Do you ever wonder what would have happened had you married Calvin?" Genevieve asked.

"Sure. It's not something I think about often. I'm sure we'd be happy—we both are happy in our own marriages. But it certainly would've been different for all of us. Lawrence and I have made a great team. I learned to appreciate his writing talent over the months we spent apart. We've strengthened each other in many ways and helped each other as we've pursued both our individual and shared dreams. Those early months of remote courtship helped us build a solid friendship, teaching us both the value of patience and self-discipline. But I know we'd both agree that our marriage is as strong as it is today because of the foundation of faith on which we built our relationship."

"Except the Lord build the house, they labor in vain that build it," Lawrence added. "I learned that proverb first from Julia as we corresponded. Reverence, hope and charity were all fairly uncommon in my family of origin, but when I began tagging along with my brother to church on Sundays, I started recognizing that light was penetrating a part of my heart and soul I didn't even know existed. Hope and charity, at least for me, became a byproduct of those early steps into reverence. When I first visited the farm and the town of Niederbipp and witnessed the results of practicing the keys of joy on a community level, I was convinced that the joyful life was really the only life I wanted to pursue, and that Julia was the only person I wanted to pursue it with."

"You're lucky to have found each other," Matt suggested.

Lawrence smiled but shook his head. "I don't know if luck had anything to do with it. When you follow the path of joy, if you'll open your eyes and heart, you'll soon recognize that there are no coincidences. Miracles, big and small, become weekly if not daily occurrences, and somehow there is always enough time and resources to keep things moving forward in the direction you should be traveling."

"Yes, but there are still plenty of surprises along the way," Julia acknowledged. "We thought we had this assignment pretty well figured out when we heard from Ruby and Pops that a space had opened up for you to be able to spend the summer here, Genevieve. It felt like an answer to many years' worth of prayers—to be able to share some of the stories and secrets from Harmony Hill with our readers just as a transition was taking place in the ownership and control of the magazine. What we didn't count on was that an exponent, far larger than we ever could've dreamed, might come into play.

"The Yiddish proverb, 'Man plans, and God laughs,' comes to mind," Lawrence added. "We recognized we were rather selfishly looking at one small aspect of what was going on here, not realizing there was far more at play than we ever could've imagined."

"When we learned that you'd accepted the offer, and that you'd found a partner to share both the joys and the burdens, we wept with joy and relief," Julia admitted. "We can't imagine a more hopeful continuation of this legacy. As you know, more than three hundred years have passed since Johann and Mary Zwahlen crossed the Allegheny and began homesteading here on Harmony Hill. I've wondered many times if Mary's vision was long enough to see how her matchmaking work would continue to influence individuals, couples, and families for generations to come. It may take you two the rest of your lives to fully appreciate the work that you'll do here. By then, Lawrence and I will surely be gone, cheering you on from the other side of heaven."

"Absolutely," Lawrence continued. "All the happiness I know in life—all the joy I've experienced and value—it all has a close tie to the things I've learned and the wisdom I've gained from learning the keys of joy and marrying the woman who taught and shared them with me. I owe a great debt of gratitude to Pops and Ruby and all those who came before them, who bucked against the trends and drifts of the world and taught timeless virtues and principles that truly invite joy. This is the magic we hope to share with our readers."

"I'm curious about that," Matt admitted. "Is it converts you're looking for?"

Lawrence and Julia glanced at each other before they both shook their heads.

"True conversion is a lifelong journey, not a singular, one-time destination," Julia answered. "Our hope for sharing the keys of joy with our readers is simply to offer light and hope in a world that seems to be starving for both. To me, that is what Harmony Hill and Niederbipp are all about—a proverbial city that is set on a hill, encouraging others to look up, see a brighter, better way, and to find their own path to the God who lives and loves without end. More than anything, that's the story we hope you'll tell."

"It's a beautiful ideal, but there are so many moving parts, and so many places it could go off the rails," Genevieve answered.

"It's true," Julia acknowledged. "But you've got more help than you could ever know. Light produces more light. Hope breeds added hope. Truth spawns additional truth. And when it is founded on light, hope and truth, joy multiplies exponentially, pouring forth until it echoes and shines in every heart it touches."

"We've seen that this summer, haven't we?" Genevieve responded thoughtfully as she turned to Matt.

He nodded. "Yes. Where do we sign up?"

Julia smiled warmly. "I think you already have."

They stopped walking. The Cartwright's yellow stallion stood by the roadside, his head and neck hanging over the corral fence, staring at them curiously.

"What are you looking at?" Genevieve teased.

The horse nodded, pawing the ground beneath his feet.

"Give me a minute," Genevieve responded, leaving the others on the road and approaching the horse. Just beyond his reach, she gathered an armful of tall, sweet smelling, autumn grass, ripping it from the ditch. Laying it over her arm, she walked to the corral, talking softly to the horse. The horse wore a black leather halter across his muzzle and over his ears. While he helped himself to the grass in her arms, she read the brass medallion on the side of his jaw where the leather straps joined together. "Buttercup" had been stamped into the medallion. It seemed an odd name for a stallion, especially one who'd been so fierce and unruly in the beginning. But as she spoke to him, calling him by his new name, he watched her closely with his big black eyes, calmly trusting her.

"He's a rescue horse," Genevieve shared as Julia reached out her hand to pet the bridge of his nose. "The Cartwrights adopted him—brought him here from somewhere out West when they were thinning the herds."

"He was wild?"

"To say the least. He was scary."

"He must have had a good trainer."

"Yeah, an Amish man. I watched him work with him over the last few months."

"Sounds like a lesson in patience," Julia suggested.

Genevieve nodded, opening her palm as she relinquished the last of the grass. The horse nodded as if to say, "Thank you," before moving into the shade of the tree, rolling in the rich, brown dirt.

"I hate to ask…" Julia said as they stood by the fence and watched, "but how is the article coming?" She looked uncomfortable with the crassness of the question, only two days before Genevieve's wedding, but everyone knew it had to be asked.

"I think I've begun at least two dozen times, but I haven't made much progress, to be completely honest. It's not for a lack of wanting, it's just that I've felt the need to focus on what's right in front of me. I'm sorry, but I haven't forgotten my commitment to you. I promise to have it done by mid-November at the latest."

"Oh, good! Thank you. I may have mentioned that Patrick O'Brien's photographs turned out amazing. We've already got several ideas for layout."

Genevieve nodded, staring off into the corral where Buttercup continued his dirt bath. "Do you know if he got any pictures of this horse?"

"Uh, I can't say for sure, but I would doubt it since this is off the farm. Did you have an idea?"

Genevieve nodded. "Yeah, he's coming tomorrow, right?"

"Yes. He said he would be here by sunrise. He asked if he could bring his wife; said he'd been talking up the farm for the past four months and she's been dying to see it. Why do you ask?"

"I'm sure you probably have a list of things you want him to shoot?"

"Yes, why?"

"Do you mind adding this horse to his list?"

"Not at all. Have you got an idea cooking?"

"Maybe. If not for this story, then for another one sometime in the near future."

"Okay. Sure. What's on the schedule for tomorrow?

"Chores. And baking cookies for the reception. Maybe a swim at the river if we can get it all done."

"We're here to help too. You'll put us to work, won't you?"

"I…I guess that'll be our job soon, won't it?"

Julia nodded. "We have confidence in you, Genevieve."

"Thank you. I'm gonna need that."

"You've always had it."

CHAPTER 156

The Final Frolic

Where there is love there is life.
—Mahatma Gandhi—

As promised, Patrick O'Brien was waiting for the campers the next morning just outside the bunkhouses. Great, white billowy clouds, tinged with pink and gold, formed giant castles in the otherwise ultramarine sky. The cottonwood trees outside the big house glowed like a giant amber Buddha, demanding reverence with their five stories worth of shimmering gold coins, quaking in the morning breeze.

Patrick's wife, dressed in brand new farm clothes and a cowboy hat, looked like a poser; way too clean and done up to be a real farm worker. But she was pretty and smelled good and quickly caught every man's eye, which only drew more disdain from the women.

Patrick did his best to capture glimpses of each of the chores in real time, making his way as quickly as he could between the milk barn, the chickens, the laundry, the kitchen, and what was left of the garden. He tried not to linger too long with any one of the chores so he could fit it all in, but he couldn't help himself with the laundry. He admitted that the idea of washing clothes by bicycle power had been intriguing when he saw it on his shoot list but seeing it in person was uniquely inspiring. Having been teamed up in the laundry that day with Ephraim, Genevieve did her best to let Patrick and his wife, Erika, have their space. They'd come through the door just as they were beginning the rinse cycle. After five months of perfecting the balance and rhythm of the contraption, Ephraim and Genevieve made it look easy as Patrick moved around them, his shutter clicking incessantly.

"Would you like to try?" Genevieve asked Erika who was standing back, trying to stay out of the shots.

"It looks fun, but I don't want to mess anything up."

"No, this thing's practically bombproof," Genevieve responded. "Come, take my place." She jumped off the saddle and coaxed the pretty girl forward.

Erika immediately attempted to pump the pedals but failed as Ephraim tried not to laugh. He did his best to explain the torque reset interrupter with its accompanying lever, but it quickly became clear that he was talking way over her head. Instead, he switched gears, engaging the much easier spin cycle to save himself from sounding like a complete and utter nerd.

Patrick raced to the kitchen to catch multi-hued eggs being cracked and oatmeal being boiled on the giant stove. While Pops, Julia and Lawrence managed the breakfast prep, James and Susan were sent back down to the cellar to demonstrate the task of grinding several cups of wheat into flour with the two-person mill.

While in the cellar Patrick also took loads of photos of the bottles of peaches, apricots, pears, pickles, jams and apple sauce, along with the barrels full of apples and potatoes, and winter squashes lined up on the shelves. There was order and abundance everywhere he pointed his lens, and indications of industry and thrift at every turn.

He hurried back to the laundry house where the milking crew had joined with the chicken and pig crew to help Ephraim and Genevieve hang the laundry out to dry. Fourteen pairs of socks, several pairs of overalls, colorful T-shirts and button downs were lined up next to rows of assorted underwear. They were all fodder for the eager camera shutter as it clicked away, capturing every move.

The camera continued to click as they all made their way to the big house. It clicked in the dining hall as Patrick rushed to capture the patterns of dishes and utensils lined up in neat rows up and down both sides of the table. He took photos of the yoke that hung on the wall above them, and more photos of the campers washing their hands and finding their seats. He even took photos during grace. Not wanting to change the visual dynamics of breakfast on the farm, Patrick, Erika, Lawrence and Julia stood at the pass-through counter to eat their meal, allowing the photography to continue as if the intruders weren't there at all.

The capturing of photographs continued after breakfast with cleaning up the kitchen, the making of bread for the day's kitchen staff, a spontaneous concert in the music room, and a gathering in the library. When the bread was rising, Genevieve and Matt led anyone who was interested in helping back into the kitchen to begin baking cookies. Because the dough had all been made and frozen previously, the baking went rather quickly, producing many dozens of cookies in between the baking of the bread. These were set to cool before being stacked and placed in containers.

Throughout the morning, Matt and Genevieve caught glances of each other as they hurried about getting ready for their big day. The strange reality that they were baking cookies for their own wedding that would be taking place at about that same hour the next day struck them hard with both anticipation and anxiety. They were getting married! For Matt, the reality of it all felt like an incredible gift. He'd come here for the purpose of preparing himself for marriage but had no expectations that it might happen so soon. At nearly forty-four he had no time to waste. But the dream of marriage and the hope of children and family was all quickly becoming his reality. He was absolutely ready to abandon his single life and embrace Genevieve as his wife, partner and companion.

For Genevieve, having come to the farm for a very different reason, even after several months of knowing this was coming, there were still regular moments of mild anxiety. It wasn't so much that she was getting married. Matt, she knew, was undoubtedly the best guy she'd ever met. He'd proven his goodness long before she had any interest in him, helping her know and admire both his character and disposition. There'd been many times in recent weeks when she'd been struck by a quiet sense that she'd known him for much longer than five short months. And there'd been many times that she'd wondered how a guy like Matt had made it so far in life without more women appreciating him for the good man he was. But their oversight had played out for her good. Somehow, nearly forty-four years had passed before Genevieve had been the one to appreciate him for all that he was.

If Matt were all she needed to think about, her nerves may have been much calmer. But there was also farm work and finances, cheese production and writing, camper selection and matchmaking. Much of it, she knew, would be fun, but if this summer were any indication of what her future would look like, she knew there would also be struggles with personalities, opinions and perspectives that would likely cause stress and difficulties. She knew from her conversations with Ruby that such difficulties should not be avoided. They were needed and necessary to help all the campers to grow in understanding and compassion. Opposition, they'd learned, was not only unavoidable, it was necessary for everyone to grow and develop in healthy and appropriate ways, enabling all participants to recognize that their happily ever after would never be without its bumps, thorns, or challenges.

Considering all her emotions however, the one that kept rising to the surface was gratitude. Gratitude was an emotion she'd rarely known in the twenty-nine years prior to coming to the farm. She'd never taken the time to even consider it. Work, travel, exercise and other interests had consumed her time and energy. Never had she taken time to be still on purpose. Never had she prayed with any regularity or intention. Never had she taken the time and opportunity to count her blessings and recognize the beauty all around her. As she considered the mighty change that had taken place in her heart, it was difficult not to be grateful for the weeds that needed pulling and the cows that needed milking and the people that needed understanding and loving. No longer were people just strangers she'd pass with hardly a notice on the trains or the streets; people had somehow become three-dimensional and complex, even interesting.

With the cookies baked and the chores finished, the campers packed a picnic, changed into swimsuits, and rode down Harmony Hill to the river. There was an unwelcome sense of finality in the air. It didn't help that every step and action was being photographed for inclusion in articles that would highlight their summer on the farm—the summer that was quickly coming to an end. And with that end would come the inevitable scattering of the campers. No one really wanted to talk about that even though it was the largest elephant in the room. And by the time they reached the river no one was very interested in posing for Patrick. Instead, they all jumped in the river and swam out to a sandbar that had slowly appeared over the summer as the water level had dropped.

The afternoon was cool and made cooler by the autumn breeze blowing over their wet skin. They huddled together for warmth, but also for connection, knowing this would likely be their last chance to be together, enjoying the wonders of the river. The trees along the banks were painted in warm hues, and the Niederbipp Valley, cut by the Allegheny eons ago, was on fire with all the regal pigments of autumn. There was no longer a need for bellyflop contests or one-upmanship competitions. Their egos had all been tempered and tamed, leaving much more room for agreeable conversation and love.

When Holly found a heart-shaped rock while combing through the rocks at her feet, they all began a search for a similar souvenir, not stopping until they'd found one for each of them. About that time, Pops walked to the center of the bridge, attached the bungee board, and jumped into the water below.

Stowing their rocks on the sandbar, the campers raced to meet him. For surely much longer than they'd known him, Pops had been a man who'd never acted his age when it came to fun and horseplay, and this afternoon was no exception. After Pops's graceful ride upriver on bungee power, ending with him saluting the campers before the momentum ceased and he sank below the surface, the campers took turns riding and cheering those who were gliding across the slick surface of the river. As practiced veterans of the bungee board, each of them had learned the nuances required to both stand up and maintain balance during the ride. They played until they were chilled through, the billowy clouds overhead blocking out the sun.

Gathering up their rocky souvenirs, they swam together across the deeper channel, waterlogged, but content. As they ate fresh bread smeared with hand-churned butter and homemade jam, they tried to avoid melancholic topics, focusing instead on the memories and the friendships that had been forged in this furnace of meaningful connections and joyful consciousness. So much had changed in five months that really nothing remained the same.

An obvious halo of curiosity hovered over Patrick and Erika as they listened silently to the campers' talk. At first, no one addressed it, though they all silently recognized it; none of them were interested in taking the time for interruptions and questions from the interlopers who surely wouldn't understand.

But things changed when Holly invited Erika to sit with the women while Patrick wandered downstream to capture a few shots of the bridge and the men skipping rocks. Coming into the circle, Erika's curiosity could no longer be restrained, and the campers were met with a barrage of questions ranging from "How?..." and "Why?..." to in-depth inquiries regarding personal stories. As she watched Erika learning and working her way toward understanding, Genevieve began to formulate a new direction for her groundbreaking article. For the first time since arriving in Niederbipp, she considered the boundless power of sincere questions to open doors and discover truths. For twelve lucky campers who are chosen annually to sacrifice five months of labor in exchange for a new understanding of purpose and possibility, each of these questions had profound answers. But for those who would only know of the farm from the articles she would write, the questions she would inspire in the minds and hearts of her readers would be critical to offering them a deeper understanding. The more she thought about it, the more she understood that Erika's questions were the essential questions.

Without words, Patrick seemed to understand his wife's honest inquiries, giving her the time and space, she needed to ask her questions. It was only after the men had exhausted the strength in their rock-skipping arms, and he'd explored the gathering from every aesthetically pleasing angle with his camera that he returned to the women to capture the afternoon light on their sun-kissed faces and river-washed hair. These images, they all knew, would be far from the hyper-beautified photos normally found in the pages of fashion magazines. With none of the women wearing makeup or even so much as lip gloss, and not even one designer swimsuit among them, the stories these photos would tell would be far different than those normally championed in fashion publications. There would be no airbrushing or Photoshopping to remove or alter these images of real women and men living genuine, honest lives, conversing about things that truly mattered, loving each other with pure and sincere concern, connecting in ways that transcended selfishness and egotism. There was no need for altering or enhancing these images. The authentic glow radiating from each of the campers could not be enhanced by even the best photo editors.

Patrick and Erika insisted on accompanying the campers on their ascent up Harmony Hill. These photos of the campers, first riding and then pushing their old bikes up the hill against the prismatic backdrop of the Niederbipp Valley, were stunningly beautiful. Muscles toned by five months of honest labor, bodies fueled by five months of home-grown food, and souls polished by five months of joy-filled practice marched up the hill in front of Patrick's lens. Erika stood close by, observing the procession, smiling with her whole face. The photographers leap-frogged the campers, running to get ahead of them several times as they traversed the switchbacks.

The campers waited at the top of the hill for all of them to assemble, and Patrick was quick to take advantage of the spectacle, snapping pictures from many angles and arranging them all like Tour de France teammates at the end of a triumphal race. For those who were willing, Patrick continued to shoot photos. The phone booth at the top of the hill provided a fun prop, as did the bench behind it that offered a commanding view of the valley. One by one the campers left to shower and prepare for evening activities until only Matt and Genevieve remained. With the sun hanging low in the sky, sending sunbeams out across the landscape, Patrick moved quickly but thoughtfully, capturing the happy couple on the bench, with their bikes, and as they looked down on the farm over which they would soon have stewardship.

There was a tenderness and naïveté in these photos, but it was Erika who verbally recognized that there was something more—a hope and a light that seemed to come from somewhere deep within them. As Patrick ran back to the farm to capture images of dinner preparations, Erika walked alongside Genevieve and Matt, expressing sincere envy for their positions and opportunities, recognizing the unique beauty and peace that surrounded the farm.

As Genevieve showered in the remaining tepid water, she recognized that in less than twelve hours, Erika had experienced more of the magic of the farm than she herself had discovered in the first several weeks of working and living here. This realization might have once felt like a personal condemnation, but as Genevieve considered it now, it felt more like a calm reassurance that her choices were right, and her priorities were sure.

While she brushed her wet hair, Genevieve looked up at the notes Holly had posted months earlier in the corners of the mirrors. Write it on your heart that <u>today</u> is the best day of the year! and Find Magic <u>Today!</u> She recognized that somehow out beyond the hardships and attitudes she'd endured, she had found the magic. And somehow each day had been better than the ones before it. She smiled as she dressed in the sun-dried clothes that were lightly perfumed with the scent of cows, remembering her first morning here on the farm and her manure-splattered, designer jeans. Glancing up at her suitcase, stowed above the open cubbies, she tried to remember the clothes she knew were still inside. But they were of no importance to her now. In fact, the very idea of them was repulsive to her, knowing she'd probably paid more for the impractical shoes and showy clothes than the value of all the farm duds combined. Vanity. All of it was vanity to her now. Sitting on the edge of her bed to tie her shoes, she looked up at the writing on the wall above the doorway and smiled. She didn't have to read it anymore. Its simple words had been written in her heart: *Except the Lord build the house, they labor in vain that build it.*

This lesson had been taught repeatedly over the course of the summer, but more importantly for Genevieve, it had been learned. It was truth. More perhaps than any truth she'd learned that summer, she'd learned that foundations mattered. And she knew that this foundation of truth and joy would be absolutely necessary in the coming months and years as she and Matt invited campers like them to open their hearts and to think, believe and act differently as they prepared themselves to live life on a higher plane.

She found Matt waiting for her just outside her bunkhouse, his hair still damp from his shower. Together, they walked hand-in-hand to the big house, relishing the knowledge that by this time tomorrow they'd be on their way to Niagara Falls. They joined Josh and Sonja in setting the table, making room for their four guests by squeezing one more plate onto each side and placing an extra chair on either end.

A simple dinner of grilled cheese sandwiches and tomato soup was served up hot, along with several bottles of fruit from the cellar. The conversation centered around the activities planned for the following day. Ruby announced she couldn't be much help in getting Genevieve ready for her big day as she'd been asked earlier that week to give the sermon and hadn't felt like she could turn Thomas down. The ladies, including Julia and Erika, promised to be there early to help as the men agreed to handle the morning chores as well as breakfast preparations.

After dinner, they divided their efforts between kitchen cleanup and preparations for porch games and ice cream. Because the night was cool, they cuddled together under large patchwork quilts, taking their turns on Bessie's saddle, churning milk into ice cream as they reconvened the playing of one of the summer's most memorable games: Time Machine.

Having taken a break from his camera, Patrick jumped back into action, taking lots of pictures of the magical hat and its accompanying chronometer which allowed players to travel in any direction along the space-time continuum.

They each took a turn, opening their hearts and allowing their recently-improved dreams to flow freely. They each spoke of love and marriage, family, and meaningful employment. But another common thread wove its way through each of the destinations they chose. There was joy there. Greg was the last of the campers to take to the saddle. Unlike the others, Greg rolled the chronometer backwards, to the end of May, just two weeks after they'd arrived at the farm, and began describing a talk he'd had with Holly on the bench overlooking the pond. He recalled the warm afternoon in great detail as Holly nodded and smiled, remembering the day. His one regret from that day, he admitted, had affected every day since and he was grateful for the opportunity to go back and fix what he had cowardly omitted. The words that came next from his mouth were met with both smiles and tears as he professed his love for Holly. She listened for a moment, tears streaming down her face, before her emotions led to actions. She threw off the blanket in which she was wrapped and rushed him, throwing her arms around his neck and kissing him on the mouth with such enthusiasm that they had trouble staying upright. Despite the errant display of affection, the campers erupted in applause. This was exceeded only when Greg got down on his knee, still wearing the Chrononaut hat, and asked Holly to be his wife. Of course, Patrick recorded all of this with his camera as the campers responded to Holly's affirmative reply with hoots and hollers and other joyful exclamations.

As the revelry continued, Ruby stood, leaving her blanket behind, and walked to the time machine. Greg unhitched the hat's strap from under his chin, handing it to Ruby before he and Holly returned to their seats. Quiet returned as the noble matriarch of the farm strapped the hat on her own head, turned the chronometer to twenty years in the future, and sat down on Bessie's saddle, turning her peddles slowly but deliberately as she stared out at the distant horizon to an apparition only she could see.

As she spoke, she told of happy days ahead for each of them, of exultant marriages and children and joy-filled lives. She shared her dreams of each of them finding others who could use a little help in discovering the secrets of joy and the grand meaning and purpose of life. She encouraged each of them to remember the beautiful and simple keys they'd learned this summer, promising them that as they did so, joy would never depart from them. But she also invited them to remember that joy had its recipe and could not be fully realized without each key being present and kept free of rust and tarnish.

As she looked into each of their faces, each of the campers felt her love and compassion toward them. At that moment, they knew what she said was true. Five months of toil and stretching had brought each of them to a place of understanding, gratitude and grace. And it was in this place that each of their paths forward was clear and uncomplicated, full of light and possibility.

They spoke of that possibility late into the evening, long after the ice cream had been finished and Pops and Ruby had retired, and their guests had excused themselves. With quiet and reverent words, the twelve campers shared their thoughts and dreams with each other, each of them feeling both anxious and excited to put their newly acquired tools into action and move forward with a new vision and a new hope of all that life could be.

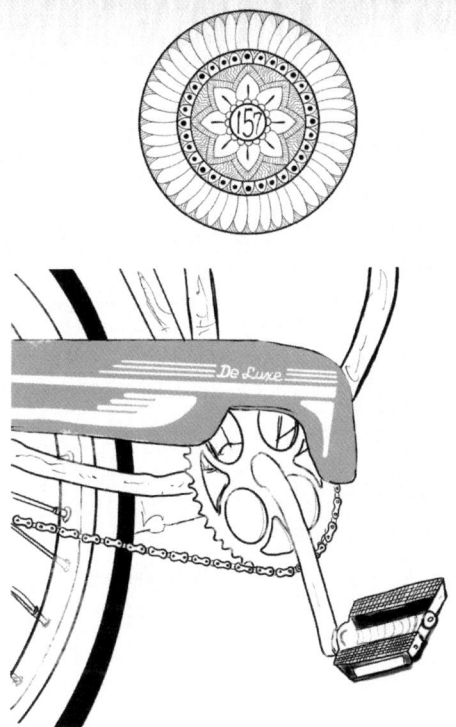

CHAPTER 157

The Last Sermon

There is only one way to get ready for immortality, and that is to love this life and live it as bravely and faithfully and cheerfully as we can.
—Henry Van Dyke—

It was a knock, not a rooster, that awoke the women the following morning, just as the day was beginning. At the mumbled invitation to 'Come in', Erika walked through the door, followed by Julia and another woman.

"Mom?" Genevieve said, sitting up as the light turned on.

The third woman smiled and nodded. "We hoped to make it up here last night, but your father got us lost. We were just checking into our room when Julia and Erika and their husbands were returning. They said we missed a fun day. I'm sorry I'm late, but I'm glad to be here. I hardly slept a wink last night, knowing my only child was getting married today. Congratulations, Honey!"

Genevieve smiled at her mother, who stood awkwardly at the end of her bed, looking worried.

"I'm glad you made it."

She turned from side to side, looking into the tired faces of the other women. "Where's your fiancé?"

"Over in the men's bunkhouse."

"The *men's* bunkhouse? Oh, I...I guess I imagined something a little different."

"What did you imagine?"

"Something a little more...communal."

"You thought I was living in a commune?"

"Your father and I didn't know what to think, and then with you announcing you were getting married after knowing this guy for just a few months, I guess we just assumed you'd gone rogue and were *way* off the reservation."

Genevieve smiled. "Mom, did you really think I'd joined a hippie commune?"

"Well, didn't you? They're kind of a thing, way out here in the woods, you know?!?"

Genevieve laughed. "I'm sorry to disappoint you, but no, this is...*very* different."

"Yes, I can see that now. Julia tried to tell us last night, but I couldn't have imagined this, no matter how hard I tried. And now look at you. You're getting married, and not to a hippie. How wonderful!"

"What? No, Mom, Matt's a dentist. This is a respectable farm."

"Whatever you say, Dear. You remember my friend, Marilyn Collins, right?"

"Uh, the one from the Junior League?" she asked, throwing back the covers and standing up.

"Yes. Her daughter, Jenny, ran off with a hippie fellow and they're growing marijuana on a farm somewhere out here in the wilds. I thought…well…what is it you grow here?"

Many of the ladies laughed.

"Wheat, oats, rye, tomatoes and berries," Genevieve managed.

"And lettuce and peppers and cucumbers, too," Crystal added.

"And all kinds of fruit in the orchard," added Susan.

"So…it's really just a *farm* farm then?" she asked, looking relieved.

Genevieve laughed. "Yes, Mom, it's just a *farm farm*."

"Oh," she said, putting her hand to her chest. "What a relief! Your father and I have been worried sick. We were imagining our grandchildren with names like Marley Lovechild and Daisy Moon Flower all the way up here. I think that's why we got lost."

"Mom? Really? Daisy Moon Flower is a great name, but Matt and I were thinking more along the lines of Happy Dawn Honey Blossom."

"And don't forget Sugar Muffin Stardust and Squeeby Juniper Rose Petal," Holly suggested, trying to keep a straight face as she approached Genevieve's mother, extending her hand of friendship.

"I'm Holly Rainbowchaser Gooseberry Fruitcake, but you can just call me Holly if you want to."

"Gooseberry…fruitcake…" she responded, looking uncertain. "I'm Sally Patterson."

"Well, welcome to the farm," Holly said, shaking her hand firmly. "Are you here to help us get your daughter ready for her wedding day?"

Sally smiled and nodded. "Where do we start?"

While Genevieve hurried to wake herself up with a cold shower, the ladies took the liberty of showing her mother Genevieve's wedding dress, but first they had a little fun, holding up a long-sleeve flannel nightgown and a pair of black muckers that might look quite handsome on a lumberjack's bride. But they couldn't hold the ruse together and burst out laughing, quickly relieving the awkward stress on Sally's face.

After dressing in the flannel nightgown to help her regain some warmth, Genevieve sat down on a chair in the middle of the room and looked into the faces of her fellow campers. "I know this probably sounds crazy, but I'm thinking I want to ride my bike to church today with all of you."

Sally looked very uncertain, but the other women smiled.

"Patrick was hoping that might be the case," Erika admitted as all eyes turned to her. "We were looking through the photos he took yesterday, and the ones of you guys on the bikes were our favorites by far. He sent me with his second camera, knowing he wouldn't be welcomed here this morning, but he was hoping I could get some decent shots of your preparations."

The women looked at each other, each of them shrugging, having grown comfortable in their own skin without makeup. It was only Sally who expressed any discomfort and asked that all pictures of her be taken only from her right side.

With a bicycle ride in mind, the women decided a braid would be the most resistant to wind displacement. Rachael quickly sketched a French braid that would wrap around Genevieve's head, forming a subtle crown with her pretty hair. Catching the vision and knowing they had a little time to play around with it, Sonja, the most accomplished braider, began with a comb, preparing Genevieve's hair on the left side of her head. Within a couple of minutes, Rachael's vision began to take shape as she and Sonja worked on different sections, sweeping up the longest part of her hair into an updo that could be sustainable with the activities planned. The braid came around the top, forming a natural headband, allowing her longer bangs to elegantly frame her face. While Sonja and Rachael focused on her hair, the other women dug into their luggage, finding bits of makeup and bottles of nail polish. Touched by the women's generosity, Genevieve selected a light peach-colored polish, and Holly meticulously painted each fingernail with precision. Offering up her own makeup bag to the ladies, they all added eyeliner and mascara, highlighting eyes that had not seen even a hint of makeup for months.

For all the women, these five months had been the longest they'd gone without makeup since they'd begun wearing it in their early teens. And though they each expressed a bit of a surprise at seeing each other with done-up faces, they also each expressed gratitude at being able to feel comfortable and even pretty without any makeup at all.

By nine o'clock, the women were mostly ready for the big day. Word that Genevieve wanted to ride her bike to church had gotten to the men, who had been creative in their own ways, wrapping the frames of two of the bicycles in toilet paper and fastening it all with several yards of scotch tape. While they waited for the women to get ready, the whole fleet of bikes was walked to the top of the hill and strings of tin cans were attached to the frames of the two lead bikes.

Before going to the big house for a quick breakfast, the women laid out their dresses on their beds, then raced to the dining hall, wolfing down the pancakes and scrambled eggs the men had prepared for them. By 9:30, with teeth brushed and dresses on, they met the men at their bunkhouse and walked together to the top of the drive. Pops and Ruby met them there, the pickup loaded with cookies, two milk cans filled with chilled milk, a few musical instruments, and two small duffle bags filled with the only non-farm dud clothing both Matt and Genevieve had. Patrick and Erika sat on the open tailgate; their cameras poised to not miss a thing.

Matt and Genevieve smiled as he helped her onto her bike, making sure her gown was free of the chain and the wheels. They smiled at each other a second time as he mounted his own bike and they began to roll forward, the tin cans clanging behind them. Riding side by side, they descended Harmony Hill for the last time as a bachelor and a bachelorette, knowing that the next time they returned to the farm they would be coming as a married couple—the next in a long tradition of matchmakers. Pops and Ruby pulled ahead when they all reached the highway, hurrying to drop off the truck bed's contents at the Parkin's pavilion before returning to the church.

Ignoring all standard traffic laws, the campers rode next to each other, two abreast, down the middle of the highway. But they didn't need to worry. Sunday traffic was light, and those who chose to pass them did so slowly, with smiles and congratulatory waves. They wove their way through town, waving at those still walking to the church. P.J. and Hazel squealed with delight when they saw the happy parade, each of them waving happily along with their parents.

The campers coasted into the courtyard and leaned their bikes against the cemetery wall as they'd been doing all summer. But it felt different this time for Matt and Genevieve. They weren't here today as visitors. They were here to become Niederbippians, to take one step closer to becoming the next matchmakers of Harmony Hill.

To their surprise, waiting for them on the bottom step were both Genevieve's and Matt's parents. Their fathers were appropriately dressed in sport coats and bow ties, looking more prepared for a regatta or a horse race than for a formal wedding. Their mothers were similarly dressed in pretty, yet simple dresses.

Quick introductions were made as they climbed the stone steps together. There was no time for awkwardness, for which all present seemed to be grateful. Genevieve's father appeared to be greatly relieved that his daughter was marrying someone who looked much more like a gentleman than the tattooed hippie he'd been imagining. And for their part, Matt's parents appeared overjoyed that their only child was finally getting married.

Joining the last of the congregants who were making their way up the stairs, they soon noticed that the chapel was nearly filled. Hildegard waved to Genevieve, inviting them to join her on the back row. And so they did, Genevieve's parents sliding in first, followed by Genevieve, Matt, and his parents.

The organ prelude filled the hall with Bach's unmistakable tune of

Jesu, Joy of Man's Desiring, inviting a gentle spirit of contemplation and drowning out the muffled sounds of Patrick's clicking shutter.

As had been done every other week, Thomas stood at the front of the chapel and warmly welcomed everyone. The congregation stood and united their voices in a rousing hymn about God's love for his children. Genevieve wasn't sure if her parents were touched by the music or if it was the fact that their only daughter was getting married, but there was obvious emotion present in each of their faces. Matt squeezed Genevieve's hand and she turned to see his mother wiping away tears of her own.

After an invocation offered by a skinny, old man dressed in a brown suit that nearly swallowed him, Thomas returned to the lectern. He announced Ruby as the morning's sermon-giver and explained that she wanted no introduction. Instead, he simply thanked her for pinch-hitting and turned the meeting over to her.

Ruby stood from the front row and walked to the lectern, setting down a collection of notes and a Bible before looking out into the congregation and smiling.

"Good morning, friends. I stand before you looking like a tired, old woman, which I surely am. But there is within my heart a vivacious and youthful spirit that feels no older than any of my summer recruits. In my nearly ninety-seven years, I've seen my share of sunshine and clouds, but I'm alive today, at least in part, because I've chosen to always look to the light, leaving the clouds to burn off or blow away.

"As most of you will know, my husband, Lorenzo, and I have made our home on Harmony Hill for the past fifty-seven years, and I'm saddened to announce that this will be the last summer I will be the matchmaker of Niederbipp."

There was some level of murmuring in the hall at this announcement, but it died down quickly.

"Fifty-seven years ago this week, Lorenzo and I married and began our stewardship of the farm. Shortly thereafter, Millie and George Smurthwaite retired and moved to Florida. They left the farm for only a couple of years, each of them returning in a pine box according to their requests, where their bones could rest in the nearest place to heaven on earth and nourish the trees on the farm.

"Lorenzo and I have made a habit of visiting the farm's cemetery on a regular basis to sit on the bench we placed there, and to consider our stewardship of the farm that was passed down to us through the hands of many good women and men who cared for the land and animals, built the farmhouse and outbuildings, and planted the trees that continue to nourish and support us today.

"I've already lived far longer than I ever hoped to, but the Good Lord has provided us with a bonus of many extra years and allowed us to find joy in every extra day. The farm and our work with our annual recruits have provided us with an extraordinary purpose. Along with our stewardship of the farm came a stewardship to love those who came to learn and grow in their understanding of the purposes and designs of God's gift of life. For these many years we've been blessed to watch the hearts of our campers swell with the light and knowledge that comes only from truth. Not a day has gone by in those fifty-seven years that we have not continued to learn and grow as we've taught and shared and considered the great mercy and grace and love of God.

"As I've grown and learned and watched virtue growing in the hearts and lives of fifty-seven years' worth of campers on Harmony Hill, I've come to the conclusion that faith is a journey, a journey that has no end, but has instead limitless invitations and encouragement to press on, to think bigger, to move further, and to stretch far beyond what is small and feeble, and embrace the full abundance of God's endless creation and love."

Genevieve squeezed Matt's hand. He glanced sideways, noticing the intensity of Genevieve's parents' attention. He turned the other way and noticed his own parents' rapt attention.

"There is within each of us a receptor of truth, but that receptor often becomes dulled or insensitive without a sense of humility and gratitude that will—with any sincerity—lead us to reverence and ultimately to faith. This is generally a unique journey for each of us. Some of us come to a place of humility and gratitude on our own accord by opening our hearts and minds to the beauties and blessings all around us. But others, perhaps most of us, come to a place of meekness and humility only after we've tried every other conceivable way to reach our desired outcome on our own. I was one of the latter. I was proud and arrogant, and I'd spent several years convincing myself that I was happy without the complications of marriage and family. Sure, I'd achieved a level of happiness in my career as a teacher and my independence from the complications of the world. But in my heart of hearts there was still much that was wanting.

"Though I'd been raised with religion, I'd wandered away from any faith in my twenties when life became something less than I thought I deserved. I'd hoped for marriage and children and a comfortable life. What I got instead made me cynical and angry, leaving me more bitter and discontent with each passing year. Of course, that attitude did little to improve anything in my life or get me closer to anything I wanted. I was a real mess when the letter arrived from my Aunt Millie, inviting me to apply to spend the summer on Harmony Hill.

Of course, I thought she was crazy. I'd never taken five months off. To do so felt irresponsible and reckless. I was nearly forty, hadn't been on a date in at least a couple of years, and I wasn't very interested in starting anything new, or stretching, or stepping out of my comfort zone, no matter what the promises looked like. I delayed responding for a couple of weeks. And then one day another piece of mail arrived from my aunt—this one a postcard. Only three words were written on the backside."

She held the postcard up so everyone could see. Even from the very back row, the yellowed card with the colored stamp in the upper right-hand corner was clearly visible. "Three words," Ruby repeated. "'Comfort retards growth.' If I was angry before, I was raging after I'd read that card. I was even more upset when the next card arrived, a week later. This one had a few more words," she said, holding it high so they all could see. "'We cannot become what we want by remaining what we are.'"[1]

Many in the congregation snickered.

"Yes, she was taunting me, and I was admittedly angry. When the third card arrived," she said, holding it up, "I was incensed. This one reads, 'It's never too late to be what you might have been.'[2] But my aunt knew me—knew what made me tick—and the night I got this last card, I lay in bed, looking up at the ceiling, angry at God, angry at the world, angry at my aunt for sticking her big nose in my business, and angry at myself for being angry instead of doing something about it. I got up in the middle of the night and sent in an application to be a camper on Harmony Hill for the summer of 1963. I remember being angry all the next day, and every day after that. I was angry that the application made me feel desperate for something I didn't know if I even wanted anymore. I was angry that I had to wait to find out. I was angry that I even cared. And I'm sure I was angry with my students who happened to be under my nose at the wrong time.

"And then one day, as I got home from work and found a letter in my mailbox, things began to change. I say *began* because the road was long indeed. Yes, I was accepted, but the acceptance was inconvenient, requiring me to leave school a month early and return a month late. I was angry as I negotiated this with my boss. I was angry when he asked for an explanation. I was angry as I waited for his deliberation. When his answer was no, I was angry that I'd dedicated seventeen years to teaching and was stuck in a thankless job. I remember looking up at the ceiling that night, too, searching my soul as the messages from my aunt's postcards echoed in the space between my ears, slowly working their way into my heart. By the time the morning came, I knew what I needed to do. I needed to get unstuck. I needed new dreams. I needed hope that life could be better."

"Fifty-seven years later, I stand before you as a living testament that life can be better, that anger stands in the way of many good things, and that life is best when joy is our goal and motivation. In the process,

I've found hope. I've learned patience. I've discovered the endless connections between gratitude and a meaningful relationship with my Creator. I've learned the thrill of self-discipline. And in the process of all of this evolution, I've discovered for myself the priceless value of joy.

"Fifty-seven years ago I arrived in Niederbipp an angry, ignorant and self-centered woman. I was quick to judge, quick to think I was better than, quick to mock and scorn and dismiss everyone as unworthy of my time and attention. And at nearly forty years old, I was here because I had nothing better to do than to make my aunt and uncle wish they'd never invited me.

She shook her head, looking humble. "And then…Niederbipp happened. It must have been a combination of a total change of environment while also being surrounded by people who were consciously and intentionally working on themselves, but my heart began to soften. My journey to humility was much slower than many of my fellow campers, most of whom had arrived ready to learn and move forward. It would take several weeks for me to begin to recognize the virtues of meekness."

"But there was a man…a handsome young devil with a difficult name, who was patient with me. He was kind. Over time he allowed me to vent thirty-nine years' worth of anger and venom until I didn't have any left. And after all that, he continued to treat me with kindness and respect, helping me work my way through each of the keys of joy, helping me fill the void in my heart with the manifestations of charity and kindness. He not only made me want to be better, he made me believe I could be better.

"But he was young. I treated him all summer like he was my little brother. He took it in stride, always returning my teasing with patience and kindness, slowly taming the shrew within me, and opening my eyes and heart to the keys of joy. He made me want to work on myself; made me want to believe there was a purpose and a plan to life; made me want to connect the dots between me and a Creator who genuinely cared for His creation.

"A farm is a fine place to discover such connections. I remember the day when the first radish seedling rose from the soil in which we'd planted them. I remember watching the magic of birth during that first lambing season. I remember observing the fruit trees blossom, form tiny, green nubs, and grow slowly through the season, fed by tiny umbilical cords until they matured and ripened, full of sweetness, color and aroma. I remember watching in awe as milk turned into cheese. And through it all I learned the pleasures that come from sharing life and laughter and joy. Those realizations softened me, making room in my hard heart for more. And every time I worried I couldn't handle any more stretching, Lorenzo was there with a kind word and reassuring smile. He made me want to believe I was worthy of love. Having lost my father in my early teens, I'd never had strong connections to any man, and those to whom I had felt connections had moved on in other pursuits.

"I remember one night, maybe halfway through that first summer, lying on my bed, staring up through the skylight in the bunkhouse at the ribbon of stars above me. It had been years since prayer had played any significant role in my life, and even then it had been relatively naive and juvenile. But on that night I felt compelled to utter a simple thank you to an unknown God whose fingerprints I was discovering everywhere I turned.

"That was the beginning for me. A simple thank you to a then unknown entity who'd created things as wonderful as strawberries, as delicate and useful as chicken eggs, and as profoundly beautiful as sunsets. I discovered God's abundance that night as I found myself leapfrogging from one beautiful creation to another, seeing the mercy and grace and playfulness of a God I began to remember. That remembrance evolved quickly into reverence as my previously cynical mind gave way to the warm feelings in my heart. Those feelings remained the next morning and grew as I began to feed them with daily portions of gratitude. With time and practice, humility came, making room for other virtues to find fertile ground. Hope. Charity. Patience. Kindness. And yes, with practice and determination, eventually self-discipline.

"In the five-and-a-half decades that have passed, close to seven hundred campers have found their way to Harmony Hill. Each of them has had their *moment* when the hand of Providence has made contact with their humble hearts. What they do with that moment and the realization of connection has the potential to set all who experience it on a higher and holier path. But the decision of whether to pursue the light is one that must be made individually and daily. As much as I would love to proclaim the glory of God from the rooftops, I'm afraid I'm no longer very stable on uneven surfaces."

Many in the congregation chuckled.

"I've lived long enough to know the wisdom of pursuing the light and seeking the fruits we most desire. As farmers and sellers of many fruits, I've come to appreciate Jesus' explanation that good fruit cannot come from bad trees. Grapes don't come from thorn bushes. And figs are never plucked from thistles. Yet many try different paths, believing maybe they will be the first to discover sweet apples growing freely under the pyracantha bushes. Many more have been injured and scratched looking for fresh peaches in the cactus garden. But regardless of who we are or how diligently we might seek, we cannot find joy where joy does not exist. No amount of wishing or hoping can change that eternal truth. Joy can neither be found nor maintained except through following joy's recipe. It cannot be found without God and his Christ. It cannot be maintained without patience, morality and self-discipline. It cannot exist without hope and charity, which, in their truest forms, share undeniable ties to Jesus Christ.

"C.S. Lewis, in his book, *The Weight of Glory,* said, 'I believe in Christianity as I believe that the Sun has risen, not only because I see it but because by it, I see everything else.' I don't know if Mr. Lewis meant to tie this statement to Christ's healing of the blind man in the 9th Chapter of John, but the story is much the same for all of us who earnestly and sincerely seek for truth and find the light that offers clarity and vision to all things. Though we may be blind from birth, through Christ alone we may find the light that leads us to see and experience the fullness of joy. Though countless souls have sought joy through alternative paths, none have ever found anything more than fool's gold at the end of their fool's errand.

"I learned recently that at the root of the word *religion* is the Latin word *religio,* meaning to *re-connect* or *re-align*. The purpose of all true religion, I believe, is to help connect the dots, and then to connect us to them, enabling us to see the whole picture.

"For thousands if not millions of years, humans have looked into the night skies, connecting dots of light and telling fantastic stories of warriors and lovers they've found scattered across the cosmos. I often look up into the heavens above the farm and remember that night in the bunkhouse, fifty-seven summers ago, when I began a glorious journey by recognizing there's really only one constellation—a masterful constellation that stretches across the entire universe, created by the Master Creator. I believe He created it all, with its hundreds of billions of stars arching across the darkest nights to inspire awe and gratitude and wonder in his boundless creations.

"The poet, William Wordsworth must have shared a similar experience before he wrote the profound lines:

Our birth is but a sleep and a forgetting:

The Soul that rises with us, our life's Star,

Hath had elsewhere its setting,

And cometh from afar:

Not in entire forgetfulness,

And not in utter nakedness,

But trailing clouds of glory do we come

From God, who is our home. [3]

"Our work with young people on the farm over these many years has taught us that our most important assignment is not to teach, but to help our kids *remember* the keys of liberty and joy they must have once known in a time before mortality and in a place much closer to the stars. Many a night we've considered Wordsworth's poetic expressions as we've sat on our porch and watched stardust leave glowing trails of sparks across the sky. In moments like these, with Wordsworth's truths in mind, I find myself honoring the sacred reality that we are much more than merely mortal women and men with expiration dates. We've watched big things change each year as our campers return to the forgotten understanding that they truly are daughters and sons of an eternal God, and as such, heirs of immortality. When we each come to this understanding, our lives suddenly have more purpose, changing how we spend and value our time. The meaning of our relationships evolves and deepens. The beautiful plan of marriage and family takes on much greater value. The way we treat each other and our physical world becomes something far more sacred and meaningful. And the use of our moral agency evolves, taking on a sacred accountability and stewardship.

"This is the way of joy. This is the way of freedom from the weighty burdens, afflictions, and liabilities of our mortal world. Too many forget their relationship to God. Too many choose the paths of least resistance, trading the promise of joy, peace and freedom for cheap, quick thrills and immediate gratification, producing instead of joy, addictions, lusts, and appetites that can never be satisfied. The keys of patience and self-discipline teach us all that we cannot reap where and what we did not till and sow. From the very beginning, when our first parents were turned out of paradise, we were told that it would by the sweat of brow that we would eat our bread until our bodies were laid down in the very dust from which we were created. [4]

"For the last decade or so, Lorenzo and I have concerned ourselves with the disposition of our stewardship of the farm on Harmony Hill. For seven generations, the farm has served this community and the world not only in its production of physically nourishing goods, but as a beacon of essential and timeless truths. As the custodial keepers of that eternal flame, Lorenzo and I have humbly given both the better part and the best years of our lives to this sacred calling. Many of you already know, but I wish to make it publicly clear that Lorenzo and I have chosen our replacements according to the duty of the stewardship passed down from Johann and Mary Zwahlen, the first matchmakers of Niederbipp and co-founders of the farm on Harmony Hill."

A murmur arose from the congregation, but Ruby plowed on.

"Genevieve, Matt. Please stand," she said, pointing her hand toward them. The handsome couple stood, dressed in the finest clothes they would likely ever wear to church in Niederbipp. All eyes in the congregation turned to face them. A spontaneous applause arose, continuing on for nearly a minute, many of the congregants standing to face them as the applause continued. For their part, Matt and Genevieve smiled, humbly nodding to the ovation they received.

"Fifty-seven years ago," Ruby continued, encouraging the congregants to end their applause and be seated, "as my Aunt Millie and Uncle George prepared to depart Harmony Hill, they gave one last bit of advice: Make this time count as a blessing for yourselves and everyone who comes here, and never forget that maintenance alone will not keep the farm going—you must be diligent in improving it.'

"What we didn't realize then was how profound this advice was. As we've worked to both maintain and improve the farm, we've discovered close ties to maintaining and improving our bodies, minds and spirits. And we've discovered for ourselves the great truths the Smurthwaites shared with us. Just as the health and fitness of a farm is dependent on the maintenance and improvements of its stewards, the health and fitness of our spiritual, mental and physical lives depend on our attention and diligence to every needful aspect. Of course, the same is true of our marriages and the relationships that matter most. Without matrimonial maintenance and regular feedings of love and the manifestations of esteem, stagnation and decay can quickly fill the void. The best defense we've discovered is a daily review of the keys of joy. The practice has helped Lorenzo and me to not only maintain the love we have for each other, but to expand and enlarge it, keeping us growing and striving to share our best selves with each other and everyone else."

Ruby took a deep breath, smiling at her audience, pausing thoughtfully. "This will be the last time I address you as my loyal community of fellow Christians. Though my spirit is willing to keep going indefinitely, my flesh is weak.₅

I have fought a good fight. I have lived much longer than I ever hoped I would. But the joy I have found from living and loving among you has sustained me through my trials and lightened my burdens. I've been blessed by knowing and loving each of you. And I hope by the time the Good Lord calls me home, you will have forgiven me for any slight or infraction I've accidentally made against you. Please know that I love you. I won't be having a funeral. They're such a fuss, you know. And the last thing I'd want is for any of you to be looking down into my casket at this old, tired face when I have no doubt I'll be rejoicing and doing cartwheels among the stars."

Again, she paused thoughtfully as she wiped her eyes. "A decade ago when I had my first cancer scare, my doctors suggested I spend whatever time I had left making good memories. I'm sure that would be good advice for most people, but by that time Pops and I had been living in the ways of joy for several decades. We didn't need to alter our plans or begin living 'extra-ordinary' lives. Joy was our companion and our way of life."

"I'm sure there are those who dream of the heaven they hope to inherit when the end finally comes, and God calls them home. I don't recall ever thinking or even hoping I deserved any better than the heaven I came to fifty-seven years ago. Harmony Hill, this town, this congregation…this man," she said extending her hand to Pops, "this is *all* heaven to me, and I know of no other that would be any better than the heaven I arrived at as a selfish and undeserving old school maid who only half-heartedly believed there was something better for me. As it turned out, there is something better for each of us. I've learned it day by day.

What began as a half-hearted slog has evolved and become a wholehearted passion: Joy! I thank you for sharing it with me, for loving me, and for helping me fall in love with each of you. I thank you for inspiring me to stretch, to think and dream bigger, and to take the time and make the effort to see the workings of God in every flower, in every face, and in every heart."

She paused for a long moment as she panned the congregation one more time, smiling into the faces of her people. "I don't know how to end my final sermon," she admitted, "so I'll simply leave you with this: I love you and pray that God will be with each of you, until we meet again."

Notes
1. Max De Pree
2. George Elliot
3. Intimations of Immortality from Recollections of Early Childhood, William Wordsworth
4. Genesis 3:19
5. Matt 26:41

CHAPTER 158

A Quaker Wedding

Joy is the best makeup.
—Anne Lamott—

There was hardly a dry eye in the congregation that day as they rose under the direction of the blue-haired old woman, and sang together the closing hymn, *There is Sunshine in My Soul Today*. For outsiders or visitors to Niederbipp, this may have seemed like an odd choice as a benedictory hymn following the final words of an old, dying woman. But for those who knew Ruby, they knew that no other hymn would be appropriate. Sunshine was not only in her soul, it had permeated it, causing her to glow from within.

Following the benediction, the entire congregation, both old and young, moved forward to embrace the old woman as sunbeams came in through the bright chapel windows.

Matt and Genevieve, pinned in on either side, stayed where they were, sharing with their parents the love and admiration they felt for Ruby and Pops and the community of Niederbipp. As the congregants began working their way to the doors, many stopped, shuffling down the aisle in front of them to shake their hands and congratulate them both on their forthcoming marriage and as the stewards-in-waiting of the farm on Harmony Hill.

While the chapel continued to clear, the campers began setting things up for the wedding. Under Thomas's direction, the first several pews were moved by the men, forming a half circle at the front. Two padded, tall-back chairs were moved in from the wings, and a table was set up in front of them, along with a fancy quill pen. Gloria and Joseph helped decorate the ends of the pew with fresh flower arrangements. Genevieve was handed a beautiful bouquet of white roses while a matching boutonnière was pinned to Matt's lapel, Patrick's camera catching it all.

As the last of the congregants made their way to the doors, the wedding party moved forward with a peaceful reverence. Though many of the townsfolk who'd been invited to the ceremony had witnessed and participated in a Quaker wedding ceremony before, this was the first for all of the campers and the parents of the bride and groom. Pops and Ruby had prepped the campers, telling them it would be much different and simpler than probably any wedding they'd attended before. There would be a time of silent worship, or stillness, to start things out, followed by the exchange of simple vows. And though Matt and Genevieve had done their best to prepare their parents, there was still an air of uncertainty as they approached the circle of pews.

Startled that things were already moving, Amy handed off her baby to Jake and walked to the table in the middle, unrolling a scroll of handmade paper that she'd illuminated with water-colored vines and flowers that framed the hand-lettered marriage vows. After using several small ceramic stones embedded with colored glass hearts to hold the paper down, she quickly returned to a second-row pew, standing next to Jake, Molly, Kai and their children, Grace and Zane.

Without pomp, music or ceremony, the handsome couple moved forward, taking their seats in the big chairs. The campers, parents and other guests followed, filling in the front row.

Hildegard sat next to Ruby and Pops, all of them beaming with joy. Susan and Paul, along with P.J. and Hazel, smiled from their seats in the second-row as Thomas officially began the ceremony by welcoming all the guests and inviting them to settle into silence. He explained that this silence welcomed the Holy Spirit to be present and sanctified the gathering, opening hearts and minds to light and truth.

Sitting down on a bench, Thomas rested his hands in his lap and closed his eyes, a pleasant smile on his face, reverently inviting others to enjoy the silence. Matt took Genevieve's hand and smiled at her before they both turned and nodded to their guests. For the next several minutes, only the soft, intermittent cooing of baby Isaac could be heard along with an occasional shuffling and the muted whispers of the other children. But in that calm and peaceful hall, enhanced and magnified by the near silence, a joyful spirit of connection and serenity descended upon them.

After five minutes, Thomas opened his eyes. He looked into each of the faces of all the guests, waiting for them to be ready. After another couple of minutes, with the feeling of serenity deepened, Thomas stood and walked to the table. He invited Matt and Genevieve to stand and take each other by the hand. Beginning with Matt, Thomas invited him to repeat the traditional Quaker wedding vows.

"In the presence of God, I take thee, Genevieve, to be my wife, promising with divine assistance to be unto thee a loving and faithful husband as long as we both shall live."

For Genevieve, the words were repeated. "In the presence of God, I take thee, Matthew, to be my husband, promising with divine assistance to be unto thee a loving and faithful wife as long as we both shall live."

As they finished, to the smiles and delight of everyone present, Thomas invited them to step forward and sign the beautifully prepared marriage certificate. When they were done, Matt took Genevieve's face gently in his hands and kissed her. The kiss was sweet and respectful, honoring the serenity that prevailed in the room while inviting the cheers of all present. They sat back down as Thomas announced that anyone who felt the Spirit prompting them to share was welcome to open their hearts and offer their joyful contents in a brief and reverential way that honored the vows and further invited divine assistance.

Over the next forty minutes, nearly everyone present took a moment in between stretches of silence to share the feelings of their heart. The peace and propinquity remained as Matt and Genevieve listened and laughed and shared with each of their guests the tender feelings of connection and love. For their parents who'd only just met their new family members, the richness of the peace offered a sense of calm assurance that all would be well. P.J and Hazel got the party laughing when they said they looked forward to visiting the farm and their new friends. The campers who stood each shared their confidence in the love and friendship they'd witnessed growing between Matt and Genevieve over the course of the summer. Ruby and Pops both shed tears as they expressed their own joy and confidence in the strength and the love of Matt and Genevieve's marriage.

When a silence fell among the guests, Genevieve stood, leaned over and kissed her new husband, and invited the guests to join them for cookies and dancing at the Parkin's estate. As the guests stepped forward to sign the wedding certificate, Hildegard pulled Genevieve and Matt aside, handing her a small gift, not much bigger than a wallet, wrapped in craft paper and tied with a twine bow. Too overcome with emotion, she simply hugged them both, saying nothing before slipping away.

Escorting the newlyweds on their bikes, the campers followed close behind, each of them smiling from ear to ear, taking up the full lane on the highway as they made their way to the Parkin's home.

Homemade cookies and milk were enjoyed, but it was the dancing that most thrilled them. Pops and Ruby, playing the guitar and fiddle, got the dancing started, but many of the others joined in, taking turns to make music for the others to enjoy.

After two hours, Matt and Genevieve walked to the center of the gazebo and thanked everyone for coming, encouraging them to stay as long as they wished, or until the cookies were gone, whichever came first. Joseph tossed Matt the keys, and the happy couple took their bags and led a small parade to the front of the house where the Volkswagen camper van was parked, *Just Married* painted on the back window, tin cans tied to the bumper.

After sharing hugs with their guests, Genevieve moved to the back of the van and turned to face it before tossing her bouquet over her head to the five female campers. The bouquet was caught fair and square by Rachael, who danced a little jig in celebration of her good fortune, drawing laughter and applause from everyone, especially the little girls. Like a well-trained gentleman, Matt helped Genevieve into the passenger side of the van, making sure the hem of her dress was tucked inside before closing the door. He walked to the other side and got in, kissing Genevieve before starting up the motor. After taking several shots of the happy couple with their joyful guests behind them, Patrick moved out of the way.

The wedding party followed, waving and cheering as they slowly drove down the arbored drive. When Matt and Genevieve came to the highway, they honked their horn and pulled away, heading north, anxious to begin their next chapter in their own Book of Joy.

CHAPTER 159

Finale

Sorrow looks back, worry looks around, faith looks up.
—Ralph Waldo Emerson—

For Pops and Ruby and the remaining ten campers, the last week of the summer was eventful and fun, though each of them suffered from bouts of melancholy as they watched the quickly approaching end of the runway.

Most of Monday and Tuesday were spent in the orchard, taking instruction as they learned from Pops about the importance of trimming back the fruit trees to encourage the best growth of fruits the following season. The giant pile of branches and twigs were set aside to dry for the following summer's campfire.

On Wednesday, they all rode their bikes to the farm stand where they each signed their names on the colorful rafters next to those of hundreds of other campers who'd spent five of the best months of their lives on Harmony Hill. They took down the solar panels from the roof and swept out the stand one last time before locking it up all for the season. Taking turns on the swing, they laughed and cried together as they recalled the sweet memories they'd created, relishing the love between them.

The connections they felt for each other ran so deep that none of them chose to do anything alone, finding every excuse to huddle together in the kitchen or the library or in the yard. When they found themselves missing Matt and Genevieve, they collectively acknowledged Pops's and Ruby's inspiration in choosing them as their replacements.

They raked leaves on Thursday, bringing most of them to the garden where they were mixed into the rich soil in preparation for next year's vegetables. Afterward, they walked to the fire ring in the orchard, happy to have some unstructured time to spend together. That night after dinner, the dining table was transformed into an assembly line as they worked together under Pops's guiding hand to create twelve hand-stitched journals for those campers who would follow in the coming year.

Ruby did not join them that night. With each passing day, the campers had reluctantly noticed Ruby's precipitous decline in her physical strength. Some of them tried to deny and ignore it. Others tried to soften the reality by being encouraging. But the facts could not be avoided, no matter their gravity. She was dying, and they silently knew she was likely only holding on for them. At nearly 97 years old, she'd earned it. But they worried about Pops. How would he cope without her? How would the farm run without her? How could they help with any of it with only a few days left before they all returned home?

On Friday morning, the campers rose as the cock crowed, knowing the cows needed milking and chickens needed feed, but they were met at the door of their bunkhouses with a chilly wind and the threat of rain. After chores and breakfast, while the women were painting over the mural they'd created during their first weeks, the men cleaned and scrubbed the creamery and moved the load of winter's hay under the barn's vaulted ceiling. It was there in the space above the stalls that they discovered the two pine caskets, sitting side by side under a tarp. It was more reality than any of them were ready for, but there they were: the simple, unadorned sarcophagi of their generous and loving hosts.

By the time Crystal and James rode their bikes into town to meet family and wedding guests that afternoon, Ruby had still not made it out of bed for the day. Not wanting to disturb her with talk or music, the remaining eight campers went for a walk, finding themselves at the little cemetery nestled in the center of the orchard. Though they all had seen it before, none of them had taken occasion to explore it. And it was there, between the Goldsteins and the Smurthwaites, that they found a headstone with Pops and Ruby's names on it, their birthdates carved into the cold, gray stone, along with blank spots patiently awaiting the dates of their deaths.

They sat in the tall grass and talked for an hour about life and death and the power of love. When the words became too heavy for him to bear, Spencer excused himself. Susan joined him, leaving the others to continue their discussion, but they returned ten minutes later with eight shovels. If Ruby was going to die, they'd decided on their way back to the big house, she ought to have a grave that was dug by the people who loved her.

Though the idea of digging a grave for a woman who was still alive felt audacious and even insensitive, it also somehow felt healing. With their shovels, Ephraim and Spencer marked the approximate dimensions of the casket in the orchard grass, and eight campers began thoughtfully hollowing out a hole in the rich, dark earth. With eight of them working together, united in the love they shared for Ruby, the work took on a deep and powerful meaning for each of them as they spoke openly of her kindness and patience, her talents and ability to love and see deeply into their souls. After what they guessed was a little over an hour of digging, they figured they'd gone deep enough. Despite their callouses, each of them had acquired blisters, and their clothes and shoes were caked in mud. But their hearts and faces shone bright with light and love.

With only eight campers at the table that night, the dining hall felt empty. Pops had taken a plate up to Ruby, but he didn't return, and the silence and unknowing was difficult to endure. When James and Crystal arrived home late, they found the others in the library, quietly consoling each other. For James and Crystal, on the eve of the happiest day of their lives, the news of Ruby's very bad day felt like a giant, unavoidable pothole on the road to happiness, but no one knew how to proceed. They quietly went to their bunkhouses, silently praying for a miracle.

The miracle arrived the following afternoon in the form of Matt and Genevieve walking their bikes down the rutted lane. Rex was the first to spot them and went running to meet the newlyweds, followed by eight of their fellow campers, James and Crystal having gone to town to spend time with family and friends on the day before their wedding. While they all caught each other up with various events of their week, the absence of both Pops and Ruby did not go unnoticed.

While the eight campers waited in the music room, Matt and Genevieve climbed the stairs for the first time, calling out to Pops. One bedroom door had been left ajar and they paused outside it, listening for voices.

Ruby's pale face brightened when she saw them, using all her strength to lean up on her elbows. They greeted her with hugs and fresh stories of the autumn colors in upstate New York and Niagara Falls. She rallied, color coming back into her face as they spoke of charming bed-n-breakfasts and magical drives over colorful scenic byways. And for the first time in two days, they coaxed her out of bed and down the stairs where she joined the campers for dinner.

Matt and Genevieve moved their meager belongings into the second bedroom that evening, leaving plenty of time to share their adventures with their fellow campers in the library, along with Pops and Ruby.

As planned, James and Crystal were married after church services the following day, and to everyone's surprise, both Ruby and Pops were there to celebrate with them. Not wanting to be upstaged by the borrowed Volkswagen camper van, James surprised everyone by renting an Amish horse and buggy, which they traded a couple miles down the road for the rental car his buddy had parked there.

The rest of the campers rode their bikes back to the farm where they enjoyed their final evening together with Pops and Ruby in the library where they all laughed and cried and shared tender memories late into the evening. Before they went to bed, Ruby asked to pray with them. She opened her heart, inviting all the blessings of heaven to be theirs as they chose to live and practice the keys of joy. As they left the library that evening, drying their tears and hugging each other, they made arrangements to gather at the Parkin's estate on the fifteenth of October the following year for a weekend retreat and reunion.

For their last night all together, Matt and Genevieve both went back to their respective bunk houses where they stayed up late talking about dreams and plans for their futures. The women offered to help Genevieve with her articles if she needed material, and she in turn offered to help them remember the keys of joy with free subscriptions to her magazine.

The men fell asleep early after listening to Matt's stories of his honeymoon and joy of feeling so close to the woman he loved. As he stared up through the skylight that night, he thanked God he would never have to sleep alone in a twin bed again—unless, of course, he wanted to.

The campers were up early to work on their final chores. When the laundry was hung and the animals cared for, they walked together, arm in arm, to the big house where Matt and Genevieve, along with Pops and Ruby, had cooked a generous breakfast of eggs, oatmeal and pancakes. Ephraim made sure they all enjoyed the last of the Wisdom Cookies, sending them all off on a high note.

With the flatbed trailer hitched to the truck and their bags loaded in the bed, they hiked to the top of the rutted drive one last time. Then, with their bellies and their hearts full, they took it all in, memorizing the colorful fence with its unique finials, the pond where they'd all fished in vain for the giant brown trout, and the farmhouse with its generous porch that had hosted the most charming and remarkable gatherings of hearts and minds that any of them had ever before experienced.

As they stood at the top of the hill together, their arms over each others' shoulders, they looked out across the farm with great love and affection. In that moment, they forgot the work and the toil of the past five months, remembering only the love and the treasures they'd gained. Without its leaves, the giant cottonwood no longer blocked the view of the fields beyond the big house where they'd worked together to till and plant the grain that would nourish next year's campers. From this vantage point, the vast garden, now cleared of its vegetables, looked much smaller, while the walk to the cow shed looked shorter. Viewing the laundry hanging to dry in the autumn sun, they were certain none of them would ever forget the endless heaps of dirty clothes that had met them every morning, nor the unique contraption that taught them all how balance, order, rhythm and harmony were necessary elements to effectively work together.

Climbing aboard the flatbed trailer, they noticed the hand of a small woman waving to them from her beloved front porch. For eight of them, they knew this would be the last time they would see her in mortality. Tears fell freely as they rolled forward, each of them holding onto these men and women next to them—strangers and weirdos who'd magically been transformed into the dearest of friends and even family.

Pops pulled into the old train station ten minutes before the bus was scheduled to arrive. He held up a twenty-dollar bill and asked for a volunteer to run to Sam's bakery and buy pastries for the bus ride to Pittsburgh. Susan and Spencer volunteered while the others stacked their bags on the platform. When they returned, they all embraced one last time, holding each other tight and making promises they intended to keep.

The bus rounded the corner at the appointed hour and eight campers loaded their bags into its luggage compartments before climbing aboard.

They waved and blew kisses to Pops and the matchmakers-in-waiting as the bus pulled away. And then, for the first time in fifty-seven years, Pops returned to the farm on Harmony Hill with his replacements, sitting by his side in the cab of the old pickup, each of them anxiously awaiting the adventure that lay ahead.

It does not matter how slowly you go as long as you do not stop.
—Confucius—

Three days after the campers returned to their various homes, Ruby fell while walking back to the big house from gathering eggs. Genevieve and Matt found her on their way back from the laundry shack, lying on her back and looking up into the beautiful clouds as if her repose had been a planned activity. They laid down beside her, their heads together, looking up in awe, surrounded by the wonders of God's creations. When they noticed she was chilled, they tried to help her up and get her back to the house, but she couldn't move her leg and was suddenly struck with pain in her hip.

Fearing it was broken, but knowing they had to get her out of the cold, Matt gingerly carried her tiny, frail body up to the house where they laid her on the loveseat and wrapped her in a blanket, her breaths were short and erratic as she stoically navigated the pain. Genevieve stayed with her, holding her while Matt ran to the milk barn to notify Pops.

At nearly ninety-seven years old, there was no question what this meant. After tearfully discussing their options, and Ruby adamantly refusing any medical intervention, Matt carried Ruby up the stairs and laid her on her bed where Genevieve and Pops delicately changed her into a flannel nightgown and made her comfortable. Over the next three days, Ruby received many visitors from Niederbipp. While Pops kept a vigil, Matt and Genevieve kept up on the chores and the kitchen duty, making sure Ruby had plenty of her favorite foods even when her appetite continued to wane.

On Sunday afternoon, Matt took the truck into town, returning with Hildegard and Thomas, giving each of them time to say goodbye to an old, dear friend. Via satellite phone, Julia and Lawrence said their goodbyes and expressed their love. And on Monday morning, after a long and fitful night for all of them, Ruby Swarovski, the splendidly illustrious and persuasively graceful matchmaker of Niederbipp, passed into eternity.

While Matt tearfully took care of the milking and the chickens, Genevieve and Pops dressed Ruby in her favorite Sunday dress and brushed her long hair. Before her body lost all its warmth, they wrapped her in a patchwork quilt and laid her in the pine box they'd lowered from the hay loft in the milk barn.

Per Ruby's request, there was no funeral, though several friends came up from Niederbipp to help with the burial. Jake and Amy squeezed Hildegard and Thomas into the back seat of their new car next to baby Isaac. Susan and Paul followed with P.J. and Hazel. Joseph and Gloria brought an armful of fresh white daisies, Ruby's favorite.

When all who'd been invited had gathered, the men lifted the casket onto their shoulders, and they all walked in a solemn procession to the tiny family graveyard in the middle of the orchard where six generations of the farm's loyal stewards had already been laid to rest. In the grave dug by those who loved her, they lowered Ruby's casket. And then, with tears flowing freely, all who were present helped bury her in the cold ground.

With her heart aching but her deadline looming, Genevieve got to work on her article. It came much quicker than she anticipated. Ten thousand words turned to twenty, then forty, then a hundred thousand, and still the words came as though a spigot had been turned on from heaven. Julia was thrilled with what she read, and she and Lawrence, along with their editors, began breaking the story down into sections that could be published every month.

While Pops and Matt managed the chores, Genevieve continued to write while her feelings were raw and her memories fresh, producing the best work she'd ever written to the delight of the entire magazine staff. By the time the January edition of the magazine was ready for publication in early December, the editors believed they had at least a year's worth of usable material but encouraged Genevieve to keep it coming.

Christmas was a simple affair. Matt's mother came for a few days between Christmas and New Year's, surprising all of them when she showed up with her fiancé, Joe. He was a kind and gentle widower with three adult children. They'd met the Sunday after the wedding when she'd returned to church for the first time in decades. Chatting with his future stepfather while milking the cows one morning, Matt learned that his mother had introduced Joe to five wonderful keys that had already changed both of their lives and introduced them to a joy they'd never known before.

Matt and Genevieve were delighted when they received a postcard from Paris a week later, letting them know that Genevieve's parents had also been attempting to live their lives in a way that made room for each of the five keys. They promised to visit but gave no specifics.

In January, letters of application began arriving at the mailbox at the top of Harmony Hill and several evenings a week were soon consumed with sorting through the applications. In the short winter days, Pops continued to teach Matt and Genevieve about the nuances of the farm and the how-to's and why's of the equipment and the animals. Sunday continued to be a favorite day for all of them. Between inclement weather and a lack of seasonal tourists, the chapel was rarely full. During these slower months, Matt and Genevieve each accepted Thomas's invitation to give a sermon, which they both came away from feeling like they could use more practice.

Greg and Holly married on the 15th of February. The next week Matt and Genevieve received a care package filled with photos from all of their fellow campers who'd attended the wedding in Colorado. They were also pleased to announce that Spencer and Susan, after dating for several months, were engaged to be married on June 6th in San Diego. An invitation to the wedding was included, along with a kind note excusing them, recognizing they would soon be occupied with campers and sharing with them the joyful arts.

Toward the end of February, Pops began slowing down. A week later Matt and Genevieve noticed his breathing was shallow and raspy. They encouraged him to see a doctor, but Pops wanted none of it. He spent a couple of days in bed before passing away in his sleep, presumably from pneumonia. It was the way he wanted it, but it left a huge void for Matt and Genevieve. Thomas and Jake came up to the farm to help Matt dig the grave in the frozen ground, and the three of them were able to lay their friend and mentor next to his adoring wife before the end of the day.

With only the two of them working the farm, the chores took much longer. Matt and Genevieve settled into their new reality, but often found themselves looking forward to May when campers would return to lend a hand with the chores.

One afternoon while they were in town for a few groceries, Matt spotted an advertisement for swing dancing classes in Warren. On a whim, they invited Paul and Susan to join them in the excursion. For the next two months, every Tuesday evening, the couples made the round trip, enjoying the conversation and friendship as much as they enjoyed the instruction. It was on one of these trips that Susan encouraged Genevieve to write a book about her experiences with farming and marriage and joy. She didn't need to be encouraged twice, and began writing that week, writing in the evenings in the kitchen while Matt baked dozens of Wisdom Cookies for next summer's campers.

After receiving more than 1,100 applications from would-be campers, Matt and Genevieve enlisted the help of many of their friends in town to help sort through them. Slowly they narrowed the best ones down from 75 to 42 to 27 and finally 12 lucky souls from diverse backgrounds who were interested in sacrificing and dedicating five months of their lives to working the farm in exchange for a little help in the love department. Acceptance letters were mailed, along with hundreds of personalized letters from the newly formed committee kindly thanking all the applicants, inviting them to apply again, and encouraging them to come to Niederbipp for a visit. It felt like the right thing to do, even if there wasn't room for everyone who wanted to be on the farm that summer.

On the morning of the third Saturday in May, Matt and Genevieve rose early, feeling anxious and nervous with what they were about to begin. As they'd been doing every morning since the beginning, they knelt next to the ottoman in the library and humbly asked for the blessings of heaven to be with them. While Matt milked the cows, fed the animals, and hitched up the flat-bed trailer, Genevieve went to the kitchen to get lunch started for the new campers.

The first week of the summer wasn't easy. Despite their best efforts to select individuals who seemed eager to learn and be compliant with what would be requested of them, there were plenty of difficulties. In just the first three days, the toilets backed up in the women's bunkhouse, an egg fight broke out between the chicken team, two tetanus shots were required for a barbed wire incident, and the runt of the piglets was carried off by a chicken hawk, squealing and flailing to the horror of everyone who witnessed it. These minor calamities caused the garden planting to be delayed by at least a couple of days, pushing back the planting of the fields.

But by the end of the third week, after several meaningful evenings of porch games and Bessie's ice cream, the team began to gel and take shape.

Over the following weeks and months, the same brand of magic Matt and Genevieve had experienced began to take place in the hearts and minds of the campers as they each made time and space for God to touch them. This magic grew day by day as they each learned, and then embraced the keys of joy. In this optimistic environment, meaningful connections were made between each of them, games were invented, skills were learned, and joy was experienced by every one of them.

A week before the summer ended, Genevieve called Matt in from the garden one morning and handed him a small paper bag. As he opened the surprise gift, pulling out a strange piece of plastic about the size of a popsicle stick, Matt looked up to find Genevieve smiling with her whole soul. She was pregnant! They wept and rejoiced together as they considered the innumerable ramifications of this incredible news.

Three weeks later, keeping with the plans they'd made the year before, Matt and Genevieve gathered with their fellow campers at the Parkin estate for a weekend reunion. After an entire year of not seeing these friends who'd become family, Matt and Genevieve relished catching up with each of them.

Holly and Greg thrilled everyone by showing up dressed in black leather and riding a Harley Davidson. They were excited to report that things were going well. They'd formed a band with a few other musicians shortly before their marriage, and had booked several gigs throughout the summer, including the wedding of the son of a wealthy hedge fund manager. She had been so impressed with their music that she'd invited them to play at another party, and then a third. As they'd become friendly, this woman had been curious about the obvious joy that existed between Greg and Holly. When they shared with her their story of meeting each other on a matchmaking farm, she became open to hearing more about the keys of joy. The light of what they shared struck a chord. In the process of sharing more, Holly had also shared her ideas about virtual vacations for people who didn't have the time, health or money to be able to travel. Thrilled with the idea, the woman had asked them to put together a business plan. Anxious to provide proof of concept, Holly and Greg made a gamble, bought a 3-D camera, and gathered enough footage from a trip to New York City to provide viewers with three dozen hours of Virtual Reality content. They were excited to share that the woman, after only five minutes of wearing the VR goggles and viewing their content, offered them a generous contract to get their business started. The campers were delighted when they learned that Greg and Holly would be heading to Europe the following week to begin a six-week tour of four major cities and Tuscany.

Following their June wedding, Spencer and Susan spent a week honeymooning on Orcas Island in the Puget Sound, where they spent most of their time talking about their dreams for the future, ultimately deciding that they wanted to figure out a way to work together so they wouldn't have to spend so much time apart. With Spencer's vast connections with athletes and sports, and Susan's law experience, they decided they'd become sports agents, using the keys of joy as the foundation for their approach and business. Now, four months after hanging out their shingle, they were excited to announce that they were representing six professional athletes and had just quit their other jobs. They tied their success to Pops and Ruby's example of giving God the first hour of every day, the first day of every week, and the first dime of every dollar. And though their future was still uncertain, it was bright and filled with possibilities.

Ephraim was excited to announce that he'd spent the last year tinkering in his home workshop after work with a series of different designs for a bicycle-powered ice cream machine that could be folded in half and stored under a bed, or the side-by-side tandem version that could fit in a standard broom closet. He was happy to announce he had just secured a patent and found a manufacturer in Milwaukee who would be turning out the first *Calorie Neutral Ice Cream Makers*, (aka CNICMs) in the world. Though it had taken him a fat minute to find his footing in the dating world after his time on the farm, he was happy to announce that he'd been on six promising dates with a beautiful and talented librarian, Jennie, whom he'd met at his local public library while doing research.

On their first date, Ephraim had told Jennie about his five months' worth of making ice cream on a matchmaking farm and had shared with her the basics of the five keys of joy. She was interested, not only in a second date, but in learning more about the keys. They'd played croquet that second date, gone tubing on a river for their third date, rode bikes to a park for a picnic on their fourth date, picked berries at a local pick-'em-yourself berry farm and made jam for their fifth date, and baked bread for their sixth date. He reported that things were looking good, that allowing Jennie to see both his vulnerabilities and his talents had invited her to do the same, allowing their friendship and a sense of connection to develop both quickly and powerfully. He didn't know exactly where things were headed, but he openly hoped that he'd be bringing Jennie with him to next year's reunion.

James and Crystal shocked all the campers when they announced they'd be having a baby girl in March. After a tough first trimester, Crystal was beginning to feel good again, though she was generally tired and hungry. They explained that while they were on their honeymoon, they, too, had spent a lot of time talking about their future, coming to the conclusion that they would each need to restructure their life's goals. Soon after, James tendered his resignation at his law firm, moving his practice first to a home office, then to a rented space in a strip mall a short walk from their home where they set up shop. While Crystal handled the office, kept the books, and worked on marketing, James dedicated his time to working with clients. They shared how they'd decided early on to dedicate ten percent of their time or roughly four hours each week to pro bono cases, offering legal help to many low-income people who were dealing with medical, housing and employment challenges. Instead of working 70-90 hours each week as he'd done before coming to the farm, James and Crystal walked to work each morning and walked home together for dinner, five nights a week. He occasionally worked on Saturdays, but only on pro bono work, and for the past six months they'd been volunteering with the youth ministry of their congregation, finding joy as they practiced charity and reverence and shared with the teens the five keys that lead to joy.

Sonja was thrilled to introduce her fiancé, Bryan, to the rest of the campers. For the last year she'd been sharing with Bryan the things she learned at the farm as they worked together at the arboretum in Asheville.

Bryan admitted that Sonja had caught his eye two years earlier, but he had kept his distance after overhearing a phone conversation between her and a debt collector. With financial debts of his own, he'd been interested as he'd watched Sonja give up weekends and holidays, even working double shifts in an effort to become debt-free before she left for the farm.

As she'd shared with Bryan some of the basics about the keys of joy, he'd begun recognizing the power of self-discipline, even putting it into practice in some areas of his life. When she shared with him how exercising reverence had enhanced her self-discipline while giving her confidence and purpose, he recognized he was missing something. As a lapsed Christian and self-proclaimed agnostic, it had been years since he'd had anything to do with religion or spirituality. She invited him to join her at church one Sunday, then again and again. These weren't exactly dates, but they served many of the same purposes, allowing them to get to know each other and discover who the other was. With each conversation, Sonja had shared what she knew from her own experience about each of the keys of joy. And from those conversations, love had grown between them.

When he heard a few weeks before that Sonja was going to a reunion in Niederbipp, Bryan asked if he might tag along. She boldly told him that she wouldn't take him if he wasn't serious enough about her to put a ring on her finger. And so the next night, at the end of a long day, Bryan took her to dinner and thanked her for her patience, tutelage and kindness. Afterwards, they walked through the streets of town, listening to the local bluegrass and mountain music being played by buskers before sitting down on a bench in the park to enjoy the evening. After twenty minutes of warm conversation tinged with nervous tension on his part, he got down on his knee and proposed marriage, sliding a simple silver band on her finger with the promise to take her ring shopping for whatever she wanted. Over their weekend in Niederbipp, the happy couple snuck away to Castleton's Fine Jewelry Shop, returning with two simple gold bands, feeling grateful for the joys that can only be appreciated by those who chose a simple life.

Rachael was the only camper who arrived without either a spouse or a fiancé, but she was far from being upset about it. In the year that had passed, she'd focused her creativity on what she called the *soft arts*, which consisted mainly of fabric and clothing, creating a line of overalls-inspired loungewear and skirts. But she was most excited about her latest take on Christmas stockings. She was happy to announce that she was having a hard time keeping up with orders. Having found an old sock knitting machine on eBay earlier that spring, she'd been playing with Christmas stockings that challenged traditions, many of her favorites knitted with non-traditional colors and up to four feet long. As each one was different, her Etsy shop had become a phenomenon for eccentrics and collectors, and she'd already received lots of attention on social media when several celebrities mentioned her on their Twitter feeds.

The attention and the success couldn't have come at a better time. Having spent most of her life dealing with depression and anxieties, it was nice to finally be the artist formerly known as starving. Her confidence from her summer on the farm and her rising success as an artist had allowed her to move three states away from her mother who'd been the cause of so much of her angst. After fully embracing the keys of joy, this new Rachael had more hope than she'd ever known before. Love would come in its own timing for her, and she felt no need to rush it, using this time to continue to heal and be strengthened by the light and truth she'd gained on the farm.

Josh arrived at the reunion much later than expected and with a pretty woman by his side, Amelia. They explained that for the last eight months, since he'd returned to work after a weekend away for Greg and Holly's wedding, Amelia had been asking lots of questions of Josh. As his co-worker at the software company, she admitted she'd seen a big change in Josh's confidence, personality and aspirations since he'd asked for a five-month sabbatical and left for the farm. As a divorcee with two young children, Amelia admitted she'd been hyper-cautious with men, but had found Josh to be a thoughtful and sensitive man with an admirable work ethic and an unusual degree of self-discipline and optimism, especially since his return from the farm.

After many months of hearing about the keys of joy and the things Josh had learned on Harmony Hill, when she'd heard that he'd be traveling to a reunion of his fellow campers, she'd invited herself to join him, wanting to know more. They'd arrived in town that morning after a redeye flight into Pittsburgh. They spent the day visiting the places Josh had described to her: the farm stand, the sacred willow tree, the church, the charming streets of Niederbipp, and finally the farm where they'd spent several hours that afternoon sitting on the bench overlooking the orchard and the valley below. Here they'd discussed the power of the keys of joy and the possibility of a future together that embraced these keys.

Josh watched closely as Amelia threw herself into conversations with the other women, bonding with them quickly as they discussed dreams and shared experiences of living their lives in ways that promoted and invited joy.

All the campers were anxious to hear about Matt and Genevieve's first year as the matchmakers of Harmony Hill. As they shared both humorous and painful stories of growth and evolution experienced by everyone on the farm that summer, the friends reminisced late into the night, nourishing their souls with the love and connections they'd made over the most challenging and rewarding summer of their lives. They rejoiced together as they announced the forthcoming arrival of the first baby on Harmony Hill in at least a century. The realities of balancing all needful things and a baby, too, felt a little overwhelming for all of them, but with it came a gentle whisper that all would be well. They all would be watching and waiting to hear, and willing to jump in and help if Matt and Genevieve ever needed it.

The former campers were also excited to hear about Genevieve's creative ventures. She reported that in her spare time, she and Amy Kimball had collaborated on a children's book entitled, *Buttercup Comes to Niederbipp*, the story of a wild stallion who is tamed through a series of challenges, each of the challenges focusing on an aspect of the keys of joy. She showed them some of Amy's illustrations and announced that they'd just found an agent and signed a contract for a six-book deal surrounding Buttercup and his adventures in Niederbipp.

When Matt and Genevieve excused themselves to return to the farm to take care of the chores over the course of the weekend, each of the campers took turns to go with them, refreshing their minds and hearts with their sweet memories of their time on Harmony Hill. They each took a moment to walk inside the bunkhouses and reread the first lesson of the farm posted above the door: Except the Lord build the house, they labor in vain that build it. They also toured the big house, looking up at the yoke that hung above the dining table, playing a tune on one of the various instruments in the music room, resting quietly in the library as they breathed in the scent of old books while they identified each of the symbols of the keys of joy. Invariably they each patted Bessie's saddle as they walked across the porch, remembering the games and talks that opened their hearts and offered connections they'd never known before.

On Saturday night, after they'd all cooked dinner together in the Parkin's kitchen, Matt and Genevieve invited the group to join them in the living room where they shared with them the note that Hildegard had given them the day they were married. They explained that in their rush to get on their honeymoon, they'd forgotten all about the small package that Matt had placed in the chest pocket of his new suit. It had not been until earlier that spring, after Ruby and Pops had both passed away that they'd found the small package and read the enclosed letter. As they opened the package again in front of the campers, a metal ring with five small keys slid out of the folded letter.

They handed these around the circle as Genevieve read the letter written in Hildegard's hand in which she explained that this ring of five keys had been "borrowed" from Lady Liberty at the Liberty Fountain by six young men of Niederbipp and their newlywed brides on the eve of their departure for the war in Europe. The six wives had innocently encouraged the men to take the keys of liberty to the war-torn continent in hopes they might be emissaries of peace. These keys, Hildegard explained, had been returned to her along with her husband's dog tags when his flag-draped coffin, and those of his friends, had been sent back to Niederbipp for burial.

Hildegard also explained that she hoped that by entrusting them to Matt and Genevieve, more people could know the power of the keys of liberty and joy.

Matt explained that he and Genevieve had spent many hours discussing what they should do with the keys and had come to the conclusion that there was really only one appropriate response—to return them back to the town of Niederbipp so those who saw them might ask questions that could lead to answers and understanding. With this in mind, the twelve campers, armed only with a ladder and a caulking gun, walked into town under the cover of darkness to finally return the borrowed symbols of the town's most honored tradition. With warm intentions and stealth, they carried the ladder to the Liberty Fountain, and Matt quietly climbed the rungs. After reattaching the ring of keys to Lady Liberty's hand, he pulled six of Jake's handmade tiles from his pocket, one for each of the keys of joy and one of the joy cluster, and glued these to the neck of the pillar at the top of the stone column on which the statue stood. Then, as quietly as they'd come, they walked back to the Parkin's home and went to bed, feeling pleased to have been advocates of restoration and learning for those with eyes to see.

On Sunday, after attending church in Niederbipp, the former campers caravanned back up to the farm. They parked at the top of the hill next to the phone booth and walked down the rutted lane together, arm in arm, chatting and laughing like old times. Instead of going into the big house or any of the outbuildings, they walked down the forest path to the orchard. Here they gathered around the humble graves of two of the kindest, wisest, most humble and noble people any of them had ever known, collectively thanking God they'd been allowed to know them.

After a late lunch at the Parkins, the friends packed up, promising to be back next year at this same time to reunite in a spirit of love and joy. No one knew what the future held, but they were filled with hope, believing that by the grace of God, all would be well—and joy would be their companion.

The End.

None of us will ever accomplish anything excellent or commanding except when he listens to this whisper which is heard by him alone.
—Ralph Waldo Emerson—

By the time this book finds its way into your hands, twenty-five years will have passed since the good folks of Niederbipp began having conversations in my head as I worked in a borrowed pottery studio, eking out a living. These years have been a crazy journey—one I hope I don't have to repeat, but one I am eternally grateful that my family and I have traveled.

I don't think it was more than a month after my wife, Lynnette, and I were married in September of 1997 that the visitors from Niederbipp began dropping by to visit. In those early days, it was Isaac who'd come and sit on my table as I worked, poking me, nudging me, whispering that I needed to stretch and seek and open my mind and heart to bigger things, bigger ideas, bigger dreams.

At this point, twenty-five years later, I'm grateful I learned to listen. But at the time, I was easily distracted by a hundred other things, all of them happening at once as I tried to find my footing in the world of art and opportunity.

It took more than eleven years from that day Isaac first spoke to me till the first book, *Remembering Isaac*, was released. Looking back, it was unmistakably fear that kept me from progressing quicker. I had nothing *and everything* to lose by taking time away from what paid the bills to write a book. I wasn't a writer. I'd never even considered it. Many of my friends had chosen to become English majors because they loved to read and aspired to write. I, on the other hand, liked making mud pies. I'd taken all the required English classes, but it just didn't feel like it was my thing. I'd chosen my course. I'd set my sail. At twenty-four years old, I thought I knew where my life was headed.

And then there was this little voice that kept poking my heart, filling my soul with images, ideas and stories that were far beyond any wisdom and understanding I knew I could make up on my own.

I only started writing because I felt compelled to write. I was ignorant, but reluctantly willing. I wrote on weekends and late into the evenings. It was never really enough, but it was all I thought I had. I continually felt compelled to write, but I wrestled with both the angels and the demons of my better nature, not knowing how, not knowing why, not knowing what I was to do with any of it.

Somewhere out there are at least twenty versions of that first book. I learned to write by writing, revising, polishing, tearing up and throwing away, and starting over with the story and the ideas that refused to give me peace until they'd made my fingers type them up.

But I was a potter, not a writer. I couldn't understand why the story couldn't find someone else to tell it. I'm grateful now that it didn't.

Time passed. I moved from that borrowed backyard studio into a real studio with real rent and a real business partner. We taught classes and made and sold pots and had some fun. I didn't have much time for writing, nor the stillness required for hearing stories. After eighteen months, I sold my share of the shop and took the money I'd made and built a studio behind our recently purchased home. Our first child, Isaac, was born the week I began working in my own space. That same week, the Niederbippians received my forwarding address, and they moved in one night, permanently, filling the space in the walls where the insulation was supposed to be. They both taught and taunted me with their stories. I did what I could to try to appease them, but it was rarely enough.

Six months after our son was born, two planes hit the World Trade Center, and time stood still. I was twenty-seven years old. I was afraid of how I would support my family if the economy changed. All our savings had been used to build the studio. I felt naked and exposed and afraid. I got back to work, anxious to move away from fear. The Niederbippians continued their stories and their taunts.

From the time I was a child, I've appreciated Gary Larson's *The Far Side* cartoons. There's one I remember vividly of God sitting at his computer. On the monitor is a doofus walking along a sidewalk. Above his head, a giant piano is suspended precariously from a rope, and God's finger is hovering over a button on the keyboard with the word SMITE emblazoned on it.

I don't *really* believe this is the way God works, but I've often wondered about his creative techniques for getting our attention. It turns out that for most of us, if we don't *choose* to be humble, we will likely be *compelled* to become such. And that compelling can sometimes feel like a smite upside the head.

That's the way it was for me anyway, when at age 30 I was diagnosed with arthritis in my hands. I wrestled with this for several years before I finally learned to submit. I needed to be writing, but I wasn't. I'd heard the voice of God in the form of a few dozen Niederbippians, but I was busy and preoccupied with other things. I suppose I needed a good smite.

I finally listened.

The story came much quicker after that. I changed gears, giving my best time to my writing rather than the scraps that were left after I'd done everything else. I discovered that's what God had been wanting all along—my best. He asked for it. I quite humbly submitted. It's worked out much better since then. After the first book took more than 11 years, I've written and published a book every year since then. God can do amazing things with us when we're willing to give him our best.

I was just finishing the last of my Isaac series when Ruby showed up. Actually, she tried to butt in line, but I had to keep sending her to the back as I was already wrestling with other stories. She was patient for a while, but she kept reminding me that she was getting older and warning me that she would not be around forever. I felt compelled to listen. I'm glad I did.

Ruby's story was quite a revelation to me. I started out blind, not knowing where it was going or what she hoped to share with me. I'd never heard of the five keys of joy before. I remember trying to guess what they were—maybe you did the same. I was often surprised by how the story would progress around them. They felt important, valuable, and needed in a world that seems to be growing increasingly conflicted with the basic elements of joy. Many, it seems, in an effort to remove or numb the conscience and shirk accountability, have attempted to cut God out of the very world he created, while moral relativism seeks to snuff out the gentle pleadings of the inner voice. How much will we have to lose before we begin to see that the joy and liberty we seek have a very defined and certain recipe, and reverence for the Creator is a critical element in that recipe?

As opposition to all that is good and true increases, the ungodly seems to retreat further and further from the sunny, purifying light of hope. While many are choosing to give in to that hopelessness, God's light and love continue to burn like beacons, inviting us to return to the safe harbor, to come home, to ignore the siren's wanton cynicism, lay down our weapons of war, and enter into the peace and love God promises us. The storm is raging, and it will only grow louder and stronger in the coming years. It's easy to become distracted by its howls and groans at our backs. But if it's hope and love we are after, it's best to remember the first rule of climbing which Pops shared in Book 2: *Never look anywhere you don't want to go.*

Focus and balance, in a world bombarded by negative voices from every conceivable media, is difficult to both obtain and maintain. The way is lost to many simply by becoming distracted.

SQUIRREL!

See what I mean? And there are a great many "squirrels" leading us further and further away from the path of light, hope and truth.

I don't pretend to know all truth, but I do recognize that all truth is filled with light. And the more of that light we can know and feel and understand, the lighter and brighter and more joyful our lives can be.

Where do you want to go?

I think that's an important question—maybe one we should ask ourselves daily, and every time we feel distracted, unfocused or unbalanced. The Desert of Criticism is real, and its drifting dunes claim more acreage every year. But Divine Discontent is also real, producing in each of us a holy longing for something beyond the wasteland before us. At the core of every holy longing is the seed of hope. I believe life is always better when we heed the urge of that holy longing and embrace the light that awaits us as we turn our backs to the Desert of Criticism and move closer to the light and hope we desire.

Ever since I was a young child, I've consciously attempted to be a good observer, hoping to understand the hows and whys of all things. In recent years, I've focused my observations on discovering the sources of joy. If I could borrow the theme of Oscar Wilde's quote: *"To live is the rarest thing in the world. Most people exist, that is all,"* I would like to suggest that to truly live as God intended and created us, joy must be our companion. Without joy, we are limited to mere existence, living far beneath our privilege.

Joy, I've discovered from my observations, is much more of a conscious choice than it is a set of ideal circumstances. As I've watched and considered the most joyful men and women in my life, I've recognized many similarities. As Einstein observed, "When you examine the lives of the most influential people who have ever walked among us, you discover one thread that winds through them all. They have been aligned first with their spiritual nature and only then with their physical selves."

As spirituality and religion wane, an increasing emphasis is placed on the physical world. When mortal bodies become more important than the eternal spirits housed within them, an imbalance occurs. And in our world today, a great imbalance exists as all forms of media and conversation focus on indulging the carnal flesh while starving and neglecting the needs of the eternal spirit. Jesus himself warned, 'Every kingdom divided against itself will be laid waste, and every city or household divided against itself will not stand.'" [1]

The great division and imbalance are real. And though many who've built their beautiful houses upon the sand are finding themselves swept away by the storm and the raging sea, the worship of these demigods still inspires ill-placed devotion. I hear many beginning to say, "There has to be a better way." But when the humble suggest that the better way includes turning our hearts to God and allowing him to be the builder and architect of our houses, the proud push back, calling God and his people judgmental haters and bigots.

What is the answer? Where do we go from here? How do we change our world for the better? Where can we turn for peace and hope?

As a Christian, I know of no other way than to turn to God and his Christ. They alone are the sure foundation. They alone can protect us from the storm and the rising tides. It will likely require building our homes and planting our hearts on higher ground. And it will certainly require us to change our focus, paying more attention to the values and promises of eternity. It will require us to lay aside the carnal fads and the trivial pursuits of pop culture, and seek instead for timeless moral principles and the high standards of joy.

The keys of joy are not new. They've been around in one form or another since the time God spoke to our first parents in the garden. They've been practiced by faithful men and women throughout history, getting lost from time to time when the love of darkness was greater than the love of light. But they've never completely disappeared. They've been preserved by monks and martyrs, recorded in illuminated manuscripts, planted in ancient forests, hidden in the narrative depictions of stained-glass windows, and told and retold in children's stories for a hundred generations. They seem to show up when people seek them, when men and women turn their backs to the growing darkness and search diligently for the beacons of light on the distant horizon. They serve as invitations, summoning each of us to step forward, to step up, to build strong, solid, and sure foundations according to sacred blueprints.

Yes, I know each of these keys run contrary to the fads and fashions of popular culture. They always have. They always will. Unless and until our love for God is greater than our love for the world, joy will always be an extracurricular pursuit. But for those who love God and practice reverence, the pursuit of joy will be a part of everything we do. Practicing each of the five keys on their own will bring you closer to joy, but the fullness of true joy can only be wholly experienced by those whose daily walk and practice embraces each of the keys.

Reverence, Patience, Hope, Self-discipline and Charity. They work together to lift and protect, encourage and sustain, build and fortify, offering grand and innumerable blessings along the way. Few of them will likely be mastered in a weekend. Most of them will, in fact, require a lifetime to become proficient, perhaps even longer. But remember that we are each eternal beings with unlimited potential and promise. We are children of a loving God who knows our potential because he's planted its seeds within each of our souls, and provides each of us with unique opportunities for that potential to blossom and grow in meaningful and profound ways.

By harnessing the powers of self-discipline with the intensifying and expanding strength of reverence for God and all creation, we can humbly yet vigorously move toward our eternal potential. God has not left us alone, but neither does he intervene in the affairs of mankind without invitation. He stands at the door and knocks *Revelation 3:20, waiting to be invited in. And once he's in, if his host is willing and listening, he'll likely make some suggestions about the decor or cleanliness, and throw open the shades to welcome in a brighter light. When you're ready, he may suggest a move to higher ground, or a renovation of your humble home to make room for more love, more light, and more friends and visitors.

I've thought often about a passage of scripture as I've been writing this series. It comes from the 6th chapter of Deuteronomy where

Moses, after spending decades in the wilderness with the whining children of Israel, is finally getting ready to move into the promised land. After seeing numerous miracles, being fed by manna, and coming to know their relationship to God, Moses invites the Israelites to carry the commandments in their hearts. He pleads with them to teach the commandments to the children and to talk about them while at home and on the road, when they lie down at night and when they rise in the morning. And he encourages them to tie them symbolically to their hands, bind them to their foreheads, and to write them on the doorframes and gates of their homes.

The keys of joy are not the commandments, but if you'll look, you will quickly find that they encompass and champion them. Just as Pops and Ruby taught, the keys have ties to our hands, and the campers and all readers are encouraged to practice them, teach them, and talk about them in ways that encourage and promote their timeless virtues.

You may not immediately have a community of campers or friends with whom you can make these connections or build these foundations, but I encourage you to find or create these communities. You will likely find them in the churches and charities in your own town and among fellow seekers and Protopians who are looking to share light and hope. But don't be afraid to look for like-minded seekers at work, at school, at the grocery store or your favorite bakery or coffee shop. A smile and a warm heart will welcome a conversation. As you share, allow yourself to be vulnerable—it will invite others to do the same. You have much to give, and much to gain as you enlarge the place of your tent, stretch your arms out wide, and refuse to hold back the kindness and love God is anxious to give to others through you. *Isaiah 54:2

I wish you all the best as you pursue light and hope through practicing the keys of joy. I hope they will expand your life as they have mine. I've learned that seekers and Protopians often find each other at the important crossroads of life. I hope that our paths will cross some day and we'll know and recognize each other through the light we share—the light that ties us to each other as children of God. When that day comes, I hope you won't mind when I greet you with a hug. If that day does not arrive here, I have no doubt that it will on that day when all things converge, and the blinders are lifted from our eyes and we can finally see clearly.

Until then, I wish you happiness and joy. May all the love you share with others be returned to you—with interest. And may the light and hope you seek be found in wondrous places, beautiful faces and welcoming hearts.

Sincerely,
Ben Behunin
Autumn 2022

Notes
1. Matthew 12:25

About the Author

God. Family. Art. Stories. With his head, heart, and hands, Ben Behunin tries to bring his passions together to make the world a little more kind, thoughtful, and beautiful. A potter by day and a writer by night—and whenever he can get away with it, Ben maintains a studio just inches away from his home in Salt Lake City, Utah. He and his wife, Lynnette, are the happy parents of two semi-adult children, Isaac and Eve.

Information about studio visits and the Behunin's semi-annual home tours is available at www.potterboy.com.

About the Author

Personalized books can be ordered
at www.potterboy.com.
There, you can register for the email mailing list
to receive updates about upcoming books, shows, and events.

Ben enjoys hearing from his readers.
You can reach him at benbehunin@comcast.net
or through snail mail at:

Abendmahl Press
1150 East 800 South
Salt Lake City, Utah 84102

For speaking engagements including
book clubs, funerals and inaugurations
call 801-597-0741

For design information, contact
Bert Compton at bert@comptonds.com

 benbehunin

 niederbippboy

Join the Protopian Movement

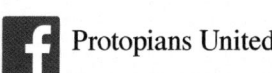 Protopians United   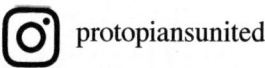 protopiansunited